WHEN DARKNESS WHISPERS

ASHES OF EDEN SERIES, BOOK 1

HEATHER L. REID

WHEN DARKNESS WHISPERS:
Book One of the Ashes of Eden Series
Previously titled PRETTY DARK NOTHING
Copyright © 2019 by Heather L. Reid

Published by Snowy Wings Publishing
www.snowywingspublishing.com

Cover Design by K.D. Ritchie www.storywrappers.com

ISBN: 978-1-948661-02-7
Second Revised Edition

In loving memory of those who believed in my dream before I even knew how to dream it. For Delia Gibson, Frank and Celia Leinbach, Jessie Easley, and for my mother, Sherry Reid. You may be gone from this world, but your spirits live on within me. I would not be who I am without you.

Shadows lingered in the corners—unhindered by the burning lights—eager for Quinn to grow careless. She ignored the weight of fear that squeezed her heart. They wouldn't have her, not tonight, not if she could help it. With shaking hands, she popped open the lid of the prescription bottle and upended the contents, tapping the bottom to make sure nothing remained. The white oval pills clattered against the porcelain and slid beneath the water. She flushed, and stared, transfixed as they swirled around and around the edge of the dark hole that waited to swallow them up. Better them than her.

She left the bathroom light on as she crept back into her bedroom, checking the clock on the bedside table for the thousandth time, willing it to race through the remaining minutes until morning. Six-thirty. Half an hour until sunrise. She wasn't sure she could last that long. A half empty energy drink sat near the clock. She downed the last dregs of cherry fizz in two gulps and threw the can into a corner. Pressing the headphones against her ears, she maxed out the volume and let Metal Mania Six shriek her awake. On the offbeat, her head banged against the antique headboard, a quick pinch of pain to ensure she hadn't nodded off.

Yawning, her eyes welled to wash away the boulders wedged beneath the lids. She hadn't slept a full night in months. She couldn't.

So tired. Maybe she could close her eyes for only the few remaining minutes. Not long enough to fall into REM sleep, but enough to give her the energy to make it through school. *Please let me sleep. Just five minutes. Please.* Metal Mania Six wailed a warning as her eyes flickered and shut. The rocking slowed then stopped. Quinn slumped to one side.

A creeping cold inched its way across her exposed skin, dotting her flesh with goosebumps. Something sinister pushed against the dead weight of her sleeping body from the other side of the headboard. The wood shuddered and groaned as the evil reached out, searching for the portal that would open with a deep sleep. Quinn's breath quickened with the thought of what was coming, but it was too late. She was helpless, already suspended in the torpor between waking and dreaming with no energy left to fight.

It only took a second for the veil between reality and nightmare to rip. Tendrils of fog splintered through the headboard and coiled around her neck. She screamed, the music in her headphones echoing that tears in her voice. The noose pulled tight, digging into her windpipe, and cut her cry short. She clawed at her throat as the coils snaked across her neck and mouth. Whips of fog were everywhere at once, twining around her body, binding her inch-by-inch with living rope. She kicked and flailed, but the fog entombed her.

The smoky mist dragged Quinn through the splintered void and held her in its dark web, dangling her over the black abyss of the tunnel below. She knew what would come next, but never when. The dreams never changed—the darkness would hold her for seconds, or hours, taunting her at the precipice of the nightmare until one by one, the tendrils unraveled and left gravity to pull her into a long, terrifying freefall.

She twisted and tumbled as she fell, hoping this time would be different, that her fingers would find some hold to stop the descent. But they never did. She grasped only air, and the ground rushed to meet her.

The thud as she hit the cold, hard earth rattled her teeth. All the air in her lungs rushed outward, and she gasped and flailed like a fish out of water. She rolled to her side and stumbled to her feet. Enormous trees stood sentry around a small clearing, their gnarled and twisted trunks mirroring the clenching inside her stomach. Hundreds of human-shaped figures hung from their branches, each draped in tattered, gray death shrouds. Mud-caked feet with jagged, black toenails peeked out from below the rags as they swayed and creaked like a disintegrating rocking chair.

Broken patterns of moonlight illuminated a narrow trail through the corpse forest and across the clearing. *Follow the light, find the way out.* Her breath came in sharp spasms. The smell of damp and decay grew stronger as she approached the first hanging body. It twisted on the end of its rope, reaching for her. But she skirted past, the end of its shroud grazing her cheek. Quinn shivered. From eyeless sockets, they watched her. She could feel their presence like a weight pressing against her skin. Dry leaves littered the forest floor; their brittle veins crunched under her black leather boots as she squeezed past two more bodies.

Each whispered a name, a word, a plea, as she passed, but she ignored them and moved on. *Keep your eyes on the light, keep moving, don't listen, it's only a dream.* She repeated the mantra to herself, numb to the thundering of her heart and the lump in her throat.

Something thudded to the ground beside her. Heart hammering within her chest, she glanced over her shoulder. An apple, blood red against the sepia-toned landscape, rolled into the moonlight and stopped at her feet.

Take a bite, the corpses whispered.

Her stomach growled. So hungry. Just one little taste. She picked up the apple, cradling the fruit in both hands. Something in the back of her mind screamed for her to drop it, but she held it tighter.

Take a bite and all your troubles will disappear.

The whispers compelled her. She swayed with their rhythm. Left, right, left, right, so soothing. Her hands lifted the fruit to her lips where she could smell its sweetness. Perfectly shiny, perfectly red. Quinn took a bite and smiled as she swallowed.

Juice trickled down her chin, and she wiped it away.. Black liquid stained the back of her fingers. She looked at the apple. Half a fat worm wriggled inside the perfect bitemark. Quinn spit and gagged, dropping the apple to the ground. Another worm swarmed out of the rapidly desiccating skin, then another, and another. They plopped to the dirt and writhed over the toes of her boots, up her ankles. She kicked free of them and darted in a circle, searching for the moonlit path to guide her way out, but it was lost in the heavy fog weaving through the maze of corpses and trees, devouring any light that dared to surface.

The trees moved closer, the corpses with them, swinging, twisting, writhing in their branches, an all-consuming darkness behind them.

What have you done? her mother's voice whispered from a nearby corpse.

It's all your fault.

Why didn't you stop it? her father's voice.

Help us. Help us.

The dark ring of fog surrounded her, moonlight absorbed by its eerie, gray-green mist. Then, like a beast pouncing on its prey, the darkness descended. Panic moved from her stomach to her feet. Blindly, she groped until her fingers found the trunk of a sturdy oak. She pressed her back against it, its rough bark catching at a strand of long hair. Trapped. Perspiration trickled down the small of her back and she shivered.

Something cold and damp brushed her leg. It felt like a human hand, a dead human hand at that, the moistness of its grave still clung to its rotting flesh. Bile rose in her throat, and she swallowed hard to keep from vomiting. She shuddered as the corporal mist found her palm, inched its way between fingers, and seized both of her wrists, binding them together. Jerking away from the smoke's grasp only succeeded in it tightening the grip of living rope until pain danced across every nerve.

Before she could blink, two new wraith vines grabbed her legs and slammed her to the forest floor. She clawed at the ground as the tendrils dragged her into the fog. Dirt lodged under her fingernails. The earthy decay, disturbed from its winter slumber, filled her nostrils.

"We're coming for you, Quinn," the fog hissed.

Earth to earth. The image of her parents throwing a handful of dirt over her coffin as it lowered into the ground came unbidden to her mind. Tears slid from her eyes. She didn't want to die.

More tendrils slithered toward her, swirling and changing into dozens of dark shadow masses. They crowded around her; their bodies blacker than the surrounding night.

"You can't get away. You have no one to protect you now." The shadows reached for her. "There's no escape, Quinn. Earth to earth. Everyone dies. Some sooner than others."

2

"No!" Quinn jolted awake, knocking over the gleaming tower of empty cans of Red Bull from her bedside table. Her alarm clock screamed, and she fumbled for the off switch. Golden-pink light oozed across the butter-yellow walls, painting the room in the warmth of sunrise. She blinked and pulled the blanket up around her chin, huddling under the covers like a child.

Hugging Mr. Snuggles, her angel-winged teddy bear to her chest, dirty and ragged from seventeen years' worth of love; she tried to shake off the lingering fear. When had these nightmares gained so much power over her? Her mind spiraled backward, picking apart every moment before her father left and every moment since. She remembered feeling it, the moment the darkness broke free and pushed forward, leaching all the color from her world. He walked out the door, and the next day, it was if the sun had been eclipsed. Cold seeped into her blood and she hadn't been warm since.

At first, the nightmares blurred with the light of morning—just dreams, but every night now, they turned more and more sinister. Their vividness bled into reality, bringing her dread

6

even in the daylight hours. Something was coming for her, and she had no idea what it wanted. Or how to stop it.

Quinn shook her head. It sounded crazy. It *was* crazy. So much so that she stopped mentioning it to her therapist and she didn't dare talk about it with anyone else. Her psychiatrist insisted the nightmares were mere manifestations of her grief, a way for her unconscious mind to cope with her father walking out on them, her fear of abandonment, her feelings of inadequacy. The doctor prescribed some sleeping pills and sent Quinn home. At first, it worked, no dreams invaded her drugged sleep, but slowly, as the months ticked by and her father didn't return, the darkness seeped back in, insidious and disturbing. The pills became a trap, locking her in with her demons and nowhere to escape. Now, her mother filled her prescriptions, and, one by one, Quinn flushed them down the toilet.

Nothing was coming for her. Dreams couldn't hurt you, no matter how vivid. Even so, she scanned the room for any movement.

The silence of an empty house washed over her, and her mind conjured the *creak, creak, creak* of the corpse forest. Quickly, she flicked the radio app on her phone to her favorite morning station and turned on her Bluetooth speaker.

"XTRM extreme music. All your favorite hits, all the time. And now, here's Skipping Zombies' new hit, 'Intensity.'"

Still clutching her angel teddy bear, Quinn slipped one foot from under the covers and let it hover above the dark space between the mattress and the floor. She chewed her bottom lip and willed herself to dip a toe into the shadow, slowly extending her leg until the sole of her foot met the cold hardwood floor. She waited. Nothing grabbed her from the recess of the bed to drag her through the cracks. She turned the volume on her phone up another notch and placed it back on the nightstand, letting the music drown out her fears, and unfolded her other leg from the tangle of covers until sunlight spilled across her bare feet, the rays charging her with courage. The floor groaned as she placed her full weight onto the solid wood boards.

The music cut off mid-note and her cell vibrated, dancing off the nightstand and onto the floor, startling her. Three deep breaths calmed her jitters. Grabbing the phone, she checked the new text message that flashed on the screen.

HAD 2 GO 2 WORK EARLY AGAIN. MORE PROBS WITH THE BUILD DESIGN. THERE'S $ ON THE COUNTER FOR PIZZA 2NITE. DON'T W8^. I'LL BE L8. LUV U. HAVE A GR8 DAY @ SCHOOL. X :-)

Mom's texts reeked of text speak lists posted on parents' websites, like how2comunic8withyourteen.com. Quinn brought up the touch screen keypad.

THANKS, MOM. SEE YOU TOMORROW. DON'T WORK TOO HARD. LOVE YOU.

Time to stop jumping at shadows and get her ass in gear, or she would be late for school, and she hated being late. But just in case, she kept her back to the lit window and eyes to the softly shadowed side of the room.

Quinn's Westland High cheerleading uniform hung on the back of the closet door, fresh from the cleaners. The shiny plastic film was a mocking reminder that she remained benched for failing algebra, of all things.

Not caring if it wrinkled, she shoved the uniform into the back of her closet. Instead, she grabbed her dad's vintage Bowie tee shirt from her dresser and pulled on a pair of dark skinny jeans. A magenta and black houndstooth scarf would keep the October chill at bay.

A pair of black boots peeked at her from under the bed. She inched forward, kicking the boots into the light, and bent to pick them up. A dead leaf clung to one of the soles. She pulled it free and brought it to her nose. The leaf smelled musty and damp, fresh from an autumn walk in the woods.

Earth to earth.

Hands shaking, she dropped the leaf, snatched one of her boots, and hammered its heel onto the golden frond until it disintegrated into brown dust.

"I-Will-Not-Be-Afraid." She snarled each word with every strike.

Quinn pulled her car into one of the last empty spaces in the school parking lot and glanced at her watch. Just enough time to get to class—if she ran. Slamming the door of her red Mustang, an unwanted bribe from her mother, she darted for the main entrance.

As she rounded the back of a white pickup, she froze. There, blocking her way, were Jeff and Kerstin, tongues throat-deep in what looked less like kissing and more like a scene from a porn movie. Quinn ducked behind the truck bed and hoped they wouldn't notice her. She wanted to look away, but her eyes were drawn to them like metal to a magnet. Jeff stroked Kerstin's hair and nuzzled her neck like he had once nuzzled Quinn's. Kerstin nibbled his ear while he laughed. They looked happy. Jeff looked happy. Yet anger swelled in Quinn's chest as she swiped at the tear rolling down her cheek.

Don't you dare cry, she told herself. *He's not worth it.* But her emotions were stubborn, and the pain of losing Jeff to that succubus was too raw. They'd been best friends their whole lives, their friendship blooming into more in eighth grade. They'd been inseparable for four years. Until the summer. Until Kerstin. *Men will always betray your trust*, her mom proclaimed. Hadn't she learned that from her father? A hard knot tightened in her stomach, and she clutched at her belly to keep her insides from ripping into a million pieces. *He's not worth it.* She repeated the mantra and choked back a sob.

Relief washed over Quinn as Kerstin grabbed Jeff's hand, and they disappeared into the building. She closed her eyes and leaned against the truck, the cool metal calming the heat rising in her cheeks. The pain in her chest eased as she released the tears she held back. At least they hadn't noticed her hiding and blubbering like a fool. The last thing she needed was Kerstin spreading more nasty rumors, a favorite hobby of hers.

Hurried footsteps approached her from the school steps and stopped on the other side of the truck. Damn, Kerstin had seen her after all and decided to come back and call her on it. Her stomach twisted again. Defending herself to Kerstin was the last thing she needed this morning.

Act natural, Quinn, like you dropped something. You stopped to pick it up. That's all, nothing to do with her and Jeff.

She wiped the last tear away and took a deep breath. Head held high, she casually adjusted her backpack and stepped out to meet the cause of her angst. Kerstin wasn't there. Nobody was there. Quinn circled the truck looking for the source of the footsteps. Someone giggled behind her. She whipped her head around, scanning the rows of parked vehicles, but she didn't see anyone.

"Kerstin!" She hoped the other girl's smirking face would appear from behind a car. "Not funny!"

Another giggle and soft footsteps echoed down the row to her right, stopping on the other side of a blue Honda.

"Kerstin. I know you're out there." She paused, waiting for a response that never came. If Kerstin wasn't playing a trick, who was?

A shadow crossed to her left. Sunlight drenched the concrete around it, intensifying the contrast of absolute blackness forming beside her. Quinn held her breath as a tremor inched up her leg. The dark silhouette lay as if painted on the concrete, long and lean, clearly defined, backpack slung across one shoulder. She twisted, and it twisted with her. Afraid of her own shadow. Talk about pathetic.

When the sun dimmed behind another bank of clouds, the silhouette faded with it, lines blurring from black to gray. Quinn released her breath in a long sigh, shaking her head at her own absurdity, and trudged toward the school entrance.

Without warning, a shiny, red apple rolled from under the white truck and into Quinn's path, stopping her short. She could almost taste the bittersweet juice on her tongue, see the squirming half-worm, black blood dripping down her wrist, shadows writhing. She kicked the apple as hard as she could. It skidded and jumped across the asphalt, bruises and tears gashing its red skin, until it landed in the grass.

She tried for the entrance again, but this time when she moved, her shadow split in two, one moving with her, the other moving to the left. Two distinct, Quinn-shaped shades stood as mirror images on each side of her.

"Kerstin?" She watched the twin shadows and took another step. The right one followed, but the left one moved a fraction of a second later, stalking her. Quinn's heart sped.

"Jeff?" She whimpered his name.

There was no one around her. Her shadow stalker leaned forward, bending at the waist until its gloomy lips touched her ear. Its cold breath sent a shiver through every muscle, freezing her in place as it murmured, "They've already gone to class with no thought of you. Look around. You're alone, Quinn."

The other shadow joined in and conspiratorially bent forward like its doppelganger. "You did see them though, right?"

Wake up. Wake up. Wake up, her mind screamed. Then she pinched her forearms hard enough to leave a mark, pain flooding her nerves. She gasped, fully awake.

"Kissing, groping. Jeff can't get enough of her. She'll give it to him. She's warm and willing, not cold and selfish, like you."

She stuck her fingers in her ears and hummed "Mary Had a Little Lamb," but the voices wouldn't hush. *Shadows don't talk. Your crazy, sleep deprived mind is making it all up.* She rocked in rhythm with the song, as if the repetition would drive them from her mind, but it only made the voices louder, more determined. Now they came from inside her.

"Did he ever kiss you like that?" one hissed. "Like he wanted to devour you?"

She didn't want to think about this. She didn't want to think about any of it. All she wanted was to go to school, to get her grades up, to get back to being captain of the cheerleading squad. She wanted her life to be normal.

"And that kiss before he left you for good?" the second asked.

The voices probed, prodded, provoked her to remember. Their last kiss, the worst kind of kiss, the kind you give a sister, a peck. Obligatory.

"No." The shadows confirmed the very question that crossed her mind. "He never loved you. Your father never loved you. Your mother doesn't love you. Sad, unlovable Quinn."

Quinn choked as her throat tightened. Now they read her thoughts. "Get out of my head."

The dark Quinns laughed and joined hands. "But we're part of you. We'll never leave you." They circled her, dancing, singing, and teasing, like sociopathic children on a playground.

"Earth to Earth." The dark masses spun past her, blurring everything in gray mist.

"Shut up," Quinn pleaded under her breath. She looked up to see a short, blond girl stop halfway up the steps to the school entrance and stare at her, mouth agape. Did the girl see them too? Quinn pulled her hands through her hair as if she were brushing it back into a ponytail. not covering her ears and talking to disembodied voices. *This is what it feels like to lose it. Padded cell, here we come.* The girl looked at the ground and hurried into the building.

"Ashes to ashes," the shadows hissed.

"Shut up," Quinn snapped.

"Dust to …"

"Shut up!" Quinn's words echoed off the cars in the empty parking lot and collided with the clang of the first period bell.

The taunting spirits snickered. "You're late, Quinn."

Balling her hand into a fist, she closed her eyes, gritted her teeth, and took a swing at a smoky face. Her fist smashed against only air, and when she opened her eyes, they were gone. She stood alone, shadow-less in the perfectly normal parking lot on a normal school day. But in that moment, everything changed. Either she had fallen asleep, or her nightmares were no longer the stuff of dreams.

aron Collier shifted his backpack over his shoulder and glanced down the hall as he deftly spun his locker combination, glancing up between numbers to make sure Quinn hadn't escaped into the cafeteria. Just fifteen rows away, she flickered in and out of his vision as the crowd of hungry students came and went.

In AP English, they'd been put in the same discussion group to debate if Hamlet really loved Ophelia. Quinn curled her hair around the pointer finger of her left hand, strangely silent, as he'd argued Hamlet's love for Ophelia was true though his need for revenge overpowered all other emotions.

"Quinn, what do you think?" he'd asked.

She'd startled at his question. Her eyes locked on his: bloodshot, tired, no makeup could have hidden the dark circles and bags. She looked as if she hadn't seen a good night's sleep in a while. He and insomnia had been toxic friends once, so he knew how hard it could be to get rid of him.

"Sorry, Aaron." She seemed dazed but her cheeks turned pink. "I was, um, a million miles away. What did you say?

"Do you think Hamlet really love Ophelia?"

"No. Hamlet was selfish. Ophelia deserved better." She'd glanced over her shoulder at Jeff, then went back to the absent-minded hair twisting while the discussion moved on. Jeff, of course. Aaron wondered how this smart, bubbly, confident girl could have changed so much in one summer. Was she really that heartbroken over Mr. Quarterback? Or was there more to it?

He'd wanted to touch her hand, to glimpse what troubled her. Give him some insight into what he could say to help her, but there was no guarantee his gift would work. A curse, a blessing, whatever enabled him to sense the truth about others through touch was unreliable at best. Then he would have had to explain an unwarranted touch. Instead, he pulled his hands inside his shirtsleeves, untrusting and defensive.

When Quinn had sat next to him in calculus, he'd smiled and she'd strained to grin back at him. The sweet apple scent of her perfume reminded him of fall, of a harvest moon, and lyrics whispered to be written down. He'd watched her. Her scarf pulled tight, a shield from the world. She tapped the end of her pencil on the back of her hand and shifted in her seat as Mr. Gordon droned on about the rules of differentiation. A can of Red Bull peeked from her backpack. She slipped her hand over the top of the can every few minutes like an addict craving their next hit.

Aaron had been distracted, too, courting his muse, and the words flowed from his pen:

UNDER THE PALE MOON, MY LIFE BEGAN
HAND IN HAND
THE SOULLESS GARDEN OF MY HEART BLOOMED
IN THE LIGHT OF YOUR EYES
TO KNOW YOU
TO LOVE YOU
ALPHA AND OMEGA
BEGINNING AND END OF LIFE AS I KNOW IT.

He had rewritten it five times to make the handwriting perfect, memorizing it as he memorized her face. He waited for Mr. Gordon to turn back to the whiteboard and folded the paper in a small square. He could casually drop the poem into her half open backpack. Maybe it would make her smile. Or maybe she'd think he was a weirdo.

The minutes ticked by. The folded piece of paper never detached from his hand, and soon, the bell rang. Quinn had snatched up her backpack and bolted before he had a chance to give his poem to her. He balled the paper in his fist and sunk it in the bottom of the wastebasket.

Now, lucky chance number three presented itself and he was determined to take it. Talk to her before her other friends show up.

Aaron rehearsed what he could say to her in his head.

I really like you, Quinn. Go out with me. We're made for each other. He shook his head. That line screamed restraining order. He could do better. *We might have some things in common.* She was just another girl, and he talked to girls all the time—had talked to her hundreds of times. They were casual friends, but he'd always wanted to get to know her better. He'd never been shy around her before, but now that she was single, his words stuck in his throat.

"Yo, Aaron! What's up?" Marcus leaned against the neighboring locker, an overly muscled shoulder blocking Aaron's view of Quinn.

Aaron shuffled to the right until her golden hair flashed back into sight.

Kerstin's petty, and Jeff's a jerk. They deserve each other, and Quinn, you deserve more. True, but maybe a little too blunt.

"Dude, you're not a Jedi. You can't use the force to pull the clothes off her body just by staring at her. Believe me, I've thought about it." Marcus turned to focus all his attention on Quinn. "Nope. Still doesn't work." He sighed and crossed his arms. "I wonder why Luke Skywalker never used his powers to see what was under Leia's gold bikini."

"Because she was his sister?" Aaron rifled through his locker for his economics book. *Hey, Quinn, are you okay? Let me know if you need anything. I'm a great listener.* Sure, if he wanted a one-way ticket to the friendzone.

"That's wrong on so many levels." Marcus shivered. "Since Quinn's not my sister, I can still fantasize about her, right?"

"No," Aaron said, his voice short.

"Look, I know you've been drooling over that one since you moved here and she's finally single, but she's damaged, man. First, Jeff breaks up with her then the cheerleading controversy, and now people are saying she was late this morning because she was talking to herself in the parking lot."

Hey, Quinn, you rock my world. That sounded like Marcus. He needed to be himself.

"Dude, are you listening?" Marcus thumped him on the ear.

Aaron flinched, still sore from the piercing he got over the weekend. "Yeah, I heard you." He slammed his locker. "So, she's a little stressed. Your ass has been late to class plenty of times. Besides, who doesn't talk to themselves occasionally? Maybe she was using one of those Bluetooth things, talking to someone on the phone."

Quinn, I felt like I knew you the day you showed me around school for the first time. You were wearing the same Bowie shirt you have on today and we talked about music and you laughed at my silly jokes. I watched you and Teresa Yang pass up the cheerleader table at lunch to sit with a freshman girl who was eating by herself. I wanted to ask you out then, but I knew you were with Jeff and didn't have a chance, but now that he's with Kerstin . . . Ok. Now he was getting closer. Sincerity felt right.

"Hey, man, I didn't mean anything by it." Marcus raised his hands in surrender. "It's just unusual for Quinn Perfect to be late, that's all. You know I'd never dis your girl."

"She's not my girl. And nobody's perfect."

"Yeah, right. Not perfect? Look at her, man! The hair, the butt, the legs leading right up into that short little cheerleading skirt." Marcus grinned. "Don't tell me you don't think about the short, little cheerleading skirt."

"The skirt's an added perk," Aaron admitted. "And her smile."

"Yeah, her face ain't bad either."

"And smart." Aaron slipped his guitar plectrum from his pocket and twirled it between his fingers, wondering how many steps stood between them.

"And still hung up on her ex. You don't get over a four-year relationship with Highlands golden boy in a matter of months." Marcus patted Aaron on the shoulder. "Trust me. She's seriously damaged goods, bro. Look but don't touch, that's my advice. Besides, we're seniors, man. You can have any girl you want. Have you seen the fresh meat walking the halls? Let's line up for the all you can eat buffet."

"I'm full, thanks." Aaron breathed deeply, ready to take the plunge. He'd do it this time. *Talk to her, ask her out.*

"Why waste another day on Quinn with so many hotties running around? Jenna's crushin' on you so bad. She's hotness personified, and you two have a lot in common: music, the band, and those raging hormones."

"Jenna's just a friend."

Fifteen steps to Quinn's locker at the most.

"What about Marie? Oh, oh, Marie, now there's a fine one. She'd give you a little something." Marcus cleared his throat and put on his best Marie impression by raising his voice an octave. *"Oh, Aaron, he's so mysterious and good looking."* He clasped Aaron's shoulder, regaining his usual deep tone. "She called you man-candy. Can you believe it? You're not as sweet as me, of course. I mean, I'm Godiva chocolate, and you, well, you're more like a Goober."

Ten long strides, twenty short ones.

"How come you never ask any of them out? I know a few who are a sure thing," Marcus said.

"Sure, Mr. Virgin. All talk and no action." Aaron punched Marcus on the shoulder.

"Hey, not so loud. You'll ruin my image." Marcus looked around like he was paranoid someone overheard then winked at Aaron. "Dude, you could have a different girl every week, and you choose to be single. What's wrong with you?"

"I don't have time for a girlfriend."

"But you'd make time for Quinn, right? Besides, who said anything about a girlfriend? I'm talking about seven minutes in Heaven, man, not commitment."

"I have other things to think about. Like family, grades, college." Aaron looked at his watch. *Come on feet, move.*

"Yeah, and I've got a leprechaun living in my locker. You suck at lying. I will admit, she is seriously F-I-N-E, fine." Marcus paused and studied Aaron. "Wait. You're serious? Were you about to ask her out? Is that why your shirt's tucked in?" He sniffed Aaron's neck. "Dude, did you bathe in that cologne this morning?"

"Shut up." Aaron untucked his shirt and mussed his hair. Looking like a poser was the last thing he wanted.

"Man, I didn't know you were serious. Forget what I said about her being damaged. If you really want her, I've got your back. Quinn is sure to need a little comforting. If you know what I mean." Marcus puckered up and made kissing noises.

"I was planning my move when your big mouth interrupted." Aaron slumped against the locker. "Anyway, it's too late now." He gestured down the hall where Quinn was joined by a group of friends.

"You gonna let them stop you? You say Quinn's not perfect, but you act like she's the only girl in the world. Grow a pair and get your butt over there."

"I don't even know what to say to her. Everything I think of sucks." Aaron rolled the plectrum he carried across his knuckles and back again, like an old magician's coin trick.

"All right, as the ladies' man of Westland High, I'll coach you."

"Right, Cyrano, let's hear it."

"Walk up to her, put your arm around her shoulder, smile, and say," Marcus paused for dramatic effect. "Quinn, you rock my world."

Aaron laughed.

"What's so funny?" Marcus crossed his arms over his chest. "The girls go crazy for that line."

"Seriously, you can't tell me it actually works. I bet you've never even used it."

"Oh, that hurts." Marcus grabbed his chest in mock pain. "I bagged a set of mega-fine twins last week with that line."

"You're mistaking your fantasies for reality." Aaron shoved the plectrum back into his pocket where it belonged.

Marcus shrugged. "Okay. I've never used that line before but trust me. It's foolproof."

"Prove it. Teresa Yang's with Quinn. I dare you to lay that foolproof line on her right now."

"No problem. Watch the master at work. She'll be mine in no time." Marcus slicked back his curly brown hair and flashed his best smile at Aaron. "Well, let's go. I'm not going alone."

Fourteen steps.

Aaron regretted the dare. Now, he'd have to talk to her.

Ten.

He couldn't stand around like a dummy at a sideshow.

Nine.

Sure, he'd talked to her before.

Eight.

But things were different now. She and Jeff weren't together anymore.

Seven.

And that meant he might have a chance.

Three tries and Quinn still couldn't get her combination to land on the right numbers. She looked over her shoulder. Her doppelgängers had disappeared, but the feeling of being watched hadn't.

The puzzle didn't fit. They had always been *night*mares. Not show-up-in-broad-daylight-to-scare-you-while-you're-awake-mares. She must've dozed while waiting for Jeff and Kerstin to finish making out, waking once the bell rang. It was the only explanation.

She jiggled the locker handle and tried again. Fourth time's a charm. Her locker opened with its usual squeak. Books with different colored covers stood in row. She replaced the literature book in the empty space next to calculus and pulled her thick, yellow, French book from between chemistry and economics.

Something tapped her shoulder. She whirled around to find Kerstin standing with her hands behind her back and a smirk on her face.

"What do you want?"

"I found this in Jeff's locker." Kerstin thrust a red, heart-shaped frame at Quinn. "He doesn't want it anymore."

Quinn swiped the frame from her hand and smiled her brightest smile.

"Thanks, Kerstin. It's so sweet of you to think of my feelings." Quinn threw as much sarcasm into her voice as she could.

"It's the least I can do, Q.T." Kerstin shot her a mocking smile.

"Only my friends are allowed to call me that."

"What? We're not friends?" Kerstin covered her mouth in feigned shock. "I'm hurt." She pouted. "But I'll get over it. See you at practice." She started to walk away but cocked her head, turning back "Oh, wait. I forgot. You're—what did Coach White call it—*taking a break?*" Kerstin mimed air quotes as she spoke. "Well, at least you should have plenty of time to study. I'll keep your captain's spot warm for you." She waited for the news to sink in.

Quinn folded her arms and glared, not giving her the satisfaction.

"What? No witty repartee? I'll turn the other cheek." Kerstin turned and stuck her right cheek out, baiting her.

Quinn wondered what it would feel like to smash her fist into that cheek, but the last thing she needed was more trouble.

"No?" Kerstin cocked a smile. "Pity. I would love to be captain permanently. Have a nice day, Quinn." She called over her shoulder, slinking off down the hallway.

"You too, bitch." Quinn whispered under her breath.

Leaning against the lockers, she traced the frame with her index finger. Her favorite picture of the two of them stared back at her. Jeff, tall and blond, wore the purple and red Westland High colors. A mustang blazed across his chest. Quinn stood beside him, dwarfed by his six-foot, two-inch frame. She'd always felt safe in his arms.

"Four years," she muttered to the picture as if it were Jeff in the flesh. "I trusted you. What do you see in her, anyway? God, I wish cameras had never been invented." She threw the picture frame into the back of her locker, slamming it shut.

"Hey. What's itching you this morning?" Teresa linked her arm through Quinn's. "Let me guess. Kerstin?"

"She's like a rash that won't go away," Quinn said. "Seriously, Reese, sometimes I want to punch the freckles right off her nose."

"I get that." Reese pulled Quinn into a hug. "But she's really not worth it. Just ignore her."

"Easy for you to say. She's not sleeping with your boyfriend."

"Ex-boyfriend."

"Rub it in, why don't you?" Quinn said.

"If he really is sleeping with that monster, then he's more of a jerk than I thought. He's so not worth it," Reese said.

"Monster? Have you looked at her lately? She's beautiful. Gorgeous red hair. Long legs. My legs are so stubby and short. And let's not forget her boobs. My chest looks like a pancake"

"Have you actually met Kerstin? Hello? Snotty, loudmouth, gossipy, shallow, liar, and, let's not forget, mean. Who in the world would want to be like her? She's not even fit to clean gum off the bottom of your shoe."

"Yeah, just good enough to sleep with my boyfriend." Quinn clipped a stray hair back with a bobby pin to keep it out of her face.

"Ex-boyfriend. I know it's not easy, but you've got to face reality. They're together. Whether he's sleeping with her or not has nothing to do with you."

"Do you really think they're sleeping together?"

"Don't know. Don't care. And neither should you."

"Easy for you to say. She didn't steal your boyfriend."

"You can't steal a guy that doesn't want to be stolen." Reese brushed her long, black hair off her shoulder.

"Hey, Q.T.! Teresa!" Ami bounded across the hall, her arms full of books, eyes flashing. "Want to hear the latest?" Ami launched into tell-all mode before either had time to answer. "Well, I just heard from Tyra who heard from Ashley that Marie is desperately in love with Aaron Collier. Do you blame her? He's so cute. I wouldn't mind going out with him. If I weren't dating Shae, of course." Ami grinned, shuffled the books in her arms, pushed her Gucci glasses back up her nose, and took a huge breath.

"Have you seen the motorcycle Aaron rides? And his earring? I've been trying to get more info on him for Marie, but he's mucho misterioso. A year of living in Westland, but nobody seems to know much about him. Marcus told Marie that Aaron lives with his dad and brother over on Oakmont, but he's never been invited over. Not the greatest neighborhood. Maybe he's too embarrassed to have anyone over, or maybe he's an axe murderer. And Marcus says he's in a band. A sexy, hot, axe murderer-musician. Oh, it gets my blood pumping! Anyway, Marie really wants him to ask her to homecoming, but he doesn't seem interested. Are you listening to me?" Ami followed Quinn's gaze across the hall. Jeff and Kerstin's lips locked together in a serious smooch fest.

"Can you believe them? Don't they ever come up for air? Get a room!" Reese yelled at the tongue wrestlers. "He's such an ass. You should be glad you're not with him anymore."

Reese and Ami moved in front of Quinn to block her view, but between now and this morning, the image had already burned itself into her memory. She knew she shouldn't care, that she should get over it, but seeing him with another girl still hurt. A dull ache started behind her right eye, rapidly spreading across her forehead. Quinn rubbed her temple and leaned against the locker, too tired to care anymore.

"Yeah, totally forget about them!" Ami added. "Kerstin will never be able to replace you. Yeah, she's with Jeff now, and Coach White appointed her as cheerleading captain while you're on academic probation, but ..."

"Who told you that?" Reese snapped.

"Nobody. It's not that hard to figure out. Coach White says it's because you're overstressed, but everyone knows that's code for academic probation. What happened, Quinn? You always get straight A's. I mean, I know you're having a bad year with your dad leaving, and the whole Kerstin stealing your boyfriend thing, but—"

"God, Ami, insensitive much?" Reese poked Ami to shut her up. "I really don't think you're helping."

It was true; Ami wasn't helping. God, she wanted to disappear. She was so very tired. Of the nightmares, of the idle gossip, of Jeff and Kerstin fondling one another. Her energy ebbed, and her lids grew heavy, the conversation between Ami and Reese a lulling rhythm. She closed her eyes for a second.

Fog seeped from the lockers and folded itself around her, cloaking her in overwhelming doom. Ami and Reese's voices sounded miles away. Their forms, eclipsed by misty darkness, faded in and out of her vision. She focused on the black-and-white tiles of the hallway floor, hoping to steady herself.

Not now. Not now. Focus, Quinn, focus on the tiles. But they swirled together, turning as gray as the mist that surrounded her.

She tried to fight, tried to reach out for her friends, tried to scream—anything to escape the drowning feeling. The floor came closer now. The cool, black-and-white tiles rushed up to soothe her troubled mind.

"Hey, ladies. What's up?" Marcus waved as he and Aaron made their way through the crowd.

Teresa waved back, but Aaron focused on Quinn. She stood between Ami and Teresa, eyes closed, face drained of color. She swayed side-to-side, like a skyscraper in the middle of an earthquake.

Quinn's knees buckled. Aaron took two giant steps toward her, pushing a helpless freshman out of the way. He scooped her in his arms before her head hit the floor. The lunch chatter, the movement in the hallway, everything around him slowed. Ami stopped mid-sentence, Reese mid-wave.

The second his skin met Quinn's, a familiar tingling gathered in the front of his brain, a flash and then the lightning strike. Before he had time to shut her out, a wave of intense fear washed through him, nearly knocking him over. Instead, he fell against the lockers and gritted his teeth, struggling to force a barrier, a psychic wall, between them.

"Dude!" Marcus's voice brought Aaron back to reality, and Quinn's fear became a low hum in the back of his brain, the tingle dissipating.

He sank to the floor, cradling her head in his lap. "Go get Mrs. Morgan," he said to the small crowd gathered around them before he bent his head to her lips. Relief washed over him as Quinn's breath warmed his cheek. "Quinn, can you hear me?"

He closed his eyes, brushed the back of his palm against her forehead, and loosened the grip on his ability. Releasing a tendril of light through the barrier, he focused on being calm, projecting love and security to Quinn. Slowly, a new tingling radiated through his skull, a spark, and then a blinding flash as he opened himself up to her unconscious.

Quinn's face appeared in his mind. Pale and shadowed, she somehow smiled as she screamed. Her pain, anger, desire, defeat, exhaustion, and fear flooded him at once. He fought to regain control, to quell her emotions and restore balance, but no matter how hard he tried, her emotions overwhelmed him. He switched tactics and tried to restore his barrier before he reached sensory overload, but it was too late. He was enthralled by the power of the connection, unlike anything he'd experienced before.

Quinn's face morphed until one face superimposed itself over the other. Her skin pulsed and changed from serene and beautiful to screaming and alien. Again, her features contorted, and her blue eyes faded to gold and back to blue again, and then back to that otherworldly gold. Black veins writhed under her skin and she scratched at herself, nails digging into flesh. Something dark wanted to consumer her. He could feel its hunger through their link and it angered him. The dream thing thrashed and clawed, ripping at her flesh from the inside out and he could feel Quinn fighting gain control. Anger wrestled with fear, wrestled with shame inside her, and the beast licked at her emotions, hungry, feeding on her pain. Suddenly, Quinn's expression settled back on her own face, and she went totally still. Her blue eyes locked on his as blood tears trickled down her cheeks.

"Help me," she mouthed before morphing again.

The dark entity, still inside Quinn, took control again and locked its golden eyes on Aaron. "You!" It hissed and leapt toward him, its form twisting into an indistinct, faceless mist. "You can't have her!"

Aaron forced all his energy toward it, and the shade erupted in a ball of light. The cord connecting him to Quinn snapped. He slammed the door of the barrier, and the sparks retreated. His heart raced, and he pulled his hand away from Quinn's forehead. He'd never felt anything that intense; nothing that dark had been able to get through his barriers, not since he'd learned to control his ability.

He had no idea how long he was gripped by Quinn's nightmare. Seconds? Minutes? He blinked and looked around. Long enough to have gathered a large crowd. He could only imagine what he looked like, bent over Quinn, staring into space like a zombie. Like a freak.

"Can someone get her some water?" he asked, but no one moved. "Are you all asleep? Can't you see she's unconscious?"

"I-I've got some." Reese handed Aaron a bottle from her backpack. "I don't know what happened. We were standing here talking. Then, bam! Maximum weirdness. She tumbled toward the floor, and you showed up like Clark Kent. You think she'll be all right?"

"Sure." Aaron stroked Quinn's hair, careful to keep tight control over his power as he touched her. "Can you open the water bottle for me? Splash a little on her face."

Reese poured some into the palm of her hand and sprinkled the drops with her fingers. Quinn's eyes blinked open, then closed again.

"Quinn? You're scaring us. Are you okay?" she said. "I wish Marcus would hurry."

"I think she's trying to say something." Aaron bent his lips to Quinn's ear. "Quinn, can you hear me?"

She licked her lips and moved her head. "Jeff," she croaked. "Why?"

Aaron stared at Jeff. The idiot stood there at the front of the crowd like a statue. He'd been just as close when Quinn fainted. Closer. Kerstin stood next to him, laughing with her friend, Spring. She snaked her left arm around Jeff's, leaving her right hand free to point as she giggled.

"Yo. Jeff. She's asking for you, man," Aaron said.

This prompted Kerstin to stop giggling and take note of the situation.

All eyes moved from Aaron to Jeff, who moved toward Quinn, but Kerstin tightened her grip on his arm. Jeff shook his head and looked at the floor. Kerstin smiled.

Aaron wanted to punch him. Hurt him for hurting Quinn. A few years ago, he would've beaten Jeff to a pulp, let emotion carry him away. Now, he swallowed the anger and let it pass. He'd learned control; he had to hold on to that.

A blinding flash of light and the shadows retreated. Unintelligible voices intruded on the darkness—alien, yet familiar. Cold needles pricked her cheek, and she felt the hard floor beneath her. A gentle hand stroked her hair. She could breathe again. What happened? Darkness swirled around the memory of Kerstin returning the picture of her and Jeff, of feeling dizzy, and then darkness. Her memory of what happened next intangible, a ghost she couldn't quite grasp. Cool fingers brushed her hot forehead. Jeff, comforting her as she lay crying on her bed the night her father left. Jeff, telling her everything would be alright, that he would always be there for her. Jeff, her safe place to fall. Why had he left her? Why had they left her? Alone, so alone. Earth-to-earth. If she died, would her father come to her funeral? Would Jeff even cry? Would either of them care if she lay pale and silent forever, buried in the ground?

She drifted backward for a moment, back to sleep, back to a faceless mass, pushing her down, choking her, taunting her. She pressed against it and a faint light strummed the gray threads of unconsciousness giving her courage. She pushed the darkness back with all her strength and she jolted awake.

Her throat felt like broken glass. She licked her lips and rolled her tongue around to work up some saliva. She willed the muscles in her neck to flex, moving her head side to side. Her body ached. She forced herself to open her eyes, but the blinding fluorescence hurt. The faint smell of lavender—Reese's perfume—comforted her.

"Welcome back to the land of the living." Reese's face came into focus, and Quinn reached out for her. "Want to sit up?"

Quinn nodded. She turned, expecting to see Jeff, but instead of Jeff's chocolate-brown eyes, her gaze met the intense green of Aaron Collier's. Why had she never noticed how beautiful his eyes were before? Deep green flecked with gold, they reminded her of a mountain stream, deep and cool and wistful.

"Are you okay?" Aaron asked.

She furrowed her brows. Was she staring at him? She felt her cheeks flush and quickly looked away. Her gaze found Jeff instead, standing arm-in-arm with Kerstin. And then it all came flooding back. Jeff was Kerstin's safe place now. Pain and humiliation welled inside her and she wished she were dead.

"Quinn? Are you okay?" Aaron repeated. "Can you stand?"

"I think so."

He offered her a hand and Reese slipped an arm around her waist, both helping her to her feet right as Marcus rounded the corner with Mrs. Morgan behind him.

"It's about time," Aaron said.

"Hey, man, I had to run all over school. I found her crouched over a plate of liver and onions in the teachers' lounge." Marcus stuck his finger in his mouth, gagged, and fell against the lockers.

"What happened, Miss Taylor?" Mrs. Morgan's breath set her head spinning again. Quinn tried to avert her nose as a wave of garlic exploded from Mrs. Morgan's mouth, but the nurse grabbed her face with thick fingers and came at her with a little flashlight, clicking it on and off in Quinn's eyes.

"I'm all right." Quinn twisted her head from Mrs. Morgan's vice grip, rubbing her eyes to clear the spots from her vision. "I didn't eat breakfast this morning. That's all. I think my blood sugar dropped or something."

Mrs. Morgan's determined black eyes searched Quinn's, then she sighed and turned her round, little body to the crowd. "This is why breakfast is so important." The nurse launched into one of her healthy-eating-habit lectures, right there in the hall-way. Everyone groaned.

"Do you want me to take you home?" Aaron asked quietly. "I have homeroom, but I'm sure Mr. Salazar won't mind. Or maybe Reese can take you, if you'd feel more comfortable." He stuttered and looked at his shoes.

Home. Alone. That was the last place she wanted to be right now. Even being locked in school with Jeff and Kerstin engaging in extreme PDA was better than what awaited her in the darkness.

"No, but, thank you." She shoved her hands in her pockets and glanced at the large hallway clock. "Coach White still expects me to attend practice after school. Torture, I know." She half smiled at him, avoiding eye contact. "I'll be okay."

She took a step to pick up her books that lay scattered on the floor, but her legs buckled, and Aaron slipped a hand against the small of her back to steady her, letting it linger for a second. A jolt of electricity ran up her spine and her heart skipped a beat.

When he pulled his hand away, a wave of sadness washed over her.

Kerstin smirked and nudged Spring with her elbow. They both broke into a snicker. Humiliation served up with a side of spite. Quinn wanted to tell them off, but before she could muster the energy, Jeff grabbed Kerstin by the arm, jerking her away from Spring and cutting her laughter short. Quinn thought she saw her eyes flash blue, then black, like ink as she tugged herself free of Jeff. A trick of the light. Then she whirled and stomped down the hallway, red hair streaming behind her like fire from a dragon's mouth.

Jeff ran a hand through his hair. Shoulders slumped, he approached Quinn. Anger and longing twisted together in her gut.

"I'm sorry about Kerstin." He stopped a few feet away and shoved his hands in his pockets.

You should be. Quinn thought, but instead, she said, "Whatever, just go after your new girlfriend and leave me alone, okay?"

"Look, I was only trying—"

"Trying to hurt her even more than you already have? She just asked you to leave her alone, man."

She wanted to tell Aaron that she could take care of herself. But her words stuck like a stale tortilla chip in the middle of her throat. Her head pounded, and she felt dizzy again. She leaned into Aaron and let him pull her protectively into the crook of his arm. Jeff tensed his jaw and Quinn relished the jealousy that flashed across his face. The two boys locked stares and looked as if they might lock horns.

"Are you her boyfriend now or something?" Jeff asked.

"I'm not Kerstin's," Aaron said.

"That's enough." Mrs. Morgan inched between them. "I think Miss Taylor has had enough excitement for the day." She pivoted to address the crowd. "The rest of you, make your way to class or wherever you're supposed to be this hour." No one moved. She clapped her hands three times. "Now, people. Or do you want to hear about the advantages of good hygiene? You to, Kristin."

"It's *Kerstin*," Kerstin said, turning on her heel and snapping her fingers at Spring, who followed in step.

The crowd dispersed. Jeff turned to follow Kerstin, disappearing into the crowd.

"I should probably get to class now, too," Quinn said.

Mrs. Morgan narrowed her eyes at Quinn, looked her up and down, and shook her head. "No, not class. I'll call your mother, Miss Taylor. I think it's best if you go home, and I don't want you trying to drive."

"No!" Quinn couldn't be home alone, not with the threat of sleep so near and the shadows so close. School was full of distractions to keep her from drifting off, but home wasn't. "Mom's in meetings all day and can't pick me up. I need some lunch, that's all. It's only another forty-five minutes. I'll grab a candy bar from the machine."

"I've never seen someone so determined to stay at school." She squinted at Quinn, deciding her fate. "I'm still calling your mother; she needs to know. But I won't send you home if you come to my office for some orange juice and cookies."

"You're not going to share your liver and onions with a starving girl, Mrs. M?" Marcus asked. "Shameful. And you're supposed to be a health professional."

She scowled at him. "That's enough from you, Mr. Woods. The three of you should get to class. I'll take it from here."

"What? I'm just trying to make the girl laugh. They say laughter is the best medicine. You're a nurse. You should know that."

"We're too late, Mrs. Morgan. We'll get detention without excuses." Reese flashed an innocent smile.

Mrs. Morgan sighed. "Fine. You can all come to my office

then, and I'll write out the excuses, but I want you three to head straight to class after that. Do you hear me, Mr. Woods?"

Marcus nodded.

"Good." Mrs. Morgan waddled down the corridor. "Let's go people," she called over her shoulder.

Quinn realized Aaron still had his arm around her, as if it were the most natural thing in the world. She looked up at him and he cleared his throat. Then they both awkwardly pulled away from each other. The moment he let go, a chill shook her to the core. One step, and the world spun. Aaron steadied her with a hand, his touch gentle and warm, and for a moment, she wanted nothing more than for him to pull her close again.

"You should let Aaron help you." Reese whispered in her ear gave Quinn a conspirator's wink.

Should she? He was more than cute with his brooding green eyes, dark hair, and rugged features. Not like pretty boy Jeff. Something about the way he looked at her, like he knew her, made her nervous. Not creepy nervous, but the excited nervous you feel the first time you ride a rollercoaster. She liked the idea of him liking her, but that didn't mean she should flirt and fawn and play the damsel in distress, even if she was in distress. She didn't want to be that girl.

"And I can help you, Reese." Marcus put his arm around her, who brushed it off and shoved him.

"That's Teresa to you, and I can find the nurse's office on my own, thanks." Reese took Quinn's arm and fell in step behind Mrs. Morgan. "We're independent women. We don't need no boys walkin' us to class; we've got our own legs. Try to keep up."

Marcus slung his bag over his shoulder and patted Aaron on the back. "Independent women. Humph."

Quinn glanced back at Aaron. He smiled. Maybe he liked her. Maybe she even liked him a little. The thought of that possibility made her feel weird, like she was betraying Jeff in some way. Which was stupid since Jeff betrayed her first. Her Jeff. She still loved him. But he had been a lie. Love was a lie. She understood that now more than ever. Even if Jeff moved on, she couldn't. Anger and hurt shadowed her heart in darkness and there wasn't room for anyone or anything else.

5

Mrs. Morgan led them into the nurse's office. Four sage-green walls held a small desk and chair. At the back stood a row of cabinets with assorted first aid materials, a sink, and a glass vase with a dozen wilting daisies bending over the side. A cot sat beneath a window overlooking the soccer fields.

"Make yourself comfortable, Miss Taylor." Mrs. Morgan gestured to the cot. "I'll bring you some cookies once I've finished writing up these excuses."

Quinn barely had time to wave at Reese before the nurse scraped the privacy curtain along the track, cloaking her away from the outside world.

Her legs dangled, her back to the window, while she waited. She wanted to pull the flimsy fabric from its hooks. Mrs. Morgan said she would give her a few cookies and send her back to class—not quarantine her like a plague victim.

A rustling of pages and the scratching of pen against paper came from the other side of the curtain. "Straight to class, no dawdling," Mrs. Morgan instructed.

"Can I at least see her before I go?" Reese asked.

"She needs to rest," Mrs. Morgan replied. "She'll be back to class after she has a nap."

Quinn chewed her bottom lip and twirled a long strand of hair around her finger. She didn't want to be alone, and she certainly didn't want to take a nap. Maybe she should have accepted Aaron's offer to take her home, but it was too late now. Besides, home would be worse, wouldn't it?

The cabinet doors creaked open, then slammed shut.

"Now, where did I put those? Ah, here we go." The curtain clattered as it opened. Mrs. Morgan held an open box of short-bread cookies and a generic juice box with a tiny white straw. Quinn went for a cookie first. "Thanks."

The shortbread had gone soft over time, melting on her tongue and tasting more of bland oatmeal than sweet cookie. Next, she took the orange juice—if it was orange juice. The warm and tangy saccharine liquid made her teeth ache. It probably had more additives than juice, but Quinn drank it without complaint.

"I feel better already." She handed the empty juice box back to Mrs. Morgan, gave her the most charming smile, and stood to leave.

"No hurry. I've told Ms. Moore you wouldn't be in class." Mrs. Morgan pulled a pillow from the cabinet and fluffed it.

"My bag?"

"It's safe by my desk. Try to take a nap. I'll give your mother a quick call." The curtain squeaked down the track again, leaving Quinn alone.

She eyed the pillow with suspicion then mashed it with her hand and let go, watching the foam spring back to shape. With nowhere to go, she lay her head down, pulling her knees to her chest and her scarf around her nose to block the mixed scent of bleach and garlic.

Any other day, a bed of nails would have been more comfortable than the lumpy, vinyl-covered cot, but exhaustion made it feel like cozy clouds of sleepy goodness. Quinn stiffened, fighting the desire to give up and relax. The shadows closed in with each breath she took, whispering for her to sleep. Her arsenal of energy drinks, caffeine pills, and phone was held hostage on the other side of that curtain. If only she could text Reese and plan a rescue operation.

The wall clock's metronome tick, along with the tap-tap-tap of Mrs. Morgan's fingers on the keyboard, lulled Quinn into a sense of calm, and her body slowly gave in.

No. No sleeping!

She lifted her head from the pillow and eased off the cot, cringing as the vinyl squeaked beneath her. She peeked around the curtain. Mrs. Morgan's back was to her as she typed; the bag lay on the floor next to her. No way to get it without being seen.

Quinn paced the small space, watching the second hand on the round, silver clock tick through the seconds. Twenty minutes to lunch.

"Come quick! The Massey boy accidentally ate something with nuts again." Quinn poked her head around the curtain as one of the lunch ladies burst in.

"That's the third time this year." Mrs. Morgan opened the lock on her fridge and pulled out an EpiPen. "Where is he? Cafeteria?"

"Yes. His face is swelling. Better get that to him quick. Principal Halstor is calling the paramedics."

Mrs. Morgan rushed out the door, leaving a forgotten Quinn on her own.

If Kevin Massey's last nut episode was anything to go by, Mrs. Morgan would have her hands full for at least an hour. Poor Kevin.

Quinn carefully checked for the all clear before grabbing her unguarded bag. She snatched two caffeine pills from the side pouch of her backpack, popped them in her mouth, and washed them down with a handful of water from the tap. Slinging the bag over her shoulder, she slipped out the door.

Instead of the nap she'd promised Mrs. Morgan, Quinn spent the rest of the day shuffling from class to class in a fog of exhaustion. Another caffeine pill before fifth period gave her the jitters but did nothing for her depleted energy. By the time the sixth period bell rang, a knot coiled inside her stomach. Nausea came in waves as she chocked down the urge to vomit. She would have to sleep soon, but how?

"You look like hell." Reese waited for Quinn by her locker, ready to walk to cheerleading practice as usual. "Maybe you should skip practice today."

"And give Kerstin more ammunition? No thanks. I can handle one more hour. And can we drop the poor-Quinn-you-look-like-crap-you-should-go-home routine?" Quinn forged ahead toward the gym. "I swear, if I hear that one more time today, I'm going to make a blanket fort and watch Netflix with a pint of ice cream."

"Yeah, fine." Reese hurried to catch up. "Can I still ride home with you? Dad's picking my car up from the garage tonight. He said he would pick me up from your house around seven, or I could grab a ride with Shonda."

"I already said you could, didn't I?"

"Yeah, I just thought with the whole not feeling well … " Quinn shot her a warning look, and Reese changed the subject. "So, only two more weeks before grades are released. I'm sure you'll be back on the squad once Coach White sees your grades are back to normal."

"Uh-huh."

"Seriously? Your AP history grade, Q.T.? Physics? You're passing now, aren't you?"

"I think I've lost the race for valedictorian." Quinn stared at her feet as she walked.

"Hell, forget about valedictorian. Have you done enough to

pass?" Quinn didn't answer, and Reese persisted. "You could ask for help, you know."

"No one can help me." Quinn stopped outside the door to the girl's locker room and across from the basketball gym where the Fillies practiced.

"I know you think you're too good for a tutor, but it's not that bad. I had one for algebra last year."

"Can you imagine what people…what Kerstin would say if I got a tutor?"

"Maybe you should stop worrying about Kerstin and start worrying about you. You're failing, you're benched, and I've seen corpses that look better than you."

A tutor won't help me get out of zombieland.

"You wouldn't understand," Quinn muttered.

"Why? Because I'm only an average student? Because I'm not Quinn Perfect? We can't all be valedictorian. God, sometimes you can be such a selfish snob."

"That's not what I meant," Quinn said with a sigh. The last thing she wanted to do was fight with her best friend.

"Yeah, well you've done nothing but shut me out and snap at me all afternoon. I'll see you after practice. Hope you enjoy your front row seat for the Kerstin show."

"Wait!" Quinn reached for Reese, but the door swung shut in her face.

She leaned against the brick wall and buried her head in her hands. It took everything in her to keep from crying. Everything went wrong. Every word, every action, they all ended in disaster. Maybe she should just disappear.

"Hey."

Quinn jumped.

Jess gestured down the hall toward the outside fields. He passed his helmet from palm to palm while avoiding eye contact. "I didn't mean to scare you. I'm just, you know, on my way to practice." He glanced over his shoulder. "Are you okay? You don't seem, you know, okay."

"Yeah, well, it's been a rough few months." Quinn stared at the ground, afraid she might catch Jeff's big brown eyes, afraid she would crumble then and there and lose herself in a flood of tears.

"Sorry," Jeff replied.

"Yeah, so you keep saying."

"I don't know what else to say." He tucked the helmet under his arm and reached out to stroke her cheek. She closed her eyes, relaxing at the familiar feel of his fingers tracing her skin. Heat radiated from him as he edged closer, his warm breath tickling her neck. She breathed him in. Jeff had always smelled of summer: sweet melons and a hint of musk from his favorite cologne. Now, he smelled of jasmine and vanilla—of Kerstin. She grabbed his hand, stilling it against her cheek, and fixed her stare on him, torn between the desire to have his lips on hers and the pain of his betrayal.

The door of the girl's locker room swung open, banging against the wall. Jeff jumped back, looking guilty. Kerstin, already in uniform, stood in the doorway.

"You forgot this." She thrust a plastic water bottle at Jeff then crossed her arms. "I was worried you might get dehydrated during scrimmage."

"Thanks." Jeff gave Kerstin an awkward kiss on the cheek, but she kept her arms crossed, returning no affection. He glanced at Quinn. "I have to go."

"Don't let me stop you." Kerstin shot Quinn a dirty look as Jeff hurried off to the football field. She waited until Jeff disappeared around the corner before turning her murderous glare on Quinn.

"Kerstin." Quinn nodded and shoved open the door to the gym, hoping Kerstin still had business in the locker room. No luck.

Kerstin's eyes followed her, like laser beams of hate boring into her skull, as she trailed Quinn across the court floor. Her silence was unnerving, and Quinn braced herself for a sharp push. At that moment, the other ten members of the Westland High Fillies giggled, gossiped, and chatted their way out of the locker room. Kerstin brushed past Quinn without a look, leaving her to wonder about retribution. Kerstin always delivered payback when she felt wronged. It was only a matter of time before Kerstin tried to get revenge.

6

*A*aron slipped out of his jeans and pulled a pair of navy swim trunks up and over his hips. Every day after school, it was the same. He and Marcus would head over to the Natatorium. Marcus would swim laps for an hour while Aaron sat beside the pool, legs tucked under his chin. Every day he told himself that he would walk into that pool and face his fears. Maybe one of these days, he'd do it.

His thoughts wandered back to Quinn and the darkness he had seen stirring in her subconscious. Should he ask her about it? What would he say? Everyone had noticed the change in her. He knew her dad leaving had hit her hard, and then Jeff. It made sense that she would be depressed. Hell, Aaron knew all too well what the black beast could be like. But what he'd felt when he touched her seemed like something more. Something sinister trying to get in.

Aaron shook his head. That sounded crazy. But did it sound any crazier than a boy who felt other peoples' emotions with one touch? He sighed and pushed his gym bag into his locker.

"FYI, Reese gave me Quinn's number." Aaron shoved his feet

into a pair of brown flip-flops and grabbed two towels from a shelf by the gym showers. "What do you think that means?" He wiped water from one of the wooden benches and sat while Marcus finished changing into his swimming trunks.

Marcus shrugged. "It means you now have Quinn's number and the next move is up to you?" He pulled a black swim cap over his ears. "Why didn't Quinn give *me* Reese's number?"

"Did you ask Quinn for Reese's number?"

"No, I asked Reese for Reese's number. She took my phone and pretended to put her number in it. When I looked later, she had written her name as Reese (You Haven't Earned It Yet) Moon with the number 555-5555 underneath. What do you think that means?" Marcus held out his hand. "My goggles, please."

"I think it means you *don't* have Reese's number and the next move is up to you." Aaron stretched the elastic strap of the swim goggles forward, creating a slingshot. He pulled the nose guard back and let go. Instead of launching into the air as he hoped, they clattered to the ground at Marcus's feet.

"Your aim sucks."

"Your advice sucks."

"Ouch, that hurt."

"So, seriously, do you think I should call her?" Aaron draped his towel over his shoulder.

"No, man. Keep it casual." Marcus shoved his bag into an empty locker and grabbed his towel from the bench. "Flirt with her, then flirt with another girl in front of her. Drive her mad with jealousy. They always want what they think they can't have." Marcus held out his fist and waited for Aaron to bump it and grinned. "See, I can give good advice, right?"

"Yeah, advice on how to get kicked in the nuts. I think you're confusing real life with what you read in that stash of mags under your bed."

"Hey, those are vintage! At least I actually read the articles." Marcus shifted and dropped his suave act. "You want my serious advice?"

"I wouldn't ask, if I didn't," Aaron said.

"She's had it rough the last couple of years, and the breakup with Jeff is the last in a long line of shit. She's going to have a few walls, some trust issues. If you really want to get to know her better, you're going to need to call her, earn her trust, be there for her when she needs someone to lean on. Besides, what's the worst she can do? Hang up on you? I've been hung up on at least a dozen times. It's not that bad. Sometimes they call back, sometimes they don't, but you gotta leave it up to them."

"Only a dozen hang-ups?"

"Maybe Reese will make it lucky thirteen. Come on lover boy, it's getting late." Marcus slapped Aaron on the back. They walked through the tiled arch and into the brightly lit Natatorium. The wall of windows captured the sun, throwing broken patterns of light across the still water off the pool.

He stopped at the edge, kicked his flip-flops off to the side, and stared, transfixed at the smooth, glassy surface. Dipping one toe into the water, he watched the ripple of tiny waves echo outward as he withdrew his foot. The scent of chlorine burned his nose. His heart beat faster, and beads of sweat formed on his forehead.

"Bombs away!" Marcus ran past him, leapt into the air, tucked his knees into his chest, and plunged, soaking Aaron from the waist down. The splash reverberated through the school's empty natatorium.

Aaron backed away, holding his breath and counting the seconds until Marcus's head popped back up above the waves.

"Dude, it's totally warm today." Marcus grinned, flipped onto his stomach and began a front crawl.

Aaron watched Marcus become one with the water. Breath,

stroke, glide through the clear blue, no fear. Marcus switched from freestyle to butterfly—his powerful muscles cutting through the water like propellers. He reached the end of his tenth lap and surfaced next to Aaron.

Marcus clicked the button on his Smartwatch to stop the timer, raised his fist, and punched the air in victory. "My fastest time yet! Watch out Bobby McGlyn, Marcus is here to smash your school record. Want to race? I'll even swim without using my arms to make it even."

He was more fish than man and determined to be state champion. When it came to water, Aaron was more chicken than man, and at the prompting of his therapist, he was determined to face his traumatic fear of water.

"You've been watching me practice for weeks, and you've barely even dipped your toe in. Jump in already. I swear, if you panic, I won't let you drown. Besides, the pool is only like five feet deep."

Yes. Time to rip the Band-Aid off. Just do it. Aaron approached the concrete lip of the pool. Each step sent a tremor through him. *Maybe Marcus is right. Don't think, just jump.* He pictured Marcus cutting through the water, fearless, alive. It was only a pool and shallow enough to stand in.

Aaron took a few steps back, breath in, breath out, using the relaxing technique he'd been taught in therapy. He detached himself from all emotion, ran forward, and jumped, pulling his knees up and sailing over Marcus.

For a moment, he forgot his fear and embraced the joy of the momentary freefall. He felt liberated. Then his body hit the surface with a jolt, and his eyes went wide, his heart like a pinball in his chest. Fingers of warm liquid pulled him under, enveloping him. The tingling started in the back of his brain, a slow burn before the lightning strike. He sank, overcome by what wouldn't stay forgotten.

The squeal of tires ripped through him, the smell of burning rubber cloying his nostrils. Screams erupted around him, through him. A hand grasped his as they flew forward, glass shattering, then the whoosh of water rushing through a broken window. He wanted out, but no amount of thrashing freed him. He gasped one last breath as waves swallowed them. Ruth's face. Quinn's face where his sister's should be, then back to Ruth. Why would Quinn's face appear where Ruth's had been? It didn't make sense. Ruth's chubby baby face floated before him in the deep blue of the river, chocolate still smeared on the corner of her mouth. A smile, as if to say: "I forgive you." Pressure like a cord around his chest pulled tighter and tighter. Darkness. Hands pulling him up, up, up.

"Aaron! Dude! Aaron, God, I'm sorry!"

Aaron coughed, sucking in humid air as he stared at the Natatorium's metal ceiling. Shaking, wet, he reveled in the solid comfort of the cold concrete beneath him. Marcus stood over him, breathing hard, dark hair dripping, eyes bulging. The shock and relief bubbled out of Aaron in a deliriously inappropriate fit of laughter.

"It's not funny." Marcus gave Aaron a stern look.

Aaron rolled over, curling himself in a ball, unable to stop.

"I'm serious. You scared me." Marcus's severe tone only made him laugh harder. "I didn't think you would actually jump." Marcus shook his head. "It's not funny." He paused, hands on his hips, and then snickered. "Okay, maybe it is a little funny. You should have seen yourself, man. It was the most ungraceful thing ever. It was like watching my cat when it tried to drink from the toilet and fell in, all screeching and thrashing." The laughter between them grew. "I thought you were going to scratch my eyes out trying to get you out of there."

This sobered Aaron. He sat up, and Marcus stopped mid-laugh. "Sorry."

"What for? It was my stupid mouth that started it. Don't ever listen to me again. You can come to the pool and sit at the edge for as long as it takes. Whenever you're ready."

"Thanks, but I don't know if I'll ever be ready."

Marcus shrugged. "Facing your fears is overrated. Who needs swimming anyway? You ever see girls go in the water?"

"One or two. Why?"

"One or two, that's what I'm sayin'. Chicks in the water are a rare occurrence. They spend most of their time sunbathing. The shore is where the action is, and you, my friend, can make the most of it. Think of all that skin waiting for sunblock. Carpe diem." Marcus, Aaron decided, really might have been clueless about the opposite sex. Marcus grabbed two towels and threw one at him. "Maybe I should give up swimming and join you on the shore." He wrapped it around his waist and shoved his feet into a pair of flip-flops. "You ready?"

"In a minute."

Marcus frowned. "I don't want to have to fish you out of there again."

Aaron gave the concrete an affectionate pat. "I'll stick to dry land."

"That's right, dry land is bikini land."

"I'll keep that in mind."

Marcus glanced at the water, looked at Aaron, and then shrugged. "I'll try not to use up all the hot water."

As Marcus disappeared around the corner into the locker room, Aaron pulled the towel around his shoulders, cocooning himself inside the soft terrycloth. Everything had changed that stormy night. In less than sixty seconds, he'd lost his family, his memories, and his life. Most days, he wasn't even sure who he was anymore. The accident had left him with an ability he didn't ask for—his memories lost to the depths of his mind— and a moment he couldn't forget, but desperately wished he could.

He envied Marcus' cavalier attitude and sunny outlook on life. If only he could learn to let go, even a little, to date and drink until he puked. To be a normal teenager. But nothing about his life was normal. Not since he'd come back from the dead.

49

*K*erstin delivered retribution between the start of practice and Reese's third lip-gloss application.

"Is it me, or has *Kristin*, oh wait, it's *Kerstin*, gone a bit psycho?" Reese pulled the screwdriver from the side of the rear tire wall. The hole blew a raspberry as the weight of the car emptied the tire's pressure.

"Great." Quinn kicked the deflated rubber then circled the car, examining it for more damage. "Know how to change a tire?"

"Yeah, flirt with a cute guy and let them offer to change it for you. Totally not a feminist take, I know."

Quinn surveyed the parking lot. Only a few cars dotted the concrete, and she recognized none of them. "Could this day get any worse?" She dropped her bag on the concrete and pushed the key fob. The car tweeted as the locks clicked open. "I am too damn tired to deal with Kerstin's crap."

"Are you sure it was Kerstin? She didn't leave that much sooner than we did."

True, and Kerstin wasn't the type to get her hands dirty—literally—if she could help it. "Spring, maybe? She'll do anything to impress her Supreme Witch." Quinn leaned over the seat, pulled the latch on the glove box, and retrieved a small, leather binder where she kept the card her mother had given her for their auto service.

"I'm not sure Spring would know what screwdriver looks like. Although, she has been hanging around with Ricky Dupree a lot lately. Maybe she used that tool to get this this tool." Reese slapped the rubber end of the screwdriver into her palm for emphasis.

"Can you hand me my phone?"

Reese pulled Quinn's phone from her backpack and tossed it to her.

Quinn typed her member number at the voice prompt and paced until an agent finally answered. "Hi, yes. I've got a flat tire. Westland High School student parking lot," she explained. "They can't come any sooner? Right. Thanks for nothing."

She hung up and Reese asked, "What did they say?"

"An hour. Can you believe it?" Quinn kicked her backpack as hard as she could. It skidded a couple of inches, scraping across the asphalt and falling over with a thud. She winced and curled her toes inside her boot.

"Feel better?"

Quinn bent and rubbed her foot. "No. Worse." She grabbed the screwdriver from Reese and twirled it between her fingers. "Maybe there are fingerprints on it."

"Yeah, yours. And mine. Guess I'll make myself comfortable." Reese settled on the curb, pulled a dandelion weed from the crack in the asphalt, and blew the white fluff into the wind.

"What did you wish for?"

"A cute guy to come and save us." Reese grinned.

"This is real life, not a movie." Quinn sighed, sat next to Reese, and picked a dandelion of her own. If this were a movie, Jeff would appear to tell her he'd broken up with Kerstin. He'd change the tire, rid her of the nightmares, and kiss her until her lips went numb. But life was not a movie.

"I could always call my dad. He might be able to leave work a little early to get us," Reese offered.

Jealous pain thumped in Quinn's chest. At least Reese had a father she could call in an emergency. Who did Quinn have? Not her dad, for sure. Once upon a time, Jeff would have been the first person she'd call. Now he would be the last. Screw this, she didn't need Jeff, or her dad, or anyone else. She did a quick search on her phone and started a video.

"What are you doing?"

"Learning how to change a tire. Go pop the trunk and see if there's something that looks like this." She swung her phone around to show Reese a picture of the jack.

"I wonder if Shonda's left yet," she grumbled. "She could drive us. She drives right past your house on her way home"

Quinn glared at her.

"Fine, I'll go check." Reese stood then grinned. "Looks like we won't need that video after all." She kicked Quinn's leg with the tip of her shoe until she looked up from her phone. Two boys exited the Natatorium and headed for the lone, white Jeep in the parking lot.

"Only works in the movies, huh? Seems to me that fate keeps throwing us in their path for a reason. Let's see you make fun of me now, ye of little faith." Reese waved as if she were a drowning victim. When they didn't notice her, Reese cupped her hands around her mouth and yelled, "Marcus! Aaron!"

Marcus looked up and nudged Aaron.

"You can stop jumping up and down now. They've seen us."

"Be nice and let them help us so we can get home before dinner."

"Hey, Teresa." Marcus enunciated each part of her name and winked.

"Oh, you can call me Reese." She flipped her hair, shamefully flirting. "We were looking for a couple of heroes, and then you two show up. Must be fate. Right, Quinn?"

"Seems we've run into a little car trouble." Quinn leaned against the back of the Mustang and pointed down.

Aaron let out a low whistle.

Marcus bent to inspect the gash in the deflated tire. "Did your car lose a knife fight?"

"More like it got screwed." The rubber handle of the screwdriver thudded against the asphalt as Quinn threw it on the ground.

"Whose Cheerios did you pee in this morning?" Marcus asked.

"Whose do you think?"

"Oh, She Who Must Not Be Named. That explains it." Aaron ran a hand through his dark hair and Quinn felt herself flush. "Do you have a spare?"

She nodded. "Sorry, I didn't mean to be so prickly. I know it's not your fault." She hit the trunk icon on the key fob, opened it, and bent over to move the jumper cables and emergency kit out of his way.

"I can do that." Aaron reached for the lever to release the cover on the tire well and his chest grazed her shoulder, his breath warm on her neck. She blushed with the sudden thought of his lips on her skin.

He brushed past her again, and she took a deep breath before sliding out of his way.

"Give me a hand, Marcus." He rolled the spare out, letting it bounce on the ground. "We'll have you back on the road in ten minutes." Aaron crouched to place the jack beneath the frame.

"You really don't have to do that; roadside assistance is on the way." She twined a strand of hair around her finger as she watched them work. She couldn't help but notice how his jeans hugged in all the right places. He was cute, in a rugged, brooding musician type of way. Fit enough, but not overly muscled. Jeff would crush him on the field with one tackle.

Aaron smiled up at her. She mirrored him then looked down and fumbled to pick up the screwdriver to keep from meeting his gaze. A nest of bees awakened in her stomach, buzzing with anger and confusion at her sudden interest in him. It's not like she had to go out with him. No harm in a little flirting, was there?"

Reese rolled her eyes. "Yeah, in an hour."

"An hour? That's crazy," Aaron said to Reese. "Call them back; tell them assistance has already arrived." He pumped the jack with his foot.

"Better do it quick, too. Aaron and I are faster than a pit crew at the Indy Five Hundred."

Aaron bent down again to help Marcus take the old tire off the rim. "Looks like multiple stab wounds. See?" He beckoned Reese to examine the tire.

Quinn crossed her arms over her chest and gawked at her best friend as she crouched next to Aaron, knee touching knee, exchanging flirtatious grins. Didn't he know it was Quinn's car, not Reese's? Annoyed at being left out, she squeezed between Reese and Aaron to get a better look. He smelled amazing—of citrus and mint, fresh from the shower.

"Quinn?" Oh God, she was staring at him.

"I better make that phone call." She stood quickly and dropped her phone in the process, but Aaron caught it before it smashed against the asphalt. His fingers grazed hers when he gave it to her. She shivered and pulled her hand away. "Thanks." She smiled. Simple chemistry, the laws of attraction, that's all it was. She was single. She could find another guy attractive.

"Are you sure this was Kerstin's work?" Aaron asked Reese. "She saw Quinn talking to Jeff earlier."

Hello, I'm right here, Quinn thought as Aaron focused all his attention on Reese.

"Oh." Aaron stared at the ground.

Marcus switched the flat for the new tire, holding it in place for Aaron while he tightened the bolts on the wheel. Marcus lowered the jack, and they loaded the ruined tire into the trunk.

"That should do it," Aaron said to Reese.

Part of Quinn burned with jealousy. "You really didn't have to do that, you know." She tried not to sound as annoyed as she felt. Even if he did like Reese and not her, it didn't give him the right to be rude.

Aaron shrugged. "It's no problem." He pulled a black, plastic guitar pick from his pocket and rolled it between his fingers, avoiding eye contact.

"Thanks." Quinn picked up her bag and threw it in the backseat. "We're heading over to Ray's to grab a soda and some fries."

"Want to join us? Aaron's buying," Marcus said to Reese.

"Thanks, but we've got a lot of homework." Quinn jumped in before Reese could answer. The last thing she wanted was to spend her evening watching two guys fawning over her best friend while she sat like a fourth wheel.

"Another time, maybe?" Reese opened the car door.

"Saturday night. Eight-ish." Marcus winked.

Reese's smile widened. "Another time was code for never."

Not missing a beat, Marcus shrugged. "Your loss, there are plenty of ladies waitin' in line for tickets to the Marcus love-fest."

"I've heard the reviews, I think I'll pass."

Marcus padded his hand across his heart, laughing. "Oh, Reese, that hurt."

"It's Teresa to you."

"But you said I could call you Reese."

Quinn watched Marcus and Reese banter while Aaron stared at her again. She dared a glance. His eyes caught hers, and heat rose in her cheeks. He frowned and looked away, breaking the connection.

"Let's go, lover boy." Aaron grabbed Marcus by the arm and dragged him across the parking lot. "See you tomorrow."

"Bye." Quinn wondered why he frowned and then wondered why she cared. She didn't like him but couldn't bear the thought of him not liking her. "Thanks again."

"Reese, you know you like me!" Marcus yelled across the parking lot as Aaron shoved him into the driver's seat of the Jeep.

"In your dreams!" Reese yelled back and slammed the car door, the final word on the matter. Then she let out a high-pitched girly squeal. "What a great guy!"

Quinn started the engine and cut Reese a surprised glance. "Who? Marcus?"

As if on cue, the white Jeep zoomed past them. Marcus honked and waved.

Reese blushed. "Well, Marcus is kind of cute, but I was talking about Aaron." Reese flipped up the passenger mirror and checked her hair.

"He's all right."

"All right? Have you met the guy?"

Quinn turned right out of the lot, catching up with the boys at a red light. Marcus danced inside the Jeep, rocking it back and forth. He sang to Aaron using his fist as a microphone. Aaron pushed his fist away, but Marcus kept coming at him until Aaron finally gave in. He sang back, punctuating each word with an exaggerated arm movement.

"I bet he has a sexy singing voice." Reese sighed. "He's clearly into you, Quinn."

The light turned green, and the boys turned left as the girls continued straight.

"No, he's not," Quinn protested.

"Um, yes he is. I saw him checking you out this morning from across the hall. It's obvious."

Quinn gripped the wheel while Reese kept talking Aaron up

to her. Block after block, she wouldn't let it go. The way she gushed about him made Quinn roll her eyes. No guy was that great. She thought Reese would finally give it up after they reached the house, but she didn't.

"You should have seen it." Reese slammed the car door. "The way he ran, pushing people out of the way to catch you in his arms before you crashed to the floor." She followed Quinn through the living room, up the stairs, and into the bedroom.

"Like Superman or something. Wow! I wish a guy would do that for me." Reese plopped into the wicker chair, folding both legs under her.

"You're exaggerating, Reese. Superman? Really." Quinn tried to downplay the hero archetype in hope that Reese would finally stop talking about Aaron and his heroics. "Can we just drop it now?"

"Well, you didn't see it. You were totally zonked. I mean, with a capital Z. No one else even tried to help. We stood there like idiots while Aaron jumped to action. And when you called out for Jeff—"

"I did what?" Quinn's blue eyes widened. "Please tell me I didn't. You're joking, right?"

Reese held her left hand up and placed her right one over her heart. "I'd never joke about that."

"I really called for Jeff?"

Reese nodded.

Quinn flopped backwards onto the bed, covered her face with a pillow, and screamed. "I'm never going back to school."

"Don't say that. I can't make it through senior year without you. Besides, there weren't that many people in the hall when you, you know, took your little nap." Reese got up and rummaged through Quinn's open closet.

"Right, only a few dozen, plus Kerstin and Jeff. It might as well be the whole school." Quinn raised herself onto her elbow. "Maybe Jeff is having second thoughts about everything. Did you see the green glow around him? Asking Aaron if he was my boyfriend? He couldn't have been more jealous."

"Be real. If he wanted to be with you, nothing would stop him." Reese pulled a shirt from the metal rod. "Hey, is this new?"

"Bought it last weekend," Quinn said.

"Cute." Reese held the black t-shift with angel wing-patterned cutouts on the back to her body. "I love the punk vibe this has, and the wings kind of look like lace." She examined herself in the full-length mirror, raising an eyebrow in contemplation. "This would be so cute with a frayed denim mini. Anyway, Jeff's been nothing but a jerk. Forget him. Let Kerstin have him."

"I know, you're right, but it's not that easy to let someone go whose been such a big part of your life for so long." Quinn joined Reese, sorting through the color-coded row of skirts. "Could you forget about our friendship that easily?"

"No." Reese conceded. "But it's not exactly the same thing."

"Isn't it? We were all friends way before Jeff and I started dating. You remember the first grade Halloween Carnival?"

"Yeah, I puked all over your shoes after riding the Ferris wheel and you told me not to worry, that it was good luck for your best friend to puke on your shoes. Then you gave me a sip of your apple cider and I knew you would be my best friend forever."

Quinn threw her arms around Reese and gave her a big hug. "You can throw up on my shoes anytime. Except for those." She pointed to a pair of designer heels. "Those were really expensive, and my mom would kill us both."

"Why don't you ever wear them? They're so cute!"

"Because they are cute but not at all comfortable. Anyway, stop distracting me with your fashion obsession."

"Sorry. You and Jeff and the first grade carnival. I'm listening."

"Right. Remember how Mrs. Jenkins dressed up as a witch

and decorated the playhouse with spider webs and played that creepy music? You had to enter the house and take the candy from her bubbling cauldron. And that cackle. I was too scared to go in."

"She was scary enough without the costume."

Quinn shot Reese a look. "I'm trying to be serious."

"Sorry, go on."

"Jeff took my hand and told me not to be afraid. When I wouldn't take the candy, he reached in to get the chocolate for me. He didn't let go of my hand the whole night. He's been a part of my life for as long as I can remember. I want to hate him. I should hate him, but I miss him, Reese. A part of me doesn't know how to exist without him. I still feel like he's going to walk through that door, grab me, and swing me around until we fall on the floor laughing. That he's going to climb the tree outside my room and bring me pizza and mint chocolate ice cream when I've had a bad day. My head knows he's with Kerstin now, but my heart can't accept it. He's my phantom limb." She pulled a denim mini from the hanger and handed it to Reese. "I'm damn mad. At him, at Kerstin. I'm hurting more than you know. But honestly, if he came over and begged for my forgiveness, wanted to get back together, I don't know if I would be strong enough to turn away from him. I can't just forget a lifetime of memories."

"Well, it looks like he has." Reese placed the skirt on the bed, shirt on top, and examined the outfit. "Not even a week after he breaks up with you, and he's with Kerstin. He's changed, Quinn. He's been different since he got back from Mexico." Grabbing the designer heels from closet, she added them to the outfit on the bed, again standing back to study the possibilities.

"I know. You're right. But he spoke to me today. For the first time in two months, he was the old Jeff. Caring, charming. He even sounded concerned. He almost kissed me until Kerstin interrupted us."

"Oh, no, you don't. You're not allowed to even think about kissing him, getting close to him, or especially getting back with him. Not even if he videoed himself tattooing the words 'I'm sorry Quinn, I'm an idiot for going out with Kerstin, I love you more than life itself' on his derrière. Not after the pieces of Quinn I had to pick up when he wouldn't return your calls. Or staying up all night with you crying after his own mother lied to you, saying he was out. And don't get me started on that jerkass breakup text. A text! A lifetime of friendship, four years as his girlfriend, and he sends you a text. Pathetic."

"You're right! What was I thinking?" Quinn cupped her hands around her head and groaned, her anger at Jeff returning tenfold. "And what a cheap excuse! 'I'm going through some personal stuff and need some space,' my ass."

"Yeah, I can see how much space that bloodsucking leech is giving him," Reese said. "I don't think she even lets him pee without her permission. Anyway, I've picked a fashion hit for tomorrow. Sure to make any boy drool, especially a boy whose name starts with A."

Quinn replaced the heels with a pair of chunky black boots and looked at Reese for approval. Reese nodded and grinned.

"I don't think I'm ready. Besides, I think he likes someone else." Quinn smoothed the edge of the duvet with a hand.

"Are you kidding? I've seen the way he looks at you."

"And I've seen the way he looks at you," Quinn mumbled.

"What?" Reese burst out laughing. "Are you that out of practice that you don't know how to read the signs anymore?"

"I'm not convinced. And even if Aaron did like me, I couldn't go out with him. I would be leading him on. That's not right."

"I don't think he would mind. If you ask me, Aaron's the best way to get over Jerky McAss. Nobody said you had to marry him or even give him your heart. Besides, kissing him might distract you from the pain of your phantom limb." Reese puckered her lips and made kissing noises.

"Very funny."

"Hey, if you don't want Aaron, can I go for him? I'm not nursing a broken heart." She beamed. "But I'll have to wear the outfit."

"I'll think about it." A pang of jealousy ran through her at the thought of Reese and Aaron together.

"The outfit or the boy?"

"Both." Quinn smoothed the wrinkles from the shirt with the palm of her hand. "Marcus likes you, and he's cute."

"If you want Aaron, just say so. You don't have to try and sell me on Marcus to distract me from your man."

Quinn looked away.

"See? You know you like him. Don't think I didn't see you checking out his butt while he changed that tire."

"Fine. I admit it. He does have a nice rear."

"Doesn't he? Now give me your phone."

"Why?" Quinn raised an eyebrow and handed her phone to Reese.

"Giving you his number, you know, in case of another emergency."

"Reese."

Reese held up her hand to stop her from protesting. "Seriously, you better make a move before someone snaps him up. There."

Quinn looked at her phone. "Superman Collier? Really, Reese."

Reese shrugged as her phone beeped. "Oh, that's my dad. He's pulling into the driveway. See you tomorrow?"

"I guess."

"You better be there."

"Do I have a choice? You've already chosen my outfit." Quinn followed Reese down the stairs.

"You better wear it." Reese kissed Quinn on the cheek. "Later, chica."

Quinn waved as Reese got into the Audi, leaving the front door open until the car was a black dot at the end of the street. If only Reese could have stayed all night, then she wouldn't have to be alone, she wouldn't have to face the rising fear as bedtime approached.

Sliding the bottom lock, she engaged the deadbolt, and set the security alarm. A breeze shifted the branches outside, their leaves scraping the windowpane like claws on glass. She filled her lungs, breathing out to calm her heartbeat as she made her way around the living room, switching on every light.

Quinn grabbed the TV remote, hit power, and the blank screen jumped to life. She tapped the volume five times, loud enough to drown out the silence, and plopped on the plush sofa. Hitting speed dial for Golden Dragon, she waited for the familiar voice on the other end.

"One sweet and sour chicken, boiled rice, and egg rolls. That's right. Number twenty-two. Twenty minutes? Yeah. Thanks."

Quinn flicked through the channels; the same reruns of old sitcoms filled the stations until primetime. Nothing new appeared on the OnDemand movie schedule. Her French and calculus homework lay untouched in her bag, along with her AP history essay marked with a red C-.

She pulled her homework from her bag and spread it on the coffee table. Grades would be out in another two weeks, not much time left to turn her F into something passable. She started with a French conjugation exercise, but the words swirled on the page as the last bits of energy drained from her body.

Forget it. There was always tomorrow. She flicked through the TV's guide one more time, settling on a nature program for background noise, and glanced at the time. Nearly seven. Jeff would be sitting down to dinner with his family right now. She missed gathering for family meals with them. Jeff and his little sister teasing each other, his parents asking each of them how their days at school went, laughing at his dad's jokes. She could always count on his family when she couldn't rely on her own. Now she sat alone waiting for takeout while her dad screwed his secretary and her mom buried herself in work. She tapped the screen of her smart phone and opened her text message menu.

JEFF, I MISS YOU.

She stared at the words. True as they were, she couldn't bring herself to send them. Deleting each letter, she closed the text box and pushed down the raw emptiness that threatened to swallow her.

Unbidden, Aaron's smile popped into her thoughts. There was something about him that she couldn't quite get her head around. Something…familiar? Safe? And she wondered if he would be having dinner right now, too. Maybe she should take Reese's advice. Opening a new text, she put in Aaron's name, or Superman's as Reese typed it.

HEY AARON, IT'S QUINN. I JUST WANTED…

Just wanted what? To use you to get over my ex? To not feel so lonely? To thank you for being a decent human being? To tell you I see shadows move and dream of demons and really need someone to talk to? That I'm afraid I'm going crazy? That I'm so tired of everything that sometimes I want to…

She shook her head, banishing the shadowed thought from her mind. *Get a grip, Quinn.* She pinched the bridge of her nose, took a deep breath, and deleted the text to Aaron.

Instead, she brought up her favorite game app and spent a few minutes matching up colored jewels to gain points. The repetition only made her sleepy. She put the phone down, peeled herself off the sofa, and did a few half-hearted jumping jacks to wake up when the doorbell startled her. Dinner at last.

Quinn tipped the delivery boy generously, re-secured the house, and settled on the sofa for some Chinese food. She took a few bites of chicken and poked holes in the sticky rice with a chopstick. In the background on the television, a lioness stalked a sick impala. She yawned and pinched herself on the leg, the pain shooting a temporary rush of adrenaline into her body. She carried the takeout boxes to the kitchen and started the coffee pot. Less water, more grounds.

A stack of mail sat on the bar. She shuffled through, looking for a new catalogue or magazine, while she waited for her caffeine to brew. Halfway through the stack, she saw it. She'd never forget her father's handwriting, the way the letters curled up at the ends. He'd finally written. She took the letter, put it back, then picked it up again.

Bringing the envelope to her nose, she breathed deeply, hoping to catch a scent of him. It smelled of paper, not a trace of her father's lemon aftershave remained. And why would it? California was a thousand miles away.

Coffee forgotten, she shoved the envelope into the pocket of her jeans and headed upstairs. As she turned, a shadow detached itself from a leg of the barstool, slithered across the floor, and disappeared into Quinn's own slim shadow. Swallowing her fear, she continued up the stairs. *And now for this special public service announcement: Remember kids, hallucinations thrive when sleep deprived.* She giggled at her absurd thoughts, the words ticking around her head like a broken record.

8

Quinn's room greeted her with its warm walls and bright, floral patterns. Shades shifted and writhed in every corner, and her stomach twisted with them. It was her own fault the hallucinations haunted her. She'd trapped herself in a vicious cycle of fear and paranoia, and her rational side would have to work overtime to break it.

"You are all in my head," she declared in false bravado. The shadows flickered and faded into normal shadows, but her hand still trembled as she fished the letter from her jeans. She traced her name on the envelope then slid a finger under the flap. Three pages of lined paper unfolded in her hands. A check fell from between the sheets.

She held it between her thumb and forefinger and slid down the wall to sit on the floor, pulling her knees to her chest. Five hundred dollars—a dollar for every day he'd been gone. It would never be enough.

Quinn flung the check away. It spun through the air and drifted down like a leaf to land a few feet from the door. The lights flickered, and a soft, tickling sensation, like a spider crawling up her neck, made her shiver. She smoothed her hair to one side until it spilled over her shoulder in one long, spiral twist. That's when she noticed a few tendrils of blond hair appeared gray, as if entwined in shadow. She blinked, running her fingers through every inch, examining the strands. Blond, gold, even a few strawberry pieces, but not one thread of gray.

Too much caffeine made her paranoid, seeing things that weren't there. She straightened out the letter and read:

DEAR QUINN,

IT'S BEEN SO LONG THAT I DON'T KNOW WHERE TO START. I'M SORRY. MAYBE THAT'S THE BEST WAY TO BEGIN.

Sorry? Was he actually saying sorry to her now? Better late than never, right? Quinn shivered as a cold draft brushed past her and settled around her neck. *God, Quinn, stop making excuses for him. You always do this—defend him. Just stop. It's too late for sorry.* What felt like a trickle of ice seeped into her ear, and she shuddered, rubbing her palm against the side of her head until the warmth returned.

I DECIDED IT WOULD BE BETTER IF I DISAPPEARED FOR A WHILE, GAVE YOU BOTH TIME TO FORGIVE ME.

You call eighteen months a while? A while is going out for milk, not for another life. Bitter dark thoughts crawled inside her mind, intensifying her anger and hurt.

But I've missed you too much. I've thought about calling a hundred times, but every time I pick up the phone, I chicken out. I thought a letter would be the best way to get my thoughts across. I didn't want to leave you, but I thought it would be better if you stayed with your mom. I hope you understand that.

Sure, I understand you are a coward and a liar.

ANYWAY, YOU REMEMBER SHERYL? WELL, SHE AND I ARE SETTLED IN CALIFORNIA.

"Don't forget cheat," the shadow voice whispered, mingling with her own. *And a cheat.* Her thoughts mirrored its words.

It's beautiful here. We've opened a restaurant right on the water, and it's packed every night. After all those years of struggling and job-hopping, I finally found my calling. Sheryl runs the business, and I get to cook and spend time talking with customers. Our house is only a mile from the beach. The only thing that would make me happier is being a part of your life again. Sheryl wants to get to know you, too.

Great.
HOW'S SCHOOL? HAVE YOU DECIDED ON A COLLEGE?

As if I would tell you.
TELL YOUR MOM NOT TO WORRY ABOUT THE EXPENSE. I KNOW I HAVEN'T BEEN MUCH OF A FATHER, BUT I'VE PUT AWAY ENOUGH MONEY TO COVER YOUR TUITION, BOOKS, HOUSING, AND ANYTHING ELSE YOU MIGHT NEED. I WANT TO DO THIS FOR YOU AND YOUR MOTHER.

Yeah, right, she'll tell you exactly where you can stick your money.
YOU MIGHT EVEN CONSIDER UCLA.

Not on your life.
IT'S ONLY THIRTY MINUTES FROM HERE. IT WOULD BE WONDERFUL TO HAVE YOU NEAR US, ALL OF US. THERE'S SOMEONE WHO WOULD ESPECIALLY LIKE TO MEET YOU.

Quinn tensed. A sick knot grew in her stomach.
YOU HAVE A NEW BABY BROTHER.

She stared at the word brother. Baby brother. She pressed a fist over her chest, her lungs squeezed tight around her heart. Breathe in, breathe out. Don't cry, don't cry, don't you dare cry.
HE'S TWO WEEKS OLD. WE NAMED HIM JACOB FRANCIS TAYLOR, AFTER YOUR GRANDFATHER. HE REMINDS ME OF YOU AS A BABY: STRONG AND ALWAYS HUNGRY. NOW I HAVE TWO LITTLE PUMPKINS.

They named him Jacob. After *her* grandfather. Tears streamed down her face, dripping on the black ink, swirling the words into nothingness. Her hands trembled as the letter slipped form her fingers.

How dare he name him after my grandfather? How dare he call him pumpkin?

Black shapes shifted against the wall, slithering closer, mirroring the storm brewing inside, urging her to focus on her pain. "Throw a little money your way and you'll forget the last two years of hell?"

Shaded voices overlapped with her thoughts, one feeding off the other.

He could have asked me to come live with him months ago.

"That's right," the shadow voice agreed.

He could have sent me a plane ticket to visit him. He didn't even tell me she was pregnant!

"He was too busy making a new life without you," it added.

Without me.

Anger, trapped for so long inside her, bubbled to the surface. She buried her head in her hands and dug her nails into her scalp, and the lights flickered and dimmed.

"The very people you love always leave."

Dad left me. A bang of her forehead against her knees punctuated each bleak thought.

"Jeff left you."

And Mom?

"She's always running away to work. She's never here when you really need her."

I really need her.

Quinn jerked her head from her hands, and the shadows scattered as the lights brightened. Wadding the letter into a tight ball, she slammed it into the trash and turned the stereo on, volume to the max. The loud frantic scream of Smashrock's lead singer matched her mood perfectly. Letting the hysteria of the music spur her anger, she kicked the trashcan. It flew into the wall. Its wicker side creaked against the force as crumpled tissues and wads of paper exploded across the room.

Broken promises, broken dreams, broken heart—nothing

but pieces of her remained. Quinn crawled on her hands and knees, banging her fists on the floor, primal pain thrumming through her. She screamed and crawled, banged and drummed, and between fits of rage, retrieved bits of Kleenex to stuff back into the trashcan. She tried stuffing down all the emotion, but the confusion in her head melted into the confusion of the music, each driving the other to a higher frenzy.

A pair of scissors gleamed from her dressing table. She grabbed them, examining the smooth, sharp edges. She put her fingers through the holes, opening and closing them, listening to the soft swish of metal grazing metal. Trembling, she dragged the cold tip across her forearm, evoking an angry, red scratch. Now her flesh reflected the raging scars on her heart. No one would care, and there wasn't anyone there to stop her. Alone. Always alone.

She stood and stared at the full-length mirror on the back of her door. Her long hair shone under the lamp. She grabbed a handful and opened the scissors wide, feeding her hair to the hungry blades. The weight fell from her, and she cut faster, clumps of blond hair floating to the floor.

"Quinn?" Her mother shoved the bedroom door open.

"Leave me alone!" Quinn screamed.

"Your hair!" Her mother dropped her briefcase on the floor and fumbled to turn off the music. "What's going on?"

"Nothing that concerns you. Why don't you leave?" Quinn fed another long chunk through the blades.

"You're my daughter, of course it concerns me. Mrs. Morgan said you fainted at school. Now I find you with a pair of scissors, chopping all your hair? My god, Quinn, what's gotten into you?"

"I told you, I just want to be left alone." Quinn slammed the scissors on the dresser, stomped over to the radio, and turned the music back on.

Her mother yanked the plug, and the music cut off mid-note.

"Honey, please talk to me." Her mother scanned the mess on the floor. "What's this?" She picked up the check, painted red lips turning into a frown. "How dare he. A bribe?" She snatched a crumpled sheet from the floor, smoothing it across her thigh and paused to read. "Quinn?" Her mother looked up, her eyebrow an arching question mark.

"A bribe. He wants to pay for school, wants me to go to UCLA. He's calling him pumpkin."

"What are you talking about?"

Quinn fished the last page from the trash and threw it at her mother. "Read for yourself."

Her mother caught it and read, her face reddening with anger. "I can see why you're upset." She balled up the letter. "I know you're hurting, but cutting your hair isn't going to help." Her mother stroked her shoulder and tried to pull her into a hug.

Quinn stiffened at her mother's touch and jerked away. "It's *my* hair." She busied herself with picking up the shorn locks.

"Talk to me." She squatted to help, eye level with Quinn. "You have to face your problems, Quinn. You can't run away from them."

"Why not? Everyone else in our family does. I'm just doing what you and Dad taught me." Quinn spat the words like venom, throwing a handful of golden hair in her mother's face.

Her mother stiffened and brushed the strands from her blouse. "Fine. I came home to check on you because I was worried. I skipped out on a meeting with a client, and for what? To be greeted by a four-year-old in a teenager's body. I'm sick of this tantrum."

"You don't know anything about me."

Her mother sighed. "How can I? You won't even talk to me. You don't think that letter hurts me too? You can talk to me."

"It's a little too late to play the caring mother."

Her mother yanked the top flap of her briefcase open,

grabbed her wallet, and threw six twenties on the floor. "That's to fix your hair. I've got to get back to work."

"That's right, Mother, go hide at your office! Drown your sorrows in your new career!" Quinn plugged the radio back in, and the music exploded.

Her mother slammed the bedroom door, and Quinn fell into a heap on the bed. All the anger poured out of her, leaving her limp and empty until exhaustion overwhelmed her. She crawled into bed, moving the decorative pillows to one side, and curled into a ball beneath the cool sheets. Why had she been so terrible to her mother? All that anger, that wasn't her. Where had it come from?

One long sigh escaped her lips, and she saw her breath, a cold, gray fog expelling from her lungs. The lights dimmed, drenching the room in darkness. Her heart jumped as shadows gathered around, inching forward. She needed a caffeine pill and another energy drink. But resisting the soft, warm comfort of her bed wasn't possible. Completely drained, her body refused her command. Even her mind slipped free of her control, drifting into unconsciousness.

Five minutes. Just five minutes. Nightmares couldn't really hurt her. That's all they were. She could let herself sleep for five minutes, right?

She tried to clear her mind, thinking only good thoughts, but the events of the day played over and over in her head. The shadows, the voices, the fog—all tumbled out of the recesses as the dream reeled her in.

Kerstin stood over her bed, red hair curling like worms around her pale face. She cocked her head and breathed out. Smoke slithered from her lips, filling the space around her until she disappeared in the swirling gray. Beside her, Quinn sensed the shadows mounting, but couldn't wake. Sleep paralysis had gripped her as her body shut down to enter REM sleep. Desperate to sleep and powerless to wake, she tried to influence the dream instead. Alone among the swirling gray where Kerstin had previously stood, she filled her lungs and blew against the fog. Her breath grew into a mighty wind, forcing the dull smoke away as she focused her thoughts on something beautiful. The lake in Colorado where she used to summer with her parents, her favorite place, appeared before her.

The darkness howled as she pushed it further to the edges of her consciousness. Now free of their influence, her mind relaxed, and she sensed a shift in the dream.

For the first time in months, she was in control.

9

"*D*ad?"

Aaron turned the key in the lock, glad to be home. He dropped his backpack and helmet on the table by the door, but the smell of bourbon—Wild Turkey, his dad's favorite—hit him hard enough that his nose burned as he as he walked into the living room. "Hey, Dad, I'm home." He turned the light on and opened the bay window. "Did you remember to pick Josh up from school?"

James Collier groaned and turned over on the couch. An empty bottle fell from his hand. "Turn the light out and leave me alone." He pulled a pillow over his eyes. "And close the damn window. Your mother hates the cold."

Aaron covered his father with a blanket and picked the bottle off the floor.

"Guess that means I'm making dinner. Want some coffee?" His father groaned. "I'll take that as a yes."

The small, bright kitchen was a drastic contrast to the stuffy, dust-filled living room. He opened the blue, retro refrigerator (retro being a euphemism for ancient), and rummaged through

73

out-of-date milk, moldy cheese, and some leftovers that now looked like moss-covered wood.

"Hey, Superman." Josh, thin and lanky, appeared at the top of the stairs, his long, curly black hair hanging loose around his shoulders. He slid down the wobbling oak banister and stuck his landing with a thud. He raised his hands above his head, bowing and blowing kisses to an imaginary audience.

"Five-point-five from the Ukrainian judge," Aaron said.

"Oh, come on, I earned at least a six. Way better than your doofus attempt this morning."

"How'd you hear about that?" Aaron placed the last filter in the coffee maker, adding two scoops of grounds from the canister on the counter.

"You mean the Superman incident? That's what Xander's sister's calling it. She witnessed every heroic moment. You'll be getting a call from the commissioner any minute; I hear there's a cat stuck in a tree over on Elm Street." Josh swung one of the mismatched dining chairs around, sitting with his arms folded over the back.

"Very funny." Aaron put the lid back on the canister.

"You'll need to make it stronger than that. I found another empty bottle in the trash."

"Today's their anniversary." He decided to add another half-scoop and left the coffee to brew.

"I forgot. So?"

"So it's been hard on him, raising us alone."

"Oh, come on. It's been over three years. I've gotten over it. Why can't he? What's for dinner, anyway?"

Aaron looked at him. "Have you?"

"Have I what?"

"Gotten over it?"

Josh hung his head, hair falling over his eyes. "I'm thinking pizza."

Aaron watched his little brother. There was no denying they

were related. Both resembled their mother: same green eyes, same full lips, and long, dark eyelashes, even the one dimple on their left cheek. Ruth had the same dimple, too, but she had copper hair, not black like the boys. Ruth.

The image of his mother's shining eyes disappearing into murky darkness was the only memory of that night Aaron never had to fight to recall. That one stayed with him, etched forever in his mind. He clapped his brother on the shoulder. "I miss them too, you know. But Dad's still here. And me, I'm here."

"Like you were right after they died?" Josh kicked the empty chair next to him so hard it spun in a half circle before crashing sideways to the linoleum. "You ran out on us. You tried to follow them. I wish you would've succeeded."

"Keep it down! Your sister's sleeping," his dad called from the living room.

"Man, eighth grade is hard enough without a drunk for a father and a psycho for a brother," Josh mumbled.

Aaron clenched his fists, counting to ten as rage swept over him. "Say what you want about me, but like it or not, he's the only father we've got."

"Whatever. Can you take me over to Xander's?"

It amazed Aaron that Josh could go from cynical to casual as quickly as Hyde turning back into Jekyll.

"Ask Dad."

"Like he'll even notice I'm gone."

"Yes, I will." James Collier pulled himself up over the edge of the couch and pointed a rough finger at his sons. "Nobody leaves the house tonight. We've got some celebrating to do."

Aaron poured the coffee into a mug and walked over to the couch. "Drink this. It's strong, just the way you like it."

His dad sat up and took a sip but missed his mouth. Dark liquid twisted its way down his white undershirt, creating a brown, amoeba-shaped stain as the mug crashed to the floor.

"Josh, get me a towel. And bring the trashcan." Aaron bent down, picked up the pieces of mug, and placed them on the coffee table.

"Get it yourself." Josh buried his head in his arms, keeping his back turned from the living room.

"Hey!" Aaron yelled.

"Aaron, go to the store and get the biggest bunch of pink roses you can find. Pink are your mamma's favorite. Pink, not red. Hurry, she'll be home soon." His dad fumbled in his pocket for his wallet. "No expense is too great for my Katy." Their wedding album lay open on the floor. His dad looked up at him from a photograph, smiling, sober.

"Dad, look at me." Aaron touched his wrist, but his father jerked away, patting his back pocket.

"I had it a minute ago," his father mumbled.

"Dad. Please." Aaron grabbed his father's hands and braced himself. "Remember where you are." Looking into his father's forlorn eyes, he opened a crack in the barrier. The familiar tingling gathered in the back of his head as their minds touched. Alcohol clouded his father's emotions. He'd been thinking about their wedding day. With the help of his powers, Aaron saw through his father's memories. His mother stood before him, young and beautiful, her dark hair piled and twisted on top of her head. Her wedding veil flowed down the back of a lacy train. He felt what his father felt, awe that Katy had said yes. An overwhelming mix of love and desire flooded him as they joined hands to say their vows.

Aaron held on to this emotion, increasing its intensity and feeding it back to his father, trying to override the underlying grief. His dad jerked his hands away from him and scrambled backward on the couch, his eyes wild.

"Who are you? Stay away from me! Leave me be!"

Aaron grabbed his father's hands again, pushing truth

through the alcohol, fear, and confusion. "Dad, she's not coming home."

As if stabbed, his dad sank onto the faded orange couch, deflated. He stared at Aaron, fear and hate etched into the lines of his wrinkled face.

"You're not my son."

Aaron's face burned. He looked at the floor and clenched his jaw, fighting the urge to punch him. It was the alcohol talking and hitting him wouldn't even begin to erase the sting his father's words had left on his heart.

The front door slammed.

"Josh!" Aaron yelled after his brother.

His dad wrapped himself in the blanket, turned away from Aaron, and wept. Aaron's anger crumbled as he watched his father's pain engulf him. He stroked his gray hair the way his mother had stroked his until the weeping turned to snores. Then he went upstairs to nurse his own wounds with the strings of his guitar.

In his room, Aaron lifted his acoustic guitar from its metal stand. He plucked the strings, listening to the tone of each note. Placing his right foot on the edge of his bed, he rested the guitar on his knee to adjust the tuning knobs and strummed. Satisfied with the sound, he paced the length of his small room, working on his newest composition.

> *The whirlwind comes and there you are broken pieces*
> *of your life.*
> *Again they're scattered near and far and you wonder*
> *why you try...*
> *to pick them up again and again...*
> *when the whirlwind comes again and again I'll tell you*
> *this...la la la la.*

Aaron leaned the guitar against the wall and flopped down on the end of his bed.

Grabbing a small spiral pad from the bed stand, he flipped to an empty page.

> Whirlwind. Wind, bend, din, end, fin, gin, in,
> pinned. Quinn. Quinn, Quinn, Quinn.

He took the pencil from behind his ear, tapping the eraser in a random rhythm on the page. He hadn't asked for her number, but Reese had given it to him anyway. "In case you want to check on her," she had said, winking as she'd saved Quinn's number in his cell. Grabbing his phone, he scrolled through his contacts and pressed SEND. It rang once, and he hung up.

Chicken. Frustrated, Aaron tossed the phone to the floor.

He needed to focus. Jenna would be annoyed if he didn't bring a new song to tomorrow night's rehearsal. Jenna. Now there was someone he should ask out. She was perfect: feisty, gorgeous, and witty. And she'd been hinting for weeks now that she wanted to be more than friends. Aaron enjoyed flirting with her, but that's as far as it went. Singing softly, he worked through some possible lyric to go with the new melody.

> To pick them up again and again,
> when the whirlwind comes again and again,
> And there's nothing left for me to mend,
> Because my life is at a bitter end.
> Tell me why I can't get this song to end!
> Why can't Quinn be my new girlfriend?

Quinn. Great, she wasn't just taking over his thoughts, but his music too. Why did every thought revolve around her? She was just a girl. Did they even have anything in common? At least he and Jenna shared a love of music. Not to mention, Quinn was clearly still hung up on someone else. Someone who could never make her happy. Not like he could.

Aaron picked up the phone and dialed again. One ring. He thought about what he would say when she answered. Two rings. He wiped sweat from his palm and shifted the phone to his other ear. Three rings. He resisted the urge to end the call. Voicemail. Relief and disappointment washed over him as he waited for the beep.

"Hey, Quinn, it's Aaron. Um, Teresa, um, gave me your number. I hope you don't mind. I wanted to make sure you were okay, you know, after what looked like a really crappy day." He winced at his own words and wished he could delete the message and start again. "Anyway, you've got my number now. Feel free to use it if you need anything." He paced as he talked. "Get some rest. See you tomorrow."

The second Aaron ended the call, small, electric shocks crackled through his brain, and a wave of fear swept through him like a tsunami. What the hell? He reeled as the electric shocks grew to a hammering pulse—a siren of sound and feeling. He gripped the bedpost, steadying himself, but the strength of emotion overwhelmed him and his knees buckled as the vision engulfed him.

10

The lake shimmered golden blue in the sun. Quinn relaxed on a pink blanket on the thin strip of beach. An empty bottle of soda, bag of chips, and a half-eaten apple from her picnic lunch sat beside her. She stretched and took a deep breath. The smell of honeysuckle floated on the breeze, warm and intoxicating.

She closed her eyes and listened to the gentle waves lapping the shore, at peace for the first time in months. She stood and kicked off her flip-flops, letting the cool waves wash over her toes as she waded along the shore. Gentle swells caressed her knees, and she raised the hem of her yellow sundress to keep it from getting wet. Content, she stopped and closed her eyes, wiggling her toes in the squishy, sandy bottom of the lake. A fish brushed the side of her leg, tickling her until she giggled.

She opened her eyes to take in the last few moments of beauty, the sky turning from pink to fiery orange, to the purple of dusk. As the sun slipped beneath the glassy surface of water, she tried to grab control of the dream, to force the sun back in the sky, but the darkness slipped past her defenses and overpowered her.

Nightfall stole all the light in the world, leaving the sky pitch-black. No moon. No stars. Strong currents churned around her legs, and goose bumps covered her flesh. She hugged herself, rubbing her bare arms in a futile attempt to keep warm as the bitter wind bit her face and whipped her hair into a million dancing strands. The joy drained out of her, opening a dark pit of hopelessness.

She stood still, blind in the darkness, and willed herself to wake up. Would her mother be home by now? Maybe if she called out, someone would hear her and shake her from the nightmare. The chilled waves pounded her thin legs, creeping past her thighs and swallowing her waist. Cupping her hands around her mouth, she yelled, "Help! Somebody! Anybody! Please help me!" The wailing of the wind tore the words from her lips, flinging them into the depths of the lake, drowning them.

She had to get back to shore, but she couldn't see which way to go. A flash of light caught her attention; it darted in and out of the trees, a beacon of hope surging in the dark. Someone searched for her!

"I'm here!" Quinn screamed and waved her hands. She tried to move forward, but sticky silt buried her feet. She pulled her left foot, yet it stayed stuck. She moved her heel and wiggled her toes to loosen the lakebed's grip and pulled once more. The mud gave way like a suction cup torn from a window. One foot free. Inch by agonizing inch, Quinn followed the light in the trees. Her muscles strained against the mud. Slurp, step, slurp, step.

Quinn's foot caught on a jagged rock, tearing the soft skin of her big toe. She fell backward into the frigid lake, her entire body enveloped in a massive splash. The icy water stung her arms and face and sent a rush of adrenaline through her whole system, propelling her back to her feet. Gagging, she sputtered and spit the fishy taste from her mouth.

Thunder rumbled behind her. Quinn turned to see a familiar fog gathering in the center of the lake. Panic filled her. Stumbling and running, sharp rocks clawed her flesh, her warm blood mixing with the icy water. She didn't care. She wanted to be back on dry land and focused all her energy on reaching the light.

"You can't get away from us," the fog whispered.

Quinn stopped and covered her ears, but fighting was futile. She swayed as the roar of the wind fought through her fingers, inside her mind, forcing her to turn and face the dread. She stood, transfixed on the mental movie playing amidst the shimmering mist. She, Quinn, a perfect and luminous spirit, floated above the waves, free of her body. While her dead flesh, heavy and cumbersome in life, sank ever further beneath the shadows of the lake. The last of her breath left her. A rush of freedom filled her as the cord tethering her soul to the gravity of life snapped. Intoxicating. She longed to be transported to a place where the chaos and fear within her would vanish, to let the wind carry her spirit far away. Is that what would happen if she let go? Would she be at peace? In heaven if she stopped fighting? She craved the promise the illusion taunted her with.

She took a step toward the swirling darkness, into deeper water. She no longer felt cold or afraid, only the desperate need to be free from her flesh, from everything.

At first, everything was blurry, a mix of sound and feeling, and it took a minute for Aaron to recognize the signature of Quinn's chaotic thoughts. What he couldn't figure out was how he'd tapped into her mind without being skin to skin. His power had never worked this way before. He'd been thinking about Quinn, and now he found himself connected to her. A psychic link through touch, he could control. This, he couldn't, and he didn't like feeling out of control. Maybe he should break the link, but curiosity and fear tugged at him until he opened his third eye wider, slipping deeper into her experience.

As the strength of their telepathic bond deepened and settled, his vision cleared. Quinn, small and pale, stood in a giant lake surrounded by a menacing-looking fog. The closest lake was three hours away. It didn't make any sense. A dream, a nightmare she desperately wanted to escape. From the middle of the lake, she called for help, her voice ragged. Something held her trapped in a nightmare. She fought to wake herself, but something held her entranced, something not human.

A knot grew in his stomach as she took a step into the darkness, the water inching over her shoulders.

"Quinn, don't!" Her fear infected him, and although he was sure it was only a dream, he couldn't help but be caught up in its vivid reality. All he knew was he had to get her out of the water. Not knowing what effect it might have, he hurled his inner voice like a spear through the connection. "Wake up!"

She tore herself from the evil mass and looked at him. Did she see him? Usually, people didn't sense him in their minds, but she stared directly right at him.

The dark shapes surrounding her exploded into a terrifying scream. A rush of wind nearly knocked her over, but she swam toward shore until she found her footing and then she ran. He edged toward the shore as well, his heart racing as he neared the waves lapping the sand. A tremor started in his legs and moved through his whole body. He backed away while waves rushed him. Instinct prompted him to turn and run.

It's only a vision. The water can't hurt you, he told himself. Quinn held out her hand, reaching for him. He swallowed hard.

Ruth's hand had reached for him the same way, and he hadn't been able to save her.

The dark gathered behind Quinn, a growing storm. She was oblivious, focused only on him.

"Quinn!" Pushing his fear away, he threw himself into the water, diving beneath an incoming wave. Panic set in as it swept him back, but he gritted his teeth and reminded himself it wasn't real. He was experiencing her dream, the immediate reality of her unconscious, while he remained safe in his room. Breaking the surface, her hand found his, and he pulled her into a tight embrace. As her body molded to his, fire burst through them, burning away everything and severing his connection.

"Wait!" he yelled as the lake disappeared and was replaced by the four walls of his bedroom. He hung his head. "No."

"They say talking to yourself is a sign of mental illness." Josh stood in the doorway, one hand in his pocket, the other brushing his curls from his eyes. "Do I need to call the men in white coats to come and take you away again?"

Aaron pinched the bridge of his nose. Pain burst behind his eyes and spread through the back of his skull as invisible ropes squeezed tight around his chest. "Not now," he growled at Josh.

Swallowing the lump in his throat, Aaron closed his eyes and tried to reconnect with Quinn, to make sure she was okay. But he wasn't sure how. He had been thinking about her when the vision took him. Maybe his mind dialed hers like a psychic cell phone. It sounded crazy, but was it any crazier than being able to read people's minds and influence their emotions?

The squeak of the bedsprings told him Josh was making himself comfortable.

"I said not now. I'm in the middle of something important." He focused on her face, on wanting to talk to her, called her name in his head. Nothing. Without touching her, he had no idea where to begin.

It was only a dream, he told himself. A vivid one, but it wasn't like she was in any real danger. She must have awakened, which then broke their connection. Aaron opened his eyes and scowled at Josh.

Josh grinned. "Oh, right, talking to yourself. So important. How rude of me to interrupt." The covers wrinkled as Josh scooted his lanky body back to lean against the headboard. "You talk to yourself a lot these days. Were you praying or something?"

"None of your business." Aaron reigned in his temper, but his words still escaped as a snarl.

Cool and in control, Josh placed his hands behind his neck, rested his head on a pillow, and stretched his spindly legs out in front of him to lounge lizard-style. "Sure looked like praying to me. On your knees, eyes closed. There is no God, you know. You might as well be talking to yourself."

"Let's just drop it, okay?" Aaron stood and flopped into the blue beanbag chair in the corner. Tired and confused, he rubbed his face with both hands. "Where have you been?"

"Out. If I had known you'd make up a little imaginary friend to talk to because you missed me so much, I might have come back sooner." Josh's sarcastic tone irked Aaron, but he tried to ignore it.

"Why did you leave?"

"What? Can't stand a little debate? Afraid your faith can't handle some skepticism?"

"What?" Aaron turned the questions around on his brother. "What about you? Can't stand to be cared about? Afraid to tell me where you went?"

Josh shrugged. "Xander's. I was hungry. There's never any food round here, and his mom fixed spaghetti. Never turn down a free meal. Especially spaghetti."

"I called Xander. He said he hadn't seen you since lunch. Where were you?"

Josh shifted on the bed, casting his eyes first on the ground, then straight into his brother's. "I forget," he said in pure defiance.

Aaron leaned forward, arms on his knees, and gave Josh a

stern look. "Right, well, you better start remembering because from now on you're going everywhere I go."

"Yeah, right." Josh leaned forward in response.

"Get used to it." Aaron stood and crossed to the bed.

"Can't make me." Josh stood, bringing himself nose to nose with Aaron.

"Wanna bet?" Aaron dared.

"How? By praying?" Josh raised an eyebrow, smirked, and sat back down on the bed.

"I said drop it." Aaron kicked the mattress and turned away from his brother.

"Maybe I should talk to God. I'll feel better, right? The truth is, life deals you crap, then it kicks you in the stomach. Or have you forgotten about pain? Oh, that's right, you forgot everything. No pain for Aaron. Losing your memory. How convenient. Wish I could lose mine."

"Well, it's all perfectly clear now. Every little detail."

Aaron couldn't tell Josh the memories weren't exactly his or how he'd fished them out of his brother's mind, his father's too, building the puzzle of his previous life from flashes of their experiences, not his own. Not exactly. Aaron pushed the door open, gesturing for Josh to leave.

Josh picked up the guitar and randomly played the only two chords he knew.

Aaron sighed and settled back in the beanbag. He didn't need to touch him to sense Josh wanted to talk, or fight—or both—and wouldn't leave until he had his say.

"What did it feel like? Being dead?" his brother wondered.

"I've told you a million times."

Josh strummed the guitar faster, moving from the first chord to the second and back to the first again. "I should have left you there, in your own pool of blood. It would have been easier."

The sickness of guilt slammed into Aaron's stomach. Josh would never forgive him. And why should he? Aaron had been selfish and stupid, but the pain told him it'd be better if he were gone. It lied to him. If he had known Josh would have come home early that day, would he have still done it? Yes. The truth shamed him.

"You owe me, Aaron. Tell me what it was like," Josh insisted.

How many times had he asked the same question? Josh knew he didn't like talking about it with him, or anyone. It was too personal. He hated the idea of being known as the boy who came back from the dead, but Josh wouldn't stop asking him and Aaron was forced to replay the event over and over as punishment.

"What do you think it's like?" Aaron waited for Josh to look up. "To wake up after three months in a hospital bed, not knowing who you are? Not recognizing anything about your life? Finding out your mother and sister are dead and feeling nothing because you can't even remember them?"

Except for Ruth. He'd always remembered her small hands and bright eyes, sinking farther and farther into the darkness.

"I woke up to a world I didn't know, a world that had gone on without me. No friends left, not that I could remember, anyway. You and dad were strangers. You think I liked that? You think I didn't want to remember my life before the accident? I tried. Months and months of therapy before I could walk again, you always pushing me to remember, Dad staring at me as if I were diseased. How would you feel? When I saw the razor, I thought it would be better for everyone. Sometimes, I still feel that way."

"I'd keep that to yourself if I were you. Maybe they let you out of the asylum a little too soon." Josh started to strum the guitar again, each strident cord irritated Aaron, but he didn't stop him.

Aaron had never told Josh the real reason he'd tried to kill himself. Awakening from the coma into a life he had no memory of was hard enough, but the visions were the real torment. Even now, eighteen months after the accident, he felt he was only half-Aaron, half a character built on the memories of others, touch-by-touch, vision-by-vision. Everything he knew about himself came from someone else. None of it was his. With each new connection, he gained pieces of himself, but he also gained the knowledge that his father would gladly trade Aaron's life to have his mother back, that Josh didn't trust him, that they both knew he wasn't the same Aaron, whoever he had been. That something awakened in him while he lay in darkness.

"Did you see Mom? Ruth?" Josh's frantic strumming softened and stopped.

"No," Aaron lied. He had seen them once, as he lay trapped in the coma. They stood by his hospital bed, bathed in light and smelling of sunshine and honey, as if waiting for something. Aaron had called to them, but they'd turned away and disappeared through a portal of light. It wasn't until he'd seen their picture on the mantel that he realized who they were.

Someone else had been there, too: a bright being holding a carved runed sword. Something tugged at the back of Aaron's mind. That sword, the light in the darkness, they were the key, but the key to what? He focused on the memory, a name slipped through his mind and dissolved before he could grab onto it.

"No, I never saw anything. Only darkness."

"Then how can you believe in a god? Why were they taken and not you?" Tears flowed down Josh's cheeks, magnifying the red rage on his face. "Answer me, Aaron! How can you believe in God? Answer me!"

"I don't know!" Aaron screamed back. "I just do. Why do you care what I believe?" Aaron waited for a response but didn't get one. He wanted to use his ability on him, but Josh would pull away if he tried to touch him, as if he knew.

"I don't believe you." Josh bolted, tears clinging to his cheeks. He slammed the door—his last word.

Aaron dissolved into tears, crying like he hadn't since before the cold steel bit his flesh. *Who am I? Why did you take them and not me? I don't understand.* He didn't really expect an answer, but a shuffling in his brain and the feeling of being watched told him something had heard him. Something familiar. Something he'd met once, on the edge of death. A name. Azrael.

11

Quinn blinked against the bright sunlight streaming through her window and threw an arm over her eyes. Her mouth felt furry, as if she'd licked a cat, and her head ached with an emotional hangover. Catching an uneven strand of hair between her fingers, the night came rushing back to her. She'd been totally out of control, screaming at her mother, cutting her hair. As if possessed. Her body twitched, and her breath caught in her throat. What if she had been taken over by something else? Sitting up, she scanned the room.

Shadows clung to the walls, silent, unmoving, normal. Dreams were dreams and this was reality. In reality, shadows don't come to life—and they don't talk to you. Not in a sane person's world.

But am I sane? Insane people don't think they're insane. Or does the fact that I'm questioning it proof I'm not crazy?

She pinched the bridge of her nose and stumbled from her bed. Her mother's cash stared at her from the floor—covered in the light golden webs of Quinn's do-it-yourself haircut. Wishing she could go back in time and make a different choice, she swiped at a tear with the back of her hand. Temporary insanity or not, she had no one to blame for her actions but herself.

She grabbed her phone to check the time. Eleven-twenty. Crap! She had slept for fifteen hours straight, through all her morning classes. In those fifteen hours, she'd missed eight calls—two from Reese, one from her mom, five from an unknown number—a ton of texts, and two voicemails.

She scanned through her text message log first.

REESE 10:45 PM: FORGOT TO TELL U. GAVE AARON YOUR #. DON'T BE MAD!

REESE 11:27 PM: *KISS* NIGHT!

REESE 7:30 AM: DID HE CALL? U HAVE TO TELL ME EVERYTHING. SEE YOU @ UR LOCKER.

REESE 8:15 AM: @LOCKER. WHERE R U?

REESE 8:30 AM: WAKE UP, SLEEPY HEAD. U R LATE!

REESE 9:47 AM: WORRIED!

REESE 10:00 AM: ANSWER UR PHONE!

REESE 10:27 AM: IF I HAVE TO SKIP ALGEBRA TO COME OVER AND CHECK ON YOU, UR SO DEAD.

REESE 10:49 AM: WHERE R U???!!!

REESE 11:09 AM: CALLING MISSING PERSONS FBI CIA IF U DON'T GET BACK TO ME IN THE NEXT 5 MINS!!!! SERIOUS!!!!

Quinn opened a new message:

QUINN 11:27 AM I'M FINE. SLEPT IN. PHONE ON SILENT. MOM LETTING ME STAY HOME. SORRY TO SCARE U. TTL.

REESE 11:27 AM THANK GOD! CALL ME AS SOON AS YOU CAN!

Next, Quinn pressed the flashing voicemail icon and waited for the first message. She winced at her mother's condescending tone.

"I tried to wake you this morning. Really, Quinn, what's wrong with you? I called your school and told them you're sick. Don't think you can make a habit of this. I've also made you an appointment with Dr. Davis. Be there at one o'clock, sharp. Then you're scheduled with Michelle to fix your hair at two-thirty. I called in a major favor to squeeze you in, so don't be late. I'm flying to Chicago this afternoon for a last-minute meeting. Maybe you'll feel like talking when I get back." Her mother paused, and her tone softened. "I do love you. I wish you felt like you could talk to me. Bye." Quinn rubbed her ear, pressed delete, and played the next message.

Aaron's voice made her heart beat faster, her cheeks flush. Something about the way he said her name reminded her of her dream. Aaron was there, calling to her, urging her to turn away from the darkness. She remembered seeing him on the shore, diving under the water and pulling her to safety. With his touch, the world exploded in a bright, hot light that burned through the nightmare, and she finally slept, at peace, dream-free.

She needed to thank him. But thank him for what? He couldn't have actually been in her dream. That sounded crazy. It was a nightmare, and Aaron... nothing but a figment of her imagination summoned by her unconscious. But why had her unconscious conjured up Aaron as her savior and not Reese, or Jeff, or someone she had a connection with?

She listened to his message again.

Hey, Quinn, it's Aaron ...

Something about him ignited an ember of trust inside her, coaxing her to share her fears with him.

Her phone buzzed with another text.

AARON (SUPERMAN) COLLIER 11:28 AM: REESE SAID YOU STAYED HOME TODAY. ARE U OK? CALL ME. AARON.

She paced. Had he known she was thinking of him? Could he read her mind? *Don't. Be. Stupid.* A slap of her palm to her forehead punctuated each word. Shared dreams, mind reading, how crazy could you get? Next, she would start believing in vampires. Earth to Quinn. It was a dream. She looked at her phone. Nearly lunchtime.

QUINN 11:29 AM I'M OK. CALL ME WHEN YOU'RE FREE.

She sat on the end of the bed and went to twist a long strand of hair around her finger, but her hair was gone. She sucked her bottom lip to hold back the tears that threatened to fall, but her phone rang, distracting her. Aaron. She took a deep breath to steady her voice, wiped her eyes, and mentally prepared herself. Not wanting to seem too eager, she let it ring two more times before picking up.

"Hello?"

"Hi, it's Aaron."

"Hey." Quinn chewed her thumbnail and tried to sound casual.

"Are you okay? I …" He paused, and she quickly filled the silence.

"I'm okay. I'm glad you called." Another round of silence took over the conversation. Face palm. She should have given him a chance to finish his sentence instead of cutting him off. "Aaron?"

"I'm here. Sorry. I'm hiding in a bathroom stall. Mr. Minks came in just as I called you."

Quinn laughed at the image of Aaron crouched in a tiny stall, talking to her.

"I didn't mean to pull you out of class."

"Geography. Yawn. You did me a favor."

She smiled. "Sorry I missed your call last night. I fell asleep, and my phone was on silent."

"It's okay. Did you have nice dreams?"

Quinn froze, mind racing.

"Quinn?"

"I'm here." He knew. He had to know. Why else would he say that? Or maybe he could read her thoughts. No, that's crazy. A mix of anxiousness and excitement gripped her. She fumbled to say something. "Dreams?"

"Yeah, you know, dreams. Those things you have at night while you sleep?" he teased. Was he fishing? Or was it a lucky guess?

"Try nightmare," she answered.

Another long pause.

"A bad one?"

She wanted to scream, *Yes!* To let the fear, the questions, the insecurity all pour out of her, but she didn't know how. Her leg trembled as the urge to trust him intensified.

"No worse than usual." She pulled at a strand of short hair that fell across her eye.

"If you want to talk about it, I'm here."

Could she really trust him? She had to talk to somebody, why not Aaron? Though she didn't know him all that well, maybe that would make it easier. He didn't know her the way Reese did. He didn't know the way she used to be.

"This is going to sound crazy."

"Trust me, it won't. I'm listening."

"The nightmares." She bit her lower lip. "They're more than nightmares. No, that sounds stupid. I don't know how to explain it."

"Try."

Quinn took a deep breath and collected her thoughts.

"So, last night, it was so weird. I was in a lake, surrounded by this fog full of darkness. The darkness pulled at me, such grief that I wanted to end it all…and then…you were there, this light in the darkness. It was so real, you know, like you were actually there, in my nightmare, with me. I felt your hand and heard your voice as clear as I'm hearing it now. You told me not to do it. I know it sounds crazy. You barely even know me, and yet I feel like I can tell you anything. You're not a dream-walker or something out of a sci-fi movie, are you?" A nervous giggle escaped her lips.

Silence.

"Crazy, right?" she asked.

Silence.

"Aaron? Are you there?"

Dial tone.

"Shit."

Maybe Mr. Minks caught him with his phone and he had to hang up. Or maybe he couldn't deal with her crazy and hung up on her. She opened her messages to text him, but before she could finish the first word, her phone buzzed with a new message.

UNKNOWN 11:32AM STAY AWAY FROM AARON COLLIER

Quinn stared at the message. Her hands shook as she typed.

QUINN 11:32 AM: WHO IS THIS?

UNKNOWN 11:32 AM: YOU KNOW WHO WE ARE, QUINN.

QUINN 11:32 AM: STOP PLAYING AROUND.

UNKNOWN 11:33 AM: HE CAN'T HELP YOU.

QUINN 11:33 AM: WHO IS THIS!!!!

UNKNOWN 11:33 AM: HE DOESN'T HAVE THAT KIND OF POWER.

QUINN 11:33AM: LEAVE ME ALONE

UNKNOWN 11:33 AM: NOBODY DOES

UNKNOWN 11:33 AM: EARTH TO EARTH

UNKNOWN 11:33 AM: ASHES TO ASHES

UNKNOWN 11:33 AM: DUST TO DUST

UNKNOWN 11:33 AM: EVERYONE DIES.

UNKNOWN 11:33 AM: HE CAN'T HELP YOU!!!!

UNKNOWN 11:33 AM: HE CAN'T HELP YOU!!!!

UNKNOWN 11:33 AM: HE CAN'T HELP YOU!!!!

UNKNOWN 11:33 AM: EVERYONE DIES, QUINN. EVERYONE.

She dropped the phone and jumped on the bed, covering her ears as dozens of new messages flooded the mobile phone. It tapped and danced across the wood floor.

"You don't scare me." She hoped the waver in her voice didn't give away her false bravado. "Leave me alone! You don't scare me!" The phone shuddered two more times, spasming like a dying fish before coming to rest in a pool of light on the opposite side of the room. Her heart hammered. She scanned the corners, waiting for something else to happen.

Ten minutes passed. The sun grew brighter, and her breathing steadied. She climbed from her perch and warily approached the now-silent phone. She kicked it, drawing her foot back in case it jumped to life. When it didn't bite her, she picked it up and turned it over. She clicked the message tab and scrolled through texts from her mom, Reese, and Aaron. The mysterious texts had vanished.

A giggle bubbled to the surface before exploding from her lips. She was cracking up. Glancing around the room, she laughed again, falling into a heap on the floor. The whole scenario was ridiculous— dark visitors, demon texts, mysterious boys from school saving her from her nightmares—all of it too bizarre to be real.

"A phone malfunction." She pointed at her shadow. "You're just my imagination gone wild." She giggled again. "You don't scare me, you're not even real." She repeated the mantra over and over as she pulled on a pair of jeans and a shirt. What would she say to Dr. Davis about all this? If she told her, would she up her meds? Give her more sleeping pills? Call the men in white coats? No, say nothing. Stick to the nightmares, to her father's letter, cutting her own hair. There would be plenty to talk about other than phantom phone demons.

"You're not real. You're not real. You're not real." The words steadied the creepy feeling crawling over her skin as she stumbled downstairs, grabbed her keys, and rushed out into the sunshine..

"Hello? Quinn? Can you hear me?" She was gone.

"Shit." Aaron pulled the phone from his ear and checked the settings. Full reception, over half battery life. He redialed her number.

"This person is not accepting calls at this time," the cold female robot on the other end informed him.

Had he pushed her too hard? Hinted too much? He replayed the conversation over again in his head. She had been about to open up to him about the nightmare, he was sure of it, and then, silence. Why would you ask someone to call you, hang up on them, and then block their number? Maybe her phone died, or she hit a wrong button and blocked him by mistake, a misunderstanding, or a phone malfunction. He shouldn't jump to conclusions. Aaron checked the number and tried again.

"This person is not accepting calls at this time." Or maybe she really didn't want to talk to him, and he should stop making excuses for her. He shoved his cell in his pocket and kicked the stall door shut. It thudded against the latch, bounced back, and thudded again.

If she didn't want to talk to him, she should have said so. He would respect her wishes and leave her alone, but to deliberately block him after she had texted him? Was she playing some kind of game? He hated games. He'd ditched class to answer her text. Why couldn't she be honest with him? Had he misjudged the situation? Misjudged her? No, he had clearly seen her pain, sensed her fear. Why couldn't she see that he wanted to help? But what if Quinn didn't want his help? Then what? Should he even bother trying? She didn't even seem to want to be friends, much less anything else. Which brought him to the thing that bugged him the most—why would she block his number? It didn't make sense.

He stood in front of the mirror and splashed cold water over his face. What was it that Marcus had said? *She's sure to have trust issues. Give her time, man.*

Maybe Marcus was right. Maybe Quinn wasn't ready. If she needed space, he should give her space. If only he could shake this cold dread that settled in the pit of his stomach. There was something more to all of this, his dream walking, their connection… something…he couldn't quite grasp.

A light breeze ruffled his hair and he spun around. Light streamed in through the window, illuminating his face in a soft glow. Then, a memory slammed into him with the force of a tornado, tossing up images and feelings so vivid, that he gripped the edge of the sink to steady himself. Since the accident, most of his memories were jumbles, pieces put together through the memories of others, not his own. This felt similar, like he had dipped into another's mind, but not.

A seven-year-old Aaron lay curled up in the middle of the street next to Bandit, a black and tan mutt with racoon markings around the eyes. Blood streaked Aaron's cheek as he buried his face into Bandit's matted fur. Bandit's legs twisted in odd angles, his cold, gray, tongue lolled to the side.

Every night for months this stray mutt snuck into their backyard and raided the trash for food. Aaron's dad called the dog a thief, and a menace, the neighborhood bandit. Not even animal control could catch this wily creature. Soon, Aaron started calling him Bandit, and before they knew it, the whole family began to think of this scruffy beast as theirs. But Bandit refused to be touched, refused to be tamed.

Aaron enticed him with food, but Bandit still raided the trash. They built Bandit a dog house and filled it with blankets, but Bandit preferred to sleep in the farthest corner of the yard, or to jump the fence and run in the woods. A treat offered in Aaron's hand would get him one or two steps closer, but the minute Aaron tried to touch him, he ran away. Bandit came and went as he pleased, with no regards to safety or loyalty or Aaron's feelings.

"It's all he's known," his father said one night after Bandit had escaped the yard again by digging a big hole under the fence. "It takes time to undo the fear that dog's been living with. He's taken care of himself his whole life, livin' free, never relying on anyone. It's instinctual now. Habit. Stop trying to change him and just love him as he is or move on."

But Aaron couldn't. What if Bandit raided a chicken coop and got shot, or coyotes attacked him in the woods. The moon was full when Aaron looked out his window. Bandit lazed in the corner of the yard, head next to an empty food bowl, tail tucked between his back legs.

Sneaking downstairs, he found a long nylon rope in the garage. He knotted it into a noose, then crept into the back yard. Tying one end to the post, he got down on all fours and crawled to Bandit. Bandit eyed him warily, the hackles on his back flaring. Before Aaron could reach him, he gave a little growl, sprang to his feet and leapt over the fence. Tires squealed, and Bandit let out a long, baleful yowl that soon faded into nothing. Aaron dropped the rope and ran, flinging open the gate. A woman got out of her car, hand over her mouth.

"He came out of nowhere," she kept repeating over, and over.

Aaron ran to Bandit and thrust his hands into his fur.

"I'm sorry. I'm so sorry." He murmured into Bandit's ear. His fur was courser than Aaron imagined, his body leaner under all the fur. And his eyes, deep honey brown, glassy and unseeing. "I should have let you be." He remembered how cold the body felt beneath his, and he wondered why he had bothered to love this wild thing that didn't want to be loved.

Aaron's mother kneeled beside him and wrapped a blanket around his shoulders as he shivered, trying to coax him away from the dead dog that he loved so much, but had never petted in life.

"I only wanted to protect him. For him to love me as much as I loved him. Why couldn't he see that, mommy?"

"Aaron, look at me." His mother cupped his cheek and stroked his hair as he stroked Bandit. "This is not your fault, okay?"

"Why did he run away when I was trying to help? Didn't he know how much I loved him?"

"Oh, honey, of course he did, but sometimes love needs room to grow and breathe. You were afraid for Bandit, but trying to control him out of fear, is not love. Love, Aaron, is not about fear, or getting what you want. It is about faith and trust. Another's love is not a thing that you can mold to your liking or set to your watch. It is theirs to keep and give when they are ready. And, sometimes, the thing you love won't love you back the way you want, but they will love you in the only way they know how. And sometimes, they may never be ready to love you at all, and it's time to let them go. And that's okay." He could hear his mother's voice as if she was with him now, and he couldn't hold back the tears that came.

"I wish I had never loved that stupid dog."

"Oh, my sweet boy, that the love you give is never wasted, even if it's not returned. The more love and kindness you put out in the world, the more you get back, just not always in the way you expected. You will learn when it's time to let go and take your love elsewhere."

"How?"

"Always trust your heart. It will know. Now, it's time to let Bandit go, sweetie. He has taken the love you gave him into the next world." She pulled his hands from his dog and guided him away. Aaron glanced over his shoulder to see his father, tears in his eyes, gently placing Bandit in a sheet.

Why this memory? Aaron asked himself. He stared at his reflection, his green eyes so like his mothers, and searched his heart. Should he stop caring about Quinn and move on, or was he supposed to give her room to learn to trust him?

Just be there when she needs you. That still, small voice inside of him whispered. His gut, his instinct, the ghost of his mother, god, whatever it was, he needed to stop and listen.

Arriving an hour early for school had its advantages. Quinn got a premium parking space, watched the sun rise, and still had time for a leisurely breakfast under her favorite oak tree. She hadn't felt this normal in months.

Breaking down in yesterday's therapy session was the best thing she's done in weeks. Dr. Davis helped her realize that she had imagined the creepy text messages from the mysterious number. It was her way of avoiding trust and connection. She also explained how extreme lack of sleep can make you question your sanity and, in some cases, can even cause visual hallucinations.

Quinn wasn't crazy, just tired and stressed. Now that she'd had a night of uninterrupted sleep, she could see how stupid being afraid of shadows had been. That, and spending a full twenty-four hours without something creepy happening. No shadows followed her, and she hadn't had one nightmare since dream-Aaron pulled her from the lake and banished the darkness that stalked her.

Dr. Davis also helped her understand that the lake dream represented Quinn moving past her fear and grief, and that

Aaron represented safety and trust. Strange that he would represent those things to her and not Jeff. Maybe she really was finally moving past him.

"You're early! And you wore my outfit!" Reese clapped her hands and took a seat next to Quinn under the oak tree. "You look amazing. I missed you yesterday. You had me so worried."

"I missed you too. You have no idea how much." Quinn wrapped her arms around Reese and squeezed.

"I haven't seen you this happy and rested in months." Reese squeezed back. "It's like the old Quinn is finally back."

"So, what do you think?" Quinn turned her head over her right shoulder, put her hand under her chin, and struck a pose. "Be honest."

"I think it's adorable. You told me it was short, but wow! I love it though! And the purple highlights are wicked. Coach White is going to freak."

"I don't care. At least it's the right color. You know, showing my school spirt and all." For all the excitement she was showing Reese about her new look, she still wasn't used to it. The short cut made her head look too small and her eyes too big. It had taken the stylist two hours, and Quinn more than a few tears, to fix the damage.

"True! Maybe we can talk her into letting all of us get purple streaks in our hair. New trend!" Reese held her hand out and Quinn handed her a flask of coffee. "I still can't believe your mom let you skip school to get a haircut." Reese took a sip and made a face. "Where's the sugar? Is there even milk in this?" She unscrewed the lid and looked in the flask.

"Oh, sorry, I'm drinking it black these days."

"Gross. Why?"

Quinn shrugged. "It grows on you. Doughnut?"

"Now you're speaking my language." Reese handed the coffee back to Quinn and pulled doughy hole from the bag. "Did she really call in sick for you? She's so cool! My mom would never do that."

Quinn plucked at a leaf on the ground and sucked on her bottom lip.

"Quinn?" Reese nudged her with a shoulder. "I know that look. What aren't you telling me?"

"Well…" Quinn sighed. "My dad sent me a letter."

"He what?"

"Yeah, the kind that come in the mail, written on that weird thing called paper?" Quinn paused and traced a broken heart in the dirt with a stick. "Oh, and there was a check for a shit ton of money to make up for all that time he's been absent. And, p.s., I have a new baby brother. Surprise! "

"What the hell? He dropped that in a letter? What a dick."

Quinn nodded. "Talk about a punch in the gut."

"Why didn't you call me? I would have come over with ice cream and hugs."

"I know, but I wasn't in the right headspace." Quinn fingered the chunky, short strands that fell just below her ears.

"It gets worse." Quinn leaned her head on Reese's shoulder and Reese leaned her cheek on Quinn's head.

"I'm listening."

The memory of it all came flooding back and Quinn felt a fat tear roll down her face. "I didn't go to get my haircut, well, not like you think. I did it myself with a pair of scissors, in my room. I can't explain it, I was so angry, and so sad, all the feelings just bubbled up and I couldn't hold it in anymore. I kept cutting, and cutting, and cutting, as if losing my hair would free me of all this pain. Mom came in and freaked out. No wonder. It scared me, Reese, it really scared me, and I think I scared mom too."

Reese pulled Quinn into her arms and ran her fingers through her hair. "Oh, Quinn. It's okay. You've been through so much. You don't have to try to be strong and perfect all the time, you know that, right?"

"That's good, because I feel like a real fuck up most of the time." Quinn admitted to Reese's shoulder.

"Come on, there's only room for one fuck up in this friendship, and it's me."

Quinn laughed. "Thank you. For always being there for me, even though I've been a terrible friend lately."

Reese wiped a tear from Quinn's cheek with the sleeve of her hoodie. "I tell you what, start putting sugar in the coffee, and I'll forgive you."

"Okay. I might even put a little milk in too."

"Let's take it one step at a time." Reese smiled. "Feel better? We can always ditch first period if you want to go get some real coffee."

"No, I'm okay. Besides, don't we have a French quiz?" Quinn stood up and offered Quinn a hand.

"Qui, fille, as-tu etudie?"

"Qui! Je suis prete!"

"That's the spirit!" Reese bumped her hip on Quinn's and Quinn threaded her arm through Reese's and they headed into the building.

One minute before the first period bell, Quinn and Reese took their usual seats in front of Jeff and Kerstin. Quinn opened her French book and felt Jeff tap her on the shoulder. Crap. Didn't he realize that talking to her painted a great big target on her back? She did not need this kind of trouble today. She ignored him and continued to quickly scan over the vocabulary that would be on the quiz. He tapped he shoulder again, so she slowly turned, trying not to show her annoyance.

"You look amazing with short hair," Jeff whispered.

"Um, thanks." Quinn caught Kerstin's glare as she turned away from Jeff. A shadowy mist gathered around her head like a dark halo, its tendrils draping her in a scarf of fog. Quinn took a deep breath and started the grounding tool her therapist had taught her.

Focus on five things you can see, Quinn.

One. Kerstin's eyes flashing from blue to black and back again.

Two. Her head torqued at an odd angle.

Three. Dark blue veins popping out against pale skin.

Four. Fingernails growing long and sharp.

Five. Red hair curling tendrils of fire twined with charcoal tendrils of smoke.

It's not real. It's not real. It's not real. Quinn repeated to herself. *Just turn around and start again.* She peeled her eyes away from Kerstin. *Forget about Kerstin and focus on passing the French quiz. Ignore the chill of fear coiling around your spine. And, whatever you do, Quinn, ignore what isn't really there. Four things you can hear, Quinn.*

One. Kerstin's hissing her name. No, no, something else. The door clinking shut.

Two. Rustling pages of a book.

Three. The whine of air conditioner kicking on.

Four. Mrs. Bouchard melodious voice calling class to start in French.

Three things you can feel, Quinn.

One. Sweat trickling down the back of my neck.

Two. The hard-plastic chair on my butt.

Three. Aaron's hand in mine.

That wasn't real either, but the idea of it calmed her just the same. Her breathing came easier now, and her muscles relaxed. By the time she finished the rest of the grounding exercise the fear had dissipated.

And when she took her quiz up to the front to turn in to Mrs. Bouchard, Kerstin looked perfectly normal, sitting in her seat, chatting with Spring. The bell rang. Quinn turned to leave, but she didn't see the foot sticking out from Kerstin's desk. Her shin smacked into it and she pitched forward. Her hand shot out to try and catch herself on a desk, but the weight of her backpack unsteadied her even more and she fell into the isle, cracking her elbow on a metal leg.

"Oops, sorry." Kerstin shrugged, slid out of her desk, and slithered out into the hallway.

"Are you okay?" Jeff offered her a hand, but she didn't take it.

"I'm fine." She said through clenched teeth.

Next period, Kerstin "accidentally" dropped a textbook on Quinn's foot. After Chemistry, she "accidentally" shouldered her into a locker. It had gotten so bad that Quinn spent the rest of the morning avoiding Kerstin's attacks by taking different routes to class and ducking behind trashcans whenever Kerstin rounded the corner. Cowardly, but effective.

After the lunch bell, Quinn cracked the door to the girl's bathroom and peeked down the hall to see if the coast was clear. No Kerstin in sight, but Aaron tapped out a rhythm on the metal door of his locker as he spun the numbers of his combination. He turned, as if he sensed her watching. She fumbled the door shut and pressed herself against the tiled wall. Waiting a few seconds, she cracked the door again. Aaron switched a book from his backpack with one from his locker. He was a mix of rugged and broody with piercing green eyes—the opposite of the all-American, preppy Jeff. A pen slid from his hand and he bent to pick it up. Her cheeks grew hot. Part of her wanted, needed, to talk to him, but uncertainty held her back.

Had he hung up on her because he thought she was crazy, or had the random phone malfunction cut her off? She should just ask him. Before her courage waned, she checked her hair in the mirror, squared her shoulders, and stepped through the door.

"Hey! Watch where you're going, freak." Kerstin rammed into her, knocking her back into the bathroom.

"Just leave me alone, all right?" Quinn tried to push past her, but Kerstin wedged her arm against the doorframe.

"Now, what would Quinn Perfect be doing hiding in the bathroom?" The lights flickered, painting dark shadows across the white tiled walls.

"I wasn't hiding." Sweat trickled down the back of Quinn's neck.

Mirror

Sink

Stall

Door

Handle

"I really need to go, Kerstin." She tried not to show the fear in her voice. "Reese is waiting for me."

Anger flashed across Kerstin's face. The lightbulbs in the bathroom began to pop, the glass shattering and raining down on her like sharp snowflakes.

"Oh, I'm sure she won't notice if you're a little late." Shadows slid across the floor and gathered at Kestin's feet. They writhed up her legs, and up her torso, painting her pale skin gray, turning her red hair to ink.

Quinn stood firm, pushing her fear as far down as she could.

"What do you want?"

Kerstin advanced, the shadows advancing with her. She seemed to grow, and stretch to the ceiling, towering over Quinn.

Quinn closed her eyes. Focus on what you can hear.

Water dripping.

The hum of the heat kicking on.

Kerstin's sneakers squeaking across the tiles

Squeak, squeak, closer, closer.

She could scream. Aaron was just outside, maybe he would hear her? Would he help her?

"Help's not coming, Quinn." Kerstin hissed in a voice not her own. Quinn covered her ears as Kerstin backed her into the corner, wedging her between the sink and the wall. "It's just you, and me."

"Kerstin," she said. "I don't think you're yourself."

"Oh, I'm exactly who I want to be." Kerstin's mouth quirked in an odd angle, her breath like sulfur.

"Quinn?" Aaron knocked on the door and Kristin spun toward it, the shadows spinning with her, a black tornado.

"Quinn?" he asked again, and pushed the door open an inch. "Are you okay?"

At the sound of his voice, all the bathroom lights suddenly came back on. Quinn blinked and looked up at the ceiling, none of the bulbs were broken. Kerstin stood, her normal five foot two, facing the vanity mirror, red lipstick poised over her bottom lip as if she'd been there, primping herself, all along.

"What's wrong, Quinn?" Kerstin cocked her head and fluffed her red hair in the mirror. "You look like you've seen a ghost."

Aaron knocked on the door again, this time louder. "Quinn?"

"Yeah, I'm here. I'm coming," Quinn said, praying that he would wait for her.

"Please don't leave me, Aaron." Kerstin parroted her thoughts.

"You've had your fun for the day." Quinn hesitantly stepped past Kerstin, backing all the way to the door, not wanting to take her eyes off her enemy.

"Oh, the fun's just beginning," Kerstin winked, and Quinn thought she saw her blue eye flash to black and back again. Kerstin finished applying her lipstick and smacked her lips. "See you at the pep rally."

 aron tapped a syncopated rhythm on the edge of his locker door with his fingers as he switched his morning text books for his afternoon classes. Marcus was sitting with his swim team buddies during lunch, going over strategies for the meet, so he'd decided to get in a little quiet writing time in the library. A new song unfurled inside him and he wanted to capture it while it sang so loudly. Jotting another fragment of lyric in his leather-bound journal, he heard a soft creak behind him. He turned to see a hint of blonde and purple hair disappearing into the girl's bathroom. Quinn. Had she been watching him? Sweat suddenly slicked the palm of his hands, and he rubbed them on his jeans.

He'd been waiting for a chance to talk to her all morning, but she'd been so elusive, rushing out of class the moment the bell rang, ducking behind corners, disappearing into crowds. At first, he thought she'd been avoiding him, that she really had blocked his calls. Until he noticed the way Quinn hunkered down in her seat when Kerstin entered a room. Then, in the hallway between classes, Kerstin shoved Quinn into the lockers, knocking her books out of her hand to spill on the floor. A cat playing with a caged bird. He'd seen the anger that flashed in Quinn's eyes. Anger that mirrored his own. Quinn's shoulders slumped as she scrambled to pick up her papers. It took everything Aaron had to hold his temper and his tongue as Kerstin laughed her way into class, but he didn't step in.

No. He'd promised himself he would give Quinn space, that he would let her come to him if she wanted to. And if she didn't? Well, he couldn't make someone trust him. And why should he? She'd never asked him to save her. It wasn't his responsibility. People had to save themselves first, that's what he'd learned in therapy.

But she'd been watching him. What if she wanted to talk to him, but felt awkward? Or maybe she wanted him to leave? The only way to find out was to ask her. He shifted his weight from left foot to right foot and glanced that the door to the girl's bathroom again. The hallway was quiet, the perfect place to confront her about this game she seemed to be playing with him. Spying on him. Blocking his number. If she *had* blocked his number. At least he could give her a chance to explain herself. But maybe she would think he was stalking her? No, she was the one hiding in the bathroom watching him. He slapped the journal on his forehead.

Go to the library. Do not pass go. Do not collect two-hundred dollars. Give. Her. Space.

He'd made it halfway down the hall when the hair on the back of his neck prickled and a cold dread crawled over his skin. When he turned, the walls narrowed like a fun house corridor until all he could see was the door to the girl's bathroom. Shadows slithered under the crack between the floor and the bottom of the door. Aaron blinked, his heart pounded a warning rhythm. He crept toward it and pressed his ear against the metal. Muffled voices rose and fell.

Aaron. Please help me. He didn't so much hear it, as felt it. This distinct plea and he knew it came from Quinn. He wasn't sure how, but he'd learned not to question moments like these.

In response, he knocked on the door.

"Quinn?"

No Answer.

He knocked louder and pushed the door open an inch. "Quinn, are you okay?"

Kerstin's voice rising against Quinn, mean, menacing, and full of snark made him clench his jaw. No more standing by while she bullied her. He knocked one more time, louder, urgent, to let them both know he wasn't going anywhere without Quinn, and if Quinn didn't answer, he would barge in, damn propriety.

"Yeah, I'm here. I'm coming." Her voice, high and full of tension.

The force of the door swinging open almost knocked him back as Quinn, pale as moonlight, pushed her way out. Not pausing to look back, she took his hand and guided him around the corner and toward the North wing. He followed her lead, swallowing the questions on his tongue. A mix of adrenaline, relief, and gratitude flooded him as her emotions poured into his. Her hand felt cool next to the heat radiating from his palm, and he wondered, for the hundredth time, why his connection with her was different than anyone else. Was he supposed to help her? Trust her? Love her? Protect her? He wanted to do all those things, but it scared him to be caught in this gravitational pull, as if he was getting sucked into a worm hole with no idea what was on the other side. An alarm bell sounded deep in the pit of his stomach, but was it for her, or for him, or for both? When they were touching, he couldn't tell where his emotions ended and hers began.

Quinn stopped at the library entrance. Aaron opened the

door and she followed him inside. He should have been surprised that she had chosen his destination without him telling her, but he wasn't. Maybe she could feel his emotions and thoughts too? Maybe she was like him and that's why he felt so drawn to her? Should he tell her about his abilities?

Together, they slowly wandered through the stacks, neither of them saying a word, until they came to the end of a secluded row near the back of the classic literature section. There they stood, alone, face to face.

"Thank you," she said and glanced at their interlaced fingers. Her cheeks blushed a light pink and she let go, folding her arms against her chest.

"Are you okay?" He suddenly felt incomplete and awkward and didn't know what to do with his now vacant hand, so he ran it through his hair. "That, um, seemed kind of weird." He leaned against the bookcase, trying to look casual.

"Weird." Quinn lovingly ran a finger over the spines of the books, not meeting his gaze. "That's one word for it."

Aaron wasn't sure what to say or do. All the questions he wanted to ask her sat on his tongue, heavy and unwieldly. Where should he begin? He walked an unstable tightrope with no net to catch him. One wrong move and it would be over. So, he waited, letting the silence fill in the gaps steadying them both. When she suddenly turned her face from the books and caught his eyes, it startled him, and he blurted out.

"—What happened with your phone—"

"—I didn't hang up on you—"

They both laughed.

"Ladies first," he said.

"The other day, when we were on the phone, I know you must think I hung up on you, but I didn't. My phone...it..." she sucked at her bottom lip. "I don't know. Died, or something." She mumbled the 'or something' and went back to pretending to browse the bookshelf. She was hiding something, he could sense it.

"You didn't block me?" He asked, leaning forward, placing himself between her and the books so she had no choice but confront him.

Her hands paused on a book, fingers gripping the spine, shoulders tense. Aaron tried to ease into the conversation, but frustration and anger reared inside him, and his suspicions spilled out like boiling water.

"Because I tried to call you back and it said that you weren't accepting calls. If you didn't want to talk to me, you could have just said so. I would have respected you and left you alone. I'm not some kind of creepy stalker."

"I don't think that!" She flinched, accidentally knocking the book she'd been clutching onto the floor, three more following with a thump, thump, thump. "Of course not!" She bent to pick them up, wiping a tear from the corner of her eye. "I'm not that kind of person."

"I'm sorry. I didn't mean to imply…" Aaron bent to help her pick them up, his hand brushing against hers. Confusion, fear, but not an outright lie. "Okay, maybe I did…" He moved away from her and rubbed the back of his neck, considering his words carefully. "I'm sorry for jumping to conclusions, it's just. One minute we were talking and the next you were gone? When I couldn't get through to you, I thought…"

Quinn's shoulders fell and she slid onto the floor with a sigh, pulling the books into her lap, like a shield. "It's complicated."

Aaron joined her, folding his hands in his lap and leaning back into the stacks. "I can handle complicated."

Quinn stared at the stack of books in her lap. Alice's Through The Looking Glass sat on top, and she began tracing the golden filigree vines and leaves on the cover with a finger.

"Have you ever felt like you were going crazy?"

Aaron stared at his hands. He thought of the first time he'd touched Josh after the accident, the secret blame buried in Josh's mind—that it had been Aaron's fault. Then came the onslaught of emotions and thoughts from every nurse, ever doctor, every person he encountered. Images he didn't want to see, knowledge he shouldn't have as he violated their privacy. It was enough to drive anyone crazy. Crazy enough to seek death. First, by fighting everyone he could, then by putting himself in increasingly dangerous situations, and when that didn't work, a knife biting into his own flesh, released him into the darkness that consumed him. Escaping death for the second time changed him. Maybe he'd been saved for a greater purpose. Maybe his new abilities weren't a curse and he could use them to help people. Instead of running from it, he embraced it. Now he could sneak in and out of the minds of others without them even knowing. Yes, he knew what it was like to feel like you were going crazy, and then some. Aaron drummed his fingers on his knee.

"We're all mad here." He finally answered, quoting the Cheshire Cat because he wasn't sure what to say. "I'm mad. You're mad."

The smile that lit Quinn's face almost knocked him over.

"How do you know I'm mad?"

"You must be, or you wouldn't have come here."

He grinned back at her and they both burst into a fit of laughter, the tension between them flying away like snowflakes in a strong wind.

"It's one of my childhood favorites." Quinn opened the book to the first chapter. "I used to insist that my dad read it to me every night before bed. He would gather me in his lap, and I would turn the pages as he read." She flipped the pages with one hand while the other reached to wind itself around a strand of hair that no longer existed. Realizing what she had done, she awkwardly tucked the shorter strands behind an ear and shifted back against the stacks. "He had different voices for each of the characters, even a high girly voice for Alice. It always made me laugh. He tried to get me to pick something else, but I always wanted Alice. I remember wishing I could go through the looking glass, to get lost in a magical world." Quinn looks up at him, eyes glassy. "Do you think Alice really just dreamed it all?"

"Does it matter? She experienced something, dream or not, and it changed her."

Quinn bit the bottom of her lip. He could feel her hesitation, like she wanted to say more, but didn't know how. He picked at invisible lint on his shirt.

"Are you and your dad close?"

"Once." Quinn closed the book with a snap and Aaron flinched. "He left my mom and me when he ran off with his secretary two years ago. Then he married her. And guess what? They have a new baby." Quinn threw her hands up in the air, letting them fall back into her lap with a smack.

Damn it. Way to go, Aaron. Say something to make it right.

"I'm sorry," he stammered. "I didn't know."

Quinn pinched the bridge of her nose. "No, I'm sorry. I just found out about my new…brother." She swallowed the word like a bitter pill. "It's kind of ripped open a slow healing wound. Ya know?"

Aaron tugged at the ends of his sleeves, pulling them down over his wrists. "I do know."

"How about you?" She handed Aaron the book. "How do you know so much about Alice?

"It was my mom's favorite." He turned it over in his hands, then placed it on the floor between them.

"Was?" Quinn asked.

Aaron nodded.

"I'm sorry. I guess we both have some old wounds that aren't quite healed." He could tell she wanted to ask him more, but didn't, and he was grateful. Those wounds went much deeper than she could even imagine.

Aaron pulled a chain out from under his shirt. A guitar plectrum dangled from the end. He pulled it over his head, opened his palm, and held it out for Quinn to see. A purple and blue striped Cheshire Cat grinned up at them from inside the black plastic background, on the other side, it said Mad Skilz. Quinn's fingers grazed his as she picked it up, and he could sense her uncertainty.

"She gave me that to me when I started playing guitar. It's silly, really, but after she died, I started wearing it around my neck. I don't know, to keep her close, I guess."

"It's not silly. I think it's beautiful." She handed it back to him and he slipped it over his neck, tucking it safely beneath his shirt.

They both startled when the bell rang. Aaron looked at his phone. "Has it really been an hour already?"

"Can't we just stay here for the rest of the day? Nestled in our nest of books?" she asked.

"It is the perfect hiding spot from Kerstin. I don't think she even knows this place exists."

Quinn laughed. "True. Wish I had thought of it earlier. I sure would have saved me a lot of pain and humiliation today."

"But then we wouldn't be here, nestled in a pile of books together."

"You're right. Hiding in the stacks is much more fun with you." Quinn closed her eyes and leaned her head on his shoulder. "Thanks, Aaron."

"For what?"

"For listening."

"You're welcome." He wrapped his arm around her waist, and she snuggled closer. It felt so natural, her leaning against him, him holding her, and he wished he could put the moment on hold forever.

"I guess I really should get to class." Quinn sighed and

stretched. "Will you walk me to Algebra like a proper gentleman?"

"Why, of course, Miss Taylor." Aaron stood up, bowed, and offered his hand to Quinn.

Quinn smiled and when she took his hand in return, Aaron couldn't help but feel like he was falling down his own rabbit hole.

The locker room smelled of hairspray and sweat. Laughter and excitement energized the Westland High Fillies as they primped before the big pep rally.

"You'll never guess what happened at lunch while you were cozied up to Aaron." Reese applied pink gloss to her full lips, handed the tube to Quinn, and fished a can of Aqua Net from her gym bag. "Marcus asked me out! Can you believe it?"

"You said no, of course," Quinn said.

"Well, no. You weren't there to back me up. You know how persistent he can be. Besides, he's cute, and homecoming's next Saturday. I didn't have a date yet, so…" Reese plastered her onyx hair down on all sides, making sure no loose ends escaped. "Besides, I don't think I should hold out for Aaron. I saw the two of you walking to class together."

"We're friends." Quinn felt herself blush at the mention of his name.

"You like him. Don't lie." Reese bumped her hip against Quinn. "You tucked your hair behind your ear and batted your lashes at him at least half a dozen times. You were flirting."

"I wasn't."

"You were. But it's okay, because Aaron's totally stuck on you too."

"How could anyone, even a freak like Aaron Collier, want leftovers like Quinn Taylor?" Kerstin shoved her way between Reese and Quinn, grabbing the hairspray from Reese's hand. "Haven't you all noticed how he wears long sleeves, even when it's ninety degrees out? What's up with that? If you ask me, he's hiding something. His dad probably beats him."

"Well, we didn't ask, and this is a private conversation. Hey, don't you think you should put on some more makeup? You wouldn't want anyone to see your real face." Quinn shoved a bag of makeup at Kerstin and smiled sweetly.

Kerstin returned her smile with a saccharine one. "At least I know how to stand on my own feet. What a desperate act from a desperate loser. If you thought that little fainting spell and a new ugly ass haircut would get Jeff back, you were wrong. He wanted to break up with you last year, you know. He only stayed with you because he felt sorry for you after your dad left."

"Shut up, Kerstin." Reese stepped in front of Quinn, fists on her hips, ready for a fight.

"What's wrong, Quinn? Missed lunch? Too weak to fight your own battles?" A shrill whistle broke the tension.

"Okay, girls, time for warm-ups." When nobody moved, Coach White blew her whistle again. "I mean now, ladies."

"Come on, Kerstin, these losers aren't worth it," Spring said. "You're right. Quinn's already humiliated herself enough. How many times have you been mistaken for a boy today with that haircut and flat chest?" Kerstin flipped her ponytail, hitting Quinn in the face. "You better hurry, Quinn, the pep rally can't start without the head cheerleader. Oh, right, that's me. Try to keep that bench warm." Kerstin and Spring laughed, slamming the door behind them.

Reese shoved the makeup bag and spray can back in her gym bag and threw it in her locker. "Don't let her get to you."

"Like water off a duck's back." Quinn forced a smile.

"That's my girl. You ready?" Reese held the door for Quinn.

"I'll be right behind you."

"Okay but hurry up. Coach White will have your ass if you're late."

Quinn took a deep breath, invoking the silence of the locker room to gather herself. She cupped her hands and splashed cool water on her face. Rivers of droplets flowed down her cheeks, pouring like tears into the shallow basin of the porcelain sink. The last thing she wanted to do was watch Kerstin lead her team while she sat on the sidelines. A part of her wanted to tell them all to go to hell, she was done with the shallow high school bullshit. She'd rather be in the library with Aaron, arm around her, talking, laughing. The sound of his voice, the touch of his hand, they erased all the confusion inside her. With him, she felt more like herself than she had in months. Maybe she could move past Jeff, with Aaron.

She reached for a paper towel to dry her face as a locker screeched and clanged shut behind her. She whirled around.

"Reese?"

No answer. Quinn turned back to the mirror to check her makeup. Steam covered the glass, like someone had taken a hot shower. The drip of the faucet, amplified by the metal gym lockers, resounded like the tapping of a spoon on a water glass. Her hand trembled as she wiped the condensation with her sleeve.

She stared into the unreality of the looking glass; her reflection peered back. A gray fog surrounded her mirror image, smothering the room in gloom. Mesmerized, she watched the cloud writhe and squirm, growing darker and denser as it twisted itself into the claws and fangs of a living nightmare.

Beware the Jabberwock, my son! The jaws that bite, the

claws that catch! Quinn thought as she pressed herself back against the lockers.

The mirror held the beast's complete image like a photograph. It sat on Quinn's shoulder and cocked its head, an oversized prune with eyes, and clicked a forked tongue. Four leathery wings sprouted from a lithe, catlike body. The fog writhed around it—one moment covering the entire beast, leaving only disembodied, glowing orange eyes—then retreating to reveal the full horror of the creature.

And, as in uffish thought he stood, The Jabberwock, with eyes of flame, came whiffling through the tulgey wood, and burbled as it came!

Unlike the boy in the poem, Quinn had no vorpal sword to slay her foe. Not daring to look away from the reflection, she tentatively inched her hand up her arm until it reached where the thing should be. Her fingers didn't find anything on her own shoulder, but the reflection showed a demon wrapping its tail around her wrist. Saliva dripped from its thick tongue as it slowly licked the back of her hand. She grabbed at the beast, tearing at her uniform to throw it off, but she clutched nothing but air and fabric.

What she saw in the glass wasn't really there at all.

She turned back to the mirror, determined her imagination ran on a creepy path that she controlled. But there it sat, crouched on her shoulder, wisps of living smoke, coiled to strike. Her chest ached as cords of panic constricted her breathing. She took a step back and groped the bench beside her in search of a weapon.

"Did you think you could hide from us forever?" The demon, the smoke, and the voice worked like one symbiotic being. Each fused with the other, their whispers and actions overlapping. "We will always find you."

Quinn shook her head. "You're not real." Her hand grasped a

hairdryer one of the girls had left out, and she hurled it at the demon. "You're not real!"

The mirror shattered. A dozen shards crashed to the floor, and, with each smash, a demon ascended through the portal of broken glass, corporeal, freed from their confinement inside Quinn's illusion.

"Aren't we?"

The gym buzzed as all six hundred students of Westland High crowded onto the bleachers for Friday's pep rally. All pep rallies were mandatory. "Have school spirit or else," was

Westland's motto.

Aaron and Marcus waded toward the gym floor with a crowd of seniors oozing with school spirit. Those who were anti-school spirit swam against the stream, clawing their way to the top of the bleachers, as far from the madness as they could get.

They watched the mascot jump around in a costume with so many faded patches it looked more like a piebald horse than a wild mustang. A girl dressed in blue and white, her face painted like a cat, shook her tail at the mustang, taunting him.

"Here, Kitty, Kitty. Here, Kitty, Kitty. STOMP!" screamed a blond girl next to Aaron, her voice picking up others as the chant roared around the gym like a hurricane. With the urging of the crowd, the mustang chased the wildcat around and around the gym, bringing roars of laughter from his adoring fans.

Aaron laughed too, caught up in the frenzy of school spirit, and chanted along. "Here, Kitty, Kitty. Here, Kitty, Kitty. STOMP!"

Cornered, the cat rolled over on her back, cowering in fear as the mustang placed its mighty, ragged hoof on her belly, raising another holey hoof in the air. Victory.

"Look, there's Reese," Marcus yelled over the racket. "She is such a hottie."

Fifteen cheerleaders, both Varsity and JV, stood in perfect formation.

Quinn was usually the first one through the doors, and she never missed a pep rally. Aaron's stomach turned. "Do you see Quinn?"

"Why? Getting bored of being Clark Kent today? You must be dying to get into your blue tights again. Man, spandex does you justice. There's not a girl in school who doesn't wish she were your Lois Lane, or should I say, Quinn Taylor. Hey, if you develop the ability to see through walls, promise me you'll take a look into the girls' locker room."

"And ruin the mystery?"

"I think it's a mystery worth solving."

"I like to use my imagination."

"All right, all right, no peeking at the cheer-goddesses in their lacy undies." Marcus sighed. "Bummer." Marcus cupped his hands and yelled down at the court. "Yo! Reese! Nice legs!" He winked at Reese, who pretended not to see him. "Ah, the thrill of the hunt." Marcus folded his arms over his chest and leaned back in satisfaction. "She's got it bad for me, you know."

"I can tell."

"So, are you going to ask Quinn to homecoming?" Marcus elbows him in the ribs and winks.

"Maybe," Aaron said.

"Picture it, bro." Marcus gestured with his arm, setting the scene. "The girls in tight dresses, you and me in our best suits.

The limo pulls up in front of the school. Paparazzi everywhere, screaming our names."

Aaron slaps Marcus on the back and laughs. "I think you're getting your fantasies confused. Besides where are we going to get money for a limo?"

"Man, you ruin everything." Marcus shook his head.

"We could take them to a fancy restaurant though."

"Now we're talking," Marcus said.

"Okay, Westland. Let's give a big cheer for your fighting mustangs." Principal Halstor pulled her powder-blue polyester pants up around her waist and tapped the top of the microphone.

The students ignored her. "Is this thing on?" The microphone screeched. A skinny kid with glasses moved a speaker out of the way until the feedback stopped.

"As I was saying, let's give a big cheer to the state champion, Westland High Mustangs." Principal Halstor pushed her glasses up with her middle finger, put the microphone under her arm, and clapped. Principal Halstor lived in a time warp. Westland hadn't won a game in two years.

"When did we become state champions?" Marcus asked. Aaron shrugged. "Twenty years ago?"

Kerstin and Reese held a six-foot sign between two poles. "Kick the Wildcats," was written in bright-red letters.

The crowd erupted in rollicking cheers as Jeff led his losing team through the sign, shredding it into a million pieces. What did Quinn ever see in him? He looked like a dumb jock, even dumber for dumping Quinn for Kerstin.

"I still don't see Quinn, do you?" Aaron drummed his fingers against his thigh and shifted in his seat. Sweat gathered on the back of his neck.

"Maybe she's fixing he hair or something."

The blond started to chant again. "Jeff. Jeff. Jeff." Others joined in, and Jeff stood, grinning and waving like a king.

"A two-year losing streak, and he's still the most popular boy in school. They all treat him like a god," Aaron said, rolling his eyes.

"A god? Maybe I should scrap the swim team and try out for football," Marcus said.

The noise in the gym dimmed as Aaron's head surged with the familiar tingle of psychic energy, stronger than the last. Waves of fear and desperation rushed him as the vision of Quinn shoved its way into his brain.

Eyes wide, Quinn backed away from her reflection. In the glass, a shadow moved behind her. A person? Who? He wasn't sure—the vision was obscured by steam from a too-hot shower. Aaron jumped as Quinn screamed.

Then she was gone.

hat had been one creature—one voice—became dozens as more of the leathery beasts appeared, taking shape from the wisps of fog that swirled around Quinn. She wanted out of the locker room—to find her friends, Coach White, anyone—but the tiny fog beasts blinked in and out of her vision like strobe lights, disorienting her, and making it impossible to find the door.

She covered her nose to block out the choking sulfurous smell that filled the air and groped for the row of lockers to her right. Demons weren't real—they only existed in bad horror movies; they didn't haunt girls' locker rooms or jump through broken mirrors. If she was going to hallucinate, why couldn't she see unicorns instead of evil, scary demons?

A rope of fog wrapped around her forearm, solidifying into a long, leathery tail, complete with scaly head and pointy claws. She screamed and grabbed for the beast, but the thing disappeared into a patch of fog and dissipated into the air. A dream, a delusion, nothing more. Sleep deprivation was known to cause hallucinations; she'd looked it up online. But how could it be lack of sleep when she'd slept a full eight hours the previous night? Or maybe all the caffeine pills and energy drinks had altered her mind, sent her on some sort of bad trip.

Blink. One monster landed on her head and laughed maliciously. Blink. One hovered over her back, the beating of its wings blowing strands of hair around her face. Quinn batted it away. Blink. One appeared on each shoulder.

"You're crazy," the left one said.

"Broken and pathetic," the right one added.

Another hovered in front of her face. Quinn stood perfectly still, back against the lockers, and gazed into its orange eyes. Her chest burned and sweat dripped from her nose. It opened its mouth in a maniacal grin, revealing three rows of teeth. Its breath smelled like rotten eggs.

Quinn heaved and covered her mouth to keep from vomiting. "What do you want?"

"Your soul," the voice boomed as the demon swiped at her cheek. She covered her face to protect her eyes, and a long talon scraped across her hand. Quinn whimpered as blood oozed from the cut. Faster and faster the beasts flew around her, disorienting her. A cacophony of shrieking ensued as they fought to be heard over one another, spewing words of hatred, each more terrible than the last.

Others filled the empty space, forging a spasmodic coffin around her. Brown ones, black ones, green ones, beating their leathery wings, screeching, jeering, and cheering the whisperers on.

Desperate, she dropped to her knees and closed her eyes. She felt along the floor, the cold, hard concrete bruising her knees as she crawled forward in search of the door. Enraged by her flight, the beasts screamed together in a macabre choir. She tried to block the sound of their shrieks by humming a tune of her own, but the louder she hummed, the louder they screamed. "Get this party started," she sang, her light melodic voice clashing with the metal on metal sound of the beasts.

The demons pulled her hair and scratched her bare skin. She jerked and flinched with each strike. They were like a swarm of bees, everywhere at once. All she could do was bat at them, tuck her chin to her chest, and keep moving. Picturing the layout of the locker room in her mind, she crawled to the right until she felt the wall.

"All right," she sang as she scooted on her knees, following the wall around until she felt the corner of the lockers.

"Gotta get this party started. Oh, yeah."

The monsters continued their hideous chorus, and she smelled their fetid breath each time one came near.

"Gonna party all night." She opened her eyes. "Gonna party just right."

She blinked as the fog pulsated around her. There, to her right, was the purple door. Tears of happiness momentarily replaced her tears of fear. She got to her feet and ran.

Quinn tore through the wall of fog. Eyes closed, she grabbed for the handle and pulled hard. A force greater than her own held it shut. She yanked until she thought her arms would rip apart. Then she tried pushing, ramming her shoulder against the metal in desperation. Buzzing around her head, the demons laughed as she kicked and screamed at the unmovable door. Another solid click, and it finally gave way, its momentum crashing it against the outside wall and bouncing it back, clipping her shoulder as she bolted through it. The dissonant choir stopped.

A wave of cool air enveloped her. She pulled in a deep breath to clear her lungs of the rancid, sulfurous air. Her heart pounded in her ears. She didn't want to open her eyes, afraid of what she might—or might not—see, afraid the demons might be playing with her, so she kept them closed. They were silent, but that didn't mean they were gone.

Hands splayed in front of her, she moved until the concrete blocks brushed against her fingers. Exhausted, she leaned her back against it, and sank to the floor. She listened for any movement, voices, anything, but all she heard was the frantic beating of her own heart. Nothing touched her, the hall smelled of dust and sweat, completely normal. Quinn sobbed hysterically, wiping at the river that poured down her cheeks. The salt stung the scratches on her hand where the beasts had clawed her. She examined her palm—a piece of glass had lodged in her skin. Scratches from the shards of broken mirror she'd been crawling over. Nothing more. Either she was crazy, and they weren't real, or she wasn't and they were. She wasn't sure which was worse.

*a*aron sprinted to the double doors that led to the locker rooms and shoved them open with an eerie, hollow squeak. Sunlight from the lobby cut through the gray gloom of the hallway, illuminating Quinn in a halo of gold. She sat against the wall, head resting on the arms around her knees, muffling her quiet, erratic sobs.

The heavy, metal door slammed shut, shrouding the hallway in dusk. He winced as its echo reverberated off the concrete walls, traveling down the corridor and into oblivion. Quinn flinched, but didn't look up. She looked as if she'd been in a fight. Red, angry scratches adorned her skin, her disheveled hair escaped the clips that held it from her face, and her legs were streaked with dirt. Had Jeff done this to her? Kerstin? Aaron bit his tongue to keep the millions of questions dancing in his mind from spilling across his lips.

He tried not to make noise as he slid down the wall. The fluorescent lights cast their otherworldly, green tint on her silky hair. A few inches separated them. He breathed in the intoxicating strawberry scent that surrounded her and listened to her sob, waiting for her to break the silence.

"Aaron?" she asked, her voice laced with uncertainty.

"Yeah. It's me. No one else."

Quinn stared out into nothingness, her tear-stained face transfixed on whatever puzzle troubled her mind.

"Quinn, are you okay? What happened?" She flinched as he moved a strand of loose hair behind her ear.

"Sorry, I just…" She stared at her hands.

"Do you want to talk about it?" he asked, resisting the urge to use his gift to seek out the answers for himself, then he would make whoever did this to her pay.

She nodded then shook her head.

"What happened? Did someone hurt you?" Aaron drummed his fingers on his knees.

A nod, and then another shake.

"You can talk to me." Aaron took her hand, but she snatched it away and tucked it under her arm before he could get a connection. Frustrated, he pushed her for answers. "You're covered in scratches and bruises, Quinn. Something happened in there." Anger welled inside him—red, hot, unflinching—and he balled his hands into fists. "Did Jeff do this to you? Kerstin? Tell me, and I'll make sure they don't hurt you again."

"Jeff would never hurt me."

The look she gave him hit him like a slap and he felt his cheeks redden.

"Really?" Aaron winced at his own sarcastic tone. "It seems like that's all he does these days, is hurt you." He couldn't believe it. After everything she still defended Jeff. Where was Jeff when she needed him? Kissing Kerstin, that's where. He took a deep breath and willed himself to calm down. "Sorry. It's just, look at you."

"It wasn't anything like that. I promise." She twisted the fabric of her cheerleading skirt in one hand. "I slipped on a puddle of water and fell against the sink. The force must have knocked the mirror from the wall. It shattered and some of the shards scratched me. Freaked me out a little, that's all."

"You seem more than a little freaked out." Aaron wanted to touch her, to search her mind for the truth, but he wanted her to tell him because she trusted him, not by using his ability.

"How did you know I needed you?" Quinn asked. "How do you always know?" She turned and looked him directly in the eyes and his heart fumbled inside his chest. Caught off guard, his tongue felt like stone as he sought the words to answer her. Telling her the truth, that they had some sort of psychic connection sounded crazy, even to him. The last thing he wanted was for her to think he was a freak, to be frightened of him the way Josh and his dad were.

"When I didn't see you on the court." He swallowed, stumbling over his words. "I had this feeling."

She twined her fingers with his and he fell, sinking fast though the dark, blue-gray of her eyes as the connection grabbed hold of him. Frightened and exhilarated, afraid of losing himself, he tried to pull back. What if the connection worked both ways? What if she could see into the darkness of his soul? What if she guessed his secret? He wasn't ready for that.

She was all around him now, her emotions pulsing through him like a soft electric current, warm, excited, making him forget all about finding the truth about what happened in the locker room. All he wanted was to run his fingers through her hair and press his lips against hers. Quinn's heart pounded, and his sped to match hers, beat for beat. She wanted him to kiss her. Longing emanated off her like a magnetic pulse. Once more, he tried to focus and break the connection, but their minds were too tightly joined. She reached for him, and he responded, pulling her onto his lap. When she ran her hands across his chest, it released a fire bolt though him that erased every reason he could think of to fight it. Their lips collided, her hands found the skin beneath his shirt, and his found the curve of her spine. Emotions roared out of her and into him and back out again and he couldn't tell where she ended, and he began. All he knew is that he didn't want this moment to ever end.

"Quinn!"

The voice startled them both and Quinn jerked her head away, leaving Aaron panting and disoriented. He tilted his head upward, toward the interruption. Jeff loomed over them, jaw set, fists balled at his sides. Before he could say anything, Quinn jumped to her feet and straightened her top.

"Coach White sent me to look for you. What the hell is going on?" Jeff took in her mussed hair, bruised knees, and scratched hands. Taking two steps toward Aaron, he arched his right arm back for a punch and Aaron crouched, ready to take a swing right at his open ribs. If Jeff wanted a fight, he was more than happy to give him one.

Before they collided, Quinn put a hand on Jeff's chest, and gently pushed him back. Aaron flexed his fingers, releasing some of the anger building within him. Part of him wanted Jeff to hit him so he could hit him back. Nothing would be quite as satisfying as seeing Jeff's nose spurting blood. Payback from all the pain he'd caused Quinn.

"I'm fine." Quinn looked from Jeff to Aaron and back again. Awkward silence bore down on the three of them. "Aaron and I were …" Quinn paused. "…talking."

Aaron couldn't believe what she was saying. Just talking? Humiliation hit him like a ten-ton weight, and he could feel heat rising in his cheeks.

"That didn't look like talking." Jeff glared at Aaron. "Are you sure you're okay?" He brushed a blond strand from Quinn's cheek.

"She's fine." Aaron took a step toward Quinn, hoping that she would back him up, but she just stared at him, frozen, not saying a word.

"Nobody asked you, Aaron." Jeff cupped Quinn's chin, lifting it until her eyes found his.

Every muscle in Aaron's neck tightened and a chill ran though him. What was this guy playing at? Couldn't Quinn see how he was manipulating her? It took everything he had not to grab Jeff shoulder and pull him away from her, but what good would that do? Quinn needed to make her own choice, to choose him over Jeff because she was ready to move on, not because he was a convenient distraction.

"The pep-rally is almost over. When you didn't show up on the court, I was worried about you." Jeff possessively stroked her back and she did nothing to stop him. "Are you sure he didn't hurt you? You can tell me."

"He wouldn't," Quinn responded, voice almost robotic. She looked mesmerized, charmed by a snake.

"Coach White wants to talk to you, so I wouldn't go anywhere, or do anything." He shot Aaron a look. "She's out for your blood."

"Thanks for the warning," she said. "I can handle coach White on my own."

"I know you can." Aaron watched, stunned, as Jeff circled her in his arms. "You've always been stronger than you think, Quinn." She breathed into him, relaxing against his chest, as if that's where she belonged. Her head fit perfectly under Jeff's chin, two pieces of the same puzzle. Star quarterback and head cheerleader. A high school cliché if he'd ever seen one.

Jeff made sure Aaron was watching when he kissed her cheek, letting it linger a little too long, claiming his prize, before disappearing back into the gym.

Aaron clenched his jaw and turned on his heel without saying a word to Quinn. He didn't want to hear her lame excuses. If she wanted to be possessed like that, what was it to Aaron? Clearly, there was no room in this picture for him.

Whatever had been between them, was over, nothing but a fantasy.

"Aaron, wait!" Quinn ran after him, but he refused to turn around, letting the door swing shut in her face with a satisfying slam.

19

uinn reeled as the door slammed in her face. She shook her head, dislodging the cobwebs from her brain. What just happened?

One-minute she had been gazing into Aaron's two pools of golden-green when something brushed against her thoughts, a soft kiss in her mind. She remembered leaning closer, inhaling the very essence of him, the ocean breeze, pine, and a hint of sunshine. Intoxicated by a burning brightness in the windows of his soul, she wanted to drown herself in his light, in his lips. The next thing she knew, her hands were on his skin, his hands were in her hair. It felt so good, so right, then Jeff had shown up and everything turned upside down.

Just talking. She slapped her palm against her forehead. What a stupid thing to say. She'd wanted to take it back the moment she had said it. She couldn't bear to look at Aaron after, to see the hurt on his face, so she'd turned away from him. And there was Jeff. Genuine concern etched the furrow of his brow and when he wrapped his arms around her, she sank into him, like she's done a million times before. Her Jeff. Why couldn't he let her move on? Or was she the one sabotaging her chances with Aaron?

Part of her heart clung to the sudden possibility of getting back together with Jeff. The other part pined for Aaron, his touch, the electricity between them. The tug-of -war confused and exhausted her. She didn't want to hurt Aaron, she cared for him, but being with Jeff was easy, they had so much history together. They'd gone from childhood friends, to best friends, to dating for four years...then, overnight, to nothing. It all happened so fast and the Jeff sized hole it left in her was bigger than she wanted to admit. She missed him. She didn't want to, but she did. And maybe, just maybe, he missed her too.

Quinn leaned against the wall and pinched the bridge of her nose. The second hand on the hall clock dragged: tick tick, a monotone metronome. If the fog reappeared, she could dart into the gym without hesitation, even if it meant certain embarrassment. If the fog was even real in the first place. She didn't know what to think anymore.

Her skin still tingled, the revenant of Aaron's touch—or Jeff's? She tasted salt as a tear dripped onto her lips. She pursed them, wondering if she would ever feel Jeff's lips on hers again—or Aaron's. She wiped her eyes with a sleeve, blinking back tears. She had bigger concerns than boys and their feelings. Everything in her life was spinning out of control, and she didn't know who to turn to. She no longer trusted her own emotions, judgment, or sanity. And if she couldn't trust herself, how could she trust anyone else?

She startled as the gym doors squeaked open. Kerstin and Spring headed the pack, grinning like deranged hyenas.

"Changing the middle basket toss to a Kewpie was brilliant. Let's keep the routine like that. You're much better at choreography than Quinn," Spring said.

"Thanks, Spring, that's a great idea. And your dismount was perfect."

Jeff, silent, walked alongside Kerstin like a dog on a leash. When they reached the locker room doors, Kerstin put her arm around his waist and kissed him.

"I'll see you at the game, baby. Love you," she said loud enough for the whole universe to hear.

"Yeah." Jeff glanced at Quinn, gave Kerstin a peck on the cheek, and then followed the others into the locker room.

With Jeff gone, Kerstin turned her attention to Quinn. "Where you been, loser?" She smirked and elbowed Spring as she took in the sight of Quinn's disheveled hair and bruised legs. "Oh. My. God. Looks like someone's spent the last hour on their knees." She doubled over with laughter. "Who's the lucky guy? Hope he paid you well for your services." She opened the locker room door and pushed Spring inside. "Later, freak."

Quinn licked her fingertips and frantically rubbed at the dirty streaks covering her pale skin. Of course she looked like a freak; she'd had a major freak out in the locker room.

"Are you okay?" Reese pulled Quinn into a corner. "What happened? I thought you were right behind me."

No. I'm not okay. I'm scared, Reese. I think I'm crazy. Do you think demons are real? Of course, you sound crazy, Quinn.

"Earth to Quinn. What the hell happened? I mean, look at you."

"I went to pee, and when I came out of the stall, I slipped and fell on a puddle of water or something. I knocked the mirror off the wall. It came crashing down, and I freaked out a little."

"God, Quinn. Are you hurt?"

"No. Well, a little bruised, but I'm fine, really." Quinn looked away and crossed her arms.

"And?"

"And what?"

"You know what." Reese tapped her foot.

"And I ran into Aaron, all right?" Quinn shrugged. Reese looked amused. "Ran into his lips more like it."

"I never said that." Quinn smoothed her hair back into place. "You didn't have to. Your smeared lipstick said it for you."

"Crap." Quinn wiped her mouth with the back of her hand.

"I know I told you to use Aaron to get over Jeff, but making out with him during the pep rally? Bad idea. Kerstin made a big deal about you not being a team player. Coach White's on the warpath." Reese ran a hand through her hair and cocked her head. "Was it worth it? At least tell me his lips were so hot they could melt ice."

Coach White shoved open the double doors, and Quinn cringed. She'd never seen her so angry and dreaded what would come next.

"Ms. Taylor, my office, now." She didn't even look at Quinn. "Ms. Moon, the locker room, pronto."

Mrs. White's cramped office smelled like sweat and stale coffee. Pictures of previous Westland High cheerleading squads hung in black frames on one side of the beige walls. On the other side were pictures of the girls' basketball teams. The gray-framed desk stood stark except for an empty jar of peanut butter and a can of diet soda.

"Have a seat, Quinn." She pointed to a faded, red vinyl chair —a startling splash of color in the otherwise bland room.

Quinn sat. The vinyl squeaked beneath her bare legs. "What happened?" Coach White leaned back in the chair.

"I—" Quinn started, her mind racing, searching for an answer that would sound more truthful than the truth.

"You missed the entire pep rally," Coach White said. "Yes, and—"

"First, your grades, now skipping out on your team. I picked you as head cheerleader because I thought you were responsible." Coach White leaned forward in her chair, slamming her hand on the edge of the desk. "Even though you're on probation, you still have a responsibility to this school and to your teammates. We had a deal. Attend all practices, help me coach, and get your grades up. Are you tired of being a cheerleader?" She stared at Quinn, waiting for an answer.

"No, ma'am." Quinn sat up straight and looked Coach White in the eye.

"You're not acting like it." Coach White leaned back in the office chair and studied Quinn. "Actions speak louder than words. I've spoken to your teachers. You're still failing."

"I still have two weeks to bring my grades up."

"One week. Grades are out next Friday, or have you forgotten? And from what I've seen, that would take a miracle. What am I supposed to do?" Coach White sighed.

Quinn's stomach rolled. She shifted in the big red chair, the temperature rising in the stuffy little room as sweat gathered on the back of her legs, the heat fusing her skin with the vinyl.

"You're a better captain than Kerstin, but my hands are tied. If you're still failing when report cards come out next week, and I know for a fact you will be, I'm suspending you for the rest of the semester."

"What? You can't!"

"Quinn, you've given me no other choice. As of today, Kerstin will permanently be captain. I must have someone reliable in that position. You understand. As of next Friday, you will be suspended, and we'll reassess at the end of the semester."

Quinn had expected a lecture, but suspended? She almost choked on the bitter pill being forced down her throat.

"I can't suspend you until I see your report card, so think of this as your last game. You will ride the bus to the game with the rest of us as usual, but you won't be allowed on the field, you won't participate in warm ups, and you won't wear your uniform. That deal is over. I want the squad to get used to Kerstin's leadership, and I can't have them divided. You'll sit in the stands and watch, take mental notes, and help Kerstin with the transition during practice next week. We leave at six o'clock sharp."

Suspended. Stupid Quinn, what did she think would happen? Shadow voices lurked in the back of her mind, urging her thoughts into a downward spiral.

"Failure."

"Irresponsible."

"Untrustworthy."

Their whispers melded with what she feared to be true. She couldn't argue. They were right: she was a failure. Tears threatened to fall, but she refused to let Coach White see her hurting. Then the whispers dissolved into nothingness, leaving the faintest echo imprinted in her mind. Her insides had been carved away, leaving an empty shell of herself. One more blow, and she would crumble into a pile of dust.

Coach White's expression softened. Putting her elbows on the table, she laced her fingers, resting her chin on her hands. "I heard about what happened yesterday. You look like you've lost some weight, and don't think I haven't noticed those dark circles. Have you been eating enough?"

Coach White's words were like a TV playing in another room. Numbed to the core, she perceived her own voice as part of that same ambient TV show. "I've been a little tired. I guess I'm a little stressed with senior stuff." Then the implications of Coach White's question sunk in, snapping Quinn out of her daze. "No, no, I'm not puking or starving myself or anything like that."

"Well, I'm glad to hear that. Promise me you'll get a tutor if you must. Do whatever it takes to get those grades up. Regional competition is in March, and we need you if we want to advance."

Her head hurt, and she wanted to get out of this oven of an office and find a deep, dark hole to hide in.

Quinn nodded. Getting her grades up by next week would be impossible. Suspension was imminent. This would be her last football game as a Westland High Filly, ever. And if she didn't get it together soon, there would be nothing left of her life worth saving.

aron weaved his motorcycle through the school parking lot. Just short of reckless, he darted down the back streets and alleyways to avoid traffic. What he really needed was a cold shower to get her out of his mind. Her smell clung to his clothes, invading his nostrils. He still felt the touch of her soft skin, the lingering passion from her thoughts.

Aaron accelerated, thrusting forward in his seat. The wind took his breath away and whipped through the fabric of his clothes, the tail of his shirt flapping behind him. He focused on the hum of the bike beneath him and let his mind go blank, invoking a state of Zen as he sped across the Westland county line and into Eastwood. He blurred past houses and bounced over bumps and potholes, trees and buildings whizzing by.

He cut a sharp left up a narrow dirt road. Bits of gravel pinged against the metal body as the tires kicked up bits of debris. The engine roared as he poured on the speed. St. Angeles Chapel stood three hundred feet before him—its stone bell tower standing stark against the bright sky.

The tires squealed as he skidded to a stop in front of the old church. Breathless, he removed his helmet and dismounted. He stood beneath the gothic stone entry arch and pushed at the large wooden door, its metal hinges groaning with the weight of heavy oak as it swung open.

His footsteps echoed off the nave's stone floor. Light streamed through the unbroken stained-glass window at the back, casting a patchwork of color across the dust-covered pews and the large cross suspended from the ceiling.

St. Angeles: his thinking place, his sanctuary. His mood lifted as he sat, cross-legged, before the disused altar. He thought about Quinn and their connection. Could she feel it too?

If she did, wouldn't she say something about it? The connection was all in his head, one-sided, a delusion. Watching how she reacted when Jeff came in was proof enough. It was Jeff she wanted and thinking anything else was a sure set-up for heartbreak, and his heart was already cracking under the weight of his obsession; he couldn't take any more.

But no matter how hard he tried to convince himself that what happened in the hallway meant nothing, the more puzzling everything became.

He was missing something. It tickled the back of his brain, a memory, something important, playing cat -and-mouse in his mind. He closed his eyes and breathed in through his nose, out through his mouth, striving for a state of meditation. He always pictured his barrier—the one he kept up in case of an accidental touch—and slowly brought it down, opening himself to psychic contact.

He focused on Quinn, her soft skin, the feel of her thoughts joined with his. He willed his gift to contact her, but nothing happened. He slammed his fists on his thighs. He had no idea how to reach her, or anyone for that matter, without touching them. Didn't this prove the connection with Quinn was all in his head, delusions concocted by his longing to be near her?

Not ready to give up, he swallowed his fear and opened himself further than he ever had, removed every brick from his wall, and sank deeper into a state of Zen. This time, instead of floating in blank space, images flashed before him: a hospital room, a curved rune sword. That name again. Azrael. Aaron repeated the name as if invoking Azrael to come forward and speak to him. Nothing.

Instead, Ruth appeared before him, her red curls framing her face. She smiled and beckoned him to follow her into a portal of light. Aaron's heart ached, and he longed to go with her, but something bound him to his flesh. He shook his head, and a flash blinded him as she disappeared, taking all the light with her. A fog gathered in the corners. Something watched him, something familiar, evil. Something he'd seen before— in Quinn's nightmare. He shrank back as a black mass rushed him.

He retreated as fast as he could, throwing up his wall to protect himself from the anger this thing directed at him.

Aaron rubbed his temples and opened his eyes. Sweat gathered on the back of his neck. His hands trembled as he ran his fingers through his mop of black hair. What did it mean? He tried to hold on to the vision, to think through what he'd seen. The answer was right in front of him, if he could just fit the pieces together. But the pieces disappeared one by one before he could form a whole picture. It was as if a black hole sucked the vision away, creating a void where the answers had been.

Shaking his head to clear the cobwebs, Aaron stretched to release the tension in his muscles. Dusk had settled around the church, and he glanced at his watch. Two hours had passed. He jumped up and dusted himself off. He was officially late for band rehearsal—again. Jenna would kill him.

On the ride to Jenna's house, he thought about the first time he'd met Jenna and Cade. A week after he had been released from the psychiatric ward at Rio Villa, he drove his motorcycle out of town with the intent of riding off into the sunset—away from the expectations of his brother and father.

He turned north down a winding dirt road that led to a small, half-ruined chapel, complete with stone bell tower, gothic arches, and a moss-covered cemetery. St. Angeles. It felt like it belonged somewhere else and in some other time, like him.

A soulful voice drifted through a broken window. He approached the derelict building where Jenna stood at the front, singing. Her twin brother, Cade, sat behind her and joined her in harmony. Aaron would never have guessed they were preacher's kids from their black nail polish, dark eyeliner, and piercings. Both were so engrossed in their music, neither had noticed Aaron.

A guitar leaned against the dusty front pew. Without thinking, he slung the strap over his shoulder and played along, improvising. He had no memory of ever having played guitar, but his fingers found the notes with ease. Playing music felt as natural as breathing, like coming home.

Neither Cade nor Jenna stopped, accepting this stranger without question. When the song finished, Jenna said, "We should start a band," and Habitual Reality was born.

Did they know they'd saved his life that day? Music, the band, they were the only things that made him feel normal.

All eyes turned to Aaron as he entered the garage, their laughter stopping as the door closed behind him.

"Where you been?" Ben twirled a drumstick in the fingers of his left hand.

"Yeah, rehearsal started half an hour ago." Jenna lay on the faded carpet in front of the door, looking through some sheet music. "Glad you decided to join us." She wore her usual tight-fitting, black t-shirt and black skinny jeans that showed off every curve. He liked curves.

"Sorry, I lost track of time."

Jenna wedged the sole of her goth boot against the door-frame, blocking his path. "Not so fast. That's the third time this week."

"I'm here now, and I seriously need to play some music and forget about my crap day." He looked down at Jenna, waiting for her to move.

"Cade, Ben, and I were just discussing kicking you out. Right, Cade?"

Cade played through some scales on the keyboard. "No, Jenna discussed kicking you out. Ben and I agreed that if she wanted to play the gig on Saturday, she would have to accept your creative temperament."

"Musicians." Jenna still blocked his path. "Say it, and I'll let you stay."

He sighed. "You're the lead singer extraordinaire. Goddess of music, queen of the band. Happy?"

"Damn, right!" She moved her leg. Aaron stepped over her, trying not to trample the long dark hair that fanned behind her, and grabbed his guitar from the stand.

"You know I would never really kick you out of the band, right?" Jenna winked at him.

"Did you finish the new song?" Cade plunked out a few notes. "My fingers are itching for a new melody."

"Copies for everyone." Aaron unzipped the front pocket of his backpack and handed a copy to Cade.

"Sweet. Hey, Jenna, want me to play through the melody for you before we start? Maybe get warmed up?" Cade asked his sister.

"Are you kidding? I've been waiting to hear this song for weeks."

Jenna rolled over on her stomach and stretched. "It better be worth the wait." She looked at Aaron. Her gray eyes narrowed as she grinned at him.

"Does that mean I'm forgiven?"

"I guess." Jenna pushed off the floor and stood in front of him, hands behind her back. "But only if you hug me." She pushed out her bottom lip in an over-exaggerated pout. Aaron pulled her into a bear hug. A consummate baker, she always smelled like something delicious—today was homemade, chocolate-chip cookies. Every time her skin touched his, he was overwhelmed by the warm, steady surge of affection mixed with a hint of nervous butterflies. Her thoughts told him she wanted to tell him she liked him, but she was scared it might jeopardize their friendship.

Jenna pulled away, breaking the connection. She placed her hands on her hips and studied him. "Until you do something else to piss me off."

Her thick, black eyeliner accentuated her soulful eyes. Her dark hair and olive skin were the opposite of Quinn. Quinn. She had made her feelings perfectly clear. She wanted Jeff. His feelings for her were turning into an unhealthy obsession and he needed to stop.

Maybe he could love bold, brave Jenna with her enthusiasm and sometimes brutal honesty. He did love her—in a calm, quiet way. When they touched, he was always careful to project warmth and friendship. But what if he didn't? What if their friendship could be more? He pictured himself kissing her. He imagined how soft her lips would be and had to stop from leaning in and finding out.

"Earth to Aaron." Jenna pinched his arm. "Are we starting, or what?" Jenna tapped the toe of her boot against the floor.

"Sorry." Aaron plugged his acoustic guitar into the amp and set his capo at the fifth fret. "Hey, did you ask your dad about using St. Angeles for our gig?"

Built by her great, great, grandfather, St. Angeles, and the land surrounding it, belonged to Pastor Lavera, Jenna's dad. He was the third and last generation Lavera to preach there. Today, the congregation met in a modern, shiny new building two miles away, leaving St. Angeles to the wind and birds.

"I told you I could talk him into anything." Jenna grinned. "He said it's fine as long as we don't do any damage. Ben's even found an old generator to power the equipment."

"We can set up lots of candles for atmosphere," Cade said.

"It will be awesome!" Jenna said, her enthusiasm spreading through them all.

"Not as awesome as you." Aaron winked at her.

"Well, that goes without saying." Jenna punched him lightly on the arm.

In that split second her thoughts moved from her fist to his mind. She pictured them meeting at the football game, holding hands, making sarcastic jokes about the cheerleaders.

Aaron liked the idea of it. "So, are you guys going to the game tonight?"

"And miss seeing Westland get their butts kicked by our offensive line? Wouldn't miss it, would we, Cade?"

"Want to meet up?" Aaron blurted it out before he had a chance to change his mind.

Jenna tried to mask her shock. "Are you asking me to go to the game with you?"

"I thought you could sit on our side, feel what it's like to be a loser for once."

She cocked her head and rubbed her chin. "A little recon? Spy on the other side? I like it. But aren't you afraid someone will see you consorting with the enemy?"

"I don't care what anyone else thinks. Sit with me. It'll be fun. I'll even buy you some nachos."

"Fine, but don't you dare tell anyone we're from Eastwood. I don't want to be stoned to death."

"Can you two stop flirting long enough to get some rehearsing in?" Cade asked.

"That wasn't flirting. I'll show you flirting." Jenna moved

closer to Aaron and batted her long-mascaraed lashes. In turn, Aaron flexed his muscles.

Cade rolled his eyes. "Please, Ben, count off, before I puke." "Let's go. One, two," Ben counted off, and Aaron lost himself in the joy of playing music—the only thing that made him feel normal.

21

Dusk settled over the stadium, flooding cones of light through every inch of the field, leaving the empty stands striped with ribbons of shadows.

Quinn mounted the steps, found a section of bench drenched in a bright patch, and took a seat. The last place she wanted to be was at the game where everything reminded her that she was a failure, a loser. What was worse—being home alone with the demons, or watching Kerstin steal everything she cared about? She put her feet on the bleacher in front of her, bringing her knees closer to her chest and pulling the end of her red shirtsleeves over her hands, tucking them under her armpits to keep from shivering.

The lights hummed, low and dull. Moths gathered around their glow, futilely beating against the cool white bulbs. Their dirty ragged wings fluttered, confused by the false radiance of the light.

Kerstin's bark broke the eerie silence of the stands. "Come on, girls. Say it with me. We're fresh. You know, the Fillies steal the show. We're too hot to handle, and we're ready to go!"

Kerstin smirked at Quinn from the sidelines as she led the squad in warm-ups.

Quinn refused to let it bother her. Instead, she let herself fantasize about shaving Kerstin's head while she slept, or accidentally elbowing her in the face, breaking her pudgy little nose. A bloody nose and two missing front teeth might improve her looks.

Quinn turned her attention to the Wildcats who were running drills on the other side of the field. Her eyes landed on Jeff, who stared at her from the sidelines. She smiled and waved. Jeff curtly waved back, turning away before anyone—Kerstin— saw him. Quinn turned away, too, but every so often she felt the resurgence of his attention. Sure enough, when she glanced his way, he was watching her. Quinn wondered what that meant. Did it mean he wasn't over her either? Could she get him back? And if she did, what then? Could she forgive him? Could they both forget about Kerstin?

Forgiving and forgetting were two different things, and she wasn't sure she could or wanted to do either. Her feelings mixed within, a dozen different smoothies blended together and no way to decipher one flavor from another. Aaron. How could she run from his lips into Jeff's arms in a matter of seconds? Guilt twisted in her gut. He must hate her. Maybe she could explain, tell him she wasn't ready, that she was still struggling to get over Jeff. Yeah, that's exactly what he'd want to hear.

Quinn turned to look at the now-crowded bleachers. She shaded her eyes from the blinding light and scanned the student's faces, looking for anyone familiar. All of them turned away the minute she made eye contact. Quinn frowned.

"Are you all right?" Breathless, Ami plopped down beside Quinn. "I'm okay. Considering." Quinn spotted Aaron standing at the top of the bleachers. A dark-haired girl she didn't recognize stepped up behind him and grabbed him around the waist. His smile lit the world, and he pulled her into a bear hug. Was she too late? Maybe Aaron wasn't as interested in her as she thought. Here she was, tying herself in knots over him, trying to figure out a way to get over Jeff and give Aaron a chance, and he hugged another girl. God, she was such a hypocrite. Hadn't she hugged Jeff like that right in front of him? Still, a pang of jealousy rose inside as he brushed a long strand from the girl's face. Quinn ran a hand through her own, short locks and wished she had never taken the scissors to them.

"It's not true, is it?"

"What's not true?" Quinn tore her eyes from Aaron and the brunette and looked at Ami.

"Oh my gosh, girl! You really don't know?" The floodgate of Ami's mouth opened, and the words washed over Quinn like a tsunami.

"Jayme told me that she heard from Keesha that Kerstin's permanently captain because Coach White caught you taking drugs before the pep rally, and that's why you're failing all your classes, and that Kerstin found a broken mirror and lines of cocaine in the girls' locker room and that you looked wild and messed up after the pep rally. I couldn't believe it. I called her a liar and said she needed to check her facts. Jayme said Lori told her she'd seen you popping pills the morning of your fainting spell. She insisted it was a drug overdose. I told her people don't faint from a drug overdose, they die, but she's always been a few colors short of a rainbow. Anyway, she insisted the rumor was true, and here you are, out of uniform, sitting alone, and I have to say to myself, 'Ami, what has this crazy world come to?'"

Ami pushed her glasses up her nose and looked over her shoulder to make sure no one was listening.

"So, dish with me, girl. You weren't really caught doing drugs, were you? I mean, not you, Quinn. Please tell me this is just a nasty rumor. I want it straight from the horse's mouth so I can use my gossip powers for good and squelch this nasty hearsay."

"Unbelievable!" Quinn folded her arms over her chest. "Next, she'll be telling everyone I'm a brain-sucking alien. Come on, Ami, you know me. Do you really think I'm some druggie?"

"Of course not, but honestly, the brain-sucking alien thing would be easier to disprove than this. This is serious. Look at the evidence. I mean, you've been acting kind of erratic lately. Your grades, the fainting thing, missing the pep rally, the suspension, your hair, the break up with Jeff …"

"Wait, wait, wait! He broke up with me, or has everyone forgotten? And what does that have to do with anything?"

"I don't know. There are so many crazy things being said, I don't even know the truth. I'm just telling you what I heard. So, tell me, what's real? As your friend, I want to hear the whole story."

Heat rose in Quinn's face. "That is the dumbest thing I've ever heard. I am not on drugs. "Here." She lifted her chin, exposing her nostrils. "Any powder on my nose?" She opened her purse and shoved it at Ami. "Go ahead, search it if you want."

"Quinn, you don't need to …" Ami pushed the purse away.

"As for why I fainted, if everyone just must know, I didn't sleep well, and I didn't eat breakfast, so my blood sugar dropped. Why I missed the pep rally is nobody's business, and neither are my grades. Never once did Coach White accuse me of being on drugs. Why? Gee, maybe because I'm not. And for the record, Jeff sent me on a one-way trip to Rejection City. I still don't know why, but I didn't summer in Druggieville. You can pass that information on to anyone and everyone you want to."

Ami squeezed Quinn around the shoulders. "I knew it wasn't true! I never believed it." She squealed, and then released Quinn from her loving constriction. "Well, I'm off to spread this news to the masses. Ciao!"

Drugs? Would Kerstin sink that low? Quinn looked back at

the crowd. Every eye in the stadium bored into her, judging her, pitying her, laughing at her. Kerstin's rumor mill was turning so fast it made her head swim.

Quinn looked up and blinked, trying to pretend she didn't know they were talking about her, that they weren't whispering her name, boldly staring at the freak show. She snapped her head back to the field, making herself as small as she could. Burying her head in her hands was her first instinct, but she didn't, she wouldn't give them the satisfaction of seeing her cower in a corner, wouldn't give them any more ammunition to throw at her by looking guilty when she wasn't.

A section of lights flickered, shading Quinn as the bulbs dimmed and darkened, one by one. A cluster of moths fluttered around her face. She batted at them, scattering them away. A large one settled on her shoulder. Its dark, gossamer wings fluttered in time with her heart. Each wing beat carried the words of her peers directly to her ear, damaging her resolve to stay calm. A tremor started in her foot and moved up her leg. All the moisture in her mouth evaporated.

"Poor Quinn." Students gossiped behind her back, spreading the lies like an STD. "No wonder Jeff left her. Brian heard she stole a hundred dollars from him to support her habit."

"I heard from Shae that he tried to get her into rehab. He drove her to a clinic and offered to check himself in with her."

"I heard that, too. I also heard she tried to stab him with a pair of scissors."

"No, no, she tried to stab herself with a pair of scissors." The story grew more ludicrous with every telling.

"Have you seen the black circles under her eyes? She's a total druggie."

Quinn resisted the tears that ached to be shed as the words ripped through her body like bullets.

"That's why her father left. He couldn't face it."

She tried to swallow, but her tongue had doubled in size, a

boulder threatening to block her airway. A sharp intake of breath sent shockwaves of pain through her chest. She wanted to tell them all they were wrong about her, but who would believe her? She didn't even believe herself. If she were in their shoes, wouldn't she be thinking the same thing? Quinn bit her bottom lip until the bitter metallic taste of blood brushed her tongue. She sucked at the wound, trying to transfer the pain from her heart to her flesh.

A moth tickled her ear.

That's what they really think of you, Quinn. Listen to what's in their minds, on their lips. Quinn. Spiraling out of control. Quinn. Unloved. Quinn. Alone. A fuck up. Her fault.

She slapped at it until it flew backward from her shoulder and hovered above her head.

You may not be a druggie, Quinn, but you're something worse. Crazy. Look at yourself. Who would believe you? Quinn swatted at the moth again. It spiraled out of reach, laughing. *Look at you. Quinn. Trembling like a leaf, batting at insects, hearing voices.*

It's not real, it's not real, I'm dreaming. I must be. Quinn pinched herself, and pain flooded her arm.

Aaron. Her thoughts always went straight to him when she felt threatened. She focused on the memory of his soft voice and reassuring touch, the way he always knew when she was in trouble. Somehow, he made her feel safe. She pictured his arms around her, protecting her.

The voices dulled inside her head as she pieced together a mental barricade. The darkness retreated from her mind, but the demon retaliated. Six mercurial threads descended from the moth as the demon tethered itself to her skull. The twisted ropes pulsed, pushing past her barriers and deep into her thoughts.

You think Aaron cares about you? He doesn't. Look, Quinn. Look for yourself. Look how much he cares.

She chanced a glance behind her. Aaron had his arm around

the dark-haired girl. He pulled her close. Their lips touched, just a peck at first. The girl pulled away, ran her hand down his arm. He leaned in again, and they kissed, urgent. A full passionate kiss. His hands roamed her body, and she returned the affection in the most blatant show of PDA she had ever seen. She had thought Aaron was different, that they had a connection. And to think she had almost trusted him. The voices were right. Aaron didn't care about her. He was no different than Jeff, ready to run off with another girl the minute she needed him most. Quinn's defenses crumbled.

You're alone. He doesn't love you. He doesn't even like you. Nobody does. Listen, Quinn. The demon shoved the thoughts into her head. *Listen to what they're saying about you. It's not a dream, Quinn. It's real. We're real. Look for yourself.*

The words from her peers found the cracks in her facade, bursting through as the last of her wall disintegrated. She rocked, hugging herself tight to keep from exploding.

"It's like she's stalking poor Jeff."

Quinn rocked faster, wiping her brow, running trembling hands through her hair, pulling the ends as each accusation hit its mark.

"I can't believe she actually came to the game. If I were her, I would switch schools."

Moths, thousands of them, spread through the crowd. Each time one landed on a shoulder, she received a stare or a point of a finger. Then, they were off again, landing on different people. Realization hit her like a head on collision, they were influencing the crowd's reaction and making sure the lies spread. A fit of laughter bubbled to the surface, and she covered her mouth.

"I see what you're doing," she murmured. "I see you." Anger, red and hot, moved from her stomach to her mouth. "I see you," she snapped. "No more hiding in the shadows."

As if in challenge, the eclipse of moths turned toward her.

Their dark wings flapped in unison, pulsing above their victims like beating hearts. One by one, they gathered into a dusky mass, an ominous storm cloud ready to explode. The cloud rushed her, and she ducked, covering her head as they spiraled her body, encasing her in a living whirlwind. Why had she provoked them? She regretted outing them, regretted mentioning that she could see what they were doing to the others.

Her breath came in quick, short bursts, and she gasped for air. Sweat trickled down her forehead as she focused on staying still. The beat of their wings grazed her skin. She swatted at her hair, her arms, and her face, but she couldn't shake them off.

"Ohmigod. She's totally lost it," a girl two rows behind her said. With a stab of laughter, the demons zoomed straight up into the sky and disappeared into the night.

All but one.

Everyone's laughing at you, Quinn. The demon still tethered to her head whispered. *They're all watching you. They all think you're crazy.*

"Am I the only one who sees you?"

Are you? the demon asked.

"She's crazy, look at her." A boy pointed.

He's right, isn't he? How else do you explain us? the demon asked. *You know where the crazies go, don't you, Quinn?*

Quinn whirled around; her bright red cheeks a stark contrast from her cool, violet -blue eyes. She folded her arms over her chest, the tension in her jaw growing. "I think she's high," the redhead whispered to her neighbor.

Pinching her lips together, she sucked in a deep breath. The whole stadium breathed with her, holding in anticipation.

"Shut up!" Quinn screamed. The demon retracted its tentacles, floated into the air, and blinked out in a puff of smoke as Quinn bolted for the exit.

*a*aron blinked as he emerged into the bright stadium lights. He scanned for Jenna but found Quinn instead, staring at Jeff with drool practically dripping down her chin. She waved at Jeff, and he waved back. Aaron frowned. He was over her drama.

"Hey, loser." Jenna snuck up behind him and covered his eyes. Her hands were warm and smelled of honey. Sparks of nervousness filtered from the ends of her fingers through his eyelids, and his wall went up in reflex.

"Hey, beautiful." Aaron turned to give her a hug. "I'm glad you made it."

"I said I would, didn't I?" She spun around and struck an exaggerated model pose, full lip pout included. "So, what do you think? Losery enough to blend in?"

Jenna wore a Westland High t-shirt that hugged in all the right places and skinny jeans that showed every curve. "Where did you get that?"

"Charity shop." She grinned.

"The loser-look works for you. No one will even suspect."

He brushed a stray hair from her face. She flushed and looked away. "It was hiding your eyes."

Jenna tucked the strand behind her ear. "Thanks."

"Where's Cade?"

"Oh, he said he wouldn't be caught dead in the enemy camp. He'll meet us after the game. Where should we sit?"

Aaron shaded his eyes from the bright floodlights and looked from row to row. "It doesn't look like we have much of a choice."

"Yo! Bro!" Marcus waved up at them.

"Subtle, isn't he?" Jenna crossed her arms.

"You cool if we sit with him?"

"He'll just follow us if we don't," Jenna said.

"You know him so well." Aaron grabbed her hand and escorted her down a few rows. His arm tingled as the sense of her emotions flitted from surprise, to joy, to doubt, and joy again. Her feelings for him ran deeper than he'd suspected. He wondered if he was doing the right thing. And why couldn't he learn to love her? People fall in love with their friends all the time. Weren't the best relationships built on friendship anyway? And at least he always knew where he stood with Jenna, unlike Quinn.

"Hey, gorgeous." Marcus winked at Jenna. "It's kind of crowded, but I saved a spot just for you." He slapped his thigh three times. "Nice and warm."

"Hey Marcus, isn't that your girlfriend waving at you from the field?" Jenna crossed her arms and cocked her head.

Gaining his attention, Reese beckoned Marcus with a finger. "Busted." Marcus handed Jenna an enormous red tub of popcorn. "I'll be right back. Try not to eat it all while I'm gone."

"We wouldn't dare." Aaron sat and patted the empty space next to him.

"What about your lap? It's not spoken for, is it?" Jenna broke into a wicked grin. "In case things get a little too crowded when he gets back."

Flirting with Jenna had always been easy. They'd been playing at it for years, innocent banter, nothing serious. Tonight, something had shifted. "My lap is unattached at the moment." He would've blushed if he'd said that cheesy line to anyone but Jenna.

She broke into a fit of laughter and plopped down next to him. "I think we're about to cross a line we shouldn't." She punched him on the shoulder, and a hint of her excitement and nerves rushed through him. Her nervousness mirrored his, and he wondered if he should take their friendship to the next level. Is that what she really wanted? Did he?

"You're the one with the dirty mind." He grabbed a handful of popcorn and savored the greasy, fake-butter flavoring.

A rush of intense rage assaulted him like a psychic punch to the stomach, and the rough seed caught in his throat. He choked and coughed. Aaron's spine prickled as his barrier cracked. Dammit, Quinn. All he wanted was to stay away from her, but how could he when one little thought of her pale, pathetic face ignited a connection between them? Mentally, he batted her away, but none of his usual blocking methods worked. Learning to control his ability through physical touch was one thing but learning to control something so random and unwarranted was something completely different.

He tried to ignore the tapping in the back of his brain, his power trying to get his attention, but every second brought him closer to losing himself until he couldn't fight it any longer.

Closing his eyes, he searched for her. Fog swirled around her thoughts, making them hard to read, but her emotions came through loud and clear. She trembled with fear, screaming inside for someone to help. Desperation bubbled up like hot, wet tears, pulling at his heartstrings, begging him to rescue her.

He refused to give in. He gritted his teeth and worked to

close the crack in his barrier. Trouble followed her like a black cloud. Why should he run after her again? That's all he ever did anymore, run to her every time she called, every time she hinted at distress. He wanted to be her boyfriend, not her puppy. She could get out of her own mess this time. The taste of metal filled his mouth, and fear knifed through his barrier. He pushed harder. The pain eased. She was gone.

"Are you okay?" Jenna patted him on the back.

"Yeah." He cleared his throat and shoved the emotion away, tightening his defenses. "It went down the wrong way." He scanned for Quinn and found her in the front row, face red with rage, hands flying as she argued with Ami.

"Want a drink?" Jenna asked. "No, I'm fine."

Quinn's humiliation lashed against his barrier as she buried her head in her hands. He was determined not to let her through and steeled his heart, his resolve, and his mental wall against her.

"Who's that?" Jenna followed his gaze to Quinn. "She looks ready to kill."

"She used to be head cheerleader. Probably some sort of cheerleader drama." Could he be anymore two-faced? Sitting with Jenna while watching Quinn and lying about knowing her. It was Quinn's fault. She was making him crazy. All he wanted was Quinn to leave him alone so he could move on.

"Oh, is she that Quinn girl who got suspended for doing drugs or something?"

"What? Where did you hear that?" Aaron whipped his attention from Quinn to Jenna.

"Everyone in Eastwood is talking about it. Haven't you heard? She doesn't look like a druggie. She looks upset, though. Do you know her?"

"Yeah, I know her," he replied in an exasperated tone. How was he supposed to forget her if people kept bringing her up?

"Annoyed much? I didn't mean to hit a nerve."

"Sorry. Can we change the subject?"

"Is it me, or is it getting chilly?" Jenna shivered and Aaron moved closer.

"Better?"

"Much."

The bleachers were alive with whispers, now that he knew to listen for them. It was obvious the topic on everyone's lips was Quinn.

Pain and humiliation knifed through him, and he tasted metal on the back of his tongue. He wasn't the only one who could hear the whispers. He clenched his jaw and tried to push her out of his mind, determined not to succumb to her psychic emotional blackmail.

Aaron put his arm around Jenna and turned to her as Quinn's desperation wrapped around him, hot, suffocating. He ran a hand across Jenna's cheek, the touch dampening the feel of Quinn's emotions. They locked eyes, and she leaned forward. He brushed his lips against hers. She tasted sweet, like chocolate. The light kiss masked Quinn's contact. Jenna was aloe on his sunburn, and he relished the relief.

As he pulled away, Quinn's mental grip tightened around his thoughts, squeezing tighter and tighter, until he thought he would drown in her psychic siren song. He repeated Jenna's name over and over in his mind as he pulled her closer, ignoring the surprise that stiffened her shoulders. He focused his resistance into a wild kiss, fierce and passionate. Quinn recoiled, and the cord between them broke. Jenna, only Jenna remained. His hands in her hair, down her back, too hot and too heavy.

Kissing Jenna had been a mistake. Her desire changed from joy to nervousness, and then anger. A sharp jolt to the shoulder snapped him back to reality, and Jenna pushed him away. She stared at him, her breath ragged, hair a tangled mess. "I think we should stop now." Aaron took her hand and probed her mind. She wanted to pull away but didn't want to hurt him. Confusion mixed with disappointment swept through her. Would this be the end of their friendship? No, he couldn't let that happen. "I'm sorry."

Jenna slowly pulled her hand from his and crossed her arms. "At first it was nice, and then … I don't know. It got weird. What's going on with you? You don't seem like yourself."

Guilt flooded Aaron. Jenna, insightful and honest to a fault, didn't deserve to be used.

"There's someone I'm trying to get over. It was wrong. I was wrong. I'm not ready. I'm sorry."

"That Quinn girl?" Aaron nodded.

"So, you used me," she said flatly.

"Not intentionally. I wanted … I like you, and I don't want to feel the way I feel about her. I thought maybe going out with you tonight would help me move on. I should never have asked you here. Please, Jenna. I'm sorry. I don't want to lose your friendship."

Jenna looked Quinn up and down as if sizing her up. "Is she really worth getting so worked up about? She looks like every other airhead cheerleader I've ever known."

"She's not though. I can't explain it. It's like she has some hold over me. I can't get her out of my mind." Jenna couldn't have any idea how literally he meant that.

"Figures. I think maybe I should go."

Aaron nodded. "I'm sorry, Jenna. I truly am."

"You should be." Jenna poked him in the chest. "Sorry for bringing me here, sorry for using me, and you should definitely be sorry for that kiss you gave me. If I had wanted to be slobbered on I would have stayed home with my Labrador." She crossed her arms and cocked her head. "As for our friendship? I'm angry now, but I'll text you when I'm over it." Jenna stared out at the field. "Good luck with that one." She pointed at Quinn. "I have a feeling you're going to need it." And with that, Jenna was gone.

Aaron slammed his palm on Jenna's empty seat. Quinn. It was always Quinn. She ruined everything. He glared at her, head buried in her hands. Pathetic. Why couldn't she leave him alone? He didn't need her kind of trouble.

Aaron found Marcus cheering for Reese from the bottom row railing.

"Yo! Why the long face? Did Jenna eat all your popcorn? You can always get more, you know."

"I'm heading home. Things with Jenna didn't go as planned." "Struck out? Man, you should have bought her the nachos.

Nothing says I love you like soggy, greasy game nachos. How do you think I got Reese to go out with me?"

"Nachos, yeah. I'll remember that next time. Later."

The gloomy underside of the bleachers smelled of imitation butter and rust with a hint of mildew. A few stragglers stood in the concession stand line, waiting for their caffeine and popcorn fix, as the Wildcat band played the opening march. Aaron ducked into the men's room to wash popcorn butter off his hands and to gather his thoughts. It should have been the one Quinn-free place in the whole stadium, but before he could even turn off the tap, two guys entered, and of course, they had to be talking about her.

"Man, Quinn's totally lost it. Did you see her yell at everyone and storm out like that?"

"Drugs, man. They can really mess up your mind."

Aaron dried his hands on his jeans and slipped out the door before he could hear any more. He was sick to death of hearing her name. The rusted entrance gate squeaked as Aaron pushed his way out into the parking lot.

He wanted to put the whole night behind him—Quinn, Jenna—he couldn't seem to do anything right. It was time to focus on other things. Quinn was a lost cause and Jenna, well, he could never start something with her until he got Quinn out of his system. She was like poison eating at him from the inside out, but he didn't know what the antidote was.

A raucous laugh exploded somewhere in front of him, followed by the crash of glass hitting the pavement. Probably some underage tailgaters getting drunk. Aaron shook his head and kept walking. Another rough snicker followed a catcall.

"Hey, sweet thing." Two boys wearing Eastwood t-shirts stumbled after a girl. He could just make out her silhouette a few feet in front of them. She had her arms crossed, head down, trying to ignore them.

Quinn. You've got to be kidding me! He balled his hands into fists and looked up at the sky. *What the hell is she doing out here? Why can't I do anything without you throwing her right in my path? Keep walking, Aaron. Don't get involved.* Getting involved led to rejection and heartache, she could take care of herself.

But he found himself moving toward her as his anger argued with his conscience. It's not about Quinn, he rationalized. He would do it for anyone in this situation. No matter how angry he was, he couldn't just leave her. He would never forgive himself if he walked away and something terrible happened— no matter who it was.

One of the boys caught up with Quinn and stepped in front of her path. "Where ya going, little Filly?" The boy's speech slurred, and he brandished a half-empty beer bottle in her face. She pushed it out of the way and picked up her pace.

"Tired of watching your team lose? Why don't you join our party?" The other boy grabbed his crotch and made a lewd gesture. "I'll give you a taste of a real winner."

His friend stopped to retch.

The first boy, the bigger of the two, grabbed her arm and pulled her to a stop. "Hey, I'm talking to you." He grabbed her face and forced her to look at him. He smiled as he swayed. "That's right. You know you want some of this."

Aaron broke into a run. Quinn stood her ground, and he

hoped she didn't do something stupid before he made it to her. "I've always wondered what it would be like to kiss an Eastwood boy," she said and leaned into him. Drunk and stupid, he took the bait. Instead of kissing him, she spit in his face. He wiped at the saliva running down his cheek and looked confused, and she took that moment to knee him in the crotch. Crumpling to the ground, he moaned in pain.

By that time, the other boy had finished retching and grabbed her from behind. Rage worked its way through Aaron, and he barreled toward his target. Quinn screamed as she dragged her nails across her captor's bare forearms and kicked him in the shin. The boy loosened his grip enough for Quinn to escape.

She bolted as Aaron plowed into him, knocking him to the ground. They rolled across the jagged asphalt, wrestling to come out on top. The pain must have sobered his opponent enough to gain the upper hand. Throwing Aaron off, they both staggered to their feet, but Aaron wasn't fast enough. The boy took a swing and caught Aaron in the jaw. Pain exploded as his neck snapped back. The bull inside Aaron was fully awake now.

The boy must have sensed it. His eyes widened as Aaron lowered his head and charged, butting him right in the stomach and knocking him to the ground. Air exploded from his opponent's lips as he curled into a ball, wheezing and gasping for breath. Aaron loomed over him, fists ready, but the fight had gone out of him.

Aaron's chest heaved. He turned to find Quinn. She'd made it halfway across the parking lot and never looked back. It would take some serious sprinting to catch her. "Quinn!" He called as he ran. "Wait."

Her jaw tensed, and she pushed him as hard as she could.

"Hey!" He gasped to catch his breath. "What's your problem? It's me."

The tension drained from her body as she doubled over and vomited into the grass.

"Oh god. I'm sorry." She said between dry heaves. "I thought you were one of them."

Aaron massaged his temples as he paced. Anger ebbed and flowed through him. He wanted to explode, to tell her how sick he was of coming to her rescue only to have her push him away. Watching her crouched in the grass, shaking and vulnerable, constrained his irritation. She'd just been attacked; he should cut her a little slack. He bent down next to her and tentatively placed a hand on her back as she emptied her stomach. When the spasms finally eased, Aaron pulled a napkin he had stuck in his pocket from the concession stand and handed it to her.

"Better?"

Quinn nodded, and then the floodgates opened. Her whole body shook as she wrapped her arms around him and buried her face in his chest. Caught off guard, he stiffened and patted her shoulder. He didn't want to encourage her, but he couldn't exactly turn her away, not after everything she'd just been through. Let her calm down, walk her to safety, and then be on his way.

"I've never been so glad to see anyone in my whole life."

When it was convenient, when she needed something from him. How many times did she have to push him away for him to get the picture? Now it was his chance to push her away, turn around, and keep walking. But his heart betrayed his head as her tears soaked his shirt, each one a bolt of lightning through his veins. She consumed him; her emotions exploded in the back of his head with a flash. He tried to maneuver through the onslaught of feeling, the deep anger, hurt, confusion, and fear, emanating off her in waves.

Their physical touch magnified the telepathic link times a thousand, and Aaron couldn't seem to sever it. In a desperate attempt to ease the intensity of her emotion, he fed calm, safe thoughts to her, giving her his strength. In return, her hunger for reassurance drew him closer. It was working; her thoughts were evening out, becoming content and less chaotic, but the more he gave, the more tangled their minds became, and he was becoming weaker every second. Jelly

replaced his knees as she leeched energy from him. He had to turn off the tap before she drained him dry.

Quinn couldn't stop shaking. The events of the night played over and over in her mind. And Aaron, there he was again, rubbing her back as she puked her guts out, comforting her while she cried. Most guys would have turned their backs, run away from an emotional basket case like her, but not Aaron.

It took everything inside her not to blurt out what she'd seen in the stadium, to tell him everything as he held her close. Her questions and uncertainty about everyone and everything ate at her from the inside out, burning a hole in her so deep she couldn't imagine being whole again. At this point she wanted to trust someone, anyone. She needed someone to tell her she wasn't crazy.

Doubt crept up on her. If she was going to trust anyone, it should be Reese, not some boy she barely knew. But Reese wasn't here, and Aaron was. The voices, or whatever they were, had said he didn't care about her, but if that were the case, why did he always arrive when she needed him most?

She hugged him tighter, and her racing heart slowed, her thoughts cleared. Being near him calmed her, restored balance in her head and made the darkness recede. When was the last time she had felt this safe? This euphoric? She could trust him, tell him everything, as long as he never let go of her again.

"Quinn." Her name sounded beautiful coming from his lips. She wanted him to say it again.

"Quinn." Cupping her cheek, he raised her eyes to his, and she tilted her head in anticipation.

"I'm sorry." Stilted words rasped against her waiting mouth, and he gently pushed her away, untangling himself from her grip. She blinked, confused. What happened? Had she done something wrong? Released from the soothing shelter of his embrace, the dark thoughts returned.

Quinn wasn't special. He would have defended anyone he saw being attacked. Of course, he didn't care about her. How stupid could she be? And to think she almost confided in him. Quinn wrinkled her nose as the memory of Aaron lip locked with that gorgeous brunette flashed across her mind. What an idiot, throwing herself at him when he was with someone else.

"You better get back to that girl you were with before she notices you're gone."

"What girl?" Aaron looked confused.

"The one with the throat you stuck your tongue down at the game. Or did you forget?" Quinn rummaged in her purse for a stick of gum to erase the bitter taste of bile.

"Jenna?" Aaron's tone suggested annoyance. "We're friends." Quinn rolled her eyes. "Right." She had no right to be angry with him, but she couldn't help herself. The thought of his lips on anyone else drove her crazy. "A friend with benefits." She ripped the gum from its wrapper and stuffed it in her mouth.

"You've got to be kidding me." Aaron kicked a rock so hard it skidded a good ten feet across the asphalt. "Why should you care who I kiss? It's not like we have a relationship. Are we even friends? You don't have any claim on me. I'm not a dog that will come running when its master calls. You're a real piece of work, Quinn."

"Me?" The sting of his words worked through her like poison. "I'm not the one who keeps showing up out of the blue like some creepy stalker." She spit back and immediately regretted it.

"Stalker?" Aaron stumbled backward. "Is that seriously what you think of me?"

Quinn covered her mouth, wishing she could take it back. "No." She stuttered, frantic to repair the damage she'd inflicted. She reached for him, but he flinched away. "I was angry. I didn't mean it. Please, I'm sorry."

"No, I'm sorry." Aaron stood several feet away, arms crossed, eyes glazed, cold. "Sorry for saving your ass over and over again with no thanks. Sorry I believed the kiss we shared meant something, that I let you get under my skin. I choose you every time. God knows why because you sure as hell wouldn't choose me over Jeff. And most of all, I'm sorry you were too blind to see how much I cared about you."

Cared? Past tense? Paralyzed by the sting of his words, her first instinct turned to anger, she wanted to defend herself, but she couldn't, not with the realization of how much she had hurt him, even if it hadn't been intentional. She had treated him like shit, and for what? Jeff? Jeff didn't give a crap about her anymore; he was with Kerstin.

"Aaron, please. Let me explain." She ran after him, reaching for his arm.

Aaron stopped cold, slapping her hand away, turning his hard gaze upon her. "Explain what? How you run back into Jeff's arms every time we get close? How you push me away every chance you get?"

"It's complicated." Quinn pulled her sleeves over her finger-tips and wiped at the tears tumbling of her chin.

"It's really not. Jeff is with Kerstin, you either like me or you don't. Simple."

She wanted it to be simple, to tell him she could see herself falling for him, but the words stuck in her throat. Falling in love with him meant letting him in and letting him in meant being vulnerable. He would see the real her, and the real Quinn was a mess.

Voices.

Shadows.

Who would stick around for that kind of crazy? She sure as hell wouldn't. When she didn't reply right away, Aaron sighed and shook his head.

"That's what I thought. You're safe now. I'm out of here. Don't expect my help again."

"You're the one who kissed someone else, not me." She took a step toward him.

Aaron closed the gap between them in two strides. "You might not have kissed Jeff right there in front of me, but I saw the way you looked at each other. You're not even close to being over him." His hands closed around her biceps, clenching and unclenching them with every breath, feverish heat spread across her skin with his touch. "Every time I get close to you, you push me away. Now I know why. I can't compete with him, Quinn. With Jenna, I wanted to have one night, one second where I didn't think about you." His voice was husky, ragged with emotion.

"And did it work? Did she help you forget?"

Two pools of golden green looked into the depths of her eyes, and her breath hitched.

"No," he whispered, breath ragged, laced with what sounded like anguish. "She didn't."

They pressed closer together, her heartbeat outracing his. He tilted his chin down and pressed his forehead to hers. She brushed her lips against his and he sighed. His kiss, tentative at first, intensified. The fierceness of it rocked her and she twined her fingers through his dark hair, matching him, desire for desire. His mouth pressed against the soft spot between shoulder and neck. Her fingers found the bare skin beneath his T-shirt, the muscles of his back flexing beneath her touch. She didn't want to stop, didn't want him to stop as the world and all her problems fell away from her like dead leaves from a tree.

"Wait." Breathless, he pulled his mouth from hers.

"What?" Quinn looked up

"You're doing it again, and I'm letting you." He closed his eyes and let out a hollow laugh.

"Doing what?"

"Manipulating me. Using me." He kissed the top of her forehead and let her go. "You're not ready for this. For us."

Panic writhed within Quinn as he walked away. Truth was, Aaron had etched himself on her heart while she wasn't looking. If she let herself, she would trust him, love him. She was ready, she knew it now.

"Wait. Please." Quinn stepped in front of him, walking backward, getting in his way every time he tried to dodge her. "I'm sorry, Aaron." She had to make him listen. "You're right. I shouldn't care that you kissed Jenna." With Jenna's name, he groaned and turned around to avoid her and walked in the opposite direction. Quinn turned too, putting herself in his path. "But I do. I've never felt so hurt and confused, and that's how I know you're wrong about Jeff." It felt good to tell him how she felt, a first step. Maybe if she could trust him with her heart, she could trust him with everything else, eventually. "That's how I know I am ready to move on."

Aaron stopped, but he wouldn't look at her. Instead, he fiddled with a guitar pick he retrieved from his pocket, avoiding her pleading eyes. "What do you want from me, Quinn?" He sighed.

She took his hands and forced him to look at her. "Maybe it's too late, but I want you to know that I choose you. Right here, right now. I don't want you to walk away from me, from us, from what could be."

Aaron didn't move. He didn't say anything. He stared at her, his eyes searching hers. Her heart hammered against her chest. A sliver of light crossed Aaron's face.

"Oh my god! Look at your cheek!" She ran a finger across

the puffy red welt rising on his usually chiseled jaw. He flinched. "It's swelling up. You should get some ice on it."

"It's fine." Aaron pushed her hand away. "I've had worse. Honest."

"You put some serious moves on that guy. I didn't know you were half ninja." He didn't even give the hint of a smile at her lame attempt at a joke. She shifted her weight from one foot to the other, not sure what else to say. As long as Aaron still stood in front of her, she might still have a chance.

Aaron shook his head. "You're right, it's too late." He didn't move.

"If you really believe that, walk away. I won't follow." Quinn gave him an out, and he didn't take it, but he still didn't look convinced. "You said you thought our kiss didn't mean anything, but it did, and that scared me. But I'm not scared now. I want to be with you, to trust you. I'm ready to see what's between us. I want you to give me one more chance. Please."

"Is that what you really want?"

Quinn nodded, afraid to breathe in case he changed his mind. "I'm a mess. I'm a fool. Please, Aaron. One more chance. I care about you."

"You have a funny way of showing it."

"Want to get out of here? Talk?" She motioned to the exit. "You have a car?"

"Motorcycle." Aaron straightened and looked at her as if he were trying to decide whether or not to buy what she was selling.

"I've never been on a motorcycle before."

"Won't you be missed?" Aaron pointed at the stadium, thawing slightly.

"Screw them. I'll be suspended by the end of the week anyway. Please, Aaron. I can't go back up to those vultures. Run away with me. Please."

Aaron sighed, took her hand, and twined his fingers around

hers. He searched her eyes, and she didn't flinch away, opening herself up to scrutiny, hoping he would see her sincerity. It must have worked because after a few seconds, he nodded.

"Okay. Where should we go?"

"As far from Westland as possible. Somewhere away from brunettes and ex-boyfriends."

He rubbed his jaw. "Okay," he said decisively and pulled her through the rows of parked cars.

Aaron's bike, slate black and silver chrome, waited in the parking lot. Her mother would freak if she saw Quinn on the back of a dangerous, teen-killing machine. Perfect.

"Ever ridden a bike before?" Aaron ran a hand through his hair and rubbed the back of his neck.

Quinn shook her head and with Aaron's help, settled herself on the bike.

"You'll have to wear this." He wiped the inside of the sapphire-blue helmet with his sleeve. "It's my brother's."

Quinn pulled the helmet over her ears. "Your brother must have a big head."

Aaron adjusted the chinstrap. His hand brushed her cheek, and she shivered. "That better?"

"A little." Her head felt like a marble inside a mayonnaise jar.

He removed his leather jacket and slipped it over her arms. The sleeves hung past her hands. "Put your feet here. When we turn, just ease your weight to that side. Follow the natural feel of the bike, don't fight it, and don't help it. Don't put your feet down when we stop. Just sit there looking pretty and hang on tight. I'll do the rest."

Aaron settled on the seat in front of her and pulled on his helmet. Quinn encircled his waist.

"You might want to hold on tighter than that." The engine sputtered and roared to life. Quinn felt unsteady on the bike as Aaron rocked forward, disengaging the kickstand with his heel, and she tightened her grip around his waist.

The first few seconds felt unnatural as they sped out of the parking lot. Making the first turn awakened the dragonflies within her heart, but when they didn't crash, her heartbeat returned to normal. As they approached the second turn, she pressed her body into Aaron's and felt what he meant about moving with the bike.

Faster and faster they rode through the night. Even with a jacket on, the wind whipped at her clothes, but she didn't care. She leaned her head on Aaron's back and sucked in the fresh scent of his cologne, a mixture of pine and cinnamon, reminding her of fall, while the steady rise and fall of his chest comforted her as she spooned him. Closing her eyes, she forced her lungs to match him breath for breath. Aaron, Quinn, free, exhilarating. She melted into his warmth. No one else existed in the world. She had no idea where they were going, and she didn't care. She wanted to ride on and on, up to the moon, far away from the voices and rumors and drunken harassers.

Aaron stopped the bike in the middle of an open field twenty minutes outside of town. Soft autumn grass dotted with white and yellow wildflowers stretched as far as the eye could see. The tops of the flowers waved in the breeze, filling the air with a sweet scent. Fireflies winked in and out, weaving their light across the open plain.

The engine sighed and cut out. He dismounted and offered his hand. Her fingers fit within his like a puzzle. Even now, he sensed the truth of her feelings through their touch. No fear, no lies. She wanted him as much as he wanted her. If he hadn't used his powers and sensed it for himself, he would have walked away and never looked back, but their connection went deeper than words, and he couldn't turn his back on that.

"We're here."

"Where's here?"

Aaron led her several feet from the bike through the ankle high grass. "Look up."

A billion stars twinkled in the inky, cloudless sky. Each celestial body seemed close enough to touch. A harvest moon glowed bright orange among them, majestic as it hung suspended in heaven. Quinn gasped.

"You wanted to be far away from everything and everyone? Will this do?"

"It's beautiful." Not taking her eyes from the sky, Quinn settled cross-legged on the grass and pulled his jacket close around her. "Chilly isn't it?"

Aaron rubbed his hands together and sat beside her. "Sorry I don't have a blanket or anything." He scooted closer, not sure if he should put his arm around her or not. Would she want him to? If he touched her hand, he could find out easily enough, but that would be cheating.

"It's okay." Quinn rested her head on his shoulder. "Mmm, you're warm."

Aaron's palms started to sweat as she curled into him, nudging him onto his back until their bodies were close enough to fuse together. He was almost scared to breathe, afraid he might wake up any moment and find it was all a dream. The ground smelled damp and sweet. Crickets chirped their night song, and an owl hooted in the distance.

"I've never seen a more beautiful sky. It's so bright tonight." Quinn pointed to a constellation. "That's Orion, I think. It's the only one I can remember."

"The Big Dipper's the only one I know." Aaron pointed to another group of stars. A jumble of questions lodged in the back of Aaron's throat, about what happened at the game, about her nightmares, about their connection. He wanted to ask them all at once, but he'd never seen Quinn so calm before, so relaxed. Her happy mood pulsed against his consciousness, and he began to trust the moment, letting his desire to be with her sweep all uncertainty away. Maybe now wasn't the time to probe her for answers. She'd had a rough night, if she wanted to forget the drama and talk about stars, why not? Maybe it was time to get to know each other better, like two people on a first date talking about normal stuff.

"What about the Ice Cream Sundae? It even has a cherry on top." Quinn indicated a dense ball of stars.

"Or the frog?" Aaron said. "Catching a fly."

"Oh! I see it! Can you imagine being born under the frog star sign?"

"Better than the sign of the fly." They both burst out laughing.

Quinn paused. "Sometimes I feel so insignificant when I look at the vastness of the universe."

The ease of their conversation surprised him. All awkwardness disappeared, and it was if they'd know each other their whole lives, spent hours under the stars just like this.

"Yeah, I know how you feel. Billions of stars and galaxies, and humans have barely scratched the surface of what's out there." Aaron caressed her arm. "We have more in common with the universe than you know. We're all part of it, made of it, of stardust."

"Carl Sagan." Quinn turned and smiled.

"You've heard of Carl Sagan?"

"My dad used to watch old videos of his show, Cosmos. He had a thing for stars, my dad ..." A worry line appeared on Quinn's brow.

"How long has he been gone?"

"Long enough." Emotion surged from Quinn, straining against his barrier. He squeezed her hand. She squeezed back, and the intensity lessened.

"Do you think they've missed me yet?"

Aaron turned on his side to face Quinn. "Kerstin's probably

celebrating your demise." He tucked a strand of hair behind her ear.

"Let her." Quinn turned so she was nose-to-nose with him. "There's no place I'd rather be." She draped her arm over his and fingered the soft flannel of his sleeve. "Why do you always wear long sleeves?" She tugged at the cuff.

Her curiosity assaulted him. Her attempt to probe his barrier felt clumsy and unfocused. He sensed a current of latent power that he guessed she didn't even know was there. She was probing him, not the other way around. The realization hit him like a mac truck; that's why they didn't always have to be skin-to-skin for him to sense her. Millions of questions rushed him, and he struggled to slow down his quivering brain. How do you tell someone they might have latent psychic ability? Would mentioning it freak her out?

Quinn played with the small, pearl button of his shirt, and a tiny piece of his wall cracked. Her power brushed against his mind, questing for an answer.

"Even when it's hot, even when everyone's in t-shirts, you're covered up. Why?"

Because reading minds and emotions wasn't his only secret, or his darkest. "I ..." Aaron's mouth went dry as he tried to compose himself, tried to patch the chink in his barrier before the whole thing collapsed. Then, she was gone, retreating behind the barrier as if she'd never been there at all.

She had no idea what she was asking him to do, the wounds that would bleed if he showed her, but something deep inside urged him to do it. And maybe telling her would bring her closer to opening up to him. He had sensed it, she wanted to. Maybe he could tell her one secret, but not the other. Start small, at the beginning. It was up to him to take the first step. Aaron took a deep breath before rolling up the sleeves of his flannel shirt. He turned his palms face up, bared his forearms, and thus, his soul.

23

Quinn stared at the thick, jagged scars that snaked up Aaron's arms. From his wrist, six inches of rough, pink, clumpy tissue embossed his pale flesh. She took his left hand in hers and traced the scar with her finger, feeling, memorizing every bump and curve. He flinched and jerked away.

"Sorry." Aaron massaged the scar and stared off into space. "It's hard for me to let anyone see them, let alone touch them."

"No, I'm sorry. I should never have pushed you."

"It's okay. You didn't make me do anything I didn't want to do." A hollow pit opened in her stomach. Staring at his scars, she didn't want to admit to herself, to anyone, that she'd contemplated the same thing. Quinn pretended to pick grass off her sweater and tried to think of the right words to fill the awkward silence.

"Why'd you do it?" She winced at herself for asking such a dumb and personal question. It was none of her business. "You don't have to tell me if you don't want to." But she wanted him to. She wanted to know him, all of him, and for him to know her in return. Every ugly part of her.

"No. I want to." Aaron hung his head, and a strand of hair fell across his furrowed brow. She wanted to smooth it back, to comfort him the way he'd comforted her so many times before, but she sensed he needed space to think through the story.

"It was a combination of things. Guilt. Anger. Grief." His voice flowed from his full lips, soft, low. "I wanted to stop the pain, to stop feeling. I thought it was the way out. That maybe it would make things right."

"Make what right?"

He turned onto his back as he spoke, gazing into Neverland. "There was an accident." He rolled down his sleeves, telling the story as if recounting something he'd heard on the news. "I don't remember much about that night. I only know what my dad told me." He paused, his Adam's apple lowering as he struggled to swallow.

"My mom, little sister, and I were on the way back from dropping my brother off at a friend's. It was raining and there were reports of flooding, so my mom had taken a different route home. We were on a bridge, and some kid in a pickup was going too fast. He lost control and hit the car smack on the driver's side." Aaron paused. "Our car crashed over the barrier and into the water. Ruth, my baby sister, was in the back. She was four." He cleared his throat. "The impact broke my window. The water was so cold. I tried to get them out. I tried, but it was dark, and I didn't know which was up. I watched her ... Ruth." He choked out her name. "I watched her sink beneath the rushing water. She reached for me. I tried ... to get to her."

"Aaron, I'm sorry." Quinn's face was wet with tears. She tried to imagine what it would be like to watch her mother die right in front of her, powerless to stop it. The demons, her father leaving, everything she'd ever been through paled in comparison. Aaron always seemed so strong and sure. No one would ever have guessed he'd been through something so tragic.

Everything about him emanated quiet strength. It's what drew her to him.

"They found me by the side of the river, dead. Nobody knows how long I'd been there. The paramedics managed to resuscitate me, but I couldn't breathe on my own. When I finally woke from the coma, I didn't know who I was. I didn't know anyone or anything. Do you know what it's like to feel completely alien in a world that should be familiar?" His eyes glistened, and he turned away, blinking.

Quinn shook her head, but she understood more than he could possibly imagine. Aaron's strength inspired her. If he could survive all that, she had no excuses for not getting her own life together.

"How long did it take to regain your memory?"

"I'll never get it all back. I'm not the same Aaron. Never will be. He's dead." Aaron balled his fist and fastened the button around his wrist, covering the last inch of his secret. "After the accident, I knew I didn't belong here. I blamed myself, so did my brother. It should be Ruth sitting here today, not me. I should be dead—I was dead. I tried to right the wrong and spent six months in the psych ward at Rio Villa for it. I still don't understand why I'm here." Aaron placed a hand on Quinn's cheek and brushed the moisture away with his thumb. "Hey, don't cry."

He pulled her to him, and she tucked her head beneath his chin, swallowing the shame rising inside. His fingers moved through her hair, consoling her as she soaked his shirt with her tears. She should be the one protecting him from his pain, not the other way around. She let him comfort her anyway and let herself contemplate falling in love with him. She'd treated Aaron like crap, pushed him away because she'd been afraid to trust him. Yet here he was again, this beautiful, damaged soul baring his broken heart and asking for nothing in return. Jeff wasn't fit to even stand in Aaron's shadow.

"Is that why you moved here?" she asked.

He nodded. "They told my dad trying to force me into my old life was too stressful. I needed to start a new one. A different life for a different Aaron."

"Does anyone else know? About the accident, about your…"

"Suicide attempt? It's okay. You can call it what it was. Yeah, Marcus, Jenna, a few others."

Jenna. That name again. Heat rose in Quinn's cheeks and she tried to untangle the knot of irrational jealousy that squeezed around her heart.

"Aaron, those scars are major. You would have bled out in minutes. How did you survive?"

Aaron stiffened. She listened to his heartbeat against her cheek.

"I didn't." His voice sounded strained.

"What do you mean?" Quinn held her body completely still. She heard her blood whooshing in her ears as her pulse quickened.

"I died. Josh found me in a pool of blood. I died in the hospital. They brought me back just before …"

"Before what?"

"I'm not sure." His frown deepened, and he shook his head. Quinn bit her lip. Had she gone too far? Aaron didn't speak, but he didn't push her away either. He lay rigid, and she tensed in response. Breath for breath, she matched him, waiting, wondering what she should do.

"I try to remember, but it slips away every time I come close." He paused and lowered his voice. "I saw something. The same something I saw the first time when I was in the coma. Something in the darkness. Watching me."

"What was it? Were you scared?" Quinn held her breath. If Aaron had seen the same thing she had, then she wasn't crazy, or alone. Could Aaron's uncanny ability to show up in her time of distress be more than coincidence? Could it have something to do with what he'd seen during his time in the coma? Quinn's heart sped. If it did, maybe they'd been brought together so he could help her understand how to defeat her own demons.

"No. Maybe. I don't know. It's all a blur."

"All I know is that I wasn't alone. I think I was sent back for a reason, but I have no idea what that reason is. Why else would I survive two near-death experiences? I know it sounds … well … kind of crazy." Aaron's face glistened in the dim shaft of moonlight. Quinn stroked his hair.

"I don't think you're crazy." Every nerve in her body was aware of him. She took his head in her hands and pulled him to her. As their lips touched, her world spun backward, turned upside-down, and all the fear and confusion drained out of her. She wanted Aaron, his lips on hers, his hand caressing her, forever. She shivered as his callused fingers edged up the back of her shirt to trace her naked spine. Passion fed on passion as the intensity of the kiss grew. As if he could read her mind, he rolled her over, pressing his body against hers. Quinn thought they might melt right through to the core of the earth.

Was this too much, too fast? Did she care? She was tired of being afraid, tired of worrying about the future. Being with Aaron, felt good. More than good, it felt cosmic, like he had been made just for her and her for him. His kiss softened, giving her the sweetest, longest, most gentle touch of his lips on hers. That's when she realized this was so much more than passion, this was genuine, this was trust, this was as close to real love as she had ever experienced.

Aaron pulled away, then curled himself around her, lips against her shoulder. "Wow. That's not usually the reaction I get when I spill my deep, dark secrets."

"Aaron?"

"Quinn?" He stroked her hair.

"I've got a deep, dark secret too."

"That you're a druggie? I heard." He kissed her neck, her cheek, eyelid, nose, and finally brushed his gentle lips on hers.

"I'm serious." Quinn's sentences, words, thoughts unraveled with every touch of his lips, making it impossible to concentrate.

"You sound serious." He continued kissing her nose, cheek, eyelids.

"Aaron. Maybe you were sent back for me." His warm breath awakened her desire for him to kiss her neck, and her heartbeat quickened.

"So I could ravage you in the moonlight?" He nipped at her collarbone.

"I'm serious," she whispered. "I need to tell you before I lose my nerve."

"Okay." Aaron sat up on his elbow and nodded. "I'm listening." When his eyes met hers, she felt naked, like he already knew what was in her soul. Tears formed in the corner of her eyes and he wiped them away with his thumb.

"It's okay., Quinn. No matter what you say, I won't judge you. I swear. You can tell me anything. You're safe."

In that moment, she knew, without a doubt, that she could trust him. The knot she'd been tying in her stomach for months began to unravel, and she began her story.

"Aaron, I …" An invisible hand wrapped around her neck, squeezing and constricting the air from her lungs. She fought to speak, but whatever held her increase its pressure every time she thought about revealing her secret to Aaron. She clutched at her throat, tried to form words, any words, but nothing came out but a raspy huff of air. She bolted upright and clawed at her throat, fighting the invisible fingers for breath.

"Are you okay?" Aaron's eyes widened, glowing in the moonlight.

No! She was trapped in one of those dreams where you scream and scream but no sound ever comes out. She looked up. A dark mass covered the moon. The darkness forced itself inside her, taking over, like a shadow crawling through her veins. Her whole body shook as she fought against it.

I won't tell him. Please, please just let me go! I swear!

She grabbed Aaron's hand, and in response he gathered her in his arms, stroking her hair, her back, her skin until his touch burned through the darkness, dispelling the shadow, and freeing her from its grip. The cords in her neck relaxed, and she gulped at the cool night air.

"Quinn? Are you okay?" Fear spiked his voice.

"Yeah, it's just … getting kind of cold." She untangled from his arms, gently pushing him away. "I should get back, anyway. Ride the bus with the others." She sat up and brushed the leaves from her hair and tried to give him a reassuring smile.

"Yeah, sure." The hurt look on Aaron's face was like a slap.

Their eyes locked, and Quinn wanted to bolt from the intensity of his stare. "I meant what I said about telling me anything."

"I know." She glanced at the moon. The ominous darkness obscured the once bright sky. "It's nothing, really." Shadows crept from every inch of the field, flickering in and out of her vision. Watching to make sure she kept her mouth shut. "We should go." Quinn got up first, heading back to the bike, followed by Aaron, followed by darkness.

Aaron could feel Quinn, tense, against him as they turned into the stadium parking lot. She gripped him tightly, too tight, as if she were afraid that she might be ripped from the back of the bike. He tried to get a reading on her, but when he reached out, he hit a cold well of nothing that set his hair standing on end.

They pulled into a spot near the back, and he cut the engine. Bitter wind hissed through the trees and he couldn't shrug off the chill settling in his bones. The concrete and steel stadium looked as grim as he felt. Westland High supporters streamed from the exits, subdued, while the opposing side whooped and clapped each other on the back.

"Looks like we lost." He dismounted and offered his hand. Quinn ignored him, her eyes fixed on the sky. He followed her gaze to the bright harvest moon and cleared his throat. She blinked and turned to him, like waking from a deep sleep. Dark circles ringed her eyes, cheeks sunken, face drawn in worry.

"What's new?" She looked behind her, shoulders tensing as she examined the long shadows of the cars on the pavement. Aaron furrowed his brow. Something wasn't right; it was as if Quinn had been replaced by a shell. When he looked at her, emptiness stared back, and he thought he'd never seen someone look so forlorn before.

"I wish I didn't have to go back." The longing in Quinn's voice persuaded him to try the telepathic link one more time. He didn't care if she didn't want him reading her thoughts. He was sick of being pushed away; it was time to push back.

"We don't. I could take you back to the field. We could start the night over." Swallowing his guilt, he took her hand and sent out another exploratory telepathic thread. An endless void yawned before him. He groped through it, searching for a thought, a feeling, for any sign of their psychic connection, but her mind was lost to him, surrounded by an endless, dark wasteland he couldn't penetrate. He was blind, his gift useless.

She shook her head. "No. I'll be in enough trouble as it is. I can't hide for the rest of my life. Thank you for taking me to the stars." She pulled him into an embrace. "Aaron, I … I really like you."

He waited for the "but." It never came. "I really like you, too."

"I'm a mess, I know I am. I'm trouble."

"I like trouble." He cupped her chin in his hand to look at her in earnest.

"So, you want to see me again?"

"Yes. How about tomorrow night? My band's playing a gig. Marcus is going, and he's bringing Reese. We can all go out for pizza after, if you want." Aaron rested his chin on her shoulder. "Do you?"

"What time?"

"Yo!" Marcus ran toward them. "Where have you two been? Reese is looking for you. And here you are, mackin' in the parking lot." He grinned. "I don't mean to interrupt the love-fest, but they're loading the bus. Reese told Coach White you were in the bathroom, but I don't know how long that story will fly. Better get over there, pronto."

"Thanks. I'll be right there." She hugged Aaron tighter. "I don't want to go," she whispered.

"You have to." He kissed the top of her head. "Quinn!" Marcus motioned for her to get going.

"One second," she shouted at Marcus. "What time tomorrow night?"

"Pick you up at six-thirty?"

"Six-thirty. Tomorrow." She brushed her lips against his.

He kissed her back, but the kiss was a semitone off, a dissonant hum instead of their previous harmony. Aaron tried his gift one last time, focusing all his energy into reaching her. Not even a glimmer emerged from the void that encompassed her.

"Quinn!" Marcus urged again. "Time's up."

"Wish me luck." She took two steps back, waved, and ran to catch up with Marcus.

24

The demons were always there now, dark masses flickering in the corners of Quinn's eyes, only to vanish the second she tried to focus on them. No amount of light banished them completely, not since last night. Now they lived where they shouldn't, boldly flaunting their presence and no longer hiding within her dreams.

She pulled another not-quite-right-for-this-date shirt over her head and threw it on the wicker chair. Kicking a discarded pile of pants out of her way, she sat on the end of her bed and fell backward into her soft floral duvet. Accepting the date with Aaron had been a bad idea. The dark things didn't like him. Closing her eyes, she tried to relax, but every time she thought about him, the shadows became agitated. Was it him, or her happiness when she was with him, they didn't like?

They pressed in on her, stroking her hair, whispering in her ear to stay away from him. Pushing their way into her head, they probed her thoughts, and she felt herself slipping into a weird trance. She should cancel. No. That wasn't what she wanted, that's what *they* wanted. She pushed back, her will against theirs, until she felt them retreat. When she jerked herself out of their grip, she found her phone in her hand, a half-written text message to Aaron, cancelling the date. She shot upright and dropped the phone, shivering at the memory of invisible fingers gripping her neck. A warning that they could control her whenever they wanted.

Pulling her knees to her chest, she rocked back and forth, uncertainty twisting around her gut. Maybe it would be better for both if she broke it off before they grew attached to one another. She picked up her phone and stared at the message again.

Send it, Quinn. Let Aaron go.

But it was too late for that. She had already crashed into love with him, hard and fast, and she couldn't bear the thought of never seeing him again.

"I swear I won't tell him anything about you. I'll do whatever you say, do whatever you want, if you leave him out of this. If you let me be with him." Quinn's eyes darted around the room, peering at every shadow, waiting for an answer, retaliation, something, but the demons retorted with silence. She took their eerie hush the way she'd wanted to, as acquiescence, but deep down she feared their silence was the calm before the storm.

She startled as her phone buzzed with a text message. Another text from Jeff. That made four in the last hour. Her finger hovered over the message icon, then hit deleted without reading any of them. Then she switched to the phone icon, dialing Reese, again.

"Hey." Reese sounded out of breath.

"Where have you been?" Quinn paced in front of her empty closet. "I've sent you three Snapchats, called your cell twice. I even sent you an e-mail."

"Sorry, I don't usually check Snapchat in the shower," Reese said. "What's up?"

"I'm having a clothing crisis, my hair is a mess, Mt. Fuji is erupting on the end of my nose, and I haven't been on a date with anyone but Jeff, ever."

"Flared black min skirt, Labyrinth t-shirt, jean jacket, black boots, hair gel, and a spot of toothpaste."

"What's the toothpaste for?"

"Mt. Fuji."

"Does that really work?"

"My mom swears by it. Look, don't be nervous. He took you stargazing, and he kissed you. Three times. I think he likes you. Just be yourself."

"Thanks, Reese. I just needed a little pep talk."

"You got this. Got to go. Marcus will be here in half an hour and my hair's still wet. Later."

"Later."

Quinn grabbed her 'babe with the power' t-shirt from her dresser drawer and pulled it over her head, then she made her way down the hall and to the bathroom to dab some toothpaste on her spot. The shadows did nothing more than follow in her wake, nothing to fear. If they didn't want her to go with Aaron, they would have made a move by now. Wouldn't they?

Inside, she smiled; they would stick to the agreement. She wouldn't tell Aaron about the demons, the demons would leave her alone, and she and Aaron would live happily ever after. Everybody wins.

The doorbell chimed— Aaron was early. She was still in her underwear and hadn't put on any makeup. A pang of longing bloomed in her chest. If her mom was here, she could answer the door and tell him Quinn would be down in a minute. But she wasn't. The doorbell chimed again.

Digging through the piles of clothes, she searched for something, anything to cover her half naked butt. A pair of ripped skinny jeans peeked out from under her bed. Perfect. She pulled them on, hopping on one foot, then the other, as she made her way downstairs.

Aaron, tall and slender, held a single pink rose. He wore jeans, a pair of black Docs, and an unbuttoned green and blue plaid flannel shift over a black, Fender guitar t-shirt that hugged in all the right places.

"You're early," Quinn stammered.

"I am? I'm sorry. I can go away and come back." He turned to leave, and she grabbed his arm.

"Not so fast."

He grinned. "I knew you couldn't resist me."

"Thanks, but I couldn't resist this." Quinn took the rose. "Now you can leave." She smiled mischievously.

"Did I mention how beautiful you look?" His grin widened. "The toothpaste brings out your eyes."

Quinn's hand flew to her nose. "Oh no." She snatched a tissue from the table, rubbed at the glob, and then gestured upstairs. "I was…" She motioned over her shoulder. "I just have to put my makeup on, and I'll be ready. It'll only take a second."

"You look beautiful without it." Aaron stroked her face with the back of his hand.

She was spellbound with one touch. "I'll be quick. Just make yourself at home."

In her bedroom, she applied some pink lip-gloss, mascara, and a little blush. She pulled on her black boots, sculpted the chunky ends of her hair with some gel, and made one more plea to the agitated shadows flickering in the corner of her eye.

"I promise I won't tell him anything if you let me have this one night. I promise I won't tell him. It's just a date. He won't know anything. I'll do anything else you want." She held her breath and waited for an answer, but they hovered, silent specters, watching, waiting. For what? She didn't know. But she would do anything to have one normal night with Aaron.

"Okay, I'm ready." She shrugged into her jean jacket as she descended the stairs.

"Our stallion awaits, my lady." Aaron handed her Josh's helmet and helped her adjust it to fit her head.

"I like the blue, but do you think we can find a helmet to match my homecoming dress? I'm thinking something in purple."

She grinned at the shocked look on Aaron's face.

"Are you asking me to homecoming?" he stuttered.

"No. I'm hinting for you to ask me."

"Oh!" Aaron ran a hand through his hair. "Wow!"

"Only if you want to."

"Of course, I want to. I mean…" Aaron got down on one knee, took her hand, and cleared his throat. "Smart, funny, beautiful, star-loving, Quinn. Will you give me the honor of escorting you to the Westland High homecoming dance?"

"Well, will there be dinner first?" She pretended to think it over.

"Wherever you want to go."

"And chocolate cake?"

"As much as you can eat?"

"And kissing?"

Aaron stood up, put his hand around her waist, and drew her to him. His lips traced up her neck, teased the line of her jaw, and came to rest, firmly on her lips.

"How can I say no to that?" She asked.

"You don't." His warm breath sent shivers through her as he whispered in her ear. "You say, yes, if you want me."

"Yes." She said, cupping his chin and bringing his lips back to hers.

Dark masses twisted and swirled around them. The demons were angry, but she didn't care. Let them try to tear them apart. Being with Aaron made her happy and she refused to let them ruin what little happiness she had. She would keep quiet, and they would stay in the background. That was the deal, but, as she settled on the bike behind Aaron, she looked up at the sky.

Above them, storm clouds gathered, and a bolt of dread struck the center of her heart.

Twenty minutes later, they arrived at the ruins of St. Angeles. Quinn's skin crawled as she stood in front of the Gothic chapel. Its aging stone edifice appeared cloaked in a murky web of writhing gray mist. When a gust of wind blew through the four arches of the bell tower, the iron giant within began tolling, low and sonorous. A tremor started in her legs and worked its way up her spine. Quinn gripped Aaron's hand while shadows stalked the adjacent cemetery, camouflaged among the moss-covered grave-stones. Their heavy gaze pressed down upon her and she suddenly felt trapped like a heroine in a bad black-and-white horror move.

"Beautiful, isn't it?" Aaron kissed her cheek.

Creepy, more like it, she thought, but nodded anyway, moving closer to him. He wrapped an arm around her, the warmth of his body easing the chill creeping through her veins.

"What are you guys doing here?" Marcus feigned surprise as he slammed the driver's side door of his Jeep. He clapped Aaron on the back. "What's up, man?"

Reese, still in the passenger seat, mashed her hand against the car horn.

"What's wrong? Your arm broken or something?" Marcus shrugged. "Women."

Reese mashed the horn again, this time not letting up on the pressure. Marcus covered his ears and walked over to the passenger side to open the door.

Reese smiled. "You're so sweet. You didn't have to open the door for me." She gave him a quick peck, and then ran over to Quinn. "Double dates are so fun!"

Reese grabbed Quinn's hand and they followed Aaron and

Marcus down the cobbled path to the door. Sweat beaded on the back of her neck. On either side of the entrance, two gargoyles perched on concrete plinths. As they passed through the wooden door, and into the nave, she felt their stony eyes watching her. Legends said their grotesque features are meant to drive away evil spirits, but the slight twitch of their tails proved otherwise. Quinn wanted to cut and run, but she forced one foot in front of the other, refusing to look back.

Inside the sanctuary, the hair on Quinn's arms shot upward as the knot of fear twisted tighter around her gut. Rows of black candelabras lit the interior. Hundreds of candles cast a myriad of deep shadows and bright warmth on the walls as light and dark danced and writhed around each other with each flicker of the flames. Above them loomed a large wooden cross suspended from the ceiling by iron chains. Red lights shone down on it, casting an otherworldly luminescence on the dead wood. Blood bubbled from the cracks and oozed down the rough timbers, splattering crimson threads across the altar. Drip, drip, drip, the sound of scarlet rain echoed through her ears and rattled her spine.

It's not real. It's not real. It's not real.

"Hey, you're late." Quinn startled as Jenna hopped off the makeshift stage, landing as gracefully as a cat, in front of them. When she looked back up at the cross, nothing seemed out of the ordinary. Two pieces of wood hanging by iron chains. That's all. Red lights. Not blood.

"Only five minutes." Aaron intertwined his fingers with hers. "Quinn, this is Jenna. Jenna, this is—"

"Quinn. I know." Jenna held out her hand. After Quinn shook it, Jenna rubbed her palm on her jeans then side-eyed Quinn in a you're-not-good-enough-for-him way.

Quinn felt her cheeks flush under Jenna's scrutiny, and she shifted her weight from one foot to the other. She wanted to protest, to tell Jenna that she was wrong about her, but Quinn wasn't sure.

"We've heard a lot about you. Quinn, this, Quinn that. It's all he talks about anymore."

"The place looks awesome." Aaron turned in a circle, taking in the atmosphere. "You and Cade did a great job with the decorations. Where did you find the lights?"

"Dad said we could borrow them from the auditorium. James and Ben set them up since you said you couldn't be here to help."

"James?" Aaron asked.

"James. A friend from school."

"Oh, I've just never heard you talk about him before."

Quinn thought Aaron sounded jealous. Maybe he lied when he said he didn't have feelings for Jenna. Maybe Jenna had rejected him, and he brought her here to make Jenna jealous. The deep shadows on the wall grew and flickered in agreement.

"Jealous?" Jenna echoed Quinn's thoughts as she bumped her hip on Aaron's.

"Hardly." Aaron bumped back.

Quinn scuffed the toe of her boot on the floor. She didn't like the way they looked at each other. She felt invisible as the two bantered back and forth, their obvious connection igniting a spark of envy. Quinn had risked everything to come here with Aaron, and all he could do was flirt with another girl in front of her. Had he lied about them just being friends? They seemed awfully close. Too close for Quinn's liking. She did a double take as one of the shadows grinned in delight. A trick of the light, that's all.

"Quinn, you won't believe the songs Aaron's written. He's the real talent behind the band. Writer, musician, and all-around great guy."

"But without Jenna's voice, we'd be nothing," Aaron said. "I can't wait for you to hear her sing."

"Don't lie, you know your voice is better than mine." Jenna flashed Aaron a drop-dead gorgeous smile, and Aaron pulled her into a hug.

"You ready for some warm -ups?" A dark-haired boy, the spitting image of Jenna, pulled her into the crook of his arm.

"Quinn, this is my twin brother, Cade." She pushed his arm away. "He plays keyboard. This is Quinn, Aaron's date." She annunciated Quinn's name in a caustic tone.

"It's really nice to meet you, Quinn." Cade smiled, then poked his sister in the ribs. "Come on, diva. I think James needs some help setting up your mic. People will start arriving soon."

"Oh, right. Well, I hope you enjoy the show, Quinn." Jenna turned to Aaron. "You coming?

"Yeah, give me two seconds." Aaron turned to Quinn and kissed her cheek, a chaste kiss, as if he didn't want to kiss her in front of Jenna. "We can grab a burger or something after. I promise to devote all my attention to you then."

"Sure." Quinn shrugged and chewed on her bottom lip. Being here made her uneasy and Jenna made her feel small and insignificant. It hurt that Aaron didn't acknowledge her uneasiness, but how could she tell him that without seeming needy and weak?

"Are you okay?" Aaron's brow furrowed. "You seem off."

"I'm just a little nervous." She fidgeted with the cuff of her jean jacket. "It's my first time out with a rock star, you know."

"You haven't heard me play, yet." Placing his finger under her chin, he guided her eyes to his, giving her no choice but to look into the golden-green light shining behind them. "I'm so glad you're here. This means a lot to me, you know? I mean it," he said with such sincerity it almost made her cry—like he knew exactly what she needed to hear—and then he kissed her. His lips, warm as the sun, burned away her fear and doubt, leaving her tingling from her toes to her hair. She wanted to hold onto that kiss forever.

"Ahem." Marcus cleared his throat. "Don't you have a gig to play?"

Aaron groaned and looked at his watch. "I guess I should get warmed up."

"Looks more like you need to cool down, bro." Marcus flashed a cheesy smile at Aaron. "You girls ready to find a seat?" Marcus put his arm around Reese, and she elbowed him in the ribs. "Ouch, what was that for?"

"For being ridiculous," Reese said. "Break a leg, Aaron. We'll see you after."

"Are you sure you're okay?" Aaron asked Quinn.

"Of course! I've got Marcus and Reese to take care of me. Go no." Quinn motioned to the stage. "Jenna's giving you the evil eye."

"I'll see you after." Aaron backed away, his hand holding hers until both their arms stretched as far as they could go, and then separated like the cutting of a towline, Quinn floated in a sea of uncertainty, adrift without her anchor.

Quinn's legs twitched as she stood with Reese and Marcus at the back of the sanctuary, watching the crowds gather. Marcus put his arm around Reese. She kissed him, he hugged her, she whispered in his ear, and then they would giggle like insane monkeys. Wrapped up in their new infatuation, neither had time to devote to an insecure Quinn, who had never needed a friend to babysit her before. But now she wished Reese would hold her hand the way she held Marcus's. Quinn shifted from one foot to the other, watching over her shoulder, wary of every whisper, every shade.

"We should sit in the front row." Marcus turned to Quinn. "Show our support? He's gonna be nervous."

"Yeah, me, too," Quinn mumbled. "What?" Marcus asked.

"It's up to you." She forced a smile.

"This is so exciting." Reese squealed, startling Quinn. "Your boyfriend! A real musician!"

"One date doesn't make him my boyfriend." Quinn warmed at the memory of Aaron's homecoming proposal. "But maybe a date to homecoming does."

"I knew it!" Reese squealed again. "You have to tell me everything."

Quinn's phone chirped. Pulling her phone from her pocket, she checked the text flashing on her screen. Jeff. Again. He wanted to meet her.

"Who is it?" Reese asked.

"Nobody important." Quinn ignored him and turned her phone to silent.

"What's up, y'all?" Jenna stood at the front of the altar, the band in a semi-circle behind her. She surveyed the room, making eye contact with the audience as she spoke. "Habitual Reality is in the house. Are you ready to rock?" The crowd erupted in whistles and cheers.

"Before we get started, we'd like to pay homage to the ruins of this beautiful church with a quick prayer."

Quinn tried to concentrate: head down, eyes closed, just like she should, but Jenna's prayer came through in static bits, like a bad cell connection to someone in China. She shook her head and rubbed her ears. The tiny hairs on Quinn's arms and neck stood on end. She was being watched. She opened one eye and tried to find the source of the stare, but every eye was closed, and every head was bowed. She closed her eye again, focusing on Jenna's words.

Blah, blah, blah, how much longer will this prayer last? Concentrate. Concentrate. You're supposed to be praying. What will Aaron think if you can't even sit still for a prayer?

Her palms sweated, and the oppression of her watcher intensified. She jerked her head up. Jenna's steel gray eyes penetrated hers. Her mouth moved, like a silent movie without the subtitles. She stared at her, never blinking, never losing eye contact. She raised her finger, pointing, singling her out.

"Amen," Jenna said, causing Quinn to jump.

Jenna raised her head and opened her eyes, as if she hadn't been watching her. Quinn looked around to see if anyone noticed anything out of the ordinary, but if they did, no one let on. Then, Jenna gestured to Ben to count off. One, two, three, and the drums erupted in a staccato beat. People beside her came to their feet, clapping their hands with the beat. Not wanting to look out of place, she followed their lead.

The band played through their varied set list of classic-rock covers, punk, garage, and more, spinning a seamless homage to great music through the decades.

Fearless, Aaron stood in front of the crowd and beamed at Quinn, as if she was the only person in the audience. That small gesture was the eye in the storm of her distress, and she forgot to be afraid. As he played, everything else disappeared. She was mesmerized by the way his fingers strummed the guitar strings and the melodious tenor of his voice. He shone, luminescent on stage. The fervor with which the musicians played lifted her spirits, and she forgot all about her uneasiness, the shadows, the blood on the cross, and Jenna's haunting stare.

An hour later, a final note rang out and the crowd erupted in applause. Quinn whistled and clapped as loud as she could. She couldn't remember the last time she had this much fun. Applause and cheers went on for several minutes until gestured for everyone to quiet down. When they finally fell silent, he turned his attention to Quinn.

"Before we call it a night, I have one more song I want to play. This one is an original. It's a little something I wrote for a girl who means a lot to me. Quinn, this is for you."

Reese elbowed Quinn in the ribs. And Quinn leaned her head on Reese's shoulder.

Aaron nodded to Jenna, who stepped up to the lead mic once again. The crowd sat, expectant. Soon, the a cappella notes poured from Jenna. Aaron joined her a few phrases later, his tenor harmony entwining with her clear alto.

Under the night's bright canopy, Your eyes and
    mine,
We stare into infinity, In heart, in mind.
We're made of star stuff, you and I, And I think
    about the possibility,
Of life and secrets, no more mysteries.
Nothing between us but stardust and moonlight
    and a billion years of history,
And I think about the possibility,
Of you and I, in that bright sky and wonder if you
    feel it to0.
The way I care for you.

Quinn wiped a tear with the back of her hand as her heart absorbed the meaning. She did feel it, and she cared for him too. More than cared, in that moment, she knew, without a doubt, that she loved him. Not the way she loved Jeff. This was deeper, rawer, and as soon as the concert was over, she would run up to him, wrap her arms around him, and tell him. She would tell him everything, no more secrets, nothing between them but stardust and moonlight.

Orion grant me one more kiss, One more moment
    just like this,
Beneath the stars,
To let me care for you.

Quinn blew Aaron a kiss, and he winked as he started the second verse. She held her breath in anticipation, but static crackled through the speakers, drowning the music. Quinn rubbed her ears and frowned. An intense ringing overtone drowned the music. She shook her head and glanced around, but nobody else seemed to notice anything unusual. Wind whipped through the sanctuary, blowing out the candles nearest to her, and cloaking the audience in dusk. Uneasiness kicked her heart with a thud.

The dark oak beams of the cross moved and stretched. Quinn shifted in her chair, watching the cross as it creaked and groaned, stretching itself to the four corners behind the band. Blood bubbled at the crest. Silent, crimson ribbons flowed down the dead wood, first dripping, then pouring all over the altar.

The room glowed red in the wake of the flood. The band played on, oblivious to the blood oozing down their faces, running into their eyes, down their bodies, clinging to their clothes, covering them in sheets of scarlet. Quinn swallowed a scream as Aaron disappeared under the gooey plasma.

"Quinn, are you okay? You look a little pale." Reese patted Quinn's knee.

No one else saw. She sat on her hands, fighting with the knowledge that only she could see the blood. Tremors rocked her legs as she shifted in her seat, resisting the urge to grab Reese, to run to Aaron, and drag them all away.

"I'm fine." She crossed one leg, then the other. The blood surged down the stone steps, toward the audience, toward her. Sweat beads popped up on her forehead. "It's just a little hot in here." Quinn squeezed her eyes shut, hoping the gruesome scene would disappear, but when she opened her eyes, the blood continued to envelope everything in its path. Down the stone steps it surged, toward the blind audience, toward her.

"How can you be hot? It's freezing outside. Can't you feel the draft coming through the broken windows?"

"I just am," Quinn snapped.

"Shhhhhh," a girl behind them warned.

The bloody magma continued toward Quinn's seat, turning from living gore to a giant crusted scab at her feet. Eyes wide, she forced herself to ignore the overwhelming compulsion to yank her knees to her chest and curl into a protective ball.

Instead, she sat straight as a pencil, staring forward, refusing to let fear ruin her night, refusing to believe any of it was real. Around her the blood coursed, splashing the legs of the audience, covering their shoes, creeping up to their knees, their waists, but Quinn remained untouched by the flaming flow, the dark scab swelling with each wave of crimson as the blood stopped just shy of her.

She flinched as the crusted mass at her feet cracked like a ghoulish egg, birthing shadowy wisps of smoke, her tormenting horde.

Please. Not now, not here.

One landed on her shoulder. She shuddered as it rubbed its bony head against her neck, scraping soft flesh with its sharp, pointy ears.

You're not real. Knuckles white from gripping the sides of her chair, her mind tried to rationalize the irrational. *Red lights, not blood. You're not real.*

"Oh, Quinn," the shadow-demon whispered in her ear. "You always fall back on the old 'you're not real' mantra. You still believe that?" More wisps emerged from the cracked scab, flying around her head, gathering near her feet, on her lap, her shoulders.

"Are you crazy?" One approached her left leg, eyeing the white, soft skin of her ankle and running a forked tongue over three rows of razor-sharp teeth.

No. She questioned that, too, and she wasn't sure which would be worse, them being real or her being crazy.

"Either we're real, or you're crazy. Yes?" A bigger shadow-demon knocked her tormentor sideways with a leathery wing. It knocked him back. They tumbled, biting and scratching each other, until the first one's head hit the cooling magma. It cried out in pain before blinking out of sight.

I don't know. That was the truth. She didn't know what to believe anymore.

"Maybe?" The victor blinked out and reappeared above her head, resuming the conversation his brother had started.

What do you want?

"We want you to leave."

We had a deal.

The demons laughed. "You believed what you wanted to believe. And you should know better than to deal with the devil."

I told you I wouldn't tell him anything.

"You will." The three on her lap inched closer. "We know you will. We can feel it. Here." The sharp tip of a leathery wing dug into her chest, just above her heart. "We can't have that."

The pressure took her breath away, a knife of pain exploded inside as the tip cut through her flesh like butter.

Reese shushed her and pointed to the stage, where the band played on under a blanket of blood, the crowd cheering them into an encore as if everything were normal. Aaron stood at the front, cocooned in dripping gore, eyes closed, arms raised to the ceiling.

She squeezed her eyes shut and sent a mental scream at her attackers: *Go away!*

This sent all of them roaring in hysterics. The beast withdrew its wing. She opened her eyes as it took flight with its brothers, turning, twisting, swooping, and blinking in and out of her reality. Clutching her shirt, she expected to see a red stain where the beast had cut her, but her sweater was clean, her flesh whole.

What do you want?

"Leave."

No.

"Don't draw attention to yourself."

No.

"Quietly."

"Quickly."

"You don't belong here."

No!

A beast the size of a condor rose from the oozing wound at her feet. Gore dripped from its massive wings as it pushed off the ground and hovered in front of her. The metallic tang of blood assaulted her nostrils. Dizziness gripped Quinn as its yellow glowing eyes stared into hers. Then it screamed, "GET OUT!"

Quinn struck out at the leathery beast, but it blinked out of sight. "Don't whap at the beasties," one of the demons on her shoulder mocked.

"Are you okay?" Reese whispered.

"Mosquito." Quinn tried not to whimper.

"God I hate those bloodsuckers. Did you get it?" Quinn nodded.

"Good." Reese turned back to the stage.

"If you leave, we'll leave them alone." The biggest of the demons, the ringleader, planted itself on Reese's shoulder, rolling its bulging yellow eyes until they focused on Reese's throat.

How?

"Lie. Any excuse will do. Hurry." The beast snapped its jaws at Reese.

Quinn scrambled for an answer, spewing the first idea that popped into her head. "Do you have a tampon?" Quinn ignored the slick wet ropes of crimson that snaked up Reese's legs, concentrating on her blood-free face.

"What?"

"A tampon, do you have one? It's an emergency." Quinn drummed her knee with her fingers. "An unexpected visitor."

"Oh, I hate when that happens," she whispered. "Hold on." Reese reached under the chair. "Crap. I left my purse in the car. Do you really need one right now?"

"Hurry." Its fat, greasy belly undulated as it fluttered its wings in agitation.

"I wouldn't be asking if I didn't."

The urgency in her voice prompted Reese to nudge Marcus in the ribs. "I need your car keys."

"What for?"

Still attached to Reese's shoulder, the beast licked its leathery lips with a forked tongue.

"You leaving me or something?" Marcus's eyes grew wide, and he raised his hand and sniffed his underarm. "I showered, used deodorant. Is it my breath?" He cupped his hand in front of his mouth and breathed out. Then he sucked the air back into his nostrils. "Ahhhh, minty fresh."

"Just shut up and give me your keys." Reese held out her hand, but Marcus just stared at her. "Quinn needs something out of my purse, and I left it in the car," Reese snapped. Marcus still didn't move. "It's a girl thing. Do you want me to go into detail?"

"No!"

"Keys." The demon hissed at Marcus.

"Here, take them. I don't want to know." Marcus dug in his pocket, handed the keys to Reese, and Reese dangled them in front of Quinn.

Had Marcus heard the demon? The beast smacked its cracked lips, turned its narrow head toward Reese, and inserted its slimy tongue into her ear. Quinn blanched.

"Damn mosquitoes." Reese slapped at her cheek. "Do you want me to go with you?"

Yes!

The imp narrowed its eyes at her, stroking long talons through Reese's hair.

"Um, no … I need … I think I can handle this mission on my own. Besides, I don't want you to miss anything." Quinn grabbed the keys from Reese. "Be right back." The demon laughed and blinked from Reese's shoulder to Quinn's. Its fetid breath, rank as a rotting corpse, made her stomach coil. Holding her breath, she walked up the aisle, blood parting like the red sea wherever she stepped.

Don't panic. Calm, normal steps. Nothing is wrong.

She kept her head down, pausing when she reached the stone arch. Was she abandoning Reese, Aaron, and Marcus to the bloody gore? She knew, knew it wasn't real. Still, she couldn't help but take a step back into the church.

The demon horde flew at her. She covered her face as they scratched and clawed at her exposed flesh.

"Get out!"

She sprinted through the door and into the dark. There wasn't anything she could do for them now.

More writhing shadows wrapped the outside of St. Angeles. Demon gargoyles lined the headstones in the cemetery, taking flight as Quinn raced across the dirt lot. Hundreds of wings beat behind her, their stinking breath hot on her neck. She had to lead them away. Away from Aaron and Reese. Home, she had to get home.

Quinn pushed the button on Marcus' key fob. The headlights blinked twice, illuminating the scarred bark of the oak tree in front of it. Shadows hung from the branches, like an evil, weeping willow.

Keeping her eyes on the tree—afraid at any moment it might come to life and crush her beneath the weight of all those shadows— she opened the door, got in the Jeep, and locked it. She jammed the key into the ignition, turning it hard. The motor roared to life, and she realized the Jeep was a standard.

"Great." She grumbled under her breath. "Okay, don't panic, you can do this." Quinn turned the interior light on and glanced at the gearshift. "R for reverse. That's simple." She looked in the rearview mirror for the all clear. A dozen leathery beasties leered at her through the rear window, wings beating slowly as they pecked at the glass with curved talons.

Gripping the stick shift in her hand, Quinn shoved it to the right and back. She pressed her foot on the gas, revved the engine, and let her foot off the clutch. The Jeep sped backward. The demons screeched and shot straight up. She turned the wheel to the right, then slammed her foot on the brake before she crashed into another car.

"Piece of cake." Quinn worked on relaxing her mind. "Forward? No problem." She pushed the stick up into first gear and paused.

Again, she revved the engine, took her foot off the brake, and let out the clutch. This time, the Jeep lurched forward, then died. Quinn glanced out at the tree where several of the demons perched, staring at her with beady eyes, craning their necks, daring her to abandon the Jeep, but she wouldn't give them the satisfaction. Determined, she leaned forward, gripped the stick, and tried again, doing her best to ignore the watching throng.

First, clutch, gas, lurch, stall. Clutch, gas, lurch, stall. Clutch, gas, lurch, stall.

Quinn pounded the steering wheel. "Who drives a stick shift in the twenty-first century!"

The outburst inspired her dark audience to taunt her from their twisted wooded balconies. Quinn took a deep breath and turned the radio full blast, drowning out the grating cackles—at least for the moment.

"Come on, girl," she cooed at the Jeep. "You can do it. It's not that hard. Please, baby, for me. It's just five miles." She turned the key, let out the clutch as she put her foot on the gas, and the vehicle lurched forward. This time, it didn't stall. Quinn popped the Jeep into second, making her way out onto Westland Boulevard.

Turning left onto the dirt road, Quinn shifted into third, then fourth gear. She raced through the first stop sign, not daring to look in the rearview mirror for fear of what she would see. When she hit fifty-five, Quinn shifted the Jeep into overdrive. The Jeep jerked and swayed as she sped down the potholed, winding, two-lane road.

Two more deserted intersections, two more stop signs, and dirt turned to tarmac.

"Stay green, stay green."

The light flicked from green to yellow as Quinn sped through the intersection and onto the long stretch of CR-718 from Eastwood to home.

At sixty- five miles an hour she approached the Westland turn off. She mashed the clutch with her left foot and pushed the stick shift back into first. The gears groaned, and the Jeep shuddered. She slammed her right foot on the brake. The force threw her forward, and the Jeep came to a full stop midway through the turn. Hundreds of tiny winged demons flocked around the car, claws scraping metal, clamoring against the glass, as they searched for a way to penetrate her safe-haven. And then she saw it, bright lights, headlights, speeding toward her.

"Okay, okay." She hurried to give it gas, but in her panic released the clutch too soon, and the engine died. The head-lights bore down on her. She braced herself for the collision. The thought of Aaron and his mother came flooding into her mind: speeding, car wreck—death. Quinn closed her eyes to the blinding light in front of her, her only thought now, if she survived, was the wreckage of her friendships following the wreckage of Marcus's Jeep.

"That was amazing!" Jenna hugged Aaron, and he half hugged her in return as he searched for Quinn over her shoulder. No sign of her. All night he'd been trying to get a read on Quinn, to find out what was causing her to fidget and cling to him so much, but every time he touched her, his gift was greeted by the same endless stark wasteland. It wasn't until he started singing the song he'd written for her that she reignited the thread. A crackle of connection, like changing the frequency on a radio, raced through him as she beamed up at him. A flash of warmth, a feeling of intense love overwhelmed him, making him want to sing to her in private. Well, maybe do more than just sing. Then the flash was gone, and she was lost to him again, no trace of the connection remained.

"Yeah, that was great, man." Ben put his arm around Jenna and held up his hand for a high five. "I feel like we're a real band now, playing original stuff."

"Are we going out to celebrate?" Jenna asked. "Sure, if it's okay with Quinn."

"Yeah, we wouldn't want to ruin your date." Jenna scanned

the room. "Where is she anyway? Don't tell me she left before the end." Jenna put a finger to each nostril, sniffed, and raised her eyebrow at Aaron.

"I know you don't like her, but she's not a druggie," Aaron snapped.

"Okay." Jenna rolled her eyes. "You know her better than I do."

"She'll be off somewhere with Reese. Look, there's Marcus. I'm sure he'll know." Aaron reached out to Quinn with his mind, but couldn't find her, convincing him even more that she controlled the link, not him.

"Meet us at Tony's if you find her. The pizza's on Cade." Marcus was talking to a leggy blond in a short, vinyl mini. No Quinn or Reese in sight. He tapped Marcus on the shoulder.

"Oh, hey! Great song, bro. The crowd loved it. Aaron, this is … " "Beth, Beth Adams."

"Beth, right. I told her I was with the band."

"Nice to meet you, Beth. Aaron wiped his hands on his jeans. "Sorry, my hands are kind of sweaty." He took her hand. "I'm—"

"Aaron. I know. Call me sometime." She handed Aaron a torn piece of paper with her number written in bright red ink. "See you around." She winked and smoothed a curl from her eye.

Marcus stood at the foot of the stage, hands in his pockets. "You get a number, and I get zilch. I feel so used."

"Where are the girls?"

"Reese ran into some girl she knew from cheer camp or something. I think they're giggling in some corner."

"Is Quinn with her?"

"Probably. Marcus glanced over at Beth. "Man, I don't know how you can resist such fineness." He grabbed the number from Aaron's hand. "Just in case Reese changes her mind. Or Quinn changes hers. Besides, I bet I can sell this baby to the highest bidder."

"You better not let Reese catch you with that, or you'll need the number for the nearest hospital."

"Hey." Reese came up behind Marcus, hands on her hips. "Did I hear my name?"

"Hey, baby. I was just telling Aaron how hot you look tonight. Right, Aaron?" Marcus elbowed him and winked.

"Is Quinn with you?" Aaron asked, ignoring Marcus. "No. I thought she'd come straight back here." "Straight back from where?"

"Oh, yeah. Forgot to tell you, she went outside during the last song. Girl stuff. Don't ask. TMI." Marcus shivered.

Aaron rubbed the back of his neck. "Did you check outside?" "Why would I do that? I thought she would be back by now." "What if something happened?"

"We're in the middle of nowhere. Where would she go?" Reese folded her arms in front of her and gave Aaron a defensive glare. "She's probably waiting for us at the car."

He started down the center aisle. "What are you waiting for? Come on." The parking lot was almost empty.

"She wasn't feeling well. Maybe she took a walk for some fresh air," Reese suggested.

"What the?" Marcus said.

Aaron stared at his bike and the empty space beside it. "You gave her your keys," Reese said.

"No, you gave her my keys," Marcus corrected.

"She can't drive a standard," Reese said.

"Apparently she can," Marcus said.

"She's not here now, so why don't the two of you stop fighting." Aaron handed Reese the spare helmet. "She probably went home. Marcus, you stay here in case she comes back."

"Why do I have to stay?"

Aaron pointed at Reese. "Cause she's a girl."

"That's so sexist."

If she'd really been in trouble, he would know, wouldn't he?

She always had connected with him in the past; this time wouldn't be any different. Aaron revved the engine. Reese climbed on behind him, and they were off, leaving Marcus standing in the empty spot where his Jeep used to be.

The Camaro let out a menacing cry as it sped around the Jeep. Quinn cringed at the middle finger that appeared in the Camaro's window.

"Fuck you, too!" she screamed at the dust left in the wake of the speeding car. "As if he cares." Quinn trembled as she wiped her eyes with the back of her hand. "Get a grip. Crying isn't going to get you out of the middle of this intersection." She turned the key in the ignition and grabbed the stick shift.

Turn around. Take the Jeep back. Tell them everything.

The fat, yellow-eyed demon materialized on her headrest.

"They'll hate you," it said.

"No, they won't." Quinn spoke out loud to them now.

"Call you crazy."

"Never."

"Deep down, you know they'll turn their back on you."

"Not Reese."

"Especially her." Two more fiends popped into being on the passenger seat, listening as their leader poured on words of persuasion, nodding their angled, bony heads in agreement.

"You don't even know her," Quinn argued.

"We know everything. We know all of them."

"But you told me to leave!" Quinn said. "You were threatening me. This is all your fault."

Their grinding, metallic snickers filled the car.

"Go away!" Quinn screamed.

"You stole Marcus's Jeep."

"I had to get out of there."

"You did it on purpose."

"I had no other choice. You made me!" Tears cascaded down Quinn's cheeks, twin waterfalls of confusion and frustration.

"Did we?"

"They'll understand."

"Will they?"

"I think."

"Or will they hate you? Better to lie." The demon stroked Quinn's hair with pointy, onyx claws.

Her phone buzzed in her pocket, sending shockwaves of vibration down her thigh. Aaron? Reese? They would have noticed her missing by now. Answer it and tell them everything. No, they would hate her if she told the truth. Even Reese. That was the demon talking. She shook her head. She and Reese had always shared everything, and she was sick of hiding from her best friend. What about Aaron? He had trusted her with his secret. Confiding in him would be so easy. The way he looked at her, like he saw through her damage, saw the Quinn she wanted to be. He could never hate her.

"I can't." Tremors seized her hand as she dug in her pocket. Pain raced up every nerve as the demon sunk its claws into her flesh. She whimpered and tried to squirm away, but the demon pushed a strange fog through the ends of the talons, like a syringe, working its way through her skin, invading her veins, eating away her resolve, possessing her. Maybe the demons were right. She should stop fighting them and start trusting them. They were only trying to help.

"Don't answer. You'll make things worse. Trust us. One tiny lie won't hurt them."

"Or me." Her head lolled to the side.

"That's right. Trust us." Dozens of beasts filled the back seat, whispering, urging her to listen intimidation in their yellow-eyes.

"And if I trust you?" One single tear slid down her cheek.

"We can help you."

"How?"

"Listen." More voices filled the car, bringing Quinn under their spell. They would always be with her now, on the fringes of her mind, hiding in the shadows, watching, and waiting. She could never outrun them. And why would she want to? They were her only friends, the only ones she could really trust. "Tell them you felt sick."

"I needed to go home."

"That you didn't want to disturb them."

"I didn't want to disturb them. Yes," Quinn repeated in a trance.

A black SUV sped past, horn blaring, startling Quinn. The beasts retreated, leaving her alone in the Jeep, if not in her head. In her rearview mirror, she saw one, bright headlight moving toward her. A motorcycle. Quinn slipped the Jeep into first. The Jeep sped forward, outrunning Aaron, outrunning the truth, leaving them both in the dust for the comfort of a lie.

Quinn fumbled in her purse for her house key. She swiped beads of sweat from her forehead with the back of her sleeve, dropping her keys into a puddle of darkness.

"Dammit!" She groped around the porch with no luck. The gold key ring shimmered in the wake of one headlight, turning into her driveway. Quinn grabbed it, jumped up, and shoved the key in the lock.

"Come on, come on. Don't stick now." The headlight flicked off as the dead bolt clicked. She turned the knob and shouldered the door open, slammed it, and locked it behind her.

Quinn held her breath, as footsteps ran up the driveway. She crouched on the tiled entry. She couldn't face them. Not Reese, not Marcus, and not Aaron. No, not Aaron, never again. He knocked. Quinn didn't move. The knock intensified, louder, more urgent. Quinn remained motionless. He'd go away if she didn't answer.

"Quinn, I know you're in there. I saw you on the porch when I drove up."

Quinn pressed her face against the glass blocks. A distorted face stared back at her, hand over his eyes to block the outside light.

"Come on, Quinn, I need to talk to you."

Quinn wiped tears from her eyes with the hem of her shirt. Turning on the foyer light, she cracked open the door. "What do you want?" She tapped her fingers on the metal handle and glared at Jeff. "I've been texting and calling you all night. I was worried."

"Just go." Quinn tried to shut the door, but Jeff blocked it with his foot.

"I really need to talk to you."

Quinn stomped on his foot, but his leather cowboy boot took the impact. "Well, I don't need to talk to you." She tried shoving the door again.

Jeff shoved back. "I broke up with Kerstin."

"Why do you think I care?" Quinn's tone was icy. She'd been waiting months to hear those words, and now they meant nothing.

"Look, I know I hurt you, and I don't blame you for being angry."

"Oh, I'm more than angry." She leaned against the door, defeated, as a demon settled on her shoulder.

"We were friends once, best friends. I didn't know who else to go to." Jeff shoved his hands in his pockets, imploring Quinn with those irresistible brown eyes.

"Let him in."

Quinn stiffened as the demon morphed into smoke and probed its way into her ear. Beads of sweat formed on her forehead as she fought their influence.

"No. You got what you wanted. I left Aaron. Leave me alone," she whispered through clenched teeth. To Jeff, she said "You should've thought of that before you dumped me."

"Let. Him. In." Quinn scratched at her ear and pulled on the ends of her hair, but the demon's words lashed at her resistance. Swaying her to their command. She opened the door.

"Q.T., I'm sorry." Jeff followed her into the kitchen. "I blew it with you …"

"Don't you dare call me Q.T.!" she yelled over her shoulder. "Only my friends and family call me that, and you are neither."

Quinn pulled a loaf of bread from the box on the counter and took out two slices. What she really wanted to do was claw at her own skin and beat her head against the wall until the demon expelled itself from her body. But she couldn't do that, not with Jeff watching, so she kept her hands busy. Jeff took his usual seat on the left side of the island, but instead of resting his elbows on the counter, his hands stayed shoved in his pockets.

Quinn grabbed a jar of peanut butter from the pantry. Unscrewing the red plastic lid, she stirred the creamy contents with the end of the knife, its metal scraping plastic as she tried to steady her hands. Silently she worked, and silently he watched, his stare never straying from her.

"You want a sandwich?" Quinn asked. "Sure."

"We don't have any grape jelly. We stopped buying it after you dumped me. You'll have to suffer strawberry." Quinn opened the jar, piling a glob of the red goo on the knife and plopping it onto the other piece of bread, masking her fear and anxiety under a blanket of anger. Jeff wouldn't know the difference.

"I wish you wouldn't use the word dumped. It sounds so, oh I don't know … bad."

"Well, let's see. How did you breaking up with me feel? Oh, I don't know … bad. Seems to me, dumped describes it perfectly." Quinn slammed the knife onto the bread, splitting the sandwich into two clean halves.

She'd been mooning over him, putting him on a pedestal, while he paraded Kerstin in front of her nose. Aaron had been there for her, and she pushed him away, time and time again for Jeff, for a guy who cheated on her. Hell yeah she was angry, at the demons, at herself for leaving Reese and Aaron, for the lies she would tell them if they asked. And Jeff, sitting in her house, telling her he'd broken up with Kerstin. A little too late.

"Fine, if you want to call it dumped, we'll call it dumped." Jeff eyed the knife.

"Don't worry. I don't think a butter knife would do much damage." Quinn handed Jeff half the sandwich, careful not to let her fingers brush his.

"You always did make the best PB and J," Jeff mumbled with a mouthful.

"Yeah, well, whoever said the way to a man's heart was through his stomach got it all wrong. The way to a man's heart is having big boobs. Big boobs equal no dump." Quinn balled her fist, her anger no longer a mask. All the things she'd really wanted to say to him over the last two months spewed out.

"You have no idea what you're talking about." Jeff slammed the half-eaten sandwich on the table.

Quinn turned her back on Jeff and started to unload clean dishes from the dishwasher. "That's because you never clued me in." Quinn slammed the cabinet door. "You came home from summer vacation and ignored my calls. When you did call, it was a cryptic 'uhhhh we need to break up,' and the next thing I know, you're dating Kerstin."

She spun around to face him, anger full throttle, words on stun. "Oh, and did you tell me about Kerstin? No. I heard it through gossip queen Ami on the first day of school. 'Sorry to hear about you and Jeff, Quinn. Sorry he dumped you for the bloodsucker Kerstin. What? You didn't know he was dating Kerstin? He's been dating her for weeks.' God, what an idiot I was." Quinn slumped over the island, head cradled in her hands.

"I'm ready to talk about it now." Jeff reached his hand over the island and grabbed Quinn's.

A long silence followed as Quinn let his familiar touch quell her anger. The demon quieted at his touch. It wanted her to be with Jeff, it liked Jeff. She tried to imagine life like it used to be, but the image of Kerstin and Jeff kissing haunted her.

I won't go back to Jeff. I love Aaron.

"What's there to talk about? We can't go back," Quinn said to Jeff.

"Aaron is lost to you." The demon pressed the thought into her mind.

Shut up. He cares about me. I can make him understand. Quinn pinched the bridge of her nose.

"Love?" The demon laughed.

"Kerstin was a big mistake. The way I treated you, even bigger. I'll always be sorry for it. Kerstin's history. I dumped her last night." Jeff moved behind her and put his hands on her shoulders.

"You loved Jeff once too. Or did you forget how you pushed Aaron away every time you thought Jeff was watching."

Quinn went stiff at his touch. "Why did you dump her?" She jerked away, whirling to face him. "No, what I really want to know is why did you dump me? After all we've been through?"

"It's complicated." He rubbed his temples. "I couldn't face

you after what I'd done. I had to make it right, somehow. I convinced myself to let you go, it would be better that way. I tried but couldn't stop thinking about you." Jeff reached for her, but she slapped his hand away.

"You don't love Aaron. How could you? If you did, you wouldn't have left him tonight. If he meant that much to you, you wouldn't be here with Jeff."

Quinn tried to ignore the demon's jibes, but their words stung with the venom of truth, the poison working through her second by second.

"What did you do? Sleep with her? That's not news. Were you trying to protect me from your teenage hormones? Now that you've gotten it out of your system, you're safe, and we can be together again. Until the next time you get an itch you just have to scratch, so you'll dump me again to find the first tramp you can to hook up with." Quinn turned from him, folding her arms over her chest.

"Kerstin's not a tramp. She's just insecure, and if you knew … " Jeff's warm breath was on her neck, so close, the strong smell of peanut butter mixed with the musky sent of his cologne.

"Please, Quinn. I'll do anything to get you back. I love you. I always have. I was such an asshole to give up all we had together."

"You know you want this, Quinn. Jeff still loves you," the demons whispered.

I don't want Jeff.

"You can't lie to us, lie to yourself. We see it inside you."

Shaking her head, she took a step forward, away from the pain his presence evoked.

"Defending her is so not the way to win points with me. And what do you mean if I knew? Knew what? How great she is in bed? Like I want to know all the dirty details."

"I would never do that to you." He came in close again, heated breath on her neck. "I still love you, Quinn."

"And Kerstin?" Quinn pivoted, watching in satisfaction as he squirmed, eyes downcast as he reached for an answer.

"With Kerstin, it's complicated. She's … " He grabbed her hands. "I don't love her."

Quinn smacked his hand away. "What makes you think I care?"

"Things would be so much easier if you went back with Jeff. Can you really forget all that time you spent together? You've loved him your whole, Quinn." The demons stroked her hair, cooed in her ear, fractured her defenses.

Quinn covered her ears and shook her head. "Leave me alone." It came out as a defeated sigh.

Jeff gripped her arm, fingers digging into her flesh. "Please, Quinn. Look at me. Give me one more chance. I've loved you since we were five years old, my whole life. I screwed up, I know that now. No excuse. What can I do to make it up to you? Anything. I'll do anything." Tears dripped down his cheeks. Their eyes connected, and she searched deep within them for the truth. She found no confirmation there, no deception either, just desperation.

Silence overtook them as they stood face-to-face, lips inches apart, his muscular arms an embrace away, and a dull ache inside her soul. She didn't want him; she wanted Aaron.

"He's telling the truth, Quinn. One kiss, and you'll feel it. How can you throw him away? All the history you share? Kiss him."

Then his lips were on hers, urgent and strong. At first his kiss tasted bitter, but within seconds it turned sweet, familiar, safe. It was as if the last two months were a distant memory, and the demons played on this, bringing forward a montage of every happy moment she'd ever had with Jeff until her mind was filled with nothing but him. All thoughts of Aaron fell away like dead leaves from a tree, leaving her naked and vulnerable, shivering beneath Jeff's touch.

"Quinn, are you here?" Aaron stepped through the kitchen door. "S-Sorry," he stammered.

Quinn pushed at Jeff, breaking away from his embrace.

Aaron took two steps backward as if punched. Eyes fixed on Quinn, jaw tight, he balled his right fist before stiffly turning on his heel.

"Aaron! Wait!" Quinn tripped over a stool as she fumbled past Jeff to get to him. It clattered to the floor, but Aaron didn't even turn around at the sound. Following him through the living room, Quinn tried to grasp his arm to get him to look at her, but he jerked away, flinching every time she approached. What had she done? Hot tears burned beneath her lids, bubbling out and down her cheeks.

"Quinn, thank God. We were so worried." Reese rushed to meet her, but Quinn shoved past her.

Aaron had his helmet on as Quinn appeared at the door.

"Aaron, wait. Let me explain." Quinn ran up to the bike. He jerked away as she touched his shoulder. "Please, Aaron." Her breath rasped from her throat, desperate, pleading. She had to make him see, make him understand. Aaron stared at her through the visor, eyes hard, judging.

Quinn cleared her throat. "Jeff showed up. I didn't ask him to come here. And then he kissed me, out of the blue. I know what it must look like, but I don't love him. I love—"

"Save it for someone who cares." Aaron gunned the engine, disengaged the kickstand, and sped off, leaving Quinn to suck on the fumes left in his wake.

aron disappeared into the night, the smell of gas a nauseating reminder of the hurt Quinn caused him.

"What's going on?" Reese demanded. "Why did you take Marcus's car? Is Jeff harassing you? Why did Aaron leave?"

"I'm not harassing anyone," Jeff barked.

"I don't want to talk to you, Jeff." Reese spit his name. "I want to talk to her." Reese's black eyes narrowed at Quinn. "What's going on?"

Quinn grabbed at the thoughts that flew through her mind, examining each one, trying to find an answer. This truth was stranger than fiction, but maybe Reese would believe her. Help her.

"Believe you?"

Yes. The truth.

"That you hear voices?"

I can tell her anything.

"That you see demons? Do you think she would believe you when she can't even see us? Even you don't want to accept we're real. But we are. Can your imagination do this?" Invisible claws dug into her neck, increasing in pressure with every thought of resisting their wishes. "You won't tell."

I won't tell. The demon retracted its claws, and Quinn rubbed at her neck.

"Quinn?" Reese pinched Quinn hard. "Hey. That hurt."

"Good. First thing I want to know is why you stole my boyfriend's Jeep."

She wants an answer. What will I say? I've never lied to Reese before.

"Really?" The grip around her neck tightened, and Quinn shivered.

No.

"Be a good girl. Stick to our story and we won't hurt you." Another demon blinked onto Reese's shoulder, talon's digging into her flesh. Reese winced and massaged the spot where the demon stood. "Or her."

Not until tonight.

The pressure eased. "That's right. You know what to say." The voices soothed her nerves. The truth, she would make it the truth.

"I wasn't feeling well." Quinn paused. "Kissable," the worst song ever, sounded even worse coming from Reese's pocket. "Um, I think your pants are ringing."

Reese pulled the bright pink phone from her pocket. "Hello? Your stupid Jeep is fine." She hung up. "Second thing I want to know is what's he doing here?" She pointed an accusing finger at Jeff.

"Maybe I should, you know." Jeff gestured toward his truck. "Call you later?"

Quinn nodded. Neither she nor Reese spoke as they watched Jeff drive away, his left headlight a beacon in the darkness, the right one gray as the night.

"He should get that fixed."

"What I really want to know is …" Reese's phone sang "Kissable" again. She ignored it. "What the hell is up with you, Quinn?"

"Well, I went to get your purse."

"Kissable's" sickly sweet melody grew louder. "Aren't you going to answer that?"

"Just ignore it."

"Okay. So, when I got to the Jeep. I felt major sick."

Quinn glanced at Reese's phone, clutched in her hand, singing and vibrating as if it were alive.

"I sent you a text. Didn't you get it?" she lied. Reese shook her head, clearly not buying it.

Quinn wanted to smash Reese's cell with a jackhammer. "You know, I really hate that song."

"I said ignore it. Go on."

"Jeff showed up. Oh, for God's sake!" Quinn jerked the phone out of Reese's hand, touched the answer button, and held it out for her to take.

Reese grabbed it. "No, he's not here … He drove off on his motorcycle. I don't have time to talk … Yes … I don't know … Not my problem … You have two legs, walk." She hung up. The phone sang again, and Reese answered. "What now?" She listened, and then held the phone out to Quinn. "It's for you."

Quinn mouthed the word no and shook her head.

Reese covered the mouthpiece with her hand. "I think you owe him an apology." She grabbed Quinn's hand and placed the phone in the middle of her palm.

"Hey. Yeah, the Jeep's all right." Quinn paced up the driveway. "No, not a scratch. Look, I'm sorry. I felt sick. What? Okay. Thanks, Marcus. I'll tell her. Bye."

"Now, was that so hard?" Reese sighed, put her arm around Quinn, and walked in step with her back inside the house. "So, what did he say?"

"That he's glad I'm not hurt, and he wants you to pick him

up a cheeseburger." Quinn shrugged and handed the phone back to Reese. "I can't believe he's not mad at me."

"See? Trust us," the demons whispered.

"Marcus may not be mad, but Aaron looked like he might explode, and I'm super pissed off at you. I'm not buying the whole 'I was sick' line. I'm your best friend. Talk to me!"

"Marcus wants you to come pick him up. He said it's getting cold. You should go get him." Quinn chewed her bottom lip and leaned against the doorframe.

"No way. You're not getting off that easy. He's not going anywhere. And neither am I. Not until you tell me everything, starting with what happened in that kitchen." She sat on the couch and pointed to the seat cushion next to her. "Sit. Talk."

"Jeff kissed me," Quinn started. "And Aaron saw it," Reese finished. "That about sums it up."

"And did you kiss him back?"

"No. Well, sort of." Quinn sat next to Reese. "I mean, I was yelling at him. He apologized. The next thing I know. Wham. Lip lock. Aaron walks in, and that's that." Quinn added in a whispered tone, "He says he broke up with Kerstin."

"And he wants you back."

"Yeah."

"Is that why you left?" Reese crossed her arms and rolled her eyes. "Jeff sent you a text, didn't he? That jerk. And you had to go running to him? You ran out on Aaron? Quinn, seriously. What is wrong with you?"

People believe what they want to believe, and Reese had just provided her with the perfect cover. Quinn tried to look contrite. "What was I supposed to do? He told me it was urgent. I couldn't very well ask Marcus to take me to see Jeff when I was on a date with his best friend, could I?"

"Do you know how shallow you sound right now? I don't even know who you are anymore. Aaron wrote you a song! A song, Quinn. And you didn't even have the decency to stay and tell him you liked it? You ran off to lip lock with Jeff instead? Please help me understand."

"I can't. I don't even understand it myself. I made a mistake. I know I'm a shitty person." Quinn grabbed Reese's hand and begged. "Please don't hate me. You might be the only person I have left on the planet." And she meant it.

Reese narrowed her eyes, letting Quinn stew in silence. Sighing, she squeezed Quinn's hand. "I don't hate you, I'm disappointed, and I'm hurt."

"I'm sorry."

"Yeah, seems like I've been hearing that from you a lot."

"I know." Quinn braided and unbraided the fringe that edged the couch cushion.

Reese grabbed the pillow from Quinn and punctuated each word by hitting her with it. "Don't. Shut. Me. Out. Anymore. Do you understand?"

Quinn nodded. "I mean it."

Quinn nodded again, and Reese pulled her into a hug.

"Okay, the honesty starts now." Reese slipped her flip-flops off and wiggled her toes. "Do you want to be with Jeff?"

"Maybe. No! I came here to tell him I didn't want him back."

"That's not what it looked like. You couldn't have texted him?"

"I did, but he said he would find me and ruin my date if I didn't meet him. Ami told him where I was." The demons nodded their approval of the lie. "What was I supposed to do? I was afraid he might make a scene in front of everyone. It was stupid."

"Couldn't you have met him outside or something?"

"I wasn't thinking. I told him I would meet him at the house." Reese sighed. "Big mistake."

"I know," Quinn mumbled. "Aaron deserves better than you."

"I know." Reese was totally right, Aaron did deserve better. "I have no idea why he's so in love with you."

"He's not anymore. You saw the way he looked at me. It's

over." The words caught in her throat; the truth of them ate a hole in her heart that could never be filled.

"Do you want it to be over?"

"I don't know. Everything's so confusing. Jeff and Kerstin are broken up, Reese." Quinn pulled her knees to her chest, resting her chin on top. "It's what I wanted, right? He wants me back. Four years. It's so easy to be with him. Aaron? He's sweet, but maybe we're just not meant to be. You know, rebound crush or something."

"Then why are you crying?" Reese pulled the sleeve of her sweater over the tips of her fingers and wiped the tear from Quinn's cheek.

"I'm just tired, I guess." Quinn sniffled and wiped her runny nose on her own sleeve.

"I think that's the first honest thing you've said to me all night." Reese rubbed her forehead. "What about homecoming? Are you still going with him?"

Quinn shook her head. "I think kissing Jeff constitutes an un-invite."

"Maybe I could talk to him for you." Reese hesitated. "And if that doesn't work, maybe Marcus could talk to him. He'll listen to Marcus."

"Reese, no one listens to Marcus."

"True." Reese put her elbows on her knees and let out a sigh. "I think I should let him go."

Reese's phone sang again. "Hey. I'm leaving right now ... No need to yell ... Yes, I'm really leaving ... No, I've never heard of that happening before ... It's fifty degrees outside ... Whatever. Bye." Reese put the phone back in her pocket. "I better pick him up before he 'freezes to death.'" Reese gestured the quotation marks with her fingers and rolled her eyes.

"Will you be okay?"

"Yeah. I just want to forget about this whole day. Tell Marcus I'm sorry again."

"Sure, but promise me something. No more joy rides in my boyfriend's Jeep. Okay?"

"Cross my heart."

Reese hugged her. "Call me if you need me. Love ya." "You too."

Quinn closed and locked the door and pressed her back to the wall. She listened to the now-familiar hum of the Jeep's engine as Reese backed out of the driveway. A wave of fatigue washed over her, and the call of her bed couldn't be ignored.

Quinn felt small and lost in the big, empty house, her footsteps echoing off the oak as she ascended the long, steep staircase. She had no choice. She had to make the journey. To sleep perchance to dream. The quote came into her mind, Shakespeare, she knew, but from which play, she couldn't remember. Didn't that speech have something to do with death? She shivered. Please, no dreams tonight.

She opened her bedroom door. Pieces of clothing blanketed her room like new-fallen snow. What she wouldn't give for a clothes plow. Not caring, she trampled over jeans, tops, shoes, and skirts, until she reached the mountain of her bed. Jelly replaced her bones, her muscles. Hollow thoughts, hollow heart, nothing left of her but a shell.

She kicked off her boots then collapsed on top of the heap. She stared at the flowers Aaron had brought her, still sitting where she'd left them on the nightstand. They would be dead by morning if she didn't put them in water. Brittle. Dry. Hollow. Like her. Dead by morning, and she didn't even care. Past caring, past fighting the demons, the nightmares.

Let them come. There wasn't anything else they could take from her now. Nothing mattered to her anymore but the sweet relief of an endless slumber. Burrowing down beneath a soft pile of sweaters, she curled into a little ball and fell asleep.

☙

The mountain's peak, tall and snow-covered, ripped at the night, hiding the moon's silvery body, but not its glow. Small and alone, Quinn clung to the side, an ant on a boulder. Any moment, she could tumble to her death or be crushed by a rock.

She tightened her grip, desperate to reach the top, to see the other side, to see the full, round figure of the moon again. The fog clung to the top half of the mountain like a spider—eight misty legs covering the entire mountaintop. The mountain stretched for miles, and the fog stretched with it. The tentacles reached for her; there was no escape. The shadow pushed its way into her body, gripping her tight and not letting go. There was no use resisting. She let go and fell, on and on into the darkness nothing.

The door slammed behind Aaron as he barged into the dark, stuffy house. He flipped on the kitchen light, wiping sweat from his brow. The thermostat read seventy-eight degrees. He turned the dial to seventy and opened the kitchen window.

"What are you trying to do? Freeze me out of my own house?" His dad groaned and sat up on the couch.

"Why are you sitting in the dark? And why do you have the heat up so high?" Aaron asked.

"I was sleeping, and it was cold. Is that a crime?" "Have you been drinking again?" Aaron rummaged through the cabinets, searching his father's usual hiding places for evidence. Finding nothing incriminating, Aaron poured himself a soda, drained it, and slammed the glass on the kitchen table.

"I haven't been drinking." The springs on the sofa creaked as his dad got up. "Had a long day at work, that's all."

Aaron blocked his dad in the hallway. His breath smelled of vodka.

"Why are you looking at me like that?" His dad crossed his arms and stared at his son. "What's going on?"

"It's time for you to sober up." Aaron wanted his dad to choose sobriety on his own, but how much longer could he and Josh wait? He was sick of waiting, sick of putting everyone else first. What about what he wanted, what he needed? Aaron needed a father now, needed his advice, his love, his support, and he aimed to get it, even if it meant forcing his father into reality. He grabbed his father and pulled him close, catapulting deep inside his mind. His dad tried to pull away, but Aaron tightened his grip and probed deeper, pushing away his resistance, over-powering him, giving him a virtual shake, a psychic wake-up call.

He radiated the need both he and Josh had for a parent, pushed visions of Josh struggling in school and hanging out with the wrong crowd, held a virtual mirror up to show his father what it was like for his boys to see him as a drunk. He showed him Katy, his mother, disapproving and angry. He took his father to the abyss and dangled him there, let him contemplate and face the damage. Then, he pulled him back, reminded him of love and honor. He opened himself fully and radiated forgiveness to wash away the guilt and grief. And then he let his father go

His dad blinked, and the alcohol fog faded from his eyes. "Where's Josh?"

"I'm not sure." His dad wrinkled his forehead. "Has he been in trouble lately?"

Aaron nodded. "What should I do?"

"Stop drinking." Aaron slammed cabinets as he searched for alcohol.

"I hid the bottles in the potted plant." His dad crossed his arms and motioned to the tall fern by the window.

Aaron stomped over to the base and pushed away the green fronds, taking a bottle in each hand. He poured the clear liquid into the sink, watching it swirl down the drain.

"Any more?"

His dad stared at the empty bottles on the counter and shook his head.

"I am so sick of trying to be a dad to Josh. You should be the one questioning where he is, who he's with. You should be the one worried that he's in trouble. You should be protecting us both." Aaron swiped his hand across the counter, and the bottles went flying. Glass exploded on the floor. "We lost them, too, you know!"

His dad didn't flinch. He rubbed the back of his neck and looked away.

Aaron got in his dad's face. "Don't do that. Don't look away. I need you to see me. I almost died while you drowned yourself in grief. You've wrapped your pain around you so tight that you can't see anything else. We've been patient. We've given you time, but now you have to stop being selfish." Red-faced and breathing ragged, he poked his dad in the chest. "We're hurting too. We need you. Josh needs you."

"You're better off without me." His dad scuffed a piece of worn linoleum with his foot."

"No. We're not. We need each other, now more than ever. Why can't you see that?" Aaron pleaded.

"I'm a stranger in my own house, some old man who keeps a roof over your heads and food on the table. Without your mama, I'm nothing." His dad hung his head and sighed. "She's what kept this family together. I've done nothing but screw up since she died. I've never said that out loud. She's dead Aaron, and I'm just so tired of hurting."

"I know, Dad." Anger drained from him like the alcohol down the sink.

"I failed her. I failed you. Now, Josh."

"Her death was an accident." Aaron reached for his father's strong, calloused hand and transmitted strength and forgiveness to fortify him. "It wasn't your fault, it wasn't mine, and it wasn't

Josh's. We can start being a family again, the three of us, together. It won't be easy, but we need you, Dad."

His dad nodded. "Okay. How do we start?"

"With a sandwich? I'm hungry." Aaron went to the fridge and pulled out some ham and cheese.

"Let me do that." His dad grabbed the bread and pulled out four slices, then paused and looked at his son. "Aaron." His Adam's apple bobbed. "Can I hug you?"

Aaron opened his arms and his dad pulled him into a bear hug, their tears mingling on each other's cheek. "Thank you. I promise I'll do better. I do love you."

"Sorry I missed the love fest." Josh smirked in the open doorway. "Sit down. I want to talk to you." Their dad pointed to an empty kitchen chair.

"About what?" Josh kicked the front door closed with his foot.

"I said. Sit. Down." His dad's serious tone outweighed any smartass remark that waited on the end of Josh's tongue.

"I've got some homework to do," Aaron said and made his way up the stairs.

Half an hour later, angry voices still rose from the first floor of the Collier house. Dad and Josh were hashing it out, all right. Aaron couldn't make out words, just tones, through the closed bedroom door, but he hoped Josh would at least listen.

He slammed his English book and stared at the phone on the nightstand. Had she really blown him off to meet Jeff? Seeing was believing, right? And boy had he seen it, Jeff practically doing Quinn on the kitchen counter. No denying that. She couldn't explain or apologize herself out of that one, and frankly, Aaron didn't want her to. He'd been a fool to ever open up to her in the first place. What a joke.

Throwing the English book on the floor, he turned on his back, staring at the ceiling, but that reminded him too much of staring into the sky with Quinn. He got up and grabbed his guitar, absently strumming as he thought. Jeff's sweaty handprints were all over their relationship, if they ever had one, and there was no way to change that. When he realized he'd been playing "Starlight Memory," he paused and sank to the floor. Leaning his back against the bed, he banged his head against the mattress.

Aaron stared at the phone as it rang. Was it Quinn? Let her stew; let her wonder if he would ever pick up. He imagined Quinn on the other end, desperate to apologize. And then he imagined the satisfaction he would feel when he slammed the phone down on her mid-sentence. Smirking, he picked it up on the fifth ring.

"Hello?"

"What's up, man?" "Hey, Marcus."

"Don't sound so disappointed."

"I thought maybe you were Quinn."

"Man, how could you ever get us confused? I know my voice is deeper than hers."

"Very funny."

"Look, man, I'm sorry. Reese told me what happened. Busted. I knew that girl was no good. But she does have a nice booty."

"Marcus, can't you be serious for once?"

"Dude, for real, I'm feelin' ya. Why would you want to talk to that witch anyway?"

"I don't, but I thought maybe she would call to apologize, to explain or something, and then I could hang up on her. Don't you think she owes me at least that?"

"Chicks are confusing. I say let Jeff have her. She's even more of a player than me."

"How could I have been so stupid?"

"Because you weren't thinking with your brain, you were thinking about what she looked like naked. It happens to the best of us."

"You still up at St. Angeles? Need me to come get you?" "No, Reese got me."

"What about homecoming? Don't I need to un-ask her or something?" Aaron ran his hand through his hair.

"I think she already did that for you." "Right."

"I'll hook you up."

"With who?"

"Marie."

"Burned that bridge."

"Beth. I've still got her number. It's a little wrinkled, but I can still read it."

"I don't even know her."

"I'll find you a hottie, don't stress."

"I'm not stressing because I'm not going." "Oh, you're going."

"Hello? Don't you listen? I said no. Last thing I want to do is see Quinn and Jeff together. If she's not going with me, I'm not going at all."

"You are so going. And if Quinn's not your date, you need a backup. Jenna. Now that girl is fine."

"I said I'm not going."

"Fine, but I'll make a few phone calls and send out some e-mails just in case you change your mind."

"I won't."

"You will. Oh, Reese is calling. I've got to go. Later."

"Later. And I still won't." Aaron hung up the phone before Marcus could get in the last word.

3 0

Quinn checked herself in the mirror, smoothing her hands over the bodice of her dress. Perfect hair, perfect makeup, and her homecoming gown fit to a tee. Perhaps she looked beautiful on the outside, but ugliness burned inside her like acid. Cowards don't deserve to be happy. Her ever-present shadows hung about her like non-returnable accessories.

"It's better this way. You'll see." The demons had been calm all week, quiet, almost happy in a strange, twisted dark way. If she stayed with Jeff, they would stay at bay the rest of the night, if not for the rest of her life.

"Is it? I should have explained, apologized instead of avoiding him all week," Quinn said,

"He didn't seek you out either, did he?" the demons reminded. "If he really cared, he wouldn't have let you go so easily."

"Like I let him go?" Maybe Aaron didn't care. He'd been avoiding her as much as she avoided him. It was easier for both of them that way.

"You never truly loved him. It's time to forget about him and move forward. You have what you wanted."

Quinn swayed with their influencing whispers.

"I do, don't I?" A crooked smile beamed back at her from the mirror. She did look beautiful. The voices always knew exactly what to say. Why had she been so afraid, so distrustful of them? Aaron was the rebound guy, a crush that didn't mean anything. Clearly, they weren't meant to be together. Jeff, it had always been Jeff.

They'd been back together for five days, and life was finally getting back to normal. Even the rumors had stopped, and Kerstin's attacks had become little more than dirty looks and snarky comments. Nothing but hot air. Then, at last night's homecoming game, Westland had actually won, nothing short of a miracle. And if that could happen, Quinn could get her grades up and her captain spot back before regionals. Things between her and Jeff were more than perfect, so why wasn't she happy?

"He's here, Quinn." Her mother's excited voice floated up the stairs. "Hurry up. I want to get a few pictures of the two of you before I go back to work."

"I'll be down in a second!" Olympic butterflies raced and twirled in her stomach.

"This is what you want, Quinn. Jeff is your destiny." The shadows flitted around her, whispering urging her on their chosen path.

"Oh, Q.T.! He's brought flowers!" Her mother squealed as if it were her own first date. "Roses. If you don't come down soon, I might just run off with him myself!"

"Now or never." With one last turn in the mirror, she finished her primping, grabbed the silver beaded handbag off her dresser, and walked to the head of the stairs to make her grand entrance, the demons following in her wake.

Jeff stood in the entryway, handsome as ever and groomed

to perfection. She wanted to flee, run back to her room and hide under the bed, but she was too old for hiding, and he'd already seen her. She was committed. She put on her best smile, and he beamed at her in return.

"Wow, you've never looked more beautiful." Jeff held out his hand to help her navigate the last few steps in her long, beaded gown.

"Thanks, handsome." She winked at him, trying her best to act normal.

"You two look great together." Her mother handed Quinn a white rose boutonniere to pin on the lapel of Jeff's tux.

Jeff tied a matching corsage around her slender wrist.

"Looks like you've done this before." Quinn hoped the little joke would dispel some of the awkwardness that lingered between them. Jeff chuckled.

"Let me get a few pictures by the fireplace." Her mother put one arm around Jeff and the other around Quinn, ushering them over to the stone mantle. She picked and fussed over every wrinkle and stray hair as she positioned them like mannequins. "Okay, Jeff, put your arm around her. That's great. Quinn, for God's sake, smile." Her mother snapped the picture. "Okay, just one more." She paused, looking the two of them up and down. "My little girl, all grown up."

Quinn thought she saw a tear, but before she could confirm it, the unusual mother/daughter moment morphed back into normalcy.

"Well, I've got to get back to work." Her mother kissed Quinn on the cheek. "Jeremy's expecting the final blueprints for the Expo building in the morning."

"There's the mom I know and love."

Her mother traded the camera for her keys and laptop bag. "Have a good time, and have her home by one," she added before rushing out the door.

"Bye," they responded in unison. "Since when do you have a curfew?"

"Since when does she stay home and take pictures of me going to a dance?"

"It's our last homecoming. Maybe she just wanted to be a part of it." Jeff ran his fingers down her bare arm. She shivered.

"Or maybe she was abducted by aliens. Either way, it's weird." Quinn picked at his lapel, brushing off imaginary lint and avoiding eye contact. "We should get going."

She started for the coat closet, but Jeff beat her there. He removed the long, black dress coat with the cream, faux-fur trim and helped her put it on like he had done for every homecoming, prom, spring formal, year after year.

"Thanks."

"This feels right. Doesn't it?" Jeff stared at her. This time, she didn't look away. "I …" he stammered. "I've made big mistakes, but I'm glad you said yes to homecoming. To a second chance."

Quinn peered deep into his eyes, those eyes she had gazed into hundreds of times before. She searched for the spark, the flame of hope. It felt awkward, this dance around the elephant in the room. The pretense of the date, the forced words, tentative gestures tangled with familiarity and comfort.

"I love you." Jeff stroked her hair and came in close, brushing his lips against hers. "I love you, Quinn. Only you." His whisper seemed strained, almost desperate. His arms encircled her.

She closed her eyes, trying to relax into his familiar embrace. But Aaron held her, not Jeff. His scarred arms wrapped around her, his hands ran through her hair, his lips on her neck—the memory of their electric kisses.

Stop it! Her mind hissed, jolting her back to reality. *You've been dreaming about Jeff for months. Now he's here with you, and you want to run to Aaron? Jeff. It's always been Jeff. Don't be stupid. Don't ruin it now.*

"He's what you want," the demons whispered, adding their two cents to her thoughts.

Jeff?

"Yes."

Yes.

She would make it work this time. The perfect couple. Together again, just like it should be.

"We should go." Jeff breathed in her ear, but his hands roamed down her back, pulling her closer. Leaning into him, she tilted her head, inviting a soft kiss.

Jeff kissed her back, long and soft at first, then harder and hungrier than ever. "I love you." He pulled the coat off her shoulder and found the soft, peachy crease of her neck.

Flashes of Aaron crossed her memory— Aaron in her dreams, burning through her nightmares, punching the Eastwood guy, on his bike, kissing her, singing to her, loving her. He deserved better than her.

"There's only one way to get over Aaron, only one way to make sure you never lose Jeff again. You know what he wants. You want it, too. We can feel the desire within you," the demons urged.

She'd always dreamed her first time would be with Jeff, her first love. Why had she waited? Would he have slept with Kerstin if she hadn't? The zipper eased down another inch as his lips parted against hers, gentle, exploring.

"That's right. If you had slept with him, he would never have given Kerstin a second glance."

But he did sleep with her. Nothing could change that.

As if answering her thoughts, he whispered, "I never loved her, Quinn. I swear." Jeff pulled away and cupped her chin until they were eye to eye. "Do you want me to stop?"

He wanted her, and she longed to be wanted—to be loved. He would stop if she asked him to. What would be the point of stopping now? She deserved to be happy. Jeff made her happy. Being with him made the world right.

If I do this, things will go back to normal, to the way they were before.

"If you're with Jeff, everything will go back to normal," the demons promised. "Seal the deal, and he'll be yours."

And Aaron?

"Don't worry," the demons said. "He's already over you. We've seen him with Jenna. He's picking her up for the dance on his motorcycle."

Quinn bit back tears. He could be happy with Jenna, like she was happy with Jeff. "No, the party can wait." She kissed Jeff, her fingers working the buttons of his shirt as her dress slipped to the floor.

Quinn trembled as Jeff fumbled for the zipper of her gown, his breath quick, his voice husky. "Quinn, I've always wanted you, nobody else."

And in that moment, she let herself go, surrendering to his embrace, to him, like she had never done before. She had nothing left to lose.

Quinn and Jeff found the party in full swing. The gym sparkled like a fairytale. The Student Council took the Winter Wonderland theme to the extreme, covering the floor with fake snow and painting the dance floor bluish white, like a giant ice rink. Fake Christmas trees stood with snow-laden limbs, creating a frosty forest that lined the walls. Even the stage at the far end of the gym had a snow-peaked mountain poking up from behind the band. Thousands of twinkle lights poked through black butcher paper, creating a canopy of stars. The astronomy club outdid themselves, making the lights look like real constellations, mimicking that very evening's night sky.

A pang of guilt hit Quinn as Orion stared down at her. Coward, that's what she was. She'd let Aaron believe what he wanted to believe, didn't even have the guts to tell him she was back with Jeff. The demons got what they wanted; Aaron was out of her life and Jeff was back in. Maybe they would leave her alone now. Fingering the string of pearls around her neck, Quinn watched them as they watched her from the shadows. If she had given them what they wanted, why were they still there? Hadn't she done everything they asked? She rubbed her hands over the goose bumps rising on her flesh.

Homecoming bliss, everyone partied in extreme celebration mode. Westland's win against Eastwood had been a miracle. A miracle attributed to Jeff and Quinn's reunion. A miracle powerful enough to stamp out Kerstin's rumors, and within minutes, catapulted Quinn back to the top of the social ladder.

Quinn searched the room for Reese and Marcus. A few couples cuddled at some of the tables, kissing and whispering. On the other side of the room, a handful of singles mingled by the punch bowl. Among them stood Kerstin, alone, evil-eyeing Quinn, face as green as her emerald velvet dress. Quinn had won, but watching Kerstin soured her triumph. A part of her felt sorry for her. Then she noticed Aaron standing in the corner with that brunette from his band, Jenna. Quinn's chest became a fist, squeezing her heart until she thought it might burst. Massaging the pain blooming above her breast, she closed her eyes and pictured Jeff holding her hand when they were little, their first kiss, how he'd held her after her father left while she cried. The tightness eased.

"Want some punch?" Jeff shouted over the music and pointed in the direction of the table.

"No." Quinn grabbed Jeff's hand, leading him to the far side of the dance floor before Aaron could notice them. "This is a dance. We should dance." Quinn put her arms in the air and moved in time with the frenzied beat.

"Okay, if you want to dance." Jeff paused. His dimple illuminated a mischievous smile. "Let's dance."

"Oh, no." Quinn grinned when he picked her up around her tiny waist, holding her close. "No, no, no," she squealed, closing her eyes as he twirled her around and around until a joyful laugh erupted from her. "Okay, okay. Put me down!" she yelled at him between giggles. "Put me down!"

Jeff lowered her to the floor as the music slowed. "I almost forgot how beautiful your laugh is."

"I almost forgot what a great dancer you are."

Like metal spikes on a chalkboard, the microphone crackled as Principal Halstor's giant, faded-orange corsage scraped against it, prompting all chatter to stop. She tried to adjust the mic stand to fit her lanky proportions, making the scraping sounds worse.

"Could someone help me with this thing!" she screamed, waving her hands in the air.

At once, a skinny kid with glasses bolted from the back of the gym and skittered up to the stage. He kept his head low, and with a flick of his wrist, set the mic to just the right height.

"Thank you, Horace," she said to him. "Attention, Westland High students. It's now time to introduce this year's homecoming court."

After a short, dramatic pause, she curled the ends of her dry, wrinkled lips into an odd smile. "Now, I am proud to present to you, princes of the homecoming court and nominees for homecoming king." She pushed her glasses back up her pointy nose, adjusting the paper to the right distance for her to read. "Jamshed Malik, Matt Martinez, Lee Ennis, Bryan McNally, and Jeff Abrams."

The already rowdy crowd erupted into whistles and clapping. Old Hawk Eyes peered over the top of her spectacles and cleared her throat until she had everyone's attention again. "Do I have your permission to continue? Now, where was I? Yes. The princesses of the homecoming court and nominees for homecoming queen are Irma Alvarez, Quinn Taylor, Teresa Yang, LaTisha Bowen, and Kerstin Connelly."

Students went wild, cheering and shouting Quinn's name as Jeff escorted her up the middle of the dance floor, following the other nominees through the excited crowd to take their places.

Jeff and Quinn split up as they reached the stage, one to the left, one to the right, and Quinn took the spot next to Reese. Kerstin mounted the stage last and stood next to Quinn. Principal Halstor moved to the microphone, stuck two gnarled fingers in her shrunken mouth, and added her own shrill whistle to the cheers.

Quinn smiled and waved at the crowd in royal dignity. Aaron, his date, and Marcus stood at the foot of the stage. Marcus grinned and winked at Reese, but Aaron was engrossed in a conversation with Jenna. A twinge of jealousy rose in her heart.

"Aaron looks happy with Jenna." Quinn leaned over to Reese, raising her voice just enough to be heard over the noise. "Are they?"

"Well, they've been friends a long time. I guess it makes sense that he would ask her, but I don't know if it's anything serious. Marcus pressured Aaron to come tonight. He couldn't stand the thought of not double-dating, so when you two didn't work out … well, anyway, they seem cute together, I guess. She seems nice. Why? Is something wrong?"

"No." Quinn adjusted her corsage, avoiding Reese's questioning stare.

"Liar."

"No. Really. Everything's great." Quinn forced her frown upside-down. "I'm glad he's here with Jenna. They look cute together." She choked on the word "cute."

"Maybe if you keep telling yourself that, you'll actually start to believe it." Reese smoothed the skirt on her dress. "So, how is it being back with Jeff?"

"Great." Quinn jumped at the chance to talk about Jeff—and forget Aaron in the process.

"Really?" Reese probed.

"It's almost as if the summer never happened. He said he never stopped loving me, and that Kerstin was a big mistake." Quinn raised her voice loud enough for Kerstin to hear.

Kerstin's hand shot out and caught Quinn's wrist. She jerked her forward and pressed her mouth up against Quinn's ear.

"If he's so in love with you, why did he call me last night?" Kerstin hissed, her breath like rotting eggs.

"You're hurting me." Quinn tried to squirm out of her grip, but Kerstin held tight.

"After the game, after you went to Nuevo for dinner. He dropped you off and called me from your driveway." Kerstin's whispers wormed their way into Quinn's heart, eating a hole through her confidence.

"Just stop," Quinn said. "It's not my fault that he broke up with you."

"Did he tell you we broke up?" Kerstin laughed. "He left you and came straight to my house. To talk. You know where talking to Jeff leads, don't you? No, I guess you don't. Let's just say, talking is overrated."

"Liar." Quinn spat through clenched teeth.

"No, Jeff is a liar. And you're a fool. Ask him yourself is you don't believe me." Kerstin let go of her wrist, smoothed back a strand of red hair, and smiled out at the crowd as if nothing was wrong.

"Okay, Westland High." Once the clapping died down, Principal Halstor, in true dramatic fashion, pulled a second envelope from the bodice of her dress. "I have the results for this year's homecoming king and queen."

"Good luck," Kerstin said, patronizing.

"I don't want, or need, your luck," Quinn smoothed the front of her dress and squared her shoulders. Kerstin's jealousy was nothing but hot air. No matter how hard she tried, she wouldn't let her get between her and Jeff again.

Principal Halstor ran a finger through the top of the envelope and pulled the folded blue sheet of paper from its nest. "This year's homecoming king and queen are ..."

Several people banged on tables, the floor, and the stage, simulating a drum roll.

"Jeff Abrams and Quinn Taylor."

She glanced over her shoulder as Jeff took her hand. Inky tears painted Kerstin's cheeks, spilled down her shoulders, and wrapped her arms in black. Quinn blinked, and the ink turned to normal tears flowing down a pale face.

Good. Let her cry.

Chants of "Jeff, Jeff, Quinn, Quinn," accompanied the explosive shouts and whistles that echoed through the gym.

Jeff placed the silver crown, decorated with diamond white, purple, and red rhinestones, on Quinn's head. Again, the student body clapped and cheered, and Quinn thrust her fist in the air, laughing. The demons were right, listening to them had given Quinn her life back—this is where she belonged. Her confidence surged with Jeff on her arm and Kerstin out of the picture. People cheered for her now, screaming her name, and she waved at her loyal voters. Kerstin was no longer in the competition. Quinn had won.

Everything is how it should be, Quinn thought.

"Would the royal court please join their king and queen for the traditional court dance?" Principal Halstor motioned to the DJ and the music started.

"May I have this dance, my queen?" Jeff offered his hand.

"I'd love to, my king."

Jeff escorted her down the stairs and out onto the dance floor, while the rest of the royal court paired off. Reese danced with Bryan McNally while Kerstin got stuck with Matt, who kept whooping like a wild animal, while spinning around her like a top. The entire gym broke out in hysterics, all except Kerstin.

Kerstin pulled away from Matt, leaving him spinning in circles all by himself, he didn't seem to care, and disappeared into the crowd. Quinn couldn't help but notice Jeff's eyes following her.

"I guess you didn't find that as funny as everyone else," Quinn said.

"Did you? I mean, Matt pretty much ruined the royal dance for the whole court."

"He didn't ruin it, he was just having a little fun." Quinn pushed away from Jeff and folder her arms over her chest. "Oh, you mean ruined for Kerstin."

"I think Matt was being mean, that's all."

"What did you do after you dropped me off last night?"

"What?" Jeff pretended to straighten his boutonniere. "I went home. It was late." He looked at her from under his blonde lashes, lips curving into a smile.

Quinn shook her head. "I don't believe you."

"Why would I lie?" Jeff placed his hands on her shoulders. "Come on, look at me. Let's forget about Kerstin, okay?" He brushed a stray hair from Quinn's forehead and tucked it behind her ear, turning his full attention to her.

Why would he lie? Then, again, why wouldn't he?

"Jeff, swear to me it's over between the two of you." Placing her hands on his chest, she looked up to search his eyes.

"I've told her in every way I know how. It's over." He didn't flinch from her, his gaze steady, voice sure.

Quinn sighed, releasing the tension from her body.

"Ok," she said.

Resting her head on Jeff's broad shoulder, she closed her eyes. His breath warmed her bare neck as they swayed to the music. She remembered all the dances, all the kisses, the laughter, even the tears, but the one thing she wanted to forget kept popping into her head. No matter how hard Quinn tried, Kerstin's words on the podium echoed in her mind.

Could he have cheated on me? Kerstin said he'd been at her house.

Aaron, the other thing she wanted to forget, stood a few feet away, hugging Jenna the way he used to hug her. Quinn shut her eyes to keep the tears from falling.

You have no right to him. He can dance with whoever he wants. You made your choice. Jeff. You love him. You've always loved him. Let Aaron go, let him be happy. Like you are.

"Kiss me," she whispered to Jeff. And he did.

From the moment they walked into the gym, Quinn and Jeff did nothing but rub their relationship in Aaron's face. At least that's what it felt like. He thought Quinn would at least try to explain herself, apologize, something, but avoidance was what she did best. Why would he expect more from her? He'd even waited by her locker before school, to let her know how pissed off he was, but she never showed.

When first period came on Monday, so did the news. Quinn and Jeff were back together, and that was all the answer he needed. The gossip spread faster than the black plague, killing the rest of his hope.

He avoided them the rest of the week, reducing the reality to rumor, at least for him. But now he faced the full truth of it. Everywhere he turned, there she was—with Jeff. And now they'd been crowned homecoming king and queen, dancing, laughing, twirling, and kissing in front of his face. Why was he surprised? He had seen them kissing that night. For a moment Aaron thought he had overreacted; maybe Jeff's kiss hadn't meant anything. Now he knew for sure. It was his kiss that meant nothing.

"You're not having a good time, are you?" Jenna shouted over the blaring music.

"Is it that obvious?" Aaron squeezed his eyes shut, banishing the rage and hurt that overwhelmed him. He wished he had stayed home.

Determined to double date, Marcus had tried to fix Aaron up with every girl from Texas to Canada. After days of fighting, Aaron relented. His stipulation: he would pick his own date. In the end, he asked Jenna—begged actually—and she'd taken pity on him. But only after making him promise he wouldn't try kissing her again. She would always have his back, but she wasn't interested in him anymore. Just like Jenna to be so blunt. He wasn't sure how true that was, but at least they knew where they stood with one another. Two friends going to a dance. Quinn's betrayal was still too fresh for it to be anything more.

"The way you keep staring at the two of them kind of gives it away."

"I'm sorry." Aaron raised his right hand and placed his left over his heart. "You're my date, and from this moment on, I promise to stop moping and start having fun." Holding out his hand to her, he asked, "How about another dance?"

"From the way you keep looking at her with those please-kick-me-one-more-time puppy dog eyes, I think it's going to take a lot more than another dance to turn this night fun." Jenna slid a hand through her silky dark hair. "What is it about her, Aaron? I mean, she's pretty, in a doe-eyed kind of way, but why her?"

"That's the million-dollar question, isn't it? Answer that for me, and you'll win a prize." Aaron sighed and pulled at the stiff, white cuffs of his shirt.

"She broke your heart. It's obvious you're not over her, but the best way to get back at her is to at least pretend to have a good time. Don't let her see you pining for her."

"I'm not pining."

"And I'm not a smartass. Stop lying to yourself. You need to forget about her, at least for a few minutes. I mean, it looks like she's forgotten about you." Jenna pointed at Quinn.

"Ouch." Aaron rubbed his hand over his chest. "V-harsh."

"Sorry, but it's kind of obvious they're together, like really together. The truth is painful, but you have to face it."

"I know. You're right."

"Just forget her for one minute."

"How can I with her in my face every time I turn around?"

"Look, I know I made you promise not to kiss me, but I never promised not to kiss you. If you think it will make her jealous, I'll take one for the team."

"I thought you didn't have any interest in me."

"Not you, just your lips." Jenna grinned, held up one hand and put the other over her heart. "I promise I won't fall desperately in love with you or call you my boyfriend." She made the sign of a cross over her chest. "And hope to die."

"I don't know." Aaron shook his head, and Jenna put her finger over his lips.

"Don't think. Thinking is your problem. Just go with it. Here, let me show you." Jenna grazed her soft lips over his and pulled away as he was about to kiss her back. She waved a finger in front of his face. "Not like last time. This time take it slow," she whispered and teased him again with a nibble. Warm and silky, her lips tasted of honey. She pulled away again and grinned.

Aaron grinned back and moved in with a teasing nibble of his own. Jenna's kisses were like homemade chocolate-chip cookies. Warm. Sweet. Comforting.

"Having fun now?" she whispered.

"Shhh. I don't want to think about it." Aaron circled her waist, drew her gently to him, and spent the next five minutes letting her wash all traces of Quinn from his mind.

"Want to get out of here?" Aaron asked between smooches. "Grab a bite to eat?"

"I thought you'd never ask."

The ends of Aaron's mouth turned up in a smile. "Why should I stick around here to get my heart pulverized, right?"

"I don't know. Pulverization's pretty painful."

"You said it." Aaron pulled her into a hug. "Thanks for everything."

"Like I said, just taking one for the team." She winked. "I'll need the little girl's room before we go."

"There's one by the front doors. I'll find Marcus and Reese to tell them we're leaving. Meet me by the doors to the parking lot?"

Aaron looked at Jenna. Her black strapless dress showed off her curves. Where Quinn's complexion was strawberries and cream, Jenna's was olives and sunset. Auburn hair flowed down her back, and her serene gray eyes sparkled in the lights. Jenna was different than Quinn in every way, and different was what he needed.

"Okay, be right back." Jenna ducked under a pair of dancing arms and disappeared in the crowd.

Aaron made his way through several members of the Mustang defensive line, ties around their heads, arms linked, jumping up and down like elephants on speed as the music's pounding rhythm accelerated faster and faster.

Hearing a deep, bellowing laugh, followed by a scream of delight, he knew he was getting close. On the right side of the stage, past the huge black speaker, he found Marcus with his tie around his head. Reese, slung over his back like a rag doll, beat on his back

"Playing Tarzan and Jane again?" Aaron yelled over the music. "Aaron, thank God you're here. Tell him to put me down!" Reese screamed.

"Aaron, my man!" Marcus turned around to face Aaron, knocking Reese's head into a nearby speaker.

"Hey, watch it!" she screamed and rubbed her head.

Marcus put her down, kissing the top of her head, then her ear, her neck, and finally her lips. "I'm so sorry, baby."

Reese slugged his arm, then smiled and kissed him back. "You're forgiven."

"Hello?" Aaron raised his hand to get their attention. "I'm still here."

"So, Jenna? Is she as good a kisser as she is a singer?" Marcus winked.

"As if I would tell you. Anyway, I just came over to say bye."

"Bye? The party's just getting started, and you're leaving?"

Reese whispered in his ear.

"Of course, Quinn and Jeff were kissing, he's her boyfriend!" Marcus yelled over the dance noise, then stuck his finger in his ear and wiggled it back and forth.

"You know nothing about subtlety, do you?" Reese turned to Aaron. "Sorry about that. I was trying to keep you from being reminded."

"Thanks, but I already ran into them."

"So that's why you're leaving." Marcus nodded.

"I just think it's better this way. Jenna's not having any fun, and neither am I. I think we're going to grab a slice at Tony's."

"Hey, pizza, that sounds great! And Tony makes my favorite: pepperoni and pineapple with extra anchovies. Save me a piece, will you? Make that four, I'm starving!"

"Does that mean you guys will meet us there?"

"And leave my fans wanting more? The party would die if I left. Just get mine to go and bring them back when you're done. Hide them in your suit jacket. Old Mr. Minks won't smell a thing. Thanks, buddy." Marcus clapped him on the back.

"Reese!" Quinn started, then stopped mid-wave.

Aaron had never seen a deer in headlights, but that's how he would describe the look on Quinn's face as her eyes met his.

"Oh, um, I didn't mean to interrupt. Jeff went to the bathroom." Quinn pointed behind her. "So, I thought I would make the rounds and say hi to, you know, everyone."

The silence that followed was more uncomfortable than winter in Maine.

"Hey, girl." Reese gave her a big hug. "We're glad you came over to say hi. Right, Marcus?" She poked him in the ribs with her elbow.

"Uh, yeah, it's always nice to get a visit from a real hottie. Right, Aaron?" Marcus's remark earned him another poke in the ribs from Reese.

Aaron stared at Quinn staring at him. "Well, it's been real, but I think I'll go. Later, Marcus." Aaron held out a fist, and Marcus tapped it with his own.

"Reese." He hugged her.

Pushing his hands in his pockets, Aaron forced himself to look up. "Quinn."

"You don't have to leave because of me."

"I'm not," Aaron said, matter-of-factly. "My date's waiting by the door."

"Right. Of course. Your date," Quinn said. "I should go find Jeff. He's probably looking for me."

"Yeah, that's a good idea. You wouldn't want his lips to get cold. We all know what happens when Jeff's lips get cold. Where is Kerstin anyway?" The comments spewed from Aaron's mouth like poison, each one hitting their mark with perfect precision, and it felt good, better than good. It was freeing. Until he noticed the shocked look on Quinn's face. He watched her chew on her bottom lip, the way she did when she was nervous or unsure. Then her mouth opened as if to speak.

Aaron thought she would let him have it. Instead, Quinn tapped her bare foot on the hardwood floor, folded her arms over her chest, and stared at him, her eyes glistening as if tears might pour out at any moment. Then she was gone.

Pain bloomed in Quinn's chest as she turned away from Aaron and pushed through the crowd. She couldn't breathe, she couldn't think, the gym flickered from dark to light to dark around her, pulsing with the ache she felt inside her heart. Tears--hot, angry, hurt, dripped from her chin.

"Don't cry." The voices, once malicious and unwelcome, now soothed her, comforted her, their breathy smoothness overlapping her own thoughts, making it harder and harder to tell which beliefs belonged to Quinn, and which were the demons. "Aaron doesn't know you."

How could he? He never tried. He gave up.

"He's selfish."

Jerk.

"Jealous of what you and Jeff have."

I don't need Aaron.

"You're better off without him. Trust us."

You're right.

Quinn dabbed her eyes with the back of her hand and stood up straighter.

"Q.T.! Hey, over here!" Ami waved both arms in the air. Quinn waved back.

"Congratulations!" Ami squealed as she embraced Quinn in a sisterly hug. "You and Jeff, king and queen! If you had asked me two weeks ago, I would have said no way. I mean, it sure looked like Kerstin would win, but when everyone found out you and Jeff were back together, there was no denying who was Queen.

"Then we won the game! Our first game! The whole school knows it's because you guys are back together. I haven't seen Jeff this happy in months or Kerstin this miserable, for that matter. Serves her right. You know she couldn't get anyone to bring her tonight? I heard she even begged Horace Wheeler, but he already had a date. Can you believe it? Anyway, we're so happy for you. Aren't we, Shae?"

Shae, Ami's date, looked stunned when she asked her opinion. "Yeah, of course, you and Jeff—"

"I know! Aren't they great together? I mean, there's no other perfect couple, and everyone thought it was over, but not me. I always had faith in the two of you. True love can never be denied."

"Thanks for the support, Ami," Quinn said. "Speaking of, have you seen Jeff anywhere?"

"No, not since your dance."

"I saw him talking to Kerstin," Shae said.

"No, you didn't. Don't even joke like that, Shae."

"I'm not joking." Shae raised her voice, bringing Ami to silence. "Last time I saw them they were walking toward the front doors. Kerstin looked pretty upset."

"Thanks, Shae. I guess I better go find him." Inside, Quinn's stomach turned. Did Kerstin seek Jeff out, or did Jeff look for Kerstin?

Quinn hurried through the crowd of well-wishers, getting stopped every few feet to be told how glad they were to see her back together with Jeff, how beautiful she looked, blah, blah, blah. The same people who had called her a druggie and a loser less than a week ago. What a bunch of phonies. But she smiled like a true royal and thanked them, her eyes ever searching for Kerstin and Jeff.

We all know what happens when Jeff's lips get cold. Where is Kerstin anyway? Aaron's words rang in her ears.

Frantic to find them, she rushed past the stage, the punch bowl, the tables, to the front doors—where she spied Jeff, in a shadowy corner—with Kerstin.

Kerstin gripped his biceps so hard his flesh bulged between

her short, stubby fingers. His hands caressed her shoulders; his head bent to her ear while she sobbed like a baby. Quinn moved closer but couldn't hear what they were saying. Kerstin pounded on Jeff's chest, a wild rage in her eye.

Anger prickled through Quinn, and she gritted her teeth. Why couldn't she leave Jeff alone? Jeff shook his head and pulled away from Kerstin's grip, but she wouldn't let him go. Grabbing him by the wrist, Kerstin jerked him back, bawling. Jeff shook his head and tried pulling away again, but she clung to him like a desperate child.

"Look at her. Trying to manipulate Jeff." Again."Stop her."

Rage and jealousy rose inside Quinn. Stalking up behind Kerstin, she grabbed her arm and spun her around, so they were face to face.

"I'm warning you, Kerstin, leave Jeff alone. He's made his choice, now deal."

Kerstin gaped. Tears streamed from her bloodshot eyes, down her round cheeks. "Stay out of this. It's none of your business."

"How can I stay out of it when I'm so obviously in the middle of it?"

"Not everything's about you, Quinn Perfect." The word perfect hissed out of Kerstin's mouth, reminding her of the whispers of the demons.

"I need to talk to Kerstin for a minute." Jeff turned his back on Quinn, pressing Kerstin further into the corner.

"He's avoiding you, Quinn. Like your father did when he left with that woman? Why do all the men in your life betray you?" A demon slipped from the shadows and landed on Quinn's shoulder.

Quinn's nails bit into her palms, and she narrowed her eyes at Jeff. "Let me get this straight, Jeff. You want me, your girl-friend, to leave you, my boyfriend, alone with Kerstin, the slut, who you, my boyfriend, dumped me for? Do you really think I'm that stupid?"

The demon whispered in her ear. "Have you ever wondered why they always leave, Quinn? Why the ones you love can't love you back?"

"Actually, he does think you're that stupid," Kerstin shot back.

"Just let me deal with this, okay?" Jeff begged Kerstin.

Shadows twisted and coiled around Quinn in agitation as she advanced on Jeff.

"Deal with this?" Quinn slammed her hands into Jeff's chest. "Deal with this!" She pushed with everything in her, shoving Jeff with all the hurt, anger, and disappointment she'd been carrying around, and he stumbled back. "What's there to deal with? You are my date and my boyfriend, not Kerstin's lap dog. You're being such a jerk."

"Now, wait a minute." Jeff balled his fists, face turning red. "That's not fair. Kerstin and I were just clearing up a few things."

"Not fair? Oh, that's great, Jeff. Clearing things up, right, like you did with me after you dumped me? I don't recall you ever clearing things up with me."

No one ever cleared things up with her, not her father, not Jeff, even Aaron had turned away never to look back, and she was sick of it. "You're a liar, Jeff. You were with her last night. Weren't you? She said you were. It's not over between the two of you. I see that now. You don't love me. You don't love her either. The only thing you love is yourself."

Jeff grabbed Quinn by the arm and pulled her farther into the corner. "What the hell do you call what happened tonight?" He pulled her to him, pressing his cheek to hers as he spoke in hushed tones. The sweet scent of ginger ale and strawberries from the punch lingered on his breath, making her nauseous. She struggled against him, but he held tight. "Didn't I make my feelings for you clear? Do you think it meant nothing to me? I mean, come on, Quinn, it was our first time."

Evil laughter echoed through her head as the shadows trembled and flickered. Quinn's heart dropped into her stomach. Of course, he had lied. He was still seeing Kerstin on the side, trying to have his cake and eat it, too. Just like her father. How stupid could she be?

"You mean my first time." Tears flowed down Quinn's cheeks. "Mine, not ours." She jerked away from his vice grip and rubbed the red spot left by his fingers. "How could I have been so stupid? I can't even believe I let you touch me after you've touched her."

"Well, well, well, little miss virgin no longer." Kerstin stepped around Jeff and Quinn shrank back. Kerstin's clear blue eyes were gone. Giant black marbles stared out from sunken sockets, and a dark gray shadow caped her shoulders, pulsing with a life of its own, growing with every word Kerstin spoke. "Little miss perfect's not so perfect after all. I didn't think you had it in you, to screw up this much. What's next, a little grand theft auto?"

The dark fog drew itself into a dense, swirling mass. It hovered over Kerstin like the grim reaper. Quinn trembled. The fog pulsed once, exploded with a blast of sulfurous air, and revealed a fully formed entity.

Unlike the others, this demon didn't care about Quinn. It had its claws fixed on Kerstin. Dark, black hair covered every inch of its twisted, gnarled body. It fluttered down to Kerstin's shoulder and turned its owl-like head to whisper to her. It opened its sliver of a mouth, revealing a set of long, pointy fangs and doubled tongue. Placing it in Kerstin's ear, it licked at her flesh. Saliva dribbled from the gray whip-like tongue, dripping off her lobe and down her neck. Kerstin didn't even flinch; she seemed to welcome it.

"So, Quinn, how did my leftovers taste? Sweet? Salty, maybe? Or more like spoiled?" They spoke in a round, the demon to

Kerstin, Kerstin to Quinn, its words, its voice, overlapping Kerstin's. It put the words in her mind and she repeated them like a parrot, like the crowd at the game with the moths. She flicked a glance at Jeff, but he had fixed Kerstin with an irritated glare that had nothing to do with the demon on her shoulder. Why couldn't anyone else see them?

"I used to be jealous of you. But you're just a pathetic fool, like me. We have way more in common than I ever thought. I can't believe I envied you. Quinn: perfect, beautiful, smart, head cheerleader, and Jeff's true love. You have no idea how much he talked about you last summer."

"Kerstin. Don't," Jeff warned.

"Until that night on the beach. When you kissed me. Do you remember, Jeff?" She glared at him for a moment, daring him to stop her. "Our parents just happened to pick the same resort in Cozumel. What are the odds of that? We went out for a late-night walk, just to get away from all the family fun. I shivered, and you put your arm around me, to warm me. We stopped in that secluded spot where the sands met the cliffs." Kerstin paused as her demon bent to whisper in her ear. "You called my name that night, not Quinn's. Mine."

Clutching her stomach, Quinn backed away, shaking her head. Kerstin looked from Jeff to Quinn, studying their expressions, probing them for ammunition perhaps, or waiting for the demon to tell her what to say next.

Kerstin stuck out her bottom lip in a pout. "What's wrong Jeff? You mean you never told her?" She spoke in exaggerated baby talk. "Precious Quinn doesn't know you cheated on her over the summer? Tsk, tsk, tsk, that wasn't very nice now, was it?" Kerstin softened her voice and shook her head at Quinn. "I told him he should be honest with you, to tell you right away, but he made me promise. He said he would tell you when the time was right. Well, what better time than now?"

Jeff shoved past Kerstin and took Quinn by the arm. "I

wanted to tell you. I tried to tell you." He pulled her farther from Kerstin and grabbed her face to get her to look him in the eye. "We'd both been drinking. I was missing you. I was weak, stupid, and it cost me more than you know."

Quinn wanted out, but Jeff blocked her path to the left. She looked to the right. Kerstin and her demon blocked the path to the stage. Quinn's own demons popped in and out between her and the door, laughing as a flowing fog gathered behind them.

"What is it you humans say? Once a cheater always a cheater?" The demons asked in chorus.

"Jeff was heartbroken, leaving his precious Quinn for six whole weeks, but I comforted him. It didn't take long to turn to me, did it?" Kerstin cocked her head and folded her arms over her chest. She clicked her tongue as she studied Quinn. Her thin lips turned into a spiteful grin. "Now that he's had both of us, which do you think he'll choose?"

Quinn stumbled sideways and covered her mouth to swallow a scream. She turned her back on them, to run from the pain and confusion, but the fog trapped her. It engulfed the entire gym, the floor, the ceiling, the other students, everything and everyone except for her, Kerstin, and Jeff. Jeff stroked her shoulder. She cringed and jerked away, looking for a break in the smoky darkness.

"Quinn, look at me. I love you." Jeff stepped around her until they were face to face again. The fog moved back just enough to accommodate him. Quinn wanted to believe the sincerity in his voice, the desperation in his wide brown eyes.

"I've always loved you." Jeff pulled her into a hug and stroked her hair. "Please, Quinn. Forgive me. All I've ever wanted was you." The demons were wrong; they had to be. Jeff cupped her chin and wiped a tear from her cheek. "Kerstin? A moment of weakness I'll always regret. If you knew, you would understand. It was a mistake."

"A mistake?" Kerstin shrieked at Jeff. "That's all I was to

you?" Eyes narrowed, she elbowed her way between them, getting up in his face. "Well, this mistake is carrying your baby!"

Was Kerstin for real? Crying pregnant to keep Jeff? Quinn shook her head and opened her mouth to defend him, but the look on his face stopped her cold. He didn't look shocked at the news.

Kerstin turned to Quinn. "Did you hear me, Quinn? I'm pregnant with Jeff's baby!" Kerstin screamed like a mad child, her words reverberating through the gym, overpowering even the rocking background music, an earthquake, shaking the very foundation of the school.

Quinn clutched her breast as the news ricocheted through her, killing her last shred of hope. The fog shook too, not in shock, but in joy. Mocking and cruel, the mischievous laughter echoed in Quinn's mind the way Kerstin's words echoed through the gym. Then the one fog separated into many, curling and dancing around the two girls like wisps of smoke from a burned-out candle.

Foolish, stupid, everything she'd done, everything she'd thought, played right into her enemies' claws. She could see that now. The demons had tricked her, playing on her emotions, her insecurities, manipulating her into this very moment all along. And she'd let them. There was no such thing as making a deal with the devil. They didn't deal; they did whatever they wanted. They would never let her go. Ever.

A crowd gathered around the tense battle waging in the dark corner of the gym. Silent, they converged on the oblivious threesome, jackals waiting to gorge on the leftover kill.

Aaron, Reese, and Marcus joined the pack.

"What are we watching?" Aaron asked Marcus.

"Probably the defensive line doing their version of YMCA."

"I can't see a thing over all these giants." Reese jumped to peer over the ocean of heads. "Come on." She grabbed Marcus's hand, cutting her way through the dense forest of bodies, Aaron at their heels.

Penetrating the pack's front line, they saw Quinn huddled in the corner, Jeff grabbing her face, Kerstin gloating beside him.

"Man, I could use some popcorn and a Coke to go with all this drama." The crowd shushed Marcus. "Hey, I thought this was a party, not a movie."

"You think this is funny?" Reese put her hands on her hips and glowered at him.

"Well," Marcus started. "No, no, of course not. Do you think we ought to do something?"

"Like what?"

"I don't know. Distract the onlookers, so they can have a little privacy?"

"I'm pregnant with Jeff's baby!" The concussion of Kerstin's bomb thundered over the loud music. The audience gasped.

"I think it's a little late for that." Aaron moved closer to the turmoil.

Jenna appeared beside him. "Do you really want to get in the middle of that mess?" She touched him on the arm.

Getting involved was the last thing he wanted. If only he could kill this instinctual sense of chivalry, especially when it came to Quinn.

Quinn covered her ears and shook her head. Kerstin advanced on her, oblivious to the spectators. Jeff and Kerstin hurting Quinn, her date with Jeff a disaster, the whole school watching. Wasn't she getting what she deserved?

Aaron loosened the collar of his shirt and reveled in the cool air on his neck. Sweat beaded on his forehead, his temples throbbed. Quinn burned bright hot in rage and humiliation. She was the sun, and he was trapped by her gravity, pulling at his soul, urging him to step in and save her once again.

He closed his eyes and conjured the thought of Jeff and Quinn kissing. He mulled the image over, reliving the pain until his anger replaced mercy and killed any urge to disentangle her from her current web. He opened his eyes, a mistake. Her tear-streaked face dispelled his anger quicker than the picture of the kiss took to contrive it.

Balling his fists and gritting his teeth, Aaron refused to give in, refused to let her control his every move. Whatever this spell she held over him, he wanted rid of it. He wasn't her guardian, her knight in shining armor—neither of them wanted to be in the other's life. A battle raged within him. Feelings fought against reason, instinct against fear, love against pain.

Quinn left him no choice.

"Let's get out of here." Aaron grabbed Jenna's hand, pushed through the crowd, letting the steel double doors slam behind them without even a glance back.

Quinn covered her ears to block out the bestial laughter. The wisps gathered around her, curling and uncurling, forming into beings. Mercurial demons surrounded Kerstin, too, but she didn't seem to notice their creepy hysteria. In fact, she seemed blind to everything, even that the whole school stood shocked by her terrible little secret, staring at them like zombies.

Kerstin carried Jeff's baby. Quinn had sacrificed everything to be with a liar and a cheat. And for what? Because some demonic delusion told her to? Even her so-called friends hated her. Look at them all now, standing on the sidelines ready to chew her up and spit her out.

"Covering your ears isn't going to make it any less true." Kerstin had exchanged her red-faced anger for serene smugness.

Quinn wanted to strike back at her. She wanted to lash out at Jeff, who stood there with his head down.He didn't even try to defend himself.

The laughing demons died down as the truth sank to the pit of Quinn's stomach.

"Fool," one whispered.

"You knew, didn't you? That's why you ghosted me." Quinn's accusing tone startled Jeff from his stupor.

His eyes widened. "No. I didn't. I-I mean ..." he stammered, reaching for her.

She swatted his hand away.

"Stupid," another demon said.

"You knew when you came home from Mexico."

"Blind," the demon added.

"That's why you broke up with me. How could I have been so blind?"

"Fool." Her demons laughed.

"I love you," Jeff said.

"Does he really?"

"Do you really?

"Yes. More than anything."

"She's carrying his baby."

"More than your baby? Jeff, she's pregnant."

"Are you?" The demon's question slammed into her like an iron fist, knocking the wind out of her. Quinn struggled for breath. Sleeping with Jeff had been an act of desperation, a sealing of the deal. The demons promised everything would go back to normal, and she dared to believe them. But they lied. Or had she lied to herself? Her choices, her consequences, there was no one else to blame.

The room swirled before her. Colors collided together, growing, changing into the ominous blackness she feared, here to swallow her up. The dark, dense cloud whirled around her, a tornado of malevolent design. Shrieks of glee and torturous whispers emanated from its all -encompassing smoky spiral. Darkness encircled her body, above her, below her, ever churning, spinning, tumbling, pushing her to vertigo.

"Get away from me!" she screamed, but the blackness leapt forward. She was just a girl, tiny and afraid; she didn't have the power to make it disappear. She groped for the wall, willing herself to find an exit. Her hand found the cool metal bar. She pushed it, delivering herself to the real tempest that raged on the other side of the darkness.

Aaron watched Jenna scarf down a third piece of veggie pizza.

"What?" she mumbled, covering her mouth as she swallowed. "All that drama made me hungry." She took a sip of soda to wash it down. "So, what was with the episode from Young and the Restless anyway?"

"Don't ask." Rain poured, coating the outside window like a second pane of glass. "I just want to forget it, okay?" He pictured Quinn, smiling, long lavender dress shimmering in the twinkling lights of the gym, blond hair framing her beautiful face.

"Yeah, sure." Jenna swirled her soda around with her straw. Lightning flashed, illuminating the parking lot, followed by a crack of thunder. "Wow, that's some storm. Aren't you glad I talked you into letting me drive?" Jenna grinned an I-told-you-so.

"What? The idea of riding on my bike in the rain doesn't sound romantic?" Aaron took the last slice of pizza, savoring the taste of the warm, stringy mozzarella. "Why didn't we take my bike again?"

"Hey, I'm always up for adventure, but cold and wet isn't my idea of the perfect date." Jenna scrunched her face. "Sorry, I didn't mean to say the D word."

Aaron tapped his foot on the bottom of the booth. "Well, I'm paying, so I guess that's what it is. Even with the rain, it's still better than my date with Quinn."

Thunder crashed, and water poured from the roof like a waterfall, flooding the half-filled parking lot.

"Did you really walk in on her kissing her ex?" Jenna rubbed her forehead. "There I go again. Stupid Jenna, can't you just learn to keep your mouth shut?"

"No, it's okay." Aaron stared at the red Formica tabletop. "It's true. She bolted from church the other night. Reese said she wasn't feeling well, but I walked in on her kissing Jeff and, well, she looked all right to me. I even tried to call her, talk to her about it. Stupid, isn't it?"

"No. Just human."

The bells on the door jingled, and a cold wind whipped

through the pizzeria. Aaron turned to see Reese, hair plastered to her head, mascara running black down her left cheek. Her royal blue dress, muddied and torn, peeked from under Marcus's black leather jacket.

Aaron and Jenna jumped up from their booth.

"What happened?" Aaron spurted "Where's Marcus? Are you okay?"

Reese shivered. Water dripped from every inch of her, pooling on the brick floor of the entryway and around her bare feet.

"I'll get her some coffee." Jenna banged on the counter to get the waitress's attention.

"I didn't come here for coffee. I came here for you."

"Is Marcus okay?" Aaron couldn't tell if she had been crying or if her cheeks were wet from the rain.

"He's in the Jeep. It's Quinn. Have you seen her?"

That name again. Aaron wanted to eat pizza, laugh, talk with Jenna, and forget that name.

He forced himself to ask, hating that part of him—the stupid part—that really wanted to know.

"What happened?"

Jenna appeared beside him, coffee in a to-go cup. Reese sipped at the steaming liquid, calming herself enough to continue.

"She ran out into the storm. Marcus and I tried to get to her, but the crowd blocked us. By the time we got outside, she'd disappeared."

"Maybe Jeff took her home."

"No, I mean, he started to run after her, but Kerstin was hysterical, blocking his way, screaming at him. He was way too busy trying to calm her down. He picked her up, carried her to his truck, and drove off. Marcus and I searched the campus for Quinn, but it's dark, and the rain. We didn't find her."

"Did you check her house? Maybe someone else gave her a

ride." "We went by there before we came here. No sign of her. Aaron, I'm worried. The dance is over, everyone's gone home. We could find her faster with help. I know you still care about her. Please, Aaron, you have to help us look for her."

Aaron looked at Jenna. She had every right not to want him chasing after Quinn in the rain. He was her date, after all.

"I can read it in your face, Aaron. You'll never forgive yourself if something happens to her." Jenna sighed. "You go with Marcus. Reese and I can take my car. We'll cover more ground that way." Always the voice of reason, Jenna confirmed what Aaron wanted to do in his heart.

"Thanks, Jenna." He kissed her cheek.

"Don't just stand here wasting time. Let's get going." Reese bolted out the door, covering her head with Marcus's jacket.

Jenna and Aaron followed, dodging raindrops as they raced to the shelter of the cars.

Quinn sprinted from the shelter of the school, away from the mass of mutant fog that pursued her. A barrage of rain pounded her body, icy needles in her flesh. She took off her shoes and ran. Her bare feet splashed through dark puddles as she raced across the parking lot. The rain stung her face.

The faster she moved, the harder the thin drops hit. Past the tennis courts she ran, her feet abandoning the traction of the pavement for the slick mud of the practice fields. Down she went into the cold wet earth, the grimy mire coating her flesh like a second skin. Gritty clay pushed its way between her lips, tasting of metal and earth. A primal scream erupted from her gut, and she spit and sputtered, working the saliva in her mouth to expel the mud. Her fists came down, two hammers of fury and frustration as she pounded the slick turf, spots of dirt splattering her face and hair.

Lightening burst from the sky. Its erratic pattern lighted the flooded field's grassy surface, now alive with writhing vapors, taking shape, moving closer.

Darkness again. A low rumble of thunder. Quinn squirmed

backward as the storm of demons advanced onto the inky field. Trembling, she wiped at her face to clear her vision and stumbled to her feet, running and slipping through the mud until she reached sounder ground. From grass to blacktop, she ran, across the lighted jogging track, down the back alley, following the lights that lined the asphalt drive.

Lightning crackled down. One bright streak struck the power line in front of her, separating the wire from the wooden pole. Sparks flew from the downed wire. Quinn jumped back, yelping as the line twisted in the wind like a snake, blocking her escape down the alley.

Quinn glanced back to see the throng watching her, glowing eyes closing in, twisting, changing, and materializing from the never-ending mists. Hundreds of bat-like wings added to the roar of the wind as they glided forward, a giant, moving ink stain on the landscape. Lacing her fingers through the loops in the eight-foot chain-link fence, she shook it, screaming, tears mixing with the rain pouring down her face. Razor wire glistened from the top, metal teeth set to shred any flesh that dared try to scale the wall, dashing any hope of climbing her way to freedom. The demons were closing in, and she was trapped.

Quick breaths rasped from her mud-caked lips, and her whole body trembled as she eased forward. If she could time it right, she might be able to jump over the downed cord. The silver whip hissed and jumped at her approach, and Quinn's heart jumped in response. The demons' shrieks spurred her on, and she pulled back for a running start. Judging the best course, she hurtled over the midsection of cable, barely avoiding its deadly strike as her feet thudded to the ground, aching with the impact. No time for pain, she dashed in the direction of the road.

She stumbled forward through the deluge of water, staying just ahead of the scraping claws and flapping wings of the hunters. She cried for the lightning to show her the way, its luminescence a double-edged sword, revealing both her deliverance and her doom. But the ribbons of light, once abundant, now abandoned her to shadows.

An explosion of wind drove her to her knees. Her dress ripped in sync with a rumble of thunder as she went down. Her hands scraped against the concrete, ripping both palms open as she slid forward and onto her stomach. Asphalt and gravel ground their way into her soft flesh. Shoulders hunched, she dug her elbows into the asphalt and drug herself forward, scraping her body against the ground, but every last ounce of energy poured from her open wounds, leaking out with the last of her resolve. Nothing mattered anymore. Everything she did lead to more disaster.

Rolling on her back, she tucked her injured hands to her chest and sat up, rocking in rhythm with the pulsing pain. The smell of ozone permeated the air, burning her eyes and nose. The air was alive with electrostatic from the storm. Another mass of twirling light flung itself into the fog, illuminating the darkness.

The demons gathered in the shadows, as if sensing her resignation. She could run to the ends of the earth, and they would still find her. Let them come. What else could they possibly do to her that she hadn't already done to herself? Her grades were in shambles, she was the laughing stock of Westland, and a fool to believe Jeff loved her. They approached, cautious not to startle their prey.

Blood flowed from her palms, staining her silk dress with crimson droplets. She'd slept with him while another girl carried his baby. No wonder her mom couldn't stand to be home long enough to even have dinner with Quinn the Disappointment, the reason her dad had left. All of it was on her shoulders. A green wisp writhed its way around her arm, caressing her wrist, solidifying into a small-winged dragon. And Aaron—the one person that might have believed her, might have helped her—she'd thrown him away without a second thought. What did that say about her?

"Hurt?" It cocked its narrow head and looked up at Quinn. Another wisp curled itself around her ankle, turning itself into a furry, black, cat -like demon. Standing on two legs, it rubbed itself against her shin. Clenching her stomach, she leaned over and retched. Her sides heaved as she vomited guilt and regret along with her dinner into a vile puddle, but relief evaded her.

"Pain?" The demon purred and licked her leg.

"Follow me." Another beckoned, moving back to reveal a light in the distance.

"Home."

If she could just make it home, maybe she would wake up and find it was just another horrible nightmare. Quinn got to her feet, mesmerized by the beacon in the distance. The rain slowed. Ignoring the beasts that followed, she walked toward the magnificent, glowing sphere. Warm and inviting, it floated closer with every step. The sound of running water, Bluebonnet Creek, just ahead. The faint glow of a subdivision appeared, pinpricks of light between the trees on the other side of the bank. Her subdivision. Home.

Deserted, the darkened streets melded with the barrage of rain, creating an unrecognizable, watery-gray world. The Jeep was an inadequate submarine. Aaron pressed his face against the window, searching.

"Can't you go any faster?"

Marcus mashed the accelerator to the floor. The Jeep lurched forward, fishtailing on the slick road. The force whipped Aaron and Marcus from side-to-side like pinballs in a machine. Marcus eased up on the gas, bringing the speed back down to ten miles per hour, regaining control of the vehicle.

"This must have been what Noah felt like. Wish we had an ark." Marcus tightened his grip on the steering wheel.

"Man, I can't see anything out there." Aaron checked his seatbelt, sighed, and sank back into the leather seat. The three-minute ride from Tony's to school stretched into ten. Aaron fought the urge to take the wheel by tapping the dash in rhythm with the windshield wipers.

"Are the wipers on high?"

"No, I just like driving blind." Marcus hit an unseen patch of high water. Aaron braced himself as the sound of a rushing wave crashed against the car. Marcus pumped the brakes, slowing down enough for the wave to recede.

"Hey." Aaron sat up in his seat and wiped at the glass with his shirtsleeve. "That was it!" Aaron gestured to the right.

Marcus jerked the wheel and slammed on the brakes. The tires squealed, sending them into another skid.

"You missed the parking lot!" Aaron yelled. "I know!"

"Turn around!"

"Stop yelling at me!" Marcus gripped the wheel as the Jeep slid forward, slipping into a spin. Like a top, they spun, until the back wheels sank their rubber teeth into the soggy clay earth, pulling the rest of the Jeep into the muddy front lawn of Westland High.

"Great." Marcus switched the Jeep into four-wheel drive, but the tires spun, traction-less. He wrinkled his nose at the smell of burning oil. "Just great." Marcus turned the engine off and doused the headlights. "I guess this means it's time to get out."

The school towered over them, dark and empty.

"Now or never." Aaron fumbled in the back seat for the flashlights, handing one to Marcus.

"You think the girls will be okay? Maybe we should've made them go home."

"As if we could make them do anything."

"At least they get to stay dry. Why are we getting out again?" Marcus zipped his leather jacket up around his neck.

"We can search more places on foot than the girls can on wheels."

"So, where should we start?" Marcus asked.

"I'll head through the practice fields toward the river. Maybe she ran for shelter in the field house or the alley. You start on the south side in case she headed toward Reese's house. If you don't find her soon, double back and meet me here. Is your cell phone on?"

"Yep."

"Mine, too. Call as soon as you find her. Ready?" Aaron held out his fist to Marcus.

"I guess." Marcus completed the ritual: top to bottom, bottom to top, fist to fist. "Let's get this over with."

Aaron opened the passenger door. A rush of water soaked him to the bone. Squinting through the rain, he waved the beam of light in the direction he thought the tennis courts were, its ray illuminating every glistening drop it met, reflecting toward him like a mirror. He said a silent prayer. This was going to be even more difficult than he'd thought.

3 5

Quinn trudged down the rocky bank, stepping carefully, so as not to fall on the slippery rocks that jutted from the steep riverfront. She wasn't alone. The shadows kept tabs on her movements, calming her, encouraging her with their insidious whispers. She let them, wrapping herself in their foggy lies like a soft, fuzzy blanket, smothering any fiery fight left in her. Approaching the river's edge, the rhythm of the rushing water intensified, roaring its way down Bluebonnet Creek to the Rio Grande and out to the Gulf.

Exhaustion settled into every sinewy muscle of Quinn's body. A giant boulder protruded out into the rolling waves, the perfect place to rest. With nowhere else to go, she lowered herself onto the damp crag, crossed her legs, and leaned over the edge. Water exploded upward as it met the hard opposition of the rock. Cold, black spray tickled her already soaked skin.

Minutes passed. Twigs and other debris floated by in a never-ending parade, hypnotizing with their constant swirl of water and objects speeding past. All hope of home and bed were lost with the realization that the light had been an illusion, some strange trick of the eye.

The shadows crept closer, beating their wings in rhythm with her heart. She let them surround her, let them curl up next to her like unwanted strays begging for food, stroking her drenched hair with sharp talons, purring, hissing, whispering, compelling her to slip into the water. And why not? Neither of her parents wanted to be around her. Grades meant nothing to her anymore. Jeff belonged to Kerstin now, and Aaron hated her.

Life would never go back to those happy moments she'd had when she was younger, so why try anymore? Everything she touched turned to rot and ruin, and she wanted to sink into a dark and everlasting nothingness. Quinn unfolded a leg and dipped one foot into the swift water, feeling the resistance as it flowed past her ankle, colder than she'd imagined. She pulled her knees up to her chest, hugging them close.

I wish.

"What?"

I don't know.

A sense of déjà vu overwhelmed her, and she tried to catch the memory that flitted past her conscious mind.

"Tired?"

Yes.

"Of life?"

Of dealing with it.

"With life?"

She caught the déjà vu feeling again, her dead, gray flesh, heavy and cumbersome in life, sinking into oblivion beneath the water—a lake, not a river.

I guess.

"We know."

I know.

"We can help you."

To never wake up?

"To be free."

Quinn, perfect and luminous, floated above the lake, free of her body, beautiful, like a firefly or an angel. She could soar far away— free from the guilt, the pain and heartache this terrible world had to offer. All trust in this world had shattered like ice under a chisel. She stood, wind whipping at her tattered dress as she approached the edge where the boulder met the stream. Light mist turned to heavier drops as another storm cloud hovered overhead.

No more pain.

"No more confusion."

No Kerstin.

"No Jeff."

No affairs.

"Or stepmothers."

Or unwanted baby brothers.

"No more tests."

No more suspensions.

"It will end the gossip."

End the anger.

"End the hate."

Bring me peace?

"If you want."

What about you?

"You will be free of everything."

Quinn couldn't control how she lived, but maybe she could control how she died. There was nothing left to keep her here.

Mud and grime coated the hems of Aaron's pants. Even his shoes were flooded with the oozing mire as he slogged his way to the back alley. He searched the field house, the tennis courts, and every inch of the practice fields. No sign of Quinn. No call from Marcus or the girls.

"She's probably home by now, warm and dry," he mumbled to himself. "Why am I out here again?"

The asphalt of the oval track shone silver as Aaron panned the beam over it. Quiet and empty. He continued to the back ally, waving the flashlight in an arc, seeking out every dark corner to make sure Quinn wasn't curled up in one of them. He found nothing but a Dumpster, rank with the smell of rotten eggs and old vegetables. Gagging, he covered his mouth and nose with a wet sleeve and moved farther down the path.

"Which way did you go?"

Right, down the alley and to the main road? Or left, to the south parking lot? Or did she go through the small gap in the fence and into the woods? He pulled at his once-white shirt, now sticky from the starch, inviting the air to separate it from his damp skin. With no clear answer, Aaron placed the flashlight on the ground and gave it a good spin. The light played over the fence, building, Dumpster, trees, and road. When it stopped, the clear beam cast light upon the narrow alley.

"Right it is."

Cloud cover hid the moon. In the darkness, Aaron felt as if he might be squeezed to death between the building and the wooden fence. He sucked at the cold night air, hurrying to the wider opening of the asphalt drive. A downed power line had wrapped itself around the pole, leaving its sputtering end dangling a foot from the ground. Aaron hugged the fence. Easing his way around the electric line, he followed the road as it curved around the back of the school until it dead-ended into Mustang Avenue.

With no sign of Quinn, Aaron decided to return to the Jeep, making his way to the front of Westland High by way of Bluebonnet creek. He walked at the top edge of the overflowing stream, shining his flashlight down the craggy sides.

Forty feet upstream, he saw her: arms outstretched, hair blowing behind her like a mad witch. His heart leapt in joy and trepidation. Aaron felt for the cell phone in his pocket, dialing Marcus without moving his eyes from Quinn. "I found her. Yes, behind the school on the bank of the creek, about a quarter of a mile upstream from Mustang. Yes, tell the girls. Hurry."

Aaron ended the call and scrambled down the bank. She turned around; his heart blanched. Gravity pulled her backward into the rapids, entombing her in a casket of water.

Quinn hit the hard, swirling water, her head going under first. The cold water shocked her as it rushed up her nostrils. She fought her way to the surface as her body tumbled under the rolling waves. The liquid stung her nose and throat as she expelled a silty mouthful into the waiting air. One breath. The current dragged her under again, stronger than she ever imagined, and she regretted her death wish.

The demons took the plunge with her, fluttering around her face every time she surfaced, cackling, landing on her head, pushing her under before she could scream. She gasped, bobbing to the surface from another dunking, and found a log floating next to her. Two demons swooped down, claws extended. They went for her eyes. She pushed with her legs, submerging herself to avoid the flying wisps around her. She stretched her arm to grasp the rough bark from below and scrambled up onto it, catching her breath as she raced downstream.

"Please, God, somebody, help!" she screamed as the beasts hopped along the log, making their way to peck on her hands.

The demons erupted into hideous screams, hissing and spitting at her.

"Even God can't help you now."

Pain exploded in the back of Quinn's head, and she sank

under the water, her limbs paralyzed and useless as she floated down the churning river, drifting into unconsciousness.

Aaron dropped the flashlight. Running farther downstream, he jumped over rocks and limbs like an Olympic track star, the adrenaline of fear pumping through his blood, propelling him forward. He stopped at a place where the water touched the top of the bank, readying himself for an attempt to rescue Quinn as she rushed downstream. The river ran fast, and it shouldn't take long for her to reach him. He strained to see Quinn in the dark rapids and finally spotted her twenty feet upriver, clinging to a floating limb.

The currents steered her away from his reach. A land rescue wasn't possible. Swallowing hard, he paced the shore, scanning for any sign of Marcus. Where was he? Pressure pressed on his lungs at the thought of water creeping past his waist, over his chest, into his lungs. He cleared his mind, meditating to slow his heart.

You can do this. Don't let the fear consume you. You can do this. She needs you. You couldn't save them, but you can save her.

He stripped off his shirt and shoes, ready to dive into the roiling river. Tense, he watched her log spin, pushing Quinn backward toward a downed tree. The upper half of its long trunk protruded out into the raging creek like an evil hand, waiting to shove Quinn under and hold her there.

"Quinn!" Aaron cupped his hands around his mouth, pleading with her to watch out, but the words were sucked out of his mouth and into oblivion. Tremors rocked through Aaron. *Please, Marcus, hurry. I don't know if I can do this.*

Quinn screamed seconds before the log silenced her, and she slipped beneath the inky rapids. His mind spun into the depths of his memory of Ruth, screaming as the car hit the water, her body sinking beneath the waves, her hand reaching for his.

Now. Do it now.

Calm strength filled him. He breathed in and jumped. As he hit the cold surface, lightning crackled in his mind. His perception changed as he reached for her energy. The world disappeared, and all his senses zeroed in on Quinn. Maybe it was his urgency, his fear for her life, but for the first time ever his ability transcended physical touch and catapulted through time and space until it collided with her unconscious. The void he'd sensed after their night in the field gone, and he could feel her again, not physically, but mentally. She whirled under the water, but he knew where she was.

He kicked hard against the current, his muscles straining to cut through the rapids. She ebbed farther away from him. Propelling himself downward, his lungs burned. The pressure intensified, a band around his chest, squeezing the last bit of air from his body. He felt light-headed as he reached for a ribbon of lavender silk. His fingers found the hem of her dress, and he pulled on the lifeline to reel her in. When she was close enough, he grabbed her arm and with one hard kick, shot upward.

He broke the surface, and they were back into the raging storm. He coughed and gulped at the damp air, filling his body with fresh oxygen. Quinn wasn't breathing, not even shallow breaths. He needed to get them both to shore, and fast. Land disappeared in the rainy darkness. The creek carried them around a small bend, and he spotted an outcropping. He used his right arm to hold her and his left to pull himself toward the rocky finger, his legs pumping scissor-like under the water. Rushing waves pushed them under every few seconds, blinding him, tiring him. He struggled to stay afloat as her weight dragged him down, the water resistant to letting them out of its grasp. They were being swept downstream at an alarming speed, and the more Aaron fought to make it to shore, the less progress he made.

Another downed tree skimmed the water on the left side of the shore. Aaron switched arms, dragging Quinn toward their one chance. Reaching out with his hand, he grasped the extended branch, tightening his fingers around the rough bark, and pulled with unearthly strength.

Water rushed passed, tugging at her dead weight. His hand ached as the rough wood dug into his palm. He gritted his teeth and pulled forward to secure his arm around the branch. He fought a mighty battle between water and flesh, and the water was winning.

Aaron's hope soared when Marcus appeared with the girls at the outcropping. Marcus didn't hesitate. He dove into the icy water. His steady stroke carved a straight path to them in seconds. He grabbed the branch, treading water as if it were just another day at the pool.

"Take Quinn." Aaron shouted over the roaring of the currents. Marcus nodded and pulled her into the crook of his arm.

"What about you?"

"Don't worry about me." Energy drained from Aaron with every second, but he wanted her safe. "She needs medical attention. I'll be right behind you." He gave Marcus a reassuring smile.

Marcus nodded and made it to shore, pulling Quinn behind him with powerful strokes. In seconds, they were on the bank.

At least she was safe, that's all that mattered. Cramps knotted the muscles in Aaron's arm; he would never make it back to shore on his own. Marcus left Quinn and dove back into the river, but Aaron didn't think he would make it in time. His palm slipped as the water dragged at his limbs. He scrambled to regain his grasp, but the wood ripped past his hand as he fell back into the raging river. He struggled for shore as the last of his energy seeped from him. Marcus screamed his name, he could see him cutting through the water like a torpedo, and then he disappeared around a bend as the water carried Aaron further and further away.

*A*aron woke to the light of a full moon shining down on him, illuminating calm water. The river appeared as a mirror. It no longer pushed and shoved its way around the rock. The smooth, silvery liquid hugged the giant outcropping, ice-like, but warm to the touch. Was he dead? Dreaming? The world stood still, its silence oppressive. Quinn, lifeless and pale, lay next to him.

He scrambled to her, wondering where Marcus and the girls had gone. He cradled her in his arms and pushed the wet hair out of her face, revealing blue lips. He groped for a telepathic link, but Quinn's brainwaves had gone out. He checked for breath. Nothing.

"No." Tears streamed down his cheeks, dripping onto her lifeless body. He pulled his cell from his pocket. The blank screen stared back at him, and he chucked the phone away. It shattered to pieces as it hit the rocks.

Aaron pressed his lips to hers, breathing air into her lungs with one long exhale, crying as he pumped her heart with his fists.

"I should have known you would follow her here."

Aaron whirled around. A bright light shone in his face, forcing him to shade his eyes. Something distinctly inhuman stood before him. Olive skin glowed from the inside out, a lampshade muting the brilliant bulb underneath. Coal-black hair hung straight and long around his ears, and his bright eyes pierced the darkness. He was bare-chested, a warrior from another time. Slender and tall, he stood, hands clasped in front of him, waiting. Two curved swords hung at his hips, each covered in glowing runes. One ablaze with blue, the other with golden light.

Azrael. The name of the being burned through Aaron like fire.

"I know you." Aaron said. "You were in the hospital the day I died."

"We go back further than that, Kaemon." Azrael's lips quirked into a grin. "Or do you prefer your human name now?

"Kaemon?" Aaron shook his head. "I don't understand."

"Then let me refresh your memory." Azrael grabbed Aaron by the throat and lifted him into the air. His legs dangled, a rag doll in his grip. He jerked and clawed at Azrael's hands, gasping for breath as his lungs burned. Azrael brought Aaron's forehead to his lips and kissed him. A Judas kiss.

Lightning slammed into his mind, and his body shuddered as the electricity crackled through his veins. Tossing him to the ground, Azrael extended his wings, a black shadow against the strange glittering sky. Aaron clutched his head and rolled with pain as millennia of memories seared through him. Each one stabbed at him, drawing forth a clear image of his previous life, faster and faster the images flashed until they reached the pivotal moment.

Out of sight to the mortal eye, Aaron—no, in this place he was called Kaemon— paced the length of the small hospital room, agitated and impatient. This was not at all what Aaron expected being an angel to feel like.

The woman lying on the hospital bed screamed in pain.

"Another push, Katherine. You can do it." The nurse wiped sweat from the woman's brow.

Righteous anger welled within Kaemon, a fire racing through his veins, and he slammed his fist into his palm. This was a waste of time. Guardianship was Sentinel work, he reasoned. Kaemon was Elite, a warrior, protector of the realms, not a babysitter. He despised the idea of watching a tiny, squalling, smelly thing for the rest of its short, pathetic life. It was beneath him to guard anyone, especially a child. His brothers needed him on the front line. No one knew Lilith, mother of demons and Queen of the underworld, better than he did. He should be strategizing battle plans, not pacing by the bed of this pale, fragile human woman, waiting for the demons to strike.

Kaemon ached to unfurl his wings, but the small labor room restricted his twelve-foot span of golden-red feathers. How Sentinels endured such claustrophobic situations vexed him. He fought the urge to shoot through the roof and fly free, to leave the human infant to its fate. Duty be damned, but he had no say in the matter. The Dominion's pompous directives were said to come from the top, the Light itself, and Kaemon knew all too well what happened to those who directly disobeyed the Light.

The Dominion's orders explicitly said Lilith would send her ilk to try to kill the newborn while it was at its weakest. What was so special about this one soul that both Lilith and The Light wished to lay claim to it? If it survived, Kaemon had been commanded to serve and protect the child until it was old enough to be brought to Arcadia. An eighteen-year sentence, away from his brothers, away from the front lines where he could make a real difference. Why him?

The woman screamed again, and the lights flickered. Dark

ones slithered from the corners, crawled along the seams of the ceiling, clung to the shadows on the wall, waiting. Kaemon flexed his fingers, gripped the hilt of his sword, and readied himself.

The room was charged with raw energy. Lightning crackled beneath his golden skin and he paced faster. The baby would be most vulnerable at the transition from a symbiotic soul to a lone newborn. They would attack the moment the cord that connected it to its mother was severed. Let them try; this is what he lived for. His hand caressed his sword's golden hilt.

"I see the head." The doctor locked eyes with the woman. "One more, push. That's it! That's it!"

The child burst forth into the world in a tide of blood and mucus. Perfectly pink, wrinkled, and squalling like a banshee. Kaemon stopped mid-stride and held his breath.

The child howled as the doctor cleaved the connection to its mother, as if it sensed the danger the separation brought.

Two shadows leaped forward. Kaemon drew the Qeres blade from its scabbard. The curved blue star-metal rang out the hour of the child's birth for all to hear. The beasts quailed at the sound, sensing the prophesy of their death in the rare and ancient sword's venom. The Dominions had not sent an ordinary Sentinel to watch her. Millennia of training earned Kaemon the rank of Elite, carrier of the Qeres star blade, one of the chosen few, and he would do his duty no matter his feelings.

He slashed, striking as quick as a snake. The beasts blinked and scattered before his fury. Wisps of dark smoke curled around him as he snuffed them out. One by one, the Qeres poison worked through their twisted souls, turning them to dust.

The threat gone, for now, he sheathed his weapon and stared down at the tiny bundle as it sucked life from its mother's breast. Amazed at how small and fragile it seemed, he came forward to examine it closer. A girl, like any other human baby, nothing special.

"Does this little beauty have a name?" The nurse asked.

"Evelyn," the woman said, as her husband said "Quinn." They both smiled and laughed.

"Quinn Evelyn Taylor?" The nurse asked and they nodded.

"Welcome to the world, little Quinn," the mother cooed.

Kaemon's breath hitched. Quinn *Evelyn* Taylor. Eve. No, it couldn't be. But it was. In that instant, he recognized her true soul.

"Eve." He whispered to her, reminding the ancient soul staring out of the newborn's eyes of who she really was. Kaemon stroked the porcelain skin of its hand with a finger. The child stopped sucking and looked at him. They locked eyes, and she curled her tiny fingers around his. She smiled, and lightning crackled between them as she tethered herself to him. Love, pure and strong, surged through him. In that moment, an unbreakable bond formed. The pieces of the bigger picture fell into place and he understood why he was chosen. He would need to be vigilant, unceasing.

A few remaining demons, brave enough to be witness for their master, hissed and backed into the shadows. The dark ones would be cautious now, crafty, but they would never give up. Not when the future of the all their worlds hung on the hidden power possessed within the soul of this child.

A moment later, she looked through him. Her soul had completed its journey into life, into the human realm, and she could no longer see him. He would be her invisible protector until her latent powers manifested, until she remembered who she truly was. Eve. He would never willingly leave her side again. This time would be different. This time he wouldn't let her go. And in that moment, he knew he would risk everything, even mortal death, to protect her.

The memories swirl and reform in Aaron's mind. The years Kaemon spent watching Quinn were the happiest and most agonizing of his immortal life. Like Aaron, Kaemon could touch her mind and Quinn didn't know he was there. Kaemon used his abilities to influence her. Their bond allowed him to warn her of danger, to shield her mind from Lilith's dark children, to hone, what she thought of, as intuition. Although she couldn't see him, a part of her believed something watched over her. Her guardian angel, she sometimes called him. A human construct, but close enough.

When her father broke her heart, Kaemon stayed by her side, night and day. Quinn sobbed into her father's white t-shirt. She had found it at the bottom of the laundry basket, left behind in his haste to run off with that woman. As he packed his bag, Quinn begged him not to leave. Kaemon had wanted to kill him where he stood, but killing humans was strictly forbidden.

Instead, he wrapped his golden-red wings around her, his heart breaking with hers. He probed her mind, seeking out the grief that shadowed her heart. Their bond allowed him to radiate comfort, safety, and love through the center of the pain. She relaxed, but only for a moment. A clumsy but effective wall rose to block his thoughts and keep him from influencing hers. For the first time, she deliberately shut him out.

Her reaction stung. He could push through, force her to accept his invocation, but her rejection set him to brooding. If she didn't want him there, why should he force himself on her?

"She wants the warm touch of a human. Not some cold, ethereal creature." The demons preyed on his thoughts.

His knuckles whitened as he gripped the hilt of his sword, never taking his eyes off Quinn, lying on her bed, inconsolable. "Be gone, or I'll draw the Qeres."

An empty threat. His heart had weakened in love. The fight

drained out of him with every moment of his vanity. They sensed his weakness, his thirst to live in human flesh so he could touch her.

"Look at you, Elite. Bah, we've seen Sentinels with more fight than you." The shadows circled, bold sharks waiting to feed on the turmoil. "Draw your blade, if you dare. Do you even remember how to use it?"

He took the bait, drawing the blade and pressing an attack. The demons arched back, laughing.

"Is that all you've got? She doesn't need you anymore. She's safe in the arms of another. Too long you've been tethered to this weak child. You're no warrior. The Dominion has reduced you to a common Sentinel. And for what?"

He slashed down, nicking one in the wing. It howled in pain as the poison ate through its body.

"That's it, Sentinel. Do your duty." The world exploded in wisps of evil smoke, blinking around him, fetid breath taunting him. He pressed the attack instead of defending, as the Dominion had ordered.

"They want you on a leash, Sentinel. While the other Elites win victory and honor in battle, you sit here, mooning over a human girl."

They switched their focus to Quinn, their slithering dark tendrils reaching for her.

"Don't touch her," he growled.

"Who's going to stop us?" The tendrils melted onto the skin of her hands, her face, turning her from translucent porcelain to gray as death.

Rage thrummed through him. He swung the sword in a great, sweeping arch, cutting through the tendrils as they attached themselves to Quinn. He would show them the true meaning of Elite. The ones touched by the blade screamed and withered in death. The gray scales fell from Quinn, and he pressed on. The remaining demons retreated, a murder of crows scattering across the world to hide from his wrath. Lost in a warrior's rage, he flew after them, leaving Quinn alone and forgotten.

He hunted them, one by one, tracking one to a small graveyard next to the ruins of a gothic church. It hid among the gravestones, cowering at his presence. He drew his weapon, ready to rid the world of another dark spirit.

"Wait," it pleaded. "I can help you. To be with her, as that boy is. As a human."

"Lies." But his heart wanted to believe, and so he stayed his hand.

"We know of those who hold the secrets. The Powers. They hold dominion over births and deaths, do they not? They can make you human."

"How do you know this?" Could the ancient myth be true? Was there a way to cast off his immortality? Holding Quinn in his arms would be worth the sacrifice.

"I was a Power, once, before the fall. I remember," it hissed. "Seek the Powers, and you will find the answer. Seek Azrael."

Azrael. He knew the name. He had been the Power who attended to Quinn's making. He sheathed the Qeres blade. "If you lie, I will hunt you down and kill you where you stand."

The demon's head bobbed up and down. Then he disappeared in a puff of smoke.

Azrael. He closed his eyes, sending out probing threads, searching for the hum of Azrael's psychic signature. He sensed him within the concrete walls of a hospital, a few hundred miles away. Unfurling his golden wings, he launched into the air.

A minute later, he descended through the floors of the hospital until he reached the place Azrael's signal was strongest. The sign over the door read ICU. A boy lay, pale and unmoving, on the bed in front of the angle of life and death. The boy's arms were wrapped in bandages. His chest rose and fell, machines beeping and whirring, playing death's tune. The spirits of a woman and a girl stood beside the bed, waiting for their beloved Aaron join them. A bright tunnel stretched behind them, a portal to the next realm, to the city of Arcadia.

"Ah, Kaemon. I sensed you would come."

"Then you know what I want?"

Azrael nodded.

"Perhaps there is a way." Azrael looked at the boy and smoothed his dark hair from his forehead. "Is she worth it, Kaemon? Is she worth throwing everything away?"

"Yes." Kaemon rasped through clenched teeth.

"Then give me your blade."

Kaemon hesitated.

"Your blade, before it's too late." Azrael held his open palm in expectation. "Or have you changed your mind? Is her love not everything you long for?"

He pulled the blue Qeres sword from the scabbard. It sang as it came clear. Azrael took the hilt and brandished the weapon in great, sweeping arcs. Kaemon stared, mesmerized by the rhythmic pulse of the light as it illuminated Azrael's wicked grin. Then, Azrael lashed out, dragging the blade down and across Kaemon's bare chest.

Kaemon cried out. The slow poison of the Qeres dripped into his body. His wings withered. Golden-red feathers fell, one by one like autumn leaves to the ground. He fell against the bed, panting.

Azrael shoved him backward and into the boy's waiting flesh. Pain ripped through Kaemon as he felt the boy's heart, his heart now, constrict and his body stiffen. Everything felt wrong, heavy. Kaemon's spirt struggled to fit into the constraints of this human frame. The boy's soul thrashed against Kaemon, trying to push the unwanted entity out.

"Don't resist." Azrael stroked the boy's cheek, and his spirit quieted, too weak to resist Azrael's bidding. Then Azrael placed his hand on the boy's chest. A cold burn surged through them, each crackle of lighting fusing them into one being. Aaron's soul used the last of his energy to reach for his mother and sister, but they turned from him, weeping, and disappeared into the tunnel that lead to Arcadia. The gates to paradise were closed to him forever now. Kaemon couldn't speak, couldn't breathe.

"You wanted to be mortal. Kaemon."

Kaemon could feel Aaron with him, or did Aaron feel Kaemon? He was both and he was neither. He tried to speak, but nothing came out but a low grunt. *Who am I?*

"This human's life is now yours, Kaemon, for what it's worth." Azrael held his hand up and a beam of light shot from his palm through Aaron's body. "Make the most of it, if you can." Azrael smiled as the light seared away all their combined memories. Nurses flooded into the room, unfamiliar faces crowded around him, and the boy wept for a life he no longer recognized.

Aaron's eyes widened at Azrael as the last of Kaemon's memories slid into place

"So, you finally remember, old friend?" He sneered at Aaron. "Have you enjoyed your life as this ... human? Was it everything you had hoped for?"

Aaron rolled away, panting. "You tricked him," he snarled.

"Did I?"

"You wanted Kaemon out of the way. Why?"

"He came to me. He wanted to be human and you wanted to be dead. Slitting your wrists was a cry for help, so I helped you both."

Aaron tugged at his sleeves and Azrael shrugged. "It seemed like a good solution at the time."

"Kaemon didn't do anything to you."

"Didn't he? He forgot his place, forgot his job. He let pride and vanity spur him, believing he could have a future with a human girl. The Light did not realize how deep his feelings for Eve went. If they had, they would not have left her alone with him." Anger, bright as fire flashed in Azrael's eyes. "Leaving her vulnerable was Kaemon's own doing. And now look where that folly led." Azrael motioned to Quinn's lifeless body. "I forged her soul myself. As her maker, I should have been her Sentinel, not Kaemon. I would never have left her alone. Do you know how many millennia it took me to find the human genes strong enough to contain Eve's soul? How many humans I had to manipulate into breeding to get the perfect vessel? The Light demanded it, and I obeyed. So, when I saw the chance to correct their mistake, I took it." Azrael shrugged. "The Light did not sanction it, but neither did they forbid it."

"Damn you." Aaron growled.

"Do not judge what you don't understand," Azrael said. "You may have Kaemon's memories, but you are not one of us. You are nothing but an abomination and a thorn in my side. I still don't understand how you found her."

"Maybe The Light didn't like you going rouge after all." Aaron raised his arms and exposed his chest. "Kill me if you want, Azrael, I'm tired of this life anyway. Send me to be with my mother, and Ruth, and Quinn. Leave us all in peace."

"Oh, you can't join your family, Aaron. Abominations aren't welcome in Arcadia." Azrael laughed placed the tip of the blue-star sword above Aaron's heart. "As for Quinn, you didn't really believe I would kill the one person who can tip the balance, did you? You're even a bigger fool than Kaemon."

A surge of current jolted Aaron's mind, the psychic equivalent of restarting a dead battery, and he glanced at Quinn. The fingers of her left hand twitched, then she turned on her side and curled into a tight ball. Not dead, unconscious. Tears of relief spilled down his cheeks as their connection sparked to life. Backing away from the cold blade pointed at him, he reached for her, sending strength through the tenuous link.

Aaron. Quinn thought. *Where are you? It's so dark here.*

"Don't you touch her." Rage consumed Aaron. He whirled

and snatched for the blue sword hanging on Azrael's hip. Within a blink, Azrael had moved behind him and put the sword against Aaron's throat.

"Do you know what havoc can be reaped with a Qeres blade?"

The tip of the blade pulsed against his skin, calling to his angel blood. He remembered the feel of Kaemon's sword in his hands, his sword. If only he could get it, he could destroy Azrael.

"Whose side are you on, Azrael?"

"My own."

"Your time has ended, Aaron, or would you prefer Kaemon. You've been nothing but a nuisance. I thought I had done enough to rid myself of you without getting my wings dirty. I had counted on your powers and your bond to her being erased along with your memories, but even in this mortal body you remained her Sentinel. It's time to correct my mistake." Azrael dragged his golden blade across Aaron's throat, slow and steady.

Aaron rasped a cry as his body shuttered and convulsed, the immortal poison burning its way through what was left of his angel soul while human blood spurted from his jugular. He collapsed. His life force ebbed, but he pushed himself to hold on until he dragged himself the precious inches to the pale, half-conscious Quinn. With his last breath, he pressed his lips to hers.

Don't trust Azrael. He pushed the warning deep into her mind as the last of his lifeblood drained away. Her energy surged as his waned. With a kiss, he gave her the very last of himself, his last thoughts before their link was broken forever.

"Don't worry. I'll take good care of her." Azrael kicked Aaron's body over the edge of the outcropping. There was no fight left in him. The river yanked at his lifeless limbs. He let the water overwhelm him, pulling him under, calling him to the depths of darkness, to oblivion.

Quinn awoke under a clear sky. "Aaron?" She sat up and touched her lips. Warm, as if she'd just been kissed. She remembered the blinding crack to her skull and being dragged under. Her hand went to her head, and she felt for a bump, blood, tenderness, anything that would attest to an injury, but her scalp was blemish free. The thought came to her like a rushing wind.

"So, is this Heaven or Hell?"

"Neither."

A bright and terrible being swooped down and landed in front of her. Dark wings stretched behind him, magnificent and beautiful. Quinn couldn't help but gawk, too awed to be afraid. Two swords hung at his hips. She stared, mesmerized by their glowing pulse.

"Am I dead? Where am I? Are you an angel?" If he were an angel, was he here to take her away? Quinn trembled. How would her parents deal with finding her floating, bloated and gray in the river? And what about Reese and Aaron? Aaron with his green eyes, always there for her no matter how many times she had pushed him away. If she were dead, he would never know how sorry she was, how much she really loved him.

"I am Azrael." He held out his hand to help her to her feet. "Azrael?" Something stirred inside her, uneasiness she couldn't put her finger on. "Your name. It sounds familiar."

"I'm your Sentinel, or guardian, as your kind like to call us. I've been assigned to you." His voice was a symphony of peace, layers of deep sound humming out of every syllable, soothing away her concerns.

Quinn had a vague memory of a being of light following her, comforting her, reaching into her mind. It must have been this Azrael. Her guardian.

"You summoned me. I've brought you In Between to give you time to choose, away from the demons' tongues, away from their lies and influence. To give you a clear head. Time to think about what you really want."

"What are you talking about? What do those things want from me?"

"Your death. Isn't it obvious?" Warmth radiated from Azrael though his tone seemed cold in contrast.

"Why?"

"For your powers, of course." His smile masked a slow burning annoyance.

"What powers? I don't have any powers."

"Don't you?"

"No." Girls with powers didn't poison everything they touched. And if she had powers, she would have used them already.

"You can see them, can't you? The dark ones? The demons? No one else can. You're the one they speak to. Your powers are emerging."

"That's crazy. I'm just a girl. Why would they want me dead?"

"Just a girl? No, Quinn, you're much more than that. It is prophesized that Eve will return to restore darkness unto the Light. Eve's soul lives within you, Quinn Evelyn Taylor."

Quinn shook her head. "This is a dream. I'm washed up on the beach somewhere, and my imagination is running rampant."

"This is no dream. Deep down you sense it. Why do you think the demons torment you? They knew you were vulnerable." The light radiating from Azrael brightened and dimmed, pulsing with every word.

"So why didn't you come sooner? Why haven't you been protecting me?" Quinn gritted her teeth. If he were her Sentinel, why would he let them torture her? "I demand an answer."

"I've been trying for weeks to get through to you. First, I tried influencing your dreams, but you kept blocking me. You're stronger than you know."

The light in the forest by the lake. She had thought it was Aaron, but maybe it had been this Azrael the whole time?

"You must not have tried very hard." She folder her arms over her chest and glared at him. "Why could I see demons but not you?"

"Because you were consumed by darkness within, it over-shadowed the light. Overshadowed me. You didn't want to see the truth." Azrael's wings beat in frustration. "Time grows short. I don't have time to explain every little detail. It's taking the last of my energy to hold In Between together."

"How do I know you're telling the truth? How do I know you're not one of those creatures? You could be lying to me, like they did."

"I could be. But I'm not. You were created for a purpose. Search your heart. Much lies in there, untapped, power that's been waiting to be awakened." The ground trembled, and small cracks appeared in the night sky. "I can't hold you here much longer. It's time for you to decide. Now, before it collapses, and death chooses for you!" Azrael raised his voice in competition as the sky grumbled and cracked.

"Decide what?" Quinn wiped a cold drop from her cheek and shivered. Rivulets of water trickled from the growing fissures in the false world, reality leaking through, destroying the facade.

"Life or death. It's your choice." The world faded to black, and then snapped back into focus as if someone had flipped a light switch. "I can teach you how to use your power, to destroy the dark ones and restore balance, if you want. If you live, I will be your greatest ally, be by your side and teach you how to protect yourself. I can't force you. You've been granted free will. You choose."

"It's not that easy. I don't want to go back to that craziness. I don't want anything to do with the dark ones."

"Then die." Azrael raised a hand, and the ground shook.

"Wait! I need more time!"

"There is no more time." Azrael gave her a fierce look, and she scrambled back, the light inside him dimmed further, flickering as if it might be snuffed out at any moment. "Life is never easy, not for you, not for anyone. But you can choose. I grow impatient. This bubble is about to burst." Azrael's words hurled at her like thunder. "I can end it now, and the world will fall into darkness." Azrael pulled the golden blade from his scabbard. "I can release your soul from your body. It will be quick; you won't feel a thing. The choice is yours. Do you really want to die?"

Quinn pictured her funeral. Her mother, dressed in black, weeping as they lowered her into an open grave. Her father stood beside her, a baby boy in his arms, blond hair, chubby cheeks. Her brother.

"With you gone, the demons will need a new focus."

"They wouldn't dare," Quinn growled through clenched teeth.

"Why do you care? You don't even know him. You secretly wished he didn't exist."

"Get out of my head." Quinn shoved the thoughts of her brother into a mental box.

"Good. You are learning already."

"Will they leave him alone if I say yes?" The world blinked to black and back again as the cracks widened.

"Yes. But none of them will be safe if you say no." Water tumbled, waterfalls from the edge of the world, churning the once glassy surface of the stilled river.

Quinn stood, shaking in frustration. Her heart felt as if it had been shattered in a million different pieces, and she didn't know how to put it back together again without getting cut. Saying yes meant going back to face every mistake, it meant facing her demons, her despair. Yes, filled her future with the unknown. But saying no? Choosing death? She knelt on the rock, eyes closed, searching her heart for an answer.

Images of Ami, Marcus, Reese, all her friends, filed past her coffin. Each placed a rose on her casket. Aaron. Would he even come after the way she had treated him? Quinn felt his lips on hers, the squeeze of his hand. She pictured the long, winding scars that snaked up his arms. He had told her he felt as if he had been sent back for a reason, and in that moment, she almost believed he had been sent for her. Tears streamed down Quinn's face. If he would forgive her, they might have a chance. With him, she could get through this. She longed to see him one more time, to tell him she was sorry, that she did love him.

A sudden rush of magnetic wind pulled at her.

"It is done." The earth shuddered with a loud boom. And with a rush of wind, Azrael unfurled his onyx wings and ascended into the dark sky.

"Wait!" she screamed. "I still have questions."

"And when those are answered, you will have more."

"What do I do now?" A tsunami of dark water came at her like a speeding truck and washed her away as the façade crumbled around her.

"Live." The voice echoed through her mind, reverberating through the nothingness until her head exploded in pain. That same, indescribable pain filled her chest, burning its way up through her throat, followed by an overwhelming need to vomit.

Her head spun as she leaned to the side, water spewing from her mouth. With a sputtering gasp, she inhaled like a baby filling its lungs for the first time. Her chest ached as the air forced its way into her lungs. The foreign liquid exploded outward. Her stomach rolled as she vomited with no control until nothing, liquid or solid, was left inside her.

"Thank God." She relaxed with the sound of Reese's familiar voice, her hand rubbing her back, comforting her.

"Reese," she croaked, but didn't have the strength to turn and look at her.

"Shhh, just lie still until the ambulance gets here."

Quinn felt her hand on her face, stroking the sodden hair from her forehead. In the distance, Quinn heard the whine of the sirens. Her call to life, to a second chance, to destiny.

ACKNOWLEDGMENTS

Life sometimes takes unexpected turns. Though this little book and I have been through some heart ache together, I'm thrilled that When Darkness Whispers, previously titled Pretty Dark Nothing, has found a new home with Snowy Wings Publishing.

Thank you to Lyssa Chiavari and Dorothy Dreyer for welcoming me to this wonderful co-op. Although the title and cover has changed, Quinn and Aaron couldn't have been possible without my wonderful editor, Courtney Koschel. She pushed me in ways that I wouldn't have expected, and this book is as much hers as it is mine.

Thank you to my critique partner, soul sister, and agency sister. We have been through so much together. Thank you for holding my hand through the writing and publishing journey. I wouldn't want to do it without you.

Thank you to family and friends who supported me every step of the way. Especially my parents, Rocky and Sherry Reid, for teaching me anything is possible if I work hard enough. Thank you to my sisters, Kristal Seid and Beth Allen, for being my biggest cheerleaders. A big thank you to my BFF, JaneAnn Morrison, for thirty-nine years of friendship, for a lifetime of fights, misunderstandings, love and support that comes from growing up together. Thanks for sticking with me.

Thank you to my Scottish Family. You welcomed me with open arms and loved me like one of your own. A special thanks to Linda and Drew Innes, the best Scottish parents a girl could wish for. You let me live in your house, brought me chocolate when I had a bad writing day, and always supported me in my passion. I couldn't be more blessed to be part of your clan.

Thank you to my beta readers and all those who read the early versions of what was then Pretty Dark Nothing and giving me feedback. Olivia Allen, Rebecca Niven, Stormie Brown, Dondi Markham, Brian and Marie Cordell, Teresa Hill Berting, Lucy Filmore, Christine Innes, Gillian Caitens, Rocky Hatley, Kornee Byrd, Vaughn Roycroft, Tonia Marie Harris, and Trey Walpole.

Thank you to all the members of the Writer Unboxed Facebook group who took time to engage in amazing writerly conversation and for Therese Walsh for providing an amazing community and space for learning about the craft of writing. And thank you to my fellow Mod-Squad members, Vaughn Roycroft, Valerie P. Chandler and Kim Bullock for picking up the ball when life got busy.

I wouldn't be here if it weren't for my first critique group, Dreamcatcher's. Each of you helped lay the foundations and for that you will always have a place in my heart.

And last, but certainly not least, a special thank you to my loving husband, David Innes, my strength and calm in a storm. I love and appreciate you more than words can say.

Heather L. Reid is both American and British and has called six different cities in three different countries home. Her strong sense of wanderlust and craving for a new adventure mean you might find her wandering the moors of her beloved Scotland, exploring haunted castles, or hiking through a magical forest in search of fairies and sprites. When she's not venturing into the unknown in her real life, she loves getting lost in the worlds of video games or curling up by the fire with a good story. For now, this native Texan is back in the Lone Star State, settling down with her Scottish husband and dreaming up new novels to write.

PARAGON RISING

Book Two in The Curse of the Phoenix Duology

by USA Today Bestselling Author Dorothy Dreyer

On the brink of war, the fate of the nine realms lies in Tori Kagari's hands. After her arduous efforts to infiltrate the queendom of Avarell, Tori must now escape from it in an unforeseen alliance with a runaway princess and the soldier who saved Tori's life. When the savage forces of Nostidour take hold of Avarell, Tori must seek out the rulers of the other realms and convince them to join the fight. But when the other realms discover that Tori has been lying about who she is, they are hesitant to trust her. Now Tori must find a way to prove herself, even if it means leading the battle herself and risking everything in the name of peace.